CW00971951

Kylie Tennant was born at Manly, New South Wales, in 1912 and educated at Brighton College and Sydney University. She married L. C. Rodd, a school-teacher, in 1932.

She has been a chicken farmer, book reviewer, journalist, assistant publicity officer for the A.B.C., organiser for travelling unemployed and the Unemployed Workers' Union, barmaid, church sister and publisher's literary adviser and editor.

She was lecturer for the Commonwealth Literary Fund, 1957–60, at universities in Armidale, Canberra, Adelaide and Perth. Appointed to the Advisory Board of the Commonwealth Literary Fund in 1961, she is a Life Patron of the Fellowship of Australian Writers. Two of her novels, *Tiburon* and *The Battlers*, have won the S. H. Prior Memorial Prize.

THE
HONEY FLOW

KYLIE TENNANT

SIRIUS QUALITY PAPERBACK EDITION
PUBLISHED BY ANGUS & ROBERTSON

By the same author

BIOGRAPHY
Evatt: Politics and Justice
The Man on the Headland

NOVELS
Foveaux
The Battlers
Ride on Stranger
Time Enough Later
Lost Haven
Tiburon
Tell Morning This
The Joyful Condemned

SHORT STORIES
Ma Jones and The Little White Cannibals
Editor of Summer's Tales 1 and 2

TRAVEL
Speak You So Gently

HISTORY
Australia: Her Story
Editor of Great Stories of Australia Series
Tether a Dragon (Jubilee Award Play)

JUVENILE
All The Proud Tribesmen (Children's Book Award)
Trail Blazers of the Air
Long John Silver

With L. C. Rodd
The Australian Essay

ANGUS & ROBERTSON PUBLISHERS
London • Sydney • Melbourne

First published by Angus & Robertson Publishers, Australia, 1956
A&R Classics edition 1973
This Sirius Quality Paperback edition 1983

Copyright Kylie Tennant 1956

National Library of Australia
Cataloguing-in-publication data.

Tennant, Kylie, 1912–.
  The honey flow.

  First published: Sydney: Angus & Robertson, 1956.
  ISBN 0 207 14461 3

  I. Title. (Series: Sirius quality paperbacks).

A823'.2

Printed in Hong Kong

Chapter One

EVERY time my memory opens its mouth it dribbles roads. Not so much the great bitumen and concrete flanks that cut the mountain spurs and plunge over the edge of the plateaus, but bush tracks that suit a kangaroo or a rogue bullock, but look incredible to drivers who have never had to force a great truck loaded with bee boxes or honey tins through the forests, over corduroys where the forestry gangs have thrown down a few trees to make a footing in a swamp, down into steep creek beds, over places with names like Muldoon's Mistake or The Downfall.

Places where we had to make the roads ourselves, taking trucks through the scrub, leaving tyre tracks to be followed later, twisting between trees, places where we were bogged, and the legend was that you jumped as the truck sank unless you wanted to go under the red sand with it, unloading, jacking up, inching her out, loading again, roaring on.

We were 'travelling our bees', opening up new honey country. You feel like a silkworm jerking out those roads from your very marrow, spitting them out of your vitals. You sweat and lie exhausted and swear and talk obscenities and live on bread and corned beef and creek water with a little tea to disguise the taste of the mud. The professional name for all this is migratory bee-keeping; you are a member of the Commercial Apiarists' Association, and when you attend a city conference with other apiarists, you say nothing of what you did to get your honey, but tell wild lies of the flows you have been on, and how you took off seven tins to the hive.

I am not writing this book about bees, because nobody knows enough about the Daughters of the Light to write about them, although, sometimes, when you take them up in your hands and feel the vibrant delicacy of their living bodies, you almost think you know something of them. I am writing about the men who make their living from honey, an independent and dignified set of toughs, my good friends and mates, the men I have camped with in the Nithering Range or the Pilliga Scrub, or where Cut-throat Creek runs into Hellhole.

I have been told by literary experts like Dennis Oberon Herrick that there is nothing in such men of sufficient interest for a book, that the refined reader who needs plot, pace, action and a body on the hearthrug in the first chapter will recoil from the wearisome and comical statement of our drudgery.

Well, by God, I say, rolling up my sleeves, I'm going to write the book and let whoever pleases read it or not just as they prefer. I'm writing it to clear my mind, cutting a track through a forest of bewilderment and lies and laughter. It's my road and you don't need to bring your truck in unless you want a load of honey. I may get bogged, I may have to jack up, and swear at the tough going, doing everything the hard way as usual, but when I do get through, it is to somewhere where the great eucalypts are in flower, and the silver-leaved ironbark is promising, where the bees are in good heart, and the creek runs clear and there is firewood and friendship.

'This truck is making a peculiar noise,' Dennis Oberon Herrick observed. I had brought him with me because he was suffering from drink, overwork and a nervous breakdown. It was a mistake to bring him, but he married my mother, and it was a good day for me when he did so, so I owed him a debt. Dennis hates an open-air life, but he hated the prospect of a sanatorium even more, and the doctor said he must have a complete change and an open-air life.

'Parent,' I said, 'if you notice that knock, then it is time to do something about it.'

I was driving through the Pilliga Scrub with sixty hives on the back of Nobby Wallace's truck, the Roaring Ruin. Nobby lent me the truck to help me out, but the hives were mine. The Roaring Ruin always travels to a chorus of squeaks, grunts and rattles, but this knock was deliberate and threatening. I pulled in to the side of the road and slid down from the driver's seat feeling achy and light-headed, as you do from driving too long. When I lifted the bonnet, the Parent thrust his face over the hot, oily metal, making noises of disgust and ignorance.

'What's wrong with the damn thing?' he asked.

'Pistons,' I said scientifically, so that I wouldn't spoil his faith in me. I knew that pistons knocked. I could drive the truck but about the engine I knew damn all.

The Parent, a handsome man like a Roman statue chipped by vandals, expressed his opinions. He looked at the truck as though it were the thousandth episode of 'Mrs. Prothero's Family', which is the serial he writes and the cause of his nervous breakdown. He loathes Mrs. Prothero's family and writing and producing it. He always wanted to be a great financier and back race-horses.

He began one of his orations, gathering his toga about him. 'Whenever I read about a character in a book with some peculiar bond with bees, or some uncanny influence over them, that character turns out to be an idiot. Are you listening? You are no exception. Here I am, hundreds of miles from anywhere, with the family idiot, a load of

3

bees and a broken-down forsaken truck! This is the end! I'll die in a ditch. This road isn't even marked on the map. It doesn't *go* anywhere. We'll starve to death before anyone finds us.'

While he talked, I noticed that one of the hives was leaking, and pulled some horsehair from the seat cushion to plug the leak. The Parent followed me with his oratory, but he did not go near the bees who were murmuring among themselves. There are always a few riders under the bottom boards ready to whizz out and assault you when you stop.

'Mad about bees! Now look where you've landed us. You thought that Wallace fellow was doing you a favour lending you this truck. He only wanted to collect the insurance on it. A dried-up, self-opinionated, talkative little runt! All your friends are the same. They can't even speak decent English. I've done my best to see you had a good education, and you . . . Where are you going? Don't leave me here with these damned bees, do you hear?'

It was no use appealing to his sense of humour which, with a sick man, is as rare as a cushion of snake's feathers. 'Parent,' I spoke slowly and cheerfully, 'somewhere along this road the Muirdens have their bees. They have big trucks because they are migratory men, so they must be good mechanics. All I have to do is to find the Muirdens.'

'You said they might be thirty miles away.'

'If anyone comes, get a lift to the next town. Make yourself a cup of tea. Sit in the shade. I'll be back or send someone. So long.'

The Parent was still talking ungratefully as I tramped off. This time he was saying what he thought of Julie, who is my mother. She had consulted her pet astrologer, Mr. Pollock, who had said there could be no more fortunate juncture for starting a new enterprise. Julie had worried about Dennis but not about me. According to Mr. Pollock nothing much happens in my horoscope. I am never on the scene when accidents occur. If there is excitement anywhere I have either just left or don't arrive until it is all over. By the time the astrologer forecaster reaches the Sign of the Two Poor Fish — the bottommost and last sign — the one under which I was born, he simply writes: Hard work and more hard work.

'Mallee,' I could hear the Parent calling after me. 'Come back, d'you hear?'

I sympathized with him. This was a new highway cloven through sixty miles of forest, and not finished yet. By the roadside old dead grey tree roots lay, extracted like giant teeth, the light beating down into the dirt as hard as a fire hose. Ahead were furling clouds of greenery, soft and voluptuous, that revealed their softness as skeleton trunks with shaggy, blackened bark, splintered branches, dreary leathery leaves. Broken rocks, dirt, trees — nothing but two walls of trees and a narrow split of track with a heat bar shimmering over it.

In spite of the blister rising on my left heel and a few million flies that had come for the ride and crawled round my ears, I was quite happy. Julie is right about beneficent days and adverse days. This was obviously a stinker, designed to bring out the best in one's character. What was the use of crying, 'Woe and alas!'? I was away from the city which always makes me sick. I didn't have to work in an office, which makes me sicker, or live in a flat. I was out in the open, so I could be happy on the most adverse day you could find in the calendar.

This monotony of trees and rocks might not be everyone's ideal as a dwelling place. Good bee country and Nobby would have liked it. Ironbark mainly, narrow-leaf, a bit of mugga, plenty of well-grown wattle, scrubby no-good gums, and the mallee for which I am named.

5

Before I was born, my father, who was a journalist dying of T.B., moved about for his health, and I was born in the mallee country.

I was too little to remember when he died, but I once overheard Julie telling a friend how, when he was cremated, she recalled that he always wanted to be buried at sea. So she boarded a ferry boat with the black box concealing his ashes, and when the ferry was passing the Heads she flung the black box into the water. I can just picture her in a silver fox cape and a smart hat, pretty and sentimental, and incompetent. Being Julie she hadn't thought to weight the box so it would sink, and there it floated merrily, bobbing through the waves with the crew of a passing cargo ship leaning over the rail and shouting and pointing out that she had dropped something.

So when I think of my father, it is of a black box sailing out to sea, nonchalant and don't-care-a-damn, with my inadequate and charming mother crying on a ferry boat.

I tramped on through the heat, thinking of Julie, and using the forefront of my brain for noticing trees and changes of soil and any hint of blossom. Julie was working as a barmaid when she met Dennis and he took us over. We had a one-room flat with a balcony on a street where the traffic roared all day. Julie made me promise not to play in the street while I waited for her to come home from work. One afternoon I was sitting on the top of the stairs laughing heartily at what I was reading when a grim-looking man, who reminded me of a Red Indian chief, came climbing up and asked me what was so funny. He said I shouldn't read in a bad light because it would ruin my eyes.

I explained that I was reading the Bible. I had just found the story about how the Ark of the Covenant was captured by the Philistines who bore it in great

6

triumph to their temple. In the morning they found their high god Dagon had fallen off his pedestal flat on his face, so they hastily returned the Ark of the Covenant to the Israelites.

'Just imagine their faces,' I said, unlocking the flat door with the key I wore round my neck on a string. 'They would be so surprised to see their old idol toppled over.'

'Why were you sitting on the stairs?' the old man asked, and I told him it wasn't so lonely there. He said he was my grandfather, so I made some toast. Julie came in and they had a terrible quarrel.

'You never did anything for him,' Julie said.

'He always went his own way,' my grandfather answered, and I thought of the black box slapping gaily out to sea.

Julie agreed to my staying with my grandfather in the holidays. Of course he kept bees. He had retired then from the Health Food business and left it to Uncle Beresford. Nobby Wallace really worked Grandfather's farm, on a share basis, but when Grandfather died everything had to be sold. So Nobby bought an orchard and lent me his truck so that I could move my bees.

I was trudging on when it struck me I could smell honey. I had nearly gone past without noticing the bee boxes in the clearing. They were screened from the road by trees and bushes, but there were the tyre marks of the truck that had taken them in. Someone had made a fire, leaving a few blackened sticks in the white ash, but the ash was cold.

The hives stood ranked row on row, orderly as suburban cottages, painted a metallic silver which is just about the coolest colour to paint your boxes. The smell of warm honey was strong and pungent as sweat.

In the space between the trees the bees danced, living bullets of sunlight, flinging their tiny bodies towards the

7

hives that launched them, speeding off again on their mysterious paths of air. Somewhere in that heat-shimmering tangle of tree-tops, in the imperceptible flowers, the striped bodies wriggled and burrowed towards the nectar, imbibed the minute pool, flew off to crawl into the warm, whirring dimness of familiar looming combs. They were 'bringing it in'.

It was cheering to know that, if we had to off-load the bees, they had something to live on. When I lifted the lid of a super, I found, as I expected, that it was stamped with the name of Muirden. Now I had only to find their camp, which might be fifteen miles on for all I knew. I sat down in a patch of dirt and pebbles under the shade of a prickly hakea. Reddish ants quested about and tested my socks with their mandibles. It would have been wonderful to go to sleep under the blanket of heat.

However, presently, I dragged myself up again and went on, thinking about the Muirdens. I had never met them and Nobby seemed prejudiced. Many years ago he had been an assistant to old man Muirden. He said the life he led would have made a farm dog howl and run for the scrub.

'The Muirdens are villains,' Nobby told me. 'Horace is a villain, and his brother Col is worse. I hear Horace's sons take after the old man, but I haven't met 'em. Col and Horace don't work together any longer because they couldn't put up with each other.' He added, 'They're just about the best apiarists in the state.'

When I came on the villains' camp, they were drinking tea and arguing in the shade. The place gave that mixed impression of loneliness and litter which all such temporary encampments take on. Old boots, motor tyres, petrol drums, sacks, blackened kerosene tins, clustered by the fire; an auto tent had its sides up, with a view of unmade beds. There were stacks of boxes, supers, lids, excluders, base boards and screens, a big red truck loaded with shiny new tins that reflected the blue of the sky.

A gauze-covered caravan which was the extracting house was coupled to a big grey truck with a table top on which the honey tank was set.

This extracting house folded down so that it could be towed behind the grey truck, the roof collapsing as a tight-fitting lid, and the gauze screens were taken off and piled inside. It had a motor and a small steam boiler on a kind of shelf behind. I was to have a much closer acquaintance with that extracting house. It gave the clearing a domestic and settled look because a tent is always lonely and temporary, but a roofed structure, even on wheels, has a stability and permanency about it. There was another battered little old truck with a bent mudguard by the side of the road.

As if all this gear were not enough, the Muirdens had a yard of bees in the clearing with them — about fifty boxes. The ranks stretched from the door of the auto tent, close enough for you to stumble on them, to the trees on the far side of the clearing.

When I came closer, walking up the slanted ruts that the big tyres had made across the sandy drain by the road, I saw that all this confusion was really very orderly. Everything was in its convenient place, provided you consider it convenient to live within three steps of your first row of hives.

There were five men grouped in the shade, and at first they just looked like five men, two of them in white boiler suits, and the three others in dusty khaki boiler suits, or shirts and trousers of the same colour. You did not at first distinguish those idiosyncrasies and appearances that make your friends dear and familiar.

'Hello, son,' one of them said. 'Come far?'

I had straightened my limp to a stride, and now as I

9

stood among them I pushed back the army felt I used to hold a bee veil, wiped the sweat off my forehead and surveyed them. 'You are not very observant,' I said. 'Could I have a drink?'

Three of them at once sprang towards the water bag, and a bustle of hospitality and courtesy possessed that camp. I was given an oil drum to sit on, offered a sandwich of bread and fish-paste, tea in a blue enamel mug. If I had expressed a wish for the topmost bough of an ironbark, someone would have dashed off to fetch it.

'How were we to know you were a woman with your hair cut off?' one of the villains demanded. 'In that boiler suit you look like a boy of sixteen, and not well grown at that.'

Now I was beginning to see all these people, who were to be my friends, as not just a group of men. There was Joe Muirden, a big slouching blond boy in a white boiler suit and white topee that made him look like the hero of a tropical film. Joe was a good-looking kid, strong and gentle, who pretended to be tough.

There was his brother Blaze, older and not as big as Joe, but resembling barbed wire in his disposition and tactics, in that he would tear a piece out of you when you thought you had negotiated him safely. If Joe looked like the hero of one of my scripts, Blaze was obviously cast for the assistant murderer. He too had tropical whites and a lion-hunter's hat, but he had grown himself a black scrub of beard, and he had wild black hair that stood on end like a golliwog's.

Blaze looked on dignity and reverence as a waste of time, and his main asset was his contempt. For the righteous and virtuous, the unscrupulous Blaze had a savage derision. Certainly Blaze was a villain. He had brought a tin dish of water, taken off my ski-ing boots which were too heavy for walking anyway, and was bathing my feet.

'Only wants to see what your ankles are like,' his father drawled.

Old Muirden was a long, humorous man who folded up like a carpenter's rule when he sat down. He had smashed his leg when the extracting house turned over on him last season. The leg had never healed properly and must have been hellish painful. His straight grey hair fell in a bang over his forehead, and his grey eyes looked out with an amusement that had none of Blaze's derision, but a considering and judging fun. He was beginning to be tired of the entertainment, resigned and ready to give up, but he was the kind of joker who would die with one last witticism.

Then there was Fred Connelly, my good friend Fred, who was not a Muirden at all, although at first I took him for one. He was a little hoppy man full of volubility and dogmatism and queer ideas. Fred contended that all old man Muirden had to do to get his leg well was to rub it with honey and sump oil. Honey, Fred claimed, was marvellous for dandruff, and rubbed on a bald spot it would grow hair provided you ground up charcoal and mixed it with the honey. For a stomach-ache there was nothing like honey mixed with a little kerosene. The fact that Fred was still alive showed that these remedies must be harmless and that honey gave you strength and fortitude. For childlessness, melancholia, influenza, arthritis and a tearing cough — honey.

'The only thing it's no good for is drowning,' Fred would say. 'You can't force it between their teeth.'

Fred had just dropped in on the Muirdens. Someone is always coming or going in a camp. One day a beekeeper will be sitting in his wife's kitchen at home, idle and obstructive as a government department. Next morning he is throwing his tucker-box and bedding on the truck, and murmuring that he may be away for a few days. He is away for three weeks. He can't tell his wife where he is going, because he doesn't know. He drops in at other chaps' camps for a yarn or to give them a hand and see if their bees are in good heart. Then he is off 'spotting', looking for bud that might come good or giving some sites the once over before booking them.

He interviews landholders about putting in a few hives, in the back paddock not too near the dam, and where they won't interfere with the stock, for the usual fee of a tin of honey. He never tells anyone, except the few mates with whom he 'exchanges information', where he is going to move his bees. Good country is scarce, and if there is a flow he wants to be on it. Of course information drifts around like pollen in the wind. A man picks up a hint and has to act like lightning to get his bees on a real flow. Fred was pursuing his duties in what might seem a purpose-less manner, but he was there on business and his business was honey.

The fifth member didn't rate as a human being, because he was the paid assistant, and the assistant in a bee camp is the butt, the meekest and most modest of those present. He has to be because if he speaks someone will immediately jump down his throat, or find him something unpleasant to do.

Mongo Cutts, the Muirden assistant, had lasted longer than most, almost three months. Round Tembucca, where the Muirdens lived, they were a byword for the way they treated their help. 'When the Muirdens pile boxes on a barrow,' ex-assistants swore, 'you have to take a step-ladder to get them down.' The assistant always pushed the barrow.

Now Mongo Cutts, finding there was a lady in the camp, thought to distinguish himself brilliantly, and join in the hospitality. He came hurrying forward with a grubby towel, stepped on the basin of water and sent it flying. I thanked him for the towel, and he retired in confusion. Nobody said anything. They were saving it up for him when I should not be there.

I had told them my name, Mallee Herrick, and that my father was with me but recovering from a nervous breakdown, and that Nobby Wallace had sent me to them. As soon as they heard the Roaring Ruin had broken down with sixty hives on it, Joe and Fred Connelly hurried to Fred's battered little truck.

'We'll fix it,' they called, 'or have a damned good try.' They went off like a shot out of a gun. Blaze rose up and jerked his head at Mongo. 'Work,' he said. They went off with the big barrow loaded with empty boxes. I could hear Blaze lecturing Mongo on presumption, clumsiness, the sin of putting himself forward, and his general unworthiness, as soon as he thought he was out of earshot, and from the language he was using, I realized that my presence must have been constricting his speech.

Left alone with the patriarch, I remembered the letter of introduction Nobby had given me and pulled it out of my pocket. Nobby had read it over to me with great pride before he licked the envelope down. It was written in scrawled purple pencil and addressed to Horace Muirden, Pilliga State Forest, via Atholfast.

'Ask at the first timber camp, and you'll find him,' Nobby had said. 'The forestry men always know.'

Muirden took out a pair of horn-rimmed spectacles which gave him quite an intellectual air. 'Nobby writes the way he does everything,' he observed. 'In too much of a hurry. Just like these forestry roads. You saw Mongo fall over that dish? When Nobby was young, he'd not only have managed to fall over it but brain you with it into the bargain.'

'Dear Horace,' the letter ran, 'I am sending M. Herrick to see you because she wants to be a migratory apiarist and although I tell her it is no game for a woman she is like her grandfather stubborn. You remember old Applecore Smith who made a fortune out of health foods everyone said he would go broke so nothing is impossible I worked for him for years on shares on this property but it is to be sold under the will and I am buying that orchard I wanted not too big to handle Applecore's son Beresford is trustee under the will so it will probably never be settled but if it ever is M. Herrick comes in for a chunk of money I am mentioning money because it is always a nice subject to discuss I hear you are selling your bees so if she wants to buy them do not put anything over her or I will personally come up and dong you for old times sake I do not say look after M. Herrick because she can do that for herself but give her a fair go I trust the wife is well and remember me to Col if you ever see him now. How is he the same as ever I suppose Yrs. Cromwell S. Wallace.'

It took Mr. Muirden some time to read this document and I had my boots on and was rolling a cigarette when he said, 'So you're Applecore Smith's grand-daughter. I ought to of noticed the likeness. He always came out fighting. I remember once we sold him a consignment of honey and he picked the only watery tin in the whole load. Had an instinct.'

He looked at me hopefully to see if I had inherited anything except my grandfather's face, high in the cheek-bones and wide between the eyes. 'So you're going to be a big-time apiarist?' He continued, 'Years ago when my brother and me found our first swarm on a fence post we settled down with a pencil and paper and worked out that if we had enough bees we might make as much as seventy-five pounds a year, even if the wife gave up dressmaking. Think of that! Seventy-five pounds! Big money in those days.' He shifted his leg, raising it on to another tucker box. 'What's more, you didn't have to shift your bees to the other end of the earth to get a bit of honey. When you get older, Miss Herrick, even if you haven't a bad leg, you wonder what's the use of all this tearing around in big trucks and sweating your guts out. We lost two hundred hives in a bush fire out from Sarn. We was helping a cocky keep the fire off his wheat and the wind turns round and our camp cops the lot.' I shook my head sympathetically. 'The honey was just like toffee year before last on the rivers. You couldn't extract it there was so little moisture in it. Then there was the floods.'

I could have sat forever peacefully listening to him with the obbligato of bees backing up his voice. There had been three years when bees hadn't been making tucker money. Floods on the coast drowning whole townships, hundreds of miles of inland plain a grey soup which dried to rank growth of green soon brittle under the hot winds. All the western slopes were ploughed by fire that came with the winds. From Moree to Condoblin lay a great turning axis of fire. The smoke rose round threatened homes, hurricane blasts of hot air twisted the locks of flame in the tree scalps and ripped them from the writhing boughs. The sheep, blind and kicking like crippled grubs, could not stumble through the burnt fences. Chimney stacks and blackened beams were all that were left of homesteads for sale or auction.

'Now a migratory apiarist,' Muirden went on, 'isn't a bee-keeper. He's a man that makes the bees support *him*. That's the theory anyway. But I figure by the time I pay petrol and running expenses and taxation and the mortgage, that I'm still being played for a sucker by a mob of insects. I want to save my sons from the same. Joe's always talking about joining the navy. He figures he's never heard of bees aboard a battleship.'

'When Uncle Beresford,' I interrupted, 'built a fine new home up the line, a swarm of bees came and settled in the chimney. He had it torn down to get them out. He said Grandpa was haunting him.'

'Well, maybe they even get aboard battleships,' old Muirden agreed. 'Bees ought to give a man a peaceful life, but you're always shifting them. If you're not shifting them, you're speeding over the country looking for sites and paying for sites you most likely won't use. Luckily the young lady Blaze is engaged to has got sick of it. She says straight out she don't see herself married to an absentee. So he's got to the stage when he'll take a job in Tembucca to keep his eye on her. She certainly is good-looking. And it don't do to leave such a good-looking girl too long alone.'

'So you're selling out the whole show? Cash down?'

'I'm trying to do like Nobby says,' old Muirden explained patiently, 'and give you a fair go. In the first place you don't know nothing about the work and it's tough for a man. In the second, you'll do your dough.'

'I can always get a job writing scripts,' I told him. 'I've been doing that for years.'

'How old are you?'

'I'm twenty-four,' I said. 'I've been writing scripts since I was sixteen, and I'm fed up with it.'

'What about if you get married?'

'Well, what about it? I could have got married before this.'

'I don't doubt that,' old Muirden agreed courteously. I rolled a cigarette. 'But then again you'd have to depend on assistants, which is the most heart-breaking thing there is. Why don't you go with Fred Connelly for twelve months — and learn the ropes? He'd be pleased to have you.'

That sounded sensible but I didn't like to tell him I had

a hunch this was going to be a good year and I mightn't ever find a bargain again like the Muirdens'. Four hundred full-depth hives, extracting house, truck, neuc boxes and the rest of the gear all thrown in for £3,000. Why, you couldn't buy a small-sized house for that money in the suburbs. Such a chance would never come twice.

We sat there sizing each other up while we talked. I liked old Muirden. If he was Nobby's idea of a villain, villains suited me. He was quiet and polite and his lop-sided grin indicated good-nature rather than wickedness. Certainly he thought I was a bit of a joke, but a man with a sore leg is welcome to any light entertainment he might find in the thought of me as a bee cocky. Presently the battered little truck came whizzing up as though it was on its way to an accident. Out of it stepped Dennis Oberon Herrick looking like a diplomat captured by bandits and prepared to make an international incident out of it. When he saw me, he seemed relieved. Down the track came the Roaring Ruin with the fair boy Joe at the wheel, and I hastened over marvelling that the knock was gone.

'What was it?' old Muirden called.

'No oil in the gearbox,' Joe replied, and to me, 'Didn't you notice the clutch slipping?'

'The clutch always slips in the Roaring Ruin,' I said coldly, knowing my stocks had fallen lower than a politician's conscience.

The Parent was shaking hands with everyone, even Mongo. 'Very kind of you. Too bad to trespass on your time and keep you from your work.'

'Joe' — Blaze had come over to view the new arrival — 'take Mongo and run Miss Herrick's bees up to the old camp and off-load them. Don't bother about unclipping them. Just open the entrance so they can make a cleansing flight.'

They fetched Dennis's beautiful travelling bags from the Roaring Ruin. I took off the tucker box, my old army kitbag and sleeping bag and the typewriter.

'The tent's for you,' old Muirden told me. 'The riff-raff will camp by the fire. We'll clean out the extracting house later for your father.'

'No, thank you,' I said. 'If you can fit my father in the tent, I'll just sleep the way I like it, on the ground.'

'There *are* snakes,' Blaze warned.

'Don't argue with her,' the Parent said. 'Let her have her own way.'

He went off to possess himself of Blaze's bed. Presently he was stretched out with old Muirden lounging on the other bed, in a surf of paper-backed detective stories.

The Parent was giving Horace Muirden his heaviest line of conversation, all about what his friend the Minister for the Storage of Waste Products told him the Prime Minister had said. He scattered big names. If old Muirden didn't escape from the flood of eloquence Dennis would probably sell him some shares in an oil show. The Parent has the soul of a con man. I can never understand why a man who can write dialogue as well as he does should not be content with making a steady income, but instead wants to devote his life to oil-wells and mining companies. He is director of a mysterious organization known as Northern Exploitations, and that is the reason why the one foot we have in the poor-house is always about to be joined by the other foot. Now bees are substantial and productive, but an oil-well is just a hole in the ground down which the shareholders' money is dropped.

After tea — we tuckered the Muirdens that night because we had plenty of food and they had been 'doing a starve', not wanting to go into town until they had tinned off — we sat round the fire and the Muirdens tried to persuade

18

me that I should have the tent all to myself. I won that argument and I should have put a cross up to mark the date, because I never seemed to win an argument after that. In fact, as soon as their courtesy and deference wore off, I think Mongo was better off than I was. However, apart from telling me that bees were no game for a woman, they were still on their best behaviour.

No game for a woman, I said to myself, as I wriggled down into the sleeping bag. Always that, no game for a woman. I looked up at the stars swarming to some far celestial hive, I breathed the clean dry air. Nonchalant and black and devil-may-care, the box containing my father's ashes floated off to sea. It was my secret symbol, the emblem of my inner pride. You cannot sink us even when we are dead. I curled up like a case moth in my cocoon, fidgeted a rock from under my shoulder-blade and went to sleep. The Muirdens and Fred Connelly were still talking round the camp-fire, their voices lowered, discussing something that interested them very deeply.

Chapter Two

THE range of the migratory men in New South Wales is along the slopes and plateaus of the Great Divide. They take their bees down to winter on the coast, but the reason they remain along the slopes and mountains is that here are the trees. The eucalypt is the greatest honey tree in the world, and men who allow themselves no other passions will grow bitter to see a yellow box cut down.

Eucalypts are scraggy raggy trees, writhing plumy trees, with projecting skeleton boughs and elbows, broken jagged spars and left-over sticks like old hairpins and hatpins in their feathers, great limbs wrenched off, untidy scattered timber, leathery old leaves and tender green-gold tips. They are take-it-or-leave-it trees with their pants and braces hanging down and their white arms emerging from dirty old grey flannel sweat-shirts of bark.

Their great buttress roots grip and break the rocks; their hard, fibrous runner roots toil out through clay or dry dirt in search of the last wrapping of moisture round a grain of sand. Their seeds will lie for years until the forest falls or the fire ravens, and then, in the blackened desolation, the young ones are up again in the clearing, soaring to the sun, plumbing in the dark, courageous and thirsty and hard, coming up fighting. Knock back a eucalypt to the ground and it will sucker up from the stump.

Ring-bark it until it dies, strangling and choking, chop it down, grub out the great undertooth of bony grey timber, burn it off in its immense strength and vitality, with labour and sweat and curses, and you will have the satisfaction the Australian farmer has in bringing low and ruining something greater and more splendid than himself.

The first act of men when they set foot ashore was to cut down the trees, and they have been spreading among trees like a terrible disease ever since, stripping the land bare for grass and nibbling mouths, blind mouths, so that there is only dirt, that in the heat and drought blows away on the wind, red clouds on the air where there were green clouds of leaves. The trees go down before the bulldozers and die. They are only timber useful for pit props or building houses, no value till they are dead.

But to the few who love the eucalypts, they are the crowning glory of this country, and their blossoming, when the great furls of tree-tops look as though they have been showered with snow, their clean scent and colour, the way they reflect the hard, hot light, their careless, lopsided shaggy ugliness, is more than any graceful precision of gardening. They are the creatures of the wilderness, and their flowers, careless, gracious in generosity, poured out heaped and running over with nectar, are a foam on the tree's rejoicing.

Yet if you ask people what month the white box flowers near their town, or the broadleaf or the silverleaf, they will not know. The chances are they have never noticed that passionate outburst of glancing, foaming, billowing blossom, even though every bird and insect for miles has been feasting and intoxicated with brief plenty. Their eyes starve and their hearts moulder in a mud of worries without ever lifting up high, high, to the singing and wassailing, to sip the scent and froth and gladness.

Let them eat dirt. They possess the dirt, it is their miserable heritage, and until it all blows into the sea it belongs to them. It is under their nails and in their minds and mortgages. Their cities choke in it, their arts and knowledge choke in dirt, their children breathe it in. The wild people of the forests are gone, people like shadows hunting shadows under the trees, because they could not live in the evil glare of the dirt-eaters. Buy yourself a pulp magazine full of sex and murder and read it going home over miles of concrete and asphalt to a house made of baked dirt amid other mounds of baked dirt. Let your ant mind crawl through corridors of steel and dirt, jungles of streets and houses and shops. It is wrath and iron and it serves you right.

But with daylight I was up. Fred asked me to wake him at daylight so he could get an early start. When I yelled to him, voices moaned that there was Mallee tramping round in the middle of the bloody night, so I left them and, as quietly as possible, started the Roaring Ruin. I knew if I hung around I would be an irritation and a nuisance. Men in the early morning like to rub their beard and ponder and stretch without any female brisking about, shaming them in their stubble.

Joe had set my bees down on a claypan of eroded yellow flat about five miles from the camp. There were the sixty hives, dubious and shifty-looking and battered. Nobby had not had time to paint, but he had fitted them with Ansett's patent locking cleats that clamped them firm for shifting, so that you did not have all the tiresome fuss of tin strips to be locked round the hives.

They were full-depth migratory hives with the oblongs of wire gauze ventilators in the floor of the bottom box so that a current of air can circulate upwards when the bees are travelling. All round the claypan was a thick, whippy growth of narrowleaf with my name tree, the mallee, thick in flower as boiling milk, a stuggy under-sized tree with a tremendous grip of the ground. People only know mallee now by its roots of gnarled and satin-brown timber for carving, but I know it as a rough-barked, close-growing flower-bearer with shallow cups of clear waxy white rimmed with a froth of stamens.

I gazed at my hives like a mother whose child has a dirty dress at a party. They were home-made, solid cedar from a log Nobby had bought and worked himself. But I wished they had a coat of paint, pale yellowish cream, like the flowers. The boys were always despising them aloud for a mongrelly lot of hives. 'Mallee's old butter boxes' was the best term they ever used, even after I painted them weeks later. But they only did it to get me wild.

I had my bee veil and smoker, and I needed them because the bees were astir and mad as hornets. They had come from an orange orchard with clover, and here they were dumped down on what must have seemed the other side of the moon with scouts bringing in the news of strangeness and excitement. Joe had slid back the little metal doors a tiny way. I opened them right back.

'Now, people,' I said, 'begin to live', and I went fussing and strolling about, lifting off the lids to see if any had drowned in nectar, too watery and slopping in the combs.

They had stood the trip splendidly. There were a few hives with old black queens past their prime and, of course, Joe had put those ostentatiously where anyone would look in and think what a lousy lot of bees these were, while my best hives were in the middle where nobody would notice them. Yes, they badly needed paint.

Joe had ranged them in beautiful straight rows, tidy and trim, looking towards the sun-rising east and a little north, as bees like to be. There were no tall weeds around them and, as far as I could see, no small black ants. Under one lid I killed a big spider that had travelled with us all the way, and wondered how we had come to overlook that bee-eating evildoer.

Down in the dip of land beyond the claypan was a little gully with water still seeping from pool to pool through a tangle of blackened sticks that had discoloured it. One pool was big enough for wallowing among the water beetles which skated off in a commotion at the strange uproar and tidal wave of behemoth among them. The bank was sandy with a frail, sparse covering of red-headed seed grass under the cypress. I crumpled a sprig of grey-blue cypress to smell the resinous clean sap and rubbed it on my wet skin. Bees like you to smell pleasant.

Then, with the sun coming up, by the cold black-shadowed creek, I sat gazing over at my bees and let my mind relax, not thinking, not noticing, just seeping like the creek from one impression to the next, slowly through the tangle and obstruction. I would not meet obstacles, I would evade, slip between, go around. No opposition, no arguments, just a fluid aimless wandering my own way. My grandfather had been tall and shaggy and white-headed, and death had lopped him down. My father was a black box slapped by sunlit waves; my mother, Julie, took her pleasure in the stars and the comforts of a city flat, amiable and luxurious and funny. My sister Anita flowered by herself, glossy and pretty; but I would go slipping and twisting away, and I would be with my bees in the forests.

These Muirdens were a savage tribe speaking a strange language that I must learn, so that I did not crunch over their etiquette and customs. When you introduce strange bees into a colony, you must put up a paper barrier, and by the time the barrier is nibbled through, the bees will have the hive smell and be accepted. I would put up a paper barrier against the Muirdens until they accepted me.

When I returned to the camp, I had already offended them. They realized I had been to look at my bees, and they felt wounded that I had not trusted them, so they said nothing. Later they would have shouted to ask me what the hell I meant haring off before bloody daylight to check up on my miserable, half-bred black old mongrels of bees? But they were silent and gentlemanly over their steak. They had shaved and spruced themselves. Of course, when they were used to me, they didn't bother, and grew luxuriant beards, and blamed me for everything, but in our camp that morning courtesy and manners were prevalent.

Dennis drew me aside, and asked me how long we were staying. A day or so?

'We'll see in a week's time,' I said.

Dennis drew a long breath. 'Mongo got the water for tea out of the gutter.'

'The creek.'

'Do you realize it's half mud?'

'The tea disguises the flavour.'

'Nothing but mud to wash in. My dear girl, you can't stand it. There isn't even an earth closet for the most primitive human needs. And I cannot accustom myself to putting my foot out of bed and feeling my toes on dirt. Of course I was accustomed to roughing it in the army,' Dennis added handsomely. In the army he had been one of a regiment with showers and barracks and huts and canteens and latrines. Here there was a tiny clearing with five men and nothing for thirty miles but trees. 'No privacy,' Dennis said, looking at the wilderness stretching in every direction. 'Bees,' he went on. 'I have already been stung by one of the beastly things, and there are millions of them waiting their chance. I was stung by mosquitoes. I didn't get a wink of sleep.'

Dennis was going to be a problem, so I seeped round him. 'We must make a good impression on Muirden Brothers,' I argued. 'I want to buy their bees.'

'Good God, no. You never said a word to me about buying bees when we started. You're secretive, Mallee.

25

I knew you were plotting with Wallace. I thought you merely intended to ferry your wretched hives to this Nithering and leave them there with Nobby's friend.'

We were sitting on a log on the edge of the clearing. If I had had Nobby — and the plan had been to bring Nobby until Julie insisted that Dennis should come — I would have had someone to depend on, an official interpreter and negotiator, a friend to both parties, a man who spoke the Muirden language.

Dennis ran on lamenting. 'What would you do with the damn things if you had them?' he asked at last.

'Travel them. Work them. Tin off the honey and sell it.'

'And you'd live like this?' He waved his hand. 'Like a black in the scrub?'

'I'd have a damned good try.'

Fred Connelly had forgotten he was going to leave early. He had his sleeves rolled up and was taking the Roaring Ruin apart. Bits of it were lying on the road on an old tarp. Fred would come over from time to time to announce that the timing chain was worn, or the rear shock absorber had come away from the chassis. So I crawled under the truck with him, and let him explain about oil leaks and seals. He gave me a lecture on the maintenance of vehicles and engines, while the Parent decided to do some cooking and puttered about the fire, talking to Horace Muirden and beating off blowflies about the size of small vultures.

He was explaining to Horace Muirden why he favoured soya-bean sauce as a flavouring to the casserole he was cooking in a big iron pot. Horace's leg was 'playing up' again, and he was going home with Fred. The Muirdens came from Tembucca, just a hop-step-and-a-jump away — about a hundred and fifty miles. It would be only sixty miles out of Fred's way to run him home.

The Honey Flow

Blaze and Mongo were out in the yard taking off honey, slipping frames full of honey into empty boxes on the big barrow. As soon as they had a barrowload they would come grunting and tugging through the loose sand up to the extracting house and slam them in, pile them up and go off with a load of boxes to be replaced on the hives. They worked their way down the rows, their sleeves rolled up — if you leave only your wrists exposed the bees will sting your wrists, and when they swell you can't work.

Blaze would give them a little smoke round the entrance and the lid, a few delicate puffs, not the enveloping clouds of smoke you see with a man who doesn't know his job, smoke that makes the bees sick and dazed. Mongo would lift off the lid and Blaze, with the hive tool, loosen the frames in the dark wax with which the bees had fixed them tight. Then he would take out a frame, gently shaking the bees down in front of the hive entrance. They would all start climbing in again, making a pansy-brown glowing, moving carpet about his boots. With the smoker between his knees, he handed the frame to Mongo, who dipped a brush in water, shook it and brushed off the remaining bees before setting the frame in the 'empty' on the barrow. He also had a tin in which to put burr comb, which the bees build under the lid, when they have filled the frames. Blaze never stopped a running commentary of orders, complaints, exclamations and anecdotes all the time he worked. He was not one of your silent men. If he could not joke, he sang, and the harder he worked the louder he sang and the worse his jokes became.

There are two great crimes in a honey camp. One is killing bees and the other is known as 'peaking'. It gives a bee man real suffering to see a visitor swiping at bees the way the Parent swiped at them. 'Those bees,' they say sternly, 'are worth threepence each.' Any sudden

27

movement will cause them to commit suicide by stinging some mountain of flesh near at hand. Nor is it good form to yell when you are stung. A man may remark quietly, 'They're sitting down pretty heavy today', or a big six-footer exclaim, 'Oh mother, I'm a poor sick girl', but a real complaint comes under the head of 'peaking'. When you have been lumping heavy honey tins, or seventy-pound boxes all day with a poisoned hand or a temperature and are sweating and dirty and hungry, some motorist will come and ask you to tow him out of a creek, and you are expected not only to do it, but joke about it. You must never give in even if you are dying or broke or licked. That would be 'peaking'.

One thing more dangerous than the bees to a new hand in a honey camp is the sense of humour of his mates. Anything goes, and when some practical joke leaves your mates so weak with laughing that they have to lean against trees, all you can do is drawl, 'I'll pay that one', and think up something worse to play on the man who caught you. On the third night after I joined the Muirdens, I very luckily shook my sleeping bag before I got in it and a dead snake fell out. I was saving the snake to put in Blaze's bed, but the ants got it. He nevertheless continued to shake his blankets very carefully every night. I never 'let on' I knew to whom I was indebted for the snake.

Joe had steam up in the extracting house before breakfast. It was painted all silver and green, like a small temple, and at night he would scrub it out and wash it down, working with hot water and broom and brush by the light of a small electric bulb he ran off a battery.

First thing in the morning he would have Mongo chopping wood for the boiler, and would glance at the gauge every now and then to see if he had pressure up. The steam warmed the wax reducer and the honey tank and the hot knife to uncap the combs. Without heat you cannot melt the wax.

Then he would start the motor and as soon as the put-put of the motor began in the clearing the day's work had commenced. We worked to the rhythm of the extracting house, and when the motor was cut out and the small plume of smoke vanished from over its roof the silence was so peaceful. The tea was made, we rested and joked in the shade, or, if it was evening, began on other jobs. But all day long the extracting house swayed with the whirr of the baskets in the big honey tank and the slam of the boxes being pushed in and out, the purring of the motor.

By mid-afternoon the extracting-house floor was a swamp of mud, drowned bees, bits of wax, honey and dirt. A fume, a haze of honey filled the air, stung your nostrils, and the sweat ran down your face in big drops.

The first morning I climbed into the extracting house where Joe, remote and priestlike, was slicing off the cappings from the comb with the warmed, hollow knife that had a coil of rubber tubing to convey the steam to it. He would seize a frame in his big hands, holding it tilted so that the cappings melted down before the knife into the tray of the wax reducer. Then he would twirl the frame and uncap the comb on the other side. The uncapped frame he placed ready in another aluminium drip-tray by the extractor, the big drum in which the wire baskets revolved on a central pivot.

When he had enough combs uncapped, he would place them in the wire baskets down in the drum, throw the gears in by means of a metal handle on a bar, and give the baskets a push to start them revolving. They would twirl faster and faster, the honey whipping out against the side of the drum until there was only a fine spray. Then he would stop the baskets so that they swung over, change gear, and send them round again, the centrifugal action flicking the honey from the other side of the frame. The frames are whipped out empty of honey and full ones take their place in the baskets.

When I had the hang of it, I said, 'I can do that for you, Joe.'

'This is a man's job, Mallee,' Joe said sternly. His father would have been helping in the extracting house if his leg had not given him such pain. I heard the boys swearing at him that morning when he tried to take the job. Fred would have been in the extracting house, but he was repairing the Roaring Ruin.

'You get me a box to stand on,' I argued, 'and I can reach those gears.'

They had been designed for six-footers like Joe. He could not very well throw a guest out of the extracting house, so after a few protests and growls he found a sack for me to tie on as an apron. At first I bungled the gears in a way that made him flinch, but presently I was working fast, slipping the uncapped comb into the baskets, shoving in the gears, taking out frames, sorting them into broods which are the combs with young bees and eggs in them, and stickies which are those holding honey.

Sorting is a tricky job because it is easy enough with a careless glance to mistake a frame of uncapped brood for a sticky and not notice the tiny eggs. When Joe was uncapping the comb, he would try to avoid the knife over even one brood cell, though he always slashed out drone comb. The sealed brood comb has a thickened, yellow bulging cap, not flat like the capping on honey.

Sometimes you would see the poor white grubs curled up in their tiny homes, clean and solitary, dreaming in their cell, and I would feel sorry their lives were finished before they were begun. Or there would be young bees just crawling out from under the coverlet of wax, bursting out furry and harmless and dewy, only to be swept away in the ruthless suck of the honey pump.

That pump — Joe would never let me operate it — was regulated by a lever down beside the drum, and it adjusted the flow to the big tank on the back of the truck. Any wax floated on the top of the honey, and the stuff we sold was 'tinned off' into four-gallon tins from a tap at the base of the tank.

When Mongo had nothing else to do, he was 'tinning off'. I sometimes helped him rinse out tins to rid them of dead bees and dirt. Any that showed a spark of daylight through the bottom had to be stacked separately. A honey tin with a hole in it is about as much use as a soprano to a deaf man. Mongo was always in strife for letting honey spill over the top when he was filling tins. Then he would be bawled out for not filling them enough. I was glad I didn't have the job.

Helping Joe in the extracting house made me tired enough, so tired that I ached by nightfall. I had a blue-and-green bruise on my hip from leaning over the metal rim of the extractor to reach the gears. The Muirdens, when pressing their foundation wax into the two wires stretched across, often left little bits of rusty wire twisted round nail heads on the outside of the frames. Picking these up in a hurry meant torn fingertips and festering cuts. Bees often decided to make a last stand and stung those torn fingertips, or they crawled up from the welter of the floor to stab your leg. So many of them stung me on the ankles, and they swelled up so, that I borrowed a pair of army leggings from Joe. Socks were no protection.

Hurriedly dipping my sticky hands in the water bucket and wiping them on my front meant that I splashed my sacking apron. It was always sticky and soaking before the day was over.

'Never saw anyone get as mucky as you do,' Blaze said

sympathetically one hot afternoon as he trundled up
to the extracting house a load of boxes. 'Here,' and as
I leant out he sloshed the water from Mongo's brush tin
all over me.

'Why didn't you smash a frame over his head?' Joe
asked. 'Those over there.' He pointed to a pile of old
combs set aside to be burned. He wasn't going to have me
wasting good frames. I removed the red handkerchief I
wore over my hair, because bees always dive for something
shiny, like hair or your eyes. Thoughtfully wiping my
neck, I said it was best to allow a joke to fall into a
small pool of politeness that quenched it. Besides, Blaze
was bigger than me.

When Blaze came dragging the barrow next time,
Joe roared at him to shove some wood under the boiler,
and not to go kicking it in with his foot either. 'He's
broken two gauges on me already,' he growled. 'Have to
twist tin strips round to protect them.'

I smiled because old Joe resented Blaze taking a rise
out of what he now regarded as the assistant in his
extracting house. He had reached the stage of telling me
all day long what I was doing wrong, but nobody else
was to push me about. Before they found I was useful
I had status as a guest. When I worked as an assistant,
I was treated as an assistant. In one sense I had risen in
the world, because they had forgotten I was a lady and
now ranked me just below Mongo.

Fred spent two days repairing the Roaring Ruin and
then declared himself ready to take Horace home. I
wouldn't have dared offer Fred money, but I determined
I would do him a favour some time, and thanked him so
heartily that I was asked not to sprinkle any cow confetti.

Dennis enjoyed talking by the fire at night while we
boiled our overalls and clanked round with buckets.
With bees clean clothes are part of the job. Dennis never

complained to the Muirdens. For them he put on his act and took the spotlight in mid-stage with background music. His entrance from that tent was always impressive, and some of the performances he gave by our camp-fire would have brought roars of applause from any audience. He would stay in bed most of the day, as an actor likes to do, and then emerge brisk to give of his best in the evening.

Being good raconteurs themselves and spending all their spare time yarning, those bee men were in a position to appreciate a good story, and Dennis could certainly tell a good story.

'You know your dad's a bloody marvel,' Blaze would say, enviously. 'It's no wonder he does big things in oil. If a man wasn't stuck out here in the scrub, and had half a chance . . .'

I did not disillusion him. Let him keep his boyish longings. He even picked up some tricks of speech from Dennis, and would watch him closely, when Dennis wasn't looking, to memorize his mannerisms. As it has always been my own habit in any gathering to merge into the pattern of the wallpaper, I was happy to see Dennis shining for both of us. I think they had convinced themselves that Dennis was buying their bees to humour the whim of his odd daughter, and was some bountiful Croesus scattering gold.

There we would sit, Dennis and Fred Connelly starting some story that began, 'That reminds me of the time', and Blaze sticking in his oar, with Joe and Mongo as an appreciative audience, and me too tired to do more than creak when I moved.

But there was a look in Dennis's eye that forebode a break from this clearing with walls thirty miles thick. He had realized that a convalescent home might not be so bad after all. 'Everything will be going to pieces,' he warned me. 'Julie can't keep Mrs. Prothero up by herself.'

I brought out the typewriter and had Mongo fix the mess table in the tent for him to work. He tapped away, impatient, champing and complaining, but getting a certain amount done, coming over to the extracting house to shout, 'Mallee, can you remember which confounded son married Nell?' Nell was a friend of ours who often took parts in 'Mrs. Prothero'; she could be anything from a sunny little child to a heavy foreign accent.

'Basil,' I told him. The Muirdens were quite uplifted to have an author among them. When Dennis said he would go home with Horace, who kept vowing he would be back at the end of the week, and that his leg was no trouble at all, Joe took me aside.

'Don't you believe it,' he said. 'Once Dad gets home Mum'll keep him there.'

So I set my face against Dennis going. 'Surely, Parent,' I said, 'you wouldn't leave me here unchaperoned.' I didn't want to lay it on too thick because Dennis might wake up. 'Think what Julie would say if she heard that you slunk off and left me alone with three men.'

'Just which of the three looks so dangerous?' Dennis was sarcastic. 'Anyway, you should have thought of that earlier.' By now he was almost resigned to my buying the outfit. I do not know if my objection carried any weight, but Dennis said no more and Fred went off with Horace.

'When I come back, we'll talk about that offer, Mallee,' old Horace said as I shook his hand.

I walked beside the truck wanting to clinch the deal. 'I can get a cheque any time you say,' I offered.

'Plenty of time,' the villain parried. 'We're taking off honey still.'

'You won't sell to anyone else?' I insisted.

'Talk about it when I get back.' The old devil went off, and the doctor set his leg in plaster, and that was the last I saw of him for three months.

After Horace and Fred left, the old fight about the bed started again. The boys had slung a tarpaulin over a sapling between two uprights to make me a tent and built up walls of bee boxes. It was much bigger and more comfortable than the auto tent. Now they wanted to move in the old squeaky iron bed for me. I didn't want the darn thing.

'A mule,' Blaze swore. 'Nothing but an army mule.'

'The army doesn't have mules now, does it, Parent?'

'You are not so much obstinate as wall-eyed.' Dennis sided with the opposition. There he sat, under the open sky, a man who could have been home in a comfortable flat with a whisky at his elbow disobeying the doctor's orders. He could have been at his club talking oil. He could have rung up Hubert and given him hell about the cast of 'Mrs. Prothero'. He was stuck in the scrub with a blackened kerosene tin full of overalls boiling on the fire, sitting on an upended kerosene tin, drinking tea and creek water with not even a radio. Nothing but a mousy, evil-natured stepdaughter.

If only I could have clinched old Horace on the deal before he left, but Horace was a good deal more fluid and evasive than I. He had just flowed round me for some reason. Of course I could pack up my sixty hives and go on to Nithering, but that would leave Joe short-handed in the extracting house. I sat by the fire thinking.

The rest of the team, rather disconsolate without old Horace and Fred, retired. Only Mongo silently kept me company. Not even Julie's stars, which night after night had been moving about so faithfully, tidying up the affairs of Julie's friends and bringing good luck and contrary influences to step up the prosperity or vibrate against the well-being of Mr. Pollock's clientèle. A thick haze had obscured them. Above that vapour they would be there the same as ever, shining and moving, while the grey still drift below them blanketed the forests on one little shining ball among those millions of ball-bearings in the universe.

'I think I'll have a bath,' I said aloud.

'Yes, Mallee,' Mongo said obediently. He carried the tin bath tub into the dark extracting house eager to do good. He carted over a kerosene tin half full of warm water, while I collected my soap and towel from Dennis's tent. 'And here's another billyful on the fire,' he said agreeably. 'So now you'll have plenty.'

I thanked him. I was the only person in the camp who ever thanked poor Mongo.

He trotted off to bed pleased with himself. I poured the half kerosene tin of water into the tub looking forward to going to bed really clean; not just a wallow in the creek early in the morning, but a real hot bath. Dennis was not the only one missing the luxuries of civilization. Soaping my hair, I took up the billy-can of warm water and poured it over my head. Tea! It was full of left-over tea and tea-leaves. Mongo again, just the sort of thing blasted Mongo *would* do. Glumly I tried to get the tea-leaves out of my hair.

Chapter Three

THE next day had a strange red glow over it like a bush-fire suffusing the sunlight with a smoky, sombre tinge. There had been hot winds thrashing through the bush, but our camp was protected from the dust devils curling along the road. Perhaps the weather had been getting on Dennis's nerves, because he had not really been having such a poor time. The water we drank did not come from the 'gutter', as Dennis suggested, but from a creek thirteen miles up the road where the water was still running and not stagnant.

Only our washing water came from the 'gutter'. Soon it would be necessary to cart water for the bees, setting out drums with little floating boards on which they could alight to drink. The very ground was thirsty. There is an uneasiness in forests where the last of the water is going, a dumb, agonizing complaint that communicates itself as a restlessness in human beings, even though they may still have enough to drink themselves. Misery, whether we like it or not, is shared. Now the trees had blossom, heaped and tossed in the hot light, but little nectar.

Nevertheless the extracting house was moved up to the top yard near the creek from which the drinking water came. There would be enough to make it worth while to finish going round the yards. This was the last. The Muirdens had taken off honey from three of the five before we arrived. They had finished the yard at the camp, and now there remained only the bees by the creek.

Setting up the extracting house was a fussy job. The trailer had to be backed into holes dug to take the wheels, slowly, exactly, with shouts and instructions. One of the holes was deeper than the other — Mongo again! — and had to be filled in after the extracting house was pulled out. Then the same business of backing and filling began until the house settled in a dignified way like a hen about to lay, its big tyres rolling down in the pits prepared for them. Then it had to be set firm and chocked and braced on rocks and pieces of wood, with Joe adjusting the floor plumb with a spirit level so that the moving parts of the extractor were not harmed by working on a tilt. Finally he was satisfied.

Mongo had been chopping wood and they got up steam, and while Mongo and Blaze went off with the barrow I had nothing to do but look about me at the furnace-hot, sinister landscape under a sky like something out of hell. You could almost see the leaves writhe and crackle in the heat. Weather for bush-fires, tinder dry, white hot.

Blaze was cursing Mongo for something he had done, and for once Mongo growled back at him. He said he would give the unprintable job away, and Blaze called him names that his mother would not have liked. They were taking a terrible hiding from those bees that morning. The sand was heavy for dragging the dead weight of the barrow, and the heat made you gasp. Sweat was running down inside my boiler suit in rivulets, and by lunchtime, when we crouched in what might at one time have been shade, we were all pretty beat. Mongo's nerve was cracking. He had been tongue-lashed all the morning. I suppose Blaze was worried about his father.

'Aw gee,' Mongo sighed. 'Me brother Sid's home now with his mandolin, and he'd be singing them hill-billy songs.'

'Silly muck,' Joe growled. We had endured long sagas

about Mongo's relatives. He was the second youngest of a shiftless, starveling family, but, to hear poor Mongo, his 'old man' was a noble fellow whom Mongo regarded with adoration. He kept bees — and what bees the Muirdens would tell you. 'He *starves* bees, you mean,' Blaze would interrupt.

'Aw gee,' Joe mimicked Mongo, 'here's poor old Mongo doing a starve with those Muirdens that killed their last assistant and buried him in the scrub.' And he set about baiting Mongo.

'Now shut up, Joe,' I said, because I thought Mongo, nursing his bee stings, might burst out crying. Maybe they were all savage because we were reduced to sardines and fish paste and some oranges from the half case that Nobby had sent as a present to his pal up in Nithering. A truck from the timber camp had brought us out some bread and meat, but we were out of vegetables and, of course, although we wrapped the corned beef in calico flour bags there wasn't any really cool place to hang it, and the bread was stale. 'Give Mongo a break,' I commanded.

'If he'd take that brass ring off,' Blaze insisted, 'the bees 'ud let him alone. But no, flash, flash, there he is with that ring daring them to go him.' Mongo went red in the face.

'Look here, Blaze,' I said quickly, 'let me come out in the yard with you this afternoon. I'd like to be brush boy for a change.'

'You mad?' Blaze exclaimed. 'They'd murder you. Look what they done to Mongo.'

'Let the bloody girl have her own way,' Joe told him weakly. 'You know what she's like. "Let me do that for you, Joe", and it's no use saying she can't.'

Blaze looked from me to Mongo. He realized Mongo was cracking. The glare and the heat and Blaze's temper and the pasting the bees had given him were too much. 'All right,' he said, repenting of his bad temper with a touch of compunction. 'That's all right, Mongo. You go in the house with Joe.'

Mongo said nothing. There comes a point when, if you don't relieve the strain, an otherwise quiet young fellow will go completely berserk. Mongo was very near that point. 'I can do it,' he finally croaked.

'Of course you can,' Blaze soothed. 'But silly-looking Mallee here wants to have a go. Nobody says you're peaking, Mongo.' We went off hastily to the bee yard. 'All the same,' Blaze muttered to me, 'he is. He's windy, big as he is.'

'It's your damned bad temper.'

'Right. It's my temper. But there he is with his big feet, crunch, crunch on my bees. . . .'

The oppressive glare became heavier as we worked along the rows. I stood by the side of the hive, a little behind it, taking the frames from Blaze, brushing them carefully, placing them in the empty supers.

'Getting any stings?' Blaze asked, after we had been working in silence for some time. It was heavier work for him because he would not let me push the barrow.

'No, not yet.' The bees were all around us in a thick pelter like raindrops. I had my veil down and so had he. Blaze had been scratching out stings, but then he was moving about more than I was.

'Just what I say!' he exclaimed. 'It isn't the bees, it's Mongo. He gets frightened and they know it.'

'If you gave him half a chance and didn't haze him . . .'

'Well, you stop hazing me.'

I could have shot Blaze when he made a special trip to the extracting house to tell Mongo the bees weren't stinging me. He might have spared him that, but Blaze could be mean. The red glare was now positively uncanny, and suddenly there was a wind. You could hear the roar of it like a train in the distance, and above the haze there were great clouds, the edges lit with light.

'Finish,' Blaze commanded. 'Here it comes.'

We couldn't have worked anyway. Leaves whirled past, the silence fell again, but all the time there was that roar approaching. The sun went out leaving us in dull grey dust. Joe was out of the extracting house rushing about, picking up bottom boards, lids, anything that might blow away. Then the roar was on us as we came up to the extracting house with a run. Joe locked the door. He had already turned off the motor and put out the fire. He pushed a kerosene tin under the house. One spark in that wind would be enough to send up the forest in a sheet of flame.

'Into the truck,' Blaze ordered. Not only leaves but torn twigs and small boughs of leaves were whirling past. Then he gave a shout. A bough wrenched from a tree with a kind of scream and fell toppling across the truck to which the extracting house was coupled. It missed the cab of the truck and the extracting house and whacked down in a mess of branches smashing a pile of tins into something little boys might use in place of cricket stumps but they would not be good for much else.

The howl of the gale increased. It was a funnel of force that lifted the bee boxes and trundled them across the clearing. Blaze was running out madly trying to save his beloved bees. Joe and I went after him. Mongo braced himself over a pile of boxes on the back of the truck, spreadeagled.

'Get back, you fool,' Blaze yelled at me, clawing at a box to right it. Then the rain came smashing at us. We were picking up overturned boxes, setting the frames back, splashing about in drowned bees and mud. When all the wanton damage of the wind had been righted as far as it could be repaired, the half-drowned, streaming wet objects that had been bee-men in nice white suits wrung themselves out. We found rocks to weight down the lids and hoped the worst was over.

'Look at it,' Blaze said. 'Tearing every bloody blossom off the trees. Just ripping the stuff to bits and battering it down.' What was worrying him was that the other yards might be in worse condition than this one. Now that the hurricane in front of the storm had passed on its path of destruction we could go back to camp. It would have been too dangerous to drive before. 'I ought to have seen it coming,' Blaze kept repeating. 'Trying to finish, always trying to get the job done.'

'Could of been worse,' Joe grunted.

He was looking at that great bough which had so mercifully missed by feet the extracting house and the truck. If it had hit either, they would have been dented in like the empty tins. We drove towards the camp. Great trees had fallen across the road, and we had to run up into the gutters to dodge them. You could see the track of that storm in fallen trees, smashed and pulped leafage and flower. The wind had driven ahead of the storm sucking round and round like a waterspout. And, strange to say, the other yards had missed the full force of it. There were lids blown off and drowned bees, but only a few smashed boxes, where boughs had whirled down and staved them in as though with great wooden clubs.

Luckily the Muirdens had some spare boxes on the truck and transferred the bees from the smashed boxes and broken combs as best they could. At the camp, kerosene tins had blown away, the auto tent was down, and the tarp that covered my few possessions blown down into the creek; the bedding was soaked, and Dennis was sitting in the Roaring Ruin with the windows up reading a detective story. He had saved the typewriter and his suitcases.

'It came very suddenly,' he complained, as though we had sent the fiendish willy-willy. 'One moment it was as hot as hell, and the next it was as though the whole place had blown up.'

So everybody sloshed round in the downpour collecting sodden blankets and personal belongings. My sleeping bag was lying in a pool of water, but none of the water had gone inside. The oiled silk and the swansdown had kept dry. With a fire lit and steaming garments everywhere, the storm obligingly ceased. The auto tent went up again, and the tarp which made a tent for me. I collected the empty supers and built the walls up round it tidily. The Muirdens were never more cheerful. They joked, they made fun of the rain. It appealed to their primitive sense of humour that they had been waiting for rain, pretty nearly praying for it, and now it had come and smashed the blossom off the trees.

'The sort of thing Mongo 'ud do,' they decided.

Next day was grey and threatening, so a rash of correspondence broke out in camp, everyone completing letters to be taken into Atholfast, the town thirty miles north of us. 'If anyone had told me,' Dennis commented, as he furbished himself, 'that I would be looking forward to a trip into a half-baked village, I would have laughed at him, but now, after a week of insect life, Atholfast is my Mecca.'

My letters were headed, 'Wobbygong or Woebegone Creek (take your choice)'. There would be no letters for me in Atholfast because they would be waiting at Nithering, where our friends expected we would have arrived. I elected to remain in camp anticipating a beautiful day with no men.

There is nothing a girl appreciates more than a day with no men about. They were astonished that anyone should miss a trip into town, but they let me suit myself and went off in the truck with Mongo sitting behind the load on a box with his collar turned against the grey drizzle.

After I had done the washing and rearranged the tins and remainder stores, and tidied the tents, some men from the timber camp called to borrow some flour and seemed astonished to see me in possession. When they departed I slumbered on Dennis's bed in a grey fatigue that matched the day.

Waking towards evening, I found I had another visitor, a racing pigeon which came sidling piteously into camp. The gale must have blown it off its course and it could not fly, but it seemed pleased by human company and the rice I scattered. There it was, a little scrap of grey feathers, a bewildered civilized pigeon with a ring round its leg, walking with quick steps on its delicate rapid red feet, turning its round eye sideways and thinking of some far-away loft it would never see again. It would not let us catch it to see where it belonged, although it became tame and companionable. We told the timber workers they could have it as a pet when we left. The swine ate it. You can't put anything past timber workers.

Well, after dark the team came back. Having detached Dennis from the bar of the hotel and fed themselves at a café, they had seen the first half of the picture show, but they hurried home because they thought I might be nervous. Blaze had, as usual, interviewed the Shire engineer on the state of the roads and had been thrown out of the office, the engineer contending that the road was there and they could like it or lump it. If they didn't like it, they could take their bees to hell off his road.

'Like to read my letter, Mallee?' Joe asked. Good kind Joe had brought me cigarettes. 'There's a bit in it for you.'

The letter was from Mrs. Muirden, Horace's wife. 'Dear Joe,' it ran. 'Your dad came home as you know and no sooner here than I called the doctor and he is now

in hospital with his leg in plaster again. When I see you
I will tell you what I think of you for letting him stay
that long.'

'As if we could have stopped him!' Blaze commented.

'I hear he is selling the bees to a young lady, though
what a young lady would do with them I do not know.
Years and years of bees. Your dad should be ashamed of
himself selling them but he says that is the way he feels
and he has made his mind up, he is not all that broke or
no broker than usual. So of course I still don't know
where we stand, but if it means Blaze is coming home to
marry Daphne and set up that harvester agency I can
only say it is about time and not fair to Daphne for he
will lose that lovely girl Joe if he does not take a pull and
settle down. She is not going to be married to no absentee
and she is right. You can tell him from me. I made a
lovely little silk frock for Beryl's youngest to be christened
in and am cutting out the trousseau for Betty Madison.
The garden could do with a drop of water and if you ever
find time to lay that pipe down so I do not have to carry
buckets it will be a great day.' There was some news
about the neighbours and the family cow and it ended
strangely with 'Sam has the D.T.s again. Your loving
mother.'

'She's sore as a boil,' Joe said, complacently folding his
letter away. 'But it'll wear off.'

The next morning Joe and Blaze held a long conference
in low voices as they sat side by side on a log at the edge of
the clearing, Blaze talking with his hands, Joe just sitting
there with his hands hanging loose between his knees. The
decision of the governing body was then communicated to
us. They had decided to go and have a look at Nithering.
I think Dennis must have told them he had some important papers waiting at the post office there.

'We might take up a load to bung in on spec, and

Mallee's old butter boxes, doesn't matter where *they* are,'
Blaze decided.

The big truck would take a load of bees from the top
yard where the willy-willy had hit. They would have a
look at Mallee's bees to see if they needed honey taken off,
but they wouldn't have much in anyway. Once this
decision was taken and the camp and yards set in order,
there was nothing to do but consign honey tins at the
railway, block up entrances to the hives, strap up and load
and be off.

Dennis was very pleased with his adroit move for
escaping that camp at Woebegone or Wobbygong Creek.
He had had enough of it. 'When I return to the city,' he
announced, 'I shall show these grey hairs of mine and say,
"The silver is the result of a rest cure in the pure air and
quiet of the great Pilliga scrub." '

To hear him telling of his adventures later made you
realize how modest a man could be. Alone, facing death
from the tornado, that was Dennis Oberon Herrick.
After the trip into Atholfast he had a hangover and was
much quietened, but still with a smirk of approval at his
own astuteness. He had not been able to move me, so he
had moved the Muirdens. Simple when you thought of it.

The Muirdens were addicted to the use of tin strapping
and sneered at Ansett's patent cleats as too expensive. They
whipped a strip of tin round the bottom box and supers
and pulled it tight and fastened it with a metal tab
clenched by a special gripping machine. When the hives
were set up in their new stations the tin strips were slipped
off and any kinks straightened out with a few deft taps of a
hammer. I came in for the job of straightening sheafs of
tin strips occasionally — old rusty strips of metal cutting
your hands on a burred edge. Until my hands hardened
I had to hide them for fear someone would pronounce me
unfit for work.

Chapter Four

NITHERING was not marked on most of the maps because it was too tiny and lost in a crack in the mountains. But everybody knows the Nithering Range. Ombra, the most important town, began to multiply and breed suburbs of barracks and offices when the great hydro-electric authority commenced to harness the racing green streams in the valleys of the Nithering Plateau. A great new road looped and curved from Ombra through Nithering to the High Valley Dam from which untold millions of kilowatts of electricity were to be delivered to the cities.

But the Muirdens, with their peculiar genius for finding out-of-the-way roads, had pored over maps and decided on a broken-down back track that would stagger through Lacey's Crossing and bring them out at the back of Nithering, creeping and wandering round the mountains and saving fully twenty to thirty miles. To anyone who knew the Muirdens it was a foregone conclusion that they would plump every time for a crazy old road that would give them a chance to look at the new growth on the trees. If they went through Ombra they would meet motor buses, tourist cars, big earth-moving equipment.

'Fred Connelly was up there twelve months ago and he hadn't a good word to say for the place,' Joe mentioned. 'It's a good thing you didn't tell him too much. It's either no bloody good or it's something Fred is keeping quiet about.'

'It stands to reason,' Blaze agreed, 'that if Fred says he's going to the coast, then he is going somewhere else.'

The brothers began to exchange smiles of genial cunning as they saw light. Nobby Wallace wouldn't send Mallee up there if he thought her bees might do a starve. Joe was to drive the grey Ford with Mongo and Dennis for company. Blaze would drive the Roaring Ruin.

'Can't have Mallee stuck up some place with no oil in the gearbox,' Joe remarked.

'Pistons,' Blaze said, in a high feminine voice. 'Pistons always knock.'

I said nothing, knowing I deserved it and that one of these days I would pay him out for being an arrogant, know-all pup. The red truck was to be left at the timber camp with a loyal friend of the Muirdens who would see that nobody 'ran the guts out of it'. Mongo, the human spare part, was more difficult to dispose of. If he came with us he might enjoy himself, but they could see that he did some work. If they left him behind he would do no work unless Joe stayed too. Joe was keen to go, so after many log-sittings Joe convinced Blaze that the whole mob might as well take off together.

We were up at two o'clock in the morning on the day of our departure. A few hives had been left open for stragglers, but the rest had been strapped and blocked late the night before. It was daylight before the trucks were loaded, the ropes braced over, and the last double sheepshank knotted round the metal rod that ran along under the sides of the big table-top.

The towering load of silver-painted hives made my boxes on the Roaring Ruin look insignificant, and when the Muirdens began loading neuc boxes — which are the infant hives with one frame of brood and two stickies — aboard the Ruin, I could feel the springs sag. The load those brothers expected a truck to take was staggering.

Blaze was questing round the camp like a hound for things he had forgotten, a tow-rope for the Roaring Ruin, a big funnel for petrol, and then he couldn't find his hat — had anyone seen his hat? — but finally he shrugged himself into his leather overcoat and the caravan jerked out, or rather the Roaring Ruin did. Joe had long ago grown impatient and roared away. I knew perfectly well why Dennis had elected to travel with Joe. Requests that we halt at a hotel fell on deaf ears when he was driving with me.

The Roaring Ruin was accustomed to teetering along at a sedate old-lady pace, but Blaze drove her like a fiend with no concern for the Ruin's frailties. However, I comforted myself with the thought that when the end came, as it surely must with Blaze's cornering, we would be going so fast that we would be killed outright rather than crippled for life.

I still maintain Blaze is a reckless driver. Good old Joe can drive just as fast without you catching your breath. Just to cheer me, Blaze talked on about how he and his brother, on the great claypans of the West, were accustomed to race their trucks, and then put on all the brakes to send them into a spin. 'One day when we did, the truck hit a tree root and turned clean over. You know, we got the surprise of our lives!'

When we were out of the forests, the great concrete highway flashed dead level across the wheat country, with the grey towers of the silos lonely and beautiful in the morning. Mile after mile the pale mustard weed frothed by the road, its tiny yellow flowers high as a man's waist. Some call it rape or wild turnip, but at night it has a strange fragrance. Driving with the windows down and a storm flaring pink lightning somewhere over the plains, the lit puddles splashing against the headlights, you can smell the mustard weed and remember its perfume as one of

49

those secret pure pleasures, like racing storms or being alone by a river. But it is gay by daylight, the foamy yellow mustard weed, with tall purple thistles, the creeks with rich willows, sallows and turned soil, and the blue-flowering linseed and buff straw paddocks.

Small towns swelled up bristling with road signs and white bridges to slow us down their main streets. Then far off a shadow began to stalk us. It rose along the skyline, drifted up like a smoke cloud, the Nithering Range. At first it crouched and crept, then it lay bold ahead, the broad bottom-uppermost keel of the continent, granite, rotten granite and basalt, thousands of feet high, hundreds of miles long.

We came towards it through the Cassan Valley where the drought had not broken yet. In the dry, sunbeaten land that should have been rich lucerne flats, the grass-hoppers whirled and clicked and smacked on the wind-shields like raindrops. They crawled from their holes in the pebbles, wriggled and squirmed and crawled and copulated, dying in thousands but with millions to take their places. You could see them in the flying stage sweeping, a shower over the fields, with the sun glittering on their wings. They darkened and made dreadful the cultivation.

Blaze clicked his teeth. 'Cocky farmers,' he grunted. 'Too lazy to poison them before they're flying and then they moan why doesn't the Government do something.'

We had approached the Nithering Range by such imperceptible twists and windings that when we turned off the concrete highway we were already in the foothills on a bumpy yellow road of gutters and corrugations. Then we were racing along ridges and riding high while below lay the patchwork of pasture and furrow, hundreds of homes with the eldest boy at work, trouble and good news, sickness and washing on Monday, the pedigree bull in the back paddock, and the cream cans in a little wooden hutch by the gate waiting for the truck from the butter factory to pick them up.

'Joe will be boiling the billy somewhere this side of Lacey's Crossing,' Blaze prophesied. He had been giving me a long unintelligible lecture on the types of eucalypts. 'Ironbarks over there. Silverleaf. White box. When it's dry, white box has it all its own way. The silverleaf likes it wetter. Blue gum — you'll only find that where there's good soil. Do you notice they've been having rain just here — a good lot of rain? Notice how the stringy barks come down and mix with the white box?'

The white box has a grey smooth naked trunk with always a litter of twigs and rubbish about its base.

'High up, about three thousand feet, you'll only find stringies. Messmate on top of the ridges, stringies everywhere. I know thirteen different sorts, but there must be hundreds.'

We had come out on top of the plateau where the Nithering Range spreads its greats played hand, crossed with mountain bulges and creek lines, upturned as though it begged the sky to tell its fortune. We were approaching Lacey's Crossing after which a back track must take us past the farm of Matt Kettrill, Nobby Wallace's friend, halfway between Lacey's Crossing and Nithering, out on a spur between Upper Valley and the valley in which Nithering lay.

This side of Lacey's Crossing was still mostly cleared land, dead ring-barked trees, sheet erosion and gullies, poor pasture and farmer's ruin. The nearer we came to Lacey's Crossing the colder blew the wind, with great swathes of cloud racing, purple on the underside, across the vivid green paddocks and dandelions. The colour and brilliance of the day remained, but it was the threatening brilliance of a knifeblade.

'There's Joe,' Blaze said. Joe had come almost to the outskirts of the town before drawing in to the side of the road. Mongo was boiling the billy over a fire that flung its flame sideways in the wind and belched smoke in his face. By the look of Mongo something had gone wrong. Joe did not even turn to see his brother draw up. He was standing like Napoleon, his hands behind him, his feet apart, glaring at an advertisement for the local picture show. Blaze joined him and they both stood in front of that poster garnished with bunches of legs and proclaiming, 'A Singing, Dancing Musical. "Bright Lights of Broadway".'

'It stands to reason,' Blaze said at last, 'they have to show the damn thing somewhere.'

This 'Bright Lights of Broadway' was the Muirden hoodoo show. The first time they saw it was when the extracting house turned over on the Woodenbong Road and smashed Horace's leg. The second time they had to race through bush-fires with flames reaching out on either side of the road and they lost their hives. Now here it was at Lacey's Crossing.

'The engine gasket,' Joe said heavily, 'has blown. I'd push on if it wasn't for *that.*' He nodded at the hoarding. 'We'll stop at the garage.'

Blaze smote his brow. 'Only bloody time in our lives we haven't carried the spare gasket.' His bright hopes of Nithering went out like a light. 'Will you just take a look at Mallee's bees busting out at the seams. This Nobby Wallace must be the worst hive maker in the whole bloody universe.'

'Not even a spare engine gasket?' I raised my eyebrows, like a dowager who hears that a debutante's slip is showing. I had no idea what a gasket was but I found later that it is a padding that goes between the head and the metal casing of the engine. The head is the part you take off when you are going to do something unpleasant and greasy.

'Nobody,' Blaze said hotly, 'ever carries a spare gasket, but we do because the Ford's blown three gaskets since we got her.'

'Well, where is it?'

'She's doing it deliberately,' Joe said. 'Take no notice.'

So we had a meal standing with our backs to the wind. Rain had fallen over this part of the country, good soaking rain. It was too wet to sit on the ground. Mongo had spread an old piece of tarpaulin and placed the tucker boxes on it, but nobody sat. Dennis had his nose pointed down-wind towards a splendid example of outback architecture, a hotel, far off where the few houses of Lacey's Crossing huddled towards the river. A hotel with a second storey and a white-painted veranda rail, graceful wooden posts for leaning on, and a green-painted door with the word 'Bar' in gold. Empty barrels rolled out of a wooden trapdoor in the footpath from an underground cellar. Loafers stretched on a bench with a half-witted child, grinning and helpful and inarticulate.

Dennis sniffed it from afar. He suggested that the best place for information was 'probably' the hotel and someone had better make enquiries there.

Outside the hotel the dignified road we were on became entangled with a drunken and disreputable one that lurched into it at right angles. This was, of course, the road we would be taking. The dignified one hurried on over the white bridge and down the river where it had a meeting with the great road from Ombra on its way to Nithering. But the drunken road just staggered off into the scrub and, as we found later, fell down and lost itself at Matt Kettrill's gate.

The meeting of these two roads made up Lacey's Crossing with its one pub, one store, garage and a few houses that ranged along the drunken road as though to encourage it. Certainly that noble specimen of a hotel did much to raise Lacey's Crossing to the level of a stopping place, but the garage opposite struck me as sinister. It had a space of turf and beaten mud in front and a weedy paddock at the side. The skeleton remains indicated that this was where the old cars came to die. Weeds grew through their mudguards and radiators. What looked like the spine of a dinosaur was a set of caterpillar tractor-treads waiting to be oxy-welded and sinking into the mud. The garage itself was a sagging wooden barn, but whereas the Muirdens could tell that it was equipped with every-thing from a lathe to a lighting plant, to my eye it looked exactly what it was, a converted village smithy.

We came to be good friends with Lon McKillop who owns it; and make no mistake, in a place like Lacey's Crossing where the garage mechanic ranks in importance only below the S.P. bookmaker, if you are not first-rate everybody finds you out. The evil skulduggery garage-owners live in big towns. In Lacey's Crossing there is no money and lots of debts and a man like Lon will sit up all night with an ailing tractor because someone's harvest depends on it.

We did not bring the trucks right up to the garage because bees regard petrol fumes as noisome and come out to abate the nuisance. Bee men usually buy petrol from little wayside stores. Even there they are unpopular. Blaze said that one old lady 'called him for everything', saying he left a swarm of bees hanging over her front door to discourage customers last time he called for petrol. Blaze could not convince her the petrol buyer was George the Corrugation King, a friend of his who had passed through that way. The old lady vowed she would recognize Blaze anywhere. 'George is only the ugliest man in New South Wales,' Blaze said bitterly.

We all walked up to the garage — except Dennis. He had gone across to the hotel to make his enquiries. Mongo stayed with the trucks, but I thought the garage was something I could use for 'Mrs. Prothero', so I poked along.

Outside the garage was a big rich mud-spattered sedan with a stripling mechanic fiddling under the bonnet. The man in the car had the same rather bloated opulence as his sedan. The woman beside him gave us a curious glance. She was half-listening to the garage-owner's wife who stood nursing a baby on her hip and talking in the nearest approach to perpetual motion I ever heard. Lon McKillop's wife is a buck-toothed, red-headed, dynamic woman with a clutch of small children who all live in the rear room of the garage and overflow in front of it. One little boy was pedalling a red toy motor-car gravely around the petrol bowsers.

The garage owner himself was sitting on a box under a cedar tree in the car graveyard, his hands folded on his stomach, his cronies crouched on their hams and looking up through the boughs at the gathering rain clouds.

'We were just discussing,' he said cordially, as we came over to him, 'the number of pretty women along this range.' His eyes rested on the lady in the car, beautifully lacquered, nicely painted and upholstered, with a stream-lined chassis, curved in the right places and guaranteed jewelled in every movement. When I came to know her, I appreciated Vicki Warren's capabilities for making the best of everything, particularly her appearance. She was handsome and deft and adroit and could look helpless and fluttering when it suited her, or swoop like a hawk when it did not. She was making enquiries of Mrs. McKillop about a girl who might come to work at her house. 'I'll go in to Nithering and see for myself,' she said in a firm clear voice, a little bored. The young mechanic had slammed down the bonnet and the big man in the car switched on the engine.

'How about discussing,' Blaze asked the garage owner genially, 'a gasket for a Ford truck?'

The garage owner straightened up, sprang to his feet and swooped across the stretch of mud, running like a football forward. He snatched his small son out of the toy car just as the man in the sedan shot backwards and smashed it to matchwood. Mrs. McKillop squarked like a hen taken for killing, the two in the car jumped out protesting in horror, but McKillop, waving away their expostulations, tossed the wrecked toy among the other junk and strode into the garage with his son under his arm.

'Why don't you look after the kid?' he complained to his wife. 'Last week he blows his eyebrows looking in a petrol tank with a match.' He rummaged among a dusty set of gaskets hanging from a nail on the wall, and selected one which he silently handed over to Blaze.

By this time the populace, scenting the unusual, had assembled, crawling out from under logs, appearing in ones or twos with small boys in the lead, to regard the strange spectacle of a couple of trucks that buzzed in a sonorous manner. They examined Mongo as if he was some rare exhibit, and when Joe and Lon began to take the engine head off the Ford, the group of men who used the garage as a club advanced to criticize and give advice.

The finer points of technical skill were commented on like a good stroke at cricket. They did not mind the drift of rain. They were there to watch something that was as good as a play to them. They were accustomed to stroll in and borrow all Lon's tools, yarn by the hour, leisurely reassemble the bits and pieces of their machinery, use his lathe and oxy-welding plant and go off with a gracious word and an indication that, when a far day came, they might pay something off their account.

'See that?' Lon rubbed his great thumb along the metal. 'There's your trouble. See those tiny bubbles? When I've ground her down she'll never blow another gasket.' He lounged off to his bench, the interested audience following him.

Blaze came over to me impatiently where I had been talking to Mrs. McKillop. Certainly, she told me, she knew the Kettrill place. Did I see those people who made off in the sedan without more than saying they were sorry? A big impatient brute backing over a little boy's car that his father had just made. 'That's the Warrens, just come here. Kettrill's place is out beyond theirs. Old Matt Kettrill, the mad hermit. Comes into town in an old sulky with a pack of savage dogs cleaning up the town dogs. Half starved since his niece went to Nithering to be near her husband's work. He's got a lot of relatives scattered about the ranges, all of them as hungry as dingoes waiting for the old man to die. He's as mad as a snake. Goes round with a gun scaring people off his property.'

'Look,' Blaze broke in impatiently, 'we'd better push on.' Blaze always wanted to push on.

'You go out across Cobberloi Creek,' Mrs. McKillop advised. 'You might have a bit of trouble if it's up, because we've been having a bit of rain.'

I left Blaze in Mrs. McKillop's clutches and slipped across to the bar where Dennis was curled down cosily explaining to an overflow audience from the garage that big money was to be made from bee-keeping and it was a free, magnificent life for men who had the right stuff in them.

Dennis said he would wait for Joe. 'Presently I will proceed out into the drizzle taking with me something to cheer him. And, no doubt, the garage man will work all the better for a little refreshment. I have a few arrangements to make here before we proceed. Don't worry about me, Mallee. I thought I had a chill but I have taken it in the nick of time.' He was already calling the barkeep by his first name.

Blaze and I took off. Mongo had crawled back into the Ford and gone to sleep. 'That's him all over,' Blaze snarled. 'Useless.' He called Mongo names, none of them complimentary, until the pot-holes diverted his attention and he began to curse the shire engineer and the road gang responsible for the upkeep of this by-blow of a road, a set of wool-brained gutless wonders, none of whom worked an ounce of fat off their carcasses in a month.

'There's the Warrens,' I said suddenly, 'the people in the sedan that nearly ran over the child.'

Ahead of us the sedan had stuck in Cobberloi Creek and was churning mud helplessly. This Cobberloi Creek was a formidable watercourse with picturesque fanged rocks and a beer-stained froth tearing at the tree roots.

'Serve him right. I've got no time for big fat squatters going round like they owned the earth. Getting bogged in a little drain like that!' We drew up and Blaze jumped out, demanding bags to be put over the radiator. When he found I had no corn sacks, he lashed his leather coat over the Ruin's nose. 'I s'pose I'd better get the bugger out,' he snarled. He began stripping off his clothes. I took off my shoes but he ordered me to stay where I was. 'No sense two of us getting half-drowned.'

'That's all right, mate,' he shouted back to the driver of the sedan as he stepped into the water in his underpants. 'All very well you shouting "Ladies present!"' Looking very much like a plucked fowl, he waded out with a tow-rope over his shoulder.

'Mighty nice of you to help us out,' the man in the car said easily, with an attempt at conciliation.

'Bloody silly of you to get in,' Blaze responded. 'Know how to tie on for a tow? Well, out you hop and fix it, then you can't blame me.'

The man began to remove his boots and socks while Blaze leant gracefully against the side of the car looking in at him. 'Why, you've got fallen arches!' he remarked censoriously, and to the man's wife, 'What d'you want to marry a man with fallen arches for? Now if he had a figger like mine he'd be able to take off them beautiful pants without yelling, "Ladies present!" You be careful of my new rope,' he ordered. The floundering man could cheerfully have murdered him. 'I once won a competition with my figger. The skinniest guy on the Namoi River. It's a fact. Won it!'

The woman in the car was laughing, trying hard not to. Her husband was splashing around getting more and more furious.

'You right?' Blaze abandoned his flirtation. 'When I say, "Now", you give it all you've got. In reverse. Get me?' He waded out and deftly affixed the tow-rope to the Roaring Ruin and shivered into the driving-seat. 'Now,' he yelled. The man was addressing a few crisp remarks to his wife. 'Now!' Blaze bawled. The man clashed in the gears, the tow-rope took the strain, then parted with a snap and the sedan slipped back into the hole it had churned for itself.

Blaze tramped into the creek once more, lashed the rope himself without a word, and this time towed the sedan backwards without any trouble. 'Keep more to the right,' he called. 'We'll watch you across.' The sedan did not stop when it reached the other side. The woman's hand waved gracefully, there was a jet of blue smoke from the exhaust, and the car climbed the steep cutting and vanished round the bend.

'Well, that's bloody lovely,' Blaze said disgustedly, retiring to the back of the truck to put on his clothes. 'Muck up a man's new rope and then drive off without saying kiss my foot.'

'What did you want to tease him for?'

'Well, hell — a man that'd get himself bogged in a measly little creek that he must of known because he lives the other side of it. Doesn't deserve to have a car like that or a good-looking wife. Getting bogged!' He climbed into the truck and started it cautiously into the water with a brave bow wave fanning out in ripples. The Roaring Ruin protested at being asked to swim. It churned across and I clenched my hands to help it. Just as I thought we were through, there was a feeble cough, a splutter and the Roaring Ruin lurched sideways.

Without waiting to take off my slacks and shirt, I stepped out into the water. Blaze disrobed again. He had been in too many creeks not to value dry clothing when he got out of them.

'Of course the trouble is that this truck of yours just hasn't got the extra power,' he explained.

That was the last straw. I set my teeth. 'Joe is right about you not taking enough exercise,' I told him. 'You don't strip well. You're not only skinny, you're big-mouthed, lop-eared, gabby, androgynous and dead from the neck up.'

'But then,' Blaze answered with an evil grin, 'creek beds don't show me at my best. I'm much better in the other sort.'

I'd bought that one. Swapping insults with Blaze was a waste of time. I waded round the back of the truck. In grim silence Blaze jacked up the sunken rear wheel, piled rocks under both back wheels, wiped the spark plugs, coaxed the engine into action again and got it roaring for the effort.

I shoved with all my weight behind, and a wave of mud and water sprayed up from under the wheels and took me in the face. The Roaring Ruin bumped off the jack, its wheels turned helplessly. Blaze switched off the engine.

We tried again with more rocks and big boughs wedged under the sunken wheel. I tried to drive the truck out and Blaze shoved. The rain came down and the Roaring Ruin stayed stuck.

'Now what?' I said, flapping my soaked shirt and wiping my face with a piece of waste I used for cleaning the windshield.

'Off-load her,' Blaze muttered. He flicked the rain out of his eyes. 'Look.'

Walking across the creek was an elderly man with a gun and a pair of elastic-sided boots balanced on one shoulder. On the other he bore a stout piece of timber something the size of a railway sleeper. He carried this as though it was a matchbox. Behind him splashed three cross-bred cattle dogs. He wore an old army hat like mine, pushed back on his grey curls; his beard was clipped to an argumentative jutting point, and his moustache stained gold by tobacco.

'Ned Kelly in person,' Blaze murmured.

'Every time I see a new face,' the stranger said by way of greeting, 'it's up to its axles in Cobberloi Creek. Never come within cooee of the place but someone's stuck in it.'

'There was someone in before us.'

'That was the Warrens.' He put his hat carefully over his boots on the bank. 'Didn't see why I should get rheumatism when he hadn't even got out of the car.' He must have been watching us all the time from the trees. 'Might get her out without taking off the load.'

They jacked up the rear wheel, walked all round discussing the problem, wiped the spark plugs again, pushed more rocks under the other rear tyre and set about shoving the board under the wheel which was well down. By this time we were all so wet that it would not have mattered if we had swum in the creek. But the unfortunate Blaze was blue with cold.

'Get in, Mallee,' he commanded. I got in, driving barefoot, and revved the engine. 'Steady, take it steady.'

The old lad with the whiskers shoved on the board, using it as a lever. Blaze flung his weight against the other wheel. The Ruin began to crawl out like a cockroach from the plughole of a sink. When the rear wheels were on the road, I switched off the engine. The elderly gentleman was replacing his pants under the harness strap which was supposed to hold them up, and tucking in his grey flannel shirt.

'Good thing I'm dressed for this,' he said mildly.

'If it hadn't been for Ned Kelly here,' Blaze said fervently, 'we might of been there all night. I s'pose you know everybody out this way? We're looking for a cove that leases a lot of timber country. He's a bit cracked and mean as dirt by all reports. Cove by the name of Kettrill?'

'That's right,' our friend said easily. 'Matt Kettrill's the name.'

He smiled in his beard at Blaze's apologies. He had very light hazel eyes in a network of wrinkles. He had a habit of reflectively stroking his beard, listening to a man's arguments, mildly countering with his own views. When he used to play chess with Dennis, Matt would point out courteously that if Dennis moved that piece he was likely to lose it, and that might spoil the game.

I introduced myself and said that Nobby had written to him. 'He has one big fault, Nobby,' Matt murmured. 'Always dashes down the board with his bishop. In a rush, that's his trouble. A good bloke. Did some cane-cutting with him up in Queensland.'

I introduced Blaze, explained that the other truck was following. Matt waded back across the creek with a message to be left under a pile of rocks in the road in case the rain wiped out our tyre marks. Then we got going again, the dogs galloping ahead barking. The road climbed and climbed through paddocks and stands of trees.

'The Warren place,' Matt murmured, jerking his thumb. Somehow the impression lingered that the Warrens were not popular. Their house was a dignified white weatherboard under tall pines below the shoulder of a hill.

Then the darkness and rain closed over the dirt track and we jounced across cattle grids and roared along a ridge steep like the roof of a house. At last the truck slid down a slope of yellow clay to a gate which Matt opened, the headlights showing a cottage.

The little pale shell of a house, hardly more than sheets of fibro nailed to battens and thin weatherboard, was as absurd in a high, cold climate as a paper hat. The blast ran up under the floorboards and the damp dripped from the guttering. It showed a ghostly grey square like cardboard in the grey misty half-light, with the wreck of a garden in a waste of rusty wire netting, the tangle of a honeysuckle grown to a tree, a climbing rose whipping its tentacles against the wall. An old cane lounge chair lacking a leg was propped on the veranda by the back door, and a cow lumbered away into the rain. I think it had been sheltering on the veranda, although its usual home was the shed where the sulky, its shafts down like a Turk at prayer, kept company with the fowls. Matt kept the fowl feed in the bathroom just off the chilly veranda.

'I keep the door shut otherwise the fowls get in,' Matt explained. 'There's goats too. That old billy-goat's wicked enough to eat the tyres off the sulky.'

He lit a lamp in the kitchen, a man's kitchen, soot-blackened and hung with cobwebs. A tin of washing-up water stood on the table in grey puddles and breadcrumbs.

A piece of sacking over a missing window-pane flapped up in the wind and a scatter of rain came in. Then there was a scramble and a lean cat exploded through the sacking. She spat in surprise at the visitors.

'That old mammy cat' — Matt tickled her affectionately under the ear — 'she's nervy about her little kittens. I took a pane of glass out so she wouldn't get locked out.'

There were other cats, their eyes glowing from doorways, tribes of cats, mother cats, father cats, half-grown kittens. The dogs were lapping water from a pie-dish under the dripping tap in the scullery wall. Matt showed us into two cold but airy bedrooms decorated with texts and wasps' nests built of mud. One room, which was his, he said Blaze could share; the other was for me.

'I've been batching,' he mentioned. 'We had a flea plague, but this wet 'ull clean them up. The drought's broken here a lot sooner than most other places. I dunno what could 'uv brought those fleas. I s'pose it's like colds. Every time I go into Lacey's Crossing I bring home a cold.'

'Speaking of colds, I bought this at Lacey's Crossing' — and Blaze produced a bottle of dry sherry with a flashy label. 'The brother and I don't usually drink but that creek was bloody cold.'

'Living alone drinking is no good to you,' Matt agreed. He poured the sherry into three enamel mugs.

'Well, here's to four tins to the hive,' Blaze said, 'and a rise in the price of honey.'

'Here's to Matt,' I nodded.

Matt cut off a piece of the steak Blaze had unwrapped and flung it to the eldest mother cat. 'Got a bit low on tucker. Just damper and pumpkin.' The cat sank her claws into a dog's nose as he tried to take the meat away from her. The rain splashed through the window and the piece of sacking waved a defiant bachelor's flag.

Chapter Five

M Y SHABBY old bee boxes were off-loaded almost at Matt's back door on a green slope falling rather steeply to a creek bed. Matt and Blaze walked in and out of the lit space cut from the green by the headlights of the truck, setting out those old beaten-up boxes, some small, some large, old Boultons, full-depths, and the new ones that Nobby had knocked together and had no time to paint. They looked like a set of fantastic chessmen ranking up for a strange game. Blaze's silver neuc boxes were spaced farther up the slope under an old pine.

After a supper of steak and eggs we sat with the fire roasting our faces and the cold gnawing the back of our necks, listening to Matt's views on politics, which were sanguinary and aggressive. Then we stumbled half dead to bed.

In the morning, bright and promising as a new banknote, the bees were all astir. It was a mushroom morning, tender and dewy, and as I walked across what had once been a cultivation paddock towards them, a bee flew against my arm and rested there, perhaps recognizing one of those dull walking trees that bore no flowers and leaned down their great branches to the hive to tear at its cover lid. Whirring, excited and perplexed, furious against this unplantlike barrier, smelling as no tree should smell, the bee yet hesitated to throw its life away. It was not pitched to that, the twanging shrill suicide of the guard, a tossed gambler's piece staked for the living hive.

Subtle and singular and high-pitched in some strange minor, the bees wove their music in a gamut beyond all human keys, exciting the nerves, brushing the senses, unperceived by common reason, as the tiny wings brushed the gold hairs on my arm. For their life is a life of vibration, of changes of colour and immediate electric contact. Perturbed, estranged from their known resting-place, their consultation was decided before it was voiced. Otherwise there would be a growing uneasiness in the desolated combs, the queen persuaded, propelled, launched and convoyed to the rising green horizon of safety.

The long undulations of the eucalypt forests had broken round Matt's green little level above the creek. I followed the winding track up the ridge and looked back and down where the dark pine tree by Matt's cottage made the eucalypt forests dustier gold-green by contrast. I came down the other side of the ridge, and there was another old weatherboard house. A rusty wire fence hung from wooden grey posts, the remains of a gate, a hedge of privet, an old briar rose.

The house was completely deserted. The door was open, so I went in and quested about the four rooms and the veranda where a passion vine hung by strips of rag tied to nails. A rusty meat safe swung in the draught of the entry, and there was an old clock on the mantelpiece that struck a ghostly dong when I touched it. The wallpaper pasted on the grey wooden walls was of an arsenic blue colour in a pattern of feather headdresses. Behind the house was a sturdy, large shed that could be useful for storing tins.

Later I asked Matt about the house, and he told me his niece and her husband had lived there but they found it too lonely, and had moved in towards Nithering, 'to be closer to the traffic'.

On the way back I met Blaze. He was ranging along

the ridge, standing back to throw up a rock or stick to bring down a branch with bud on it. There are veins of gold under these mountains, with old mullock heaps along the creek beds where prospectors have tried their luck, but Blaze was looking for our gold higher up, just that flush of bright yellowish green in the axils of the leaves, the small green nipples of buds, in sheaves and hanging tassels, high, high up.

'We'll need more sites,' Blaze said. 'We'll send a wire for tins.' I had been sharing the joy of the morning, but Blaze had a scowl of concentration on his face. He was thinking hard and fast, planning ahead. 'Come up here,' he said. 'Take a look at this.'

We scrambled up one of the steep slopes and were able to look miles down a long valley. It was as though we stood on the ridge of a roof with the corrugations running down the hips and slants. When you first come into the ranges, the mountains seem to run every way, knotting up like a bunch of courting snakes, but the valleys and ridges mostly run north-west, south-east, rolling folds like a crumpled green cloth.

There, tiny and far down the valley, the township of Nithering showed gold and white and silver, the white of the big bridge over the river, the white of the church with its spire on a steep little hill that the river coiled round, and houses with shining silver roofs where the trees, ascending and descending the great ridges, had been pressed back to leave a deferential space for the breathing and labours of men.

The houses were gathered in casual groups around the church on the rise, standing like a country congregation waiting for service to begin. Scattered roofs and stones under which rested, not dead, but living men and women waiting to rise at the great trump of the new road which swept down the steep on a long note of triumphant finality, cleaving the quiet of the trees, surging down to the white bridge past the gold and silver town, to prolong itself and vanish around the river bend and up higher and higher to the construction camps and the great dam.

'That's the town,' Blaze said, 'that's going to be drowned. Nothing but one big stretch of water when they put the second dam in. First they finish the one up the valley, and then they start damming below Nithering. Just a big stretch of water backing up to here almost. Funny when you think of it.'

Blaze had caught himself a cold in the head. I was not going to apologize to him for losing my temper. I could see no future in apologizing for something that was probably going to happen again, and happen often. Once you began losing your temper with Blaze, and everybody did sooner or later, there were limitless possibilities of further aggravation.

Now, dear old Matt, a courtly and well-placed apology to Matt would be met in the spirit in which it was offered. When Joe and Mongo and Dennis arrived, while we were frying bacon for breakfast, Matt's manners were perfect. He had extended hospitality to a friend of Nobby's and some bees. He had lived a blissful solitary life and now he had four large men tramping in and out his kitchen and making toast on his fire and pouring tea out of his tea-pot.

They had camped the other side of the creek all night under a tarpaulin, and Dennis, when he remembered how comfortable he might have been at the hotel, blamed me for his bed in the damp.

'I don't intend to do any more chaperoning,' he said. 'This is the finish. If you are going ahead with this idea of buying bees, you can go on your own.'

He was in a very nasty temper, but he revived after breakfast. Naturally I had kidded him that I needed him to protect me, but that was strategy. I showed him the bedroom I had been occupying with a real bed in it. He shuddered at the bath tub full of fowl feed, and the hens sitting in a row on the back of the cane settee on the veranda.

At breakfast one of the hens jumped on Matt's shoulder and pecked some crumbs out of his beard. 'If there's a thing I hate to see,' Matt said, setting it gently on the floor, 'it's fowls running away squarking when you go near them. The niece used to come over pretty regular. It used to be, "Maybe you could knock over a fowl for us, Uncle." Had them all scared at the sight of her. But the rooster pecked her legs. I've trained that rooster to fight off hawks, and now he's learning to attack foxes. I hate to kill things. These Sunday sports that come driving over the mountains — I scare the tripe out of *them*.' He fluffed up his beard and rolled his eyes. 'The mad hermit, see? Likely to put a bullet through you.'

'Have some more bacon, Matt?' Blaze asked.

Matt took the point. 'I like bacon, well cured, and if I don't have to kill the pig. There's nothing friendlier than a pig. I'd go out and scratch it under the chin, and talk to it and it'd talk back to me. Then come Christmas,' he imitated a female voice, ' "Oh, someone 'ull have to kill the pig. Matt'll do it." Got to slit the throat of me best friend.'

Blaze had come on some bees belonging to Matt, neglected in a clearing, lonely as a colony of tiny lighthouses. Matt shook his head when the Muirdens hypocritically suggested they would go elsewhere so they would not crowd his hives. 'Plenty of room. Make yourselves at home. With a flow on there's more than they can bring in. Nectar dripping out of the trees on to your beard so that you can taste it.'

He had given the bees, he explained, to his niece's

husband. 'He was always at me to get the damn things for himself, but now he never looks at them. I moved them up near their home, and no sooner did I shift them than Fay and the kids and Frank all decided to go down near Nithering. I can't see why people don't stay put.'

Matt Kettrill had spent his earlier years wandering over five states, making enough money to come back and buy this bit of wilderness. He owned five hundred acres, leased another five hundred, and the rest of the country stretching away was mainly Crown land. What was the use, he asked gently, of rushing about? The human body disliked it. Moving about, your intestines and liver and lights would complain at the change of water and food and habits. It was the same with bees. They didn't like moving, they were too sensible.

'Now take those bees of mine when I shifted them up near the niece's place. They kept coming back. They're intelligent bees. They never *did* bring in more than enough honey to feed themselves. "There's that old whiskery robber hanging around," they'd say. "Let's go on strike." '

'Re-queen them for you,' Joe offered, his mouth full of toast.

He had moved those bees, Matt repeated, up to the house over the ridge, but the bees wanted to come home. 'The first time they came home, I scooped them up in my hands and carried them, and they were *nasty* about it. Next time they were sort of resigned. But the third time they came to meet me, and settled on my flannel quiet as you please, as much as to say, "Well, here's Old Whiskers. He'll carry us back to the hive." '

The Muirdens received all this with scepticism.

'I never use a smoker,' Matt told them, his eyes twinkly. 'I just breathe on them.'

'No wonder the buggers are savage,' Blaze said.

After breakfast Matt produced his chessboard and looked hopefully for an opponent. Chess is a gentleman's game. I am inclined to get mad and heave the board at anyone who beats me, and this is frowned on in the best chess circles. Blaze and Joe didn't play, but Dennis settled down with Matt on the edge of the veranda, the hens pecking about and the dogs forming a ring.

Joe drew me aside. 'Mallee,' he complained, 'cats give me asthma. Just being in a room with a cat gives me the horrors.'

I told him about the empty house. We could rent it from Matt and live there while we were at Nithering. Joe and Blaze and Mongo drove off along the spur. They would look out sites, investigate that deserted house, and off-load bees from the Ford.

'Mallee,' Blaze yelled at parting, 'if you're going into Nithering for letters' — I had said I would drive down to the post office — 'stop at the Warren property and see if you can book up some sites there.' Naturally he wasn't going to ask a favour of a man who had broken his new tow-rope.

'While you're in Nithering,' Matt said, looking up from the chessboard, 'you might call in on the niece. Mrs. Hertz is the name.'

He shook his head when I suggested he might like the drive, gently but definitely he declined. Let everyone else charge around, he was fixed with Dennis and the chessboard. Dennis had already beaten him brilliantly once, and Matt was interested.

When two chess players get together you can forget them. Hours later Matt and Dennis would still be there. The peaceful morning drowse was disturbed only by the complaining noise of hens, the tearing and munching as Matt's white goats and the cow made havoc of

71

the remains of the rosebush, and a polite click of chessmen. They only half noticed, vaguely, that I had gone
off in the Roaring Ruin. Just another disturbance
removed, an irritating noise stilled as the Ruin topped
the rise.

The Warren house snuggled down in the hollow of the
hill's shoulder, among the warm stones in the drifts of hot
scented brown pine needles. Its garden, neat with roses
and dahlias splashed with all shades of tawny orange and
crimson and yellow, with Mexican daisies and crocus
and snapdragon, was a closed warm world where no stray
breath of storm could break through the towering tops
of the pines.

How many years had the brown pollen dust drifted
down, how many years had great pine cones burned on
the hearth scenting the house, the blue smoke ascending
among the boughs! The house and the trees in their
bronze and green and white were an oasis in bleak
stretches of paddocks cleared of all but one or two
remainder trees, grey bleating sheep drifting across the
grass. Nothing changing as the former owners grew old,
lambing, crutching, drenching, shearing, a new plough
horse maybe. Nothing changed but the shadows of old
age lengthening until the old people died, and Warren,
the rich man who owned hotels, bought the property.

His wife came to the door of the kitchen. When she
recognized me, her face lit up. 'Why, of course,' she cried,
'you were with that nice kid who pulled us out of the creek.'
She frowned slightly. 'We certainly did have an unlucky
afternoon. Harry isn't really bad-tempered. He was
worried about business.' She invited me in, talking all
the time, trying to make out the discrepancy between
my appearance and my accent.

One of the things that always made me smile about
Vicki Warren was her air of dignity, the way she drew

herself up and sailed along, pretending she was a grande
dame when she was only quick-witted, competent and
funny. She had a neat fighting face with a nippy tilt
to it as though she was cocking her ears, alert, eager,
self-confident. She never missed a trick. I knew we
were going to be friends although we were so different.
Vicki loved clothes and jewellery and furniture and
decorations, and I don't give a damn about any of those.
She liked excitement and people and moving fast, and
here she was stuck in a neck of the woods pretending
loyally to enjoy it while I didn't need to pretend. I did
enjoy it.

'My husband is out with the sheep. I'm sure he
wouldn't mind you putting some bees on the place.
We've just bought this property. We want to get it all
in order before the boys come home from school. They're
mad about the land, all three of them. The eldest is
going to an agricultural college.' She was so proud of
those boys, horrid snobbish pug-faced brats who hung
round the bees and patronized us.

When she heard we were staying with Matt she was
dubious. 'We drove down there once. It was horrible.
A great pack of dogs came barking out, so we sat in the
car. Not a sign of life, and then a clawlike hand very
slowly drew away a piece of sacking from a broken
window and a terrible bearded face peered out. I tell
you we came away in a hurry.'

'That was Matt looking to see who it was.'

'Well, what with the reputation of the place and all
those trees——' She was making a cup of tea, taking
scones out of the big oven. Everything in Vicki Warren's
kitchen was brisk and shining: the bright range, the
painted woodwork, enamelled in orange and navy blue.
There were green and white striped curtains with ruffles
at the windows. 'When you drove up, I thought it might

be the woman I'm trying to get to help in the house.
She's all I could find, but there's a separate quarters for a
married couple at the back. I've painted this whole house
myself.' She whisked me through the big rooms with
their beautiful, expensive city furniture; a separate colour
scheme for each room.

'And these are the boys' rooms. D'you think they'll
like them?' They had the look of illustrations from
some glossy woman's magazine. 'They've never had a
real home before. Only hotels and boarding schools.'
How she enjoyed having another woman, even if it was
only me, to see her handiwork! 'Of course we don't know
anyone yet, and anyway they're all so dreary. Nothing
but sheep and the price of wool. I suppose I'll get used
to it.'

I asked about the deserted house over the ridge from
Matt's place. 'But didn't you know? He bought the
property cheap years ago because nobody would have it
as a gift. There was a man with a wife and four children.
He used to sit and read his Bible every night and he got
queerer and queerer. He was an Englishman and he
wasn't used to the loneliness. Anyway one night he
murdered his wife and children. Split open their skulls
with an axe and laid their brains out round a plate. He
said the voices told him to make the sacrifice. And now,
of course, that old Matt Kettrill will probably go the same
way. His niece and her family had to get out, they
couldn't stand it.'

I was silent, eating a scone. I hoped Dennis didn't
hear all this. I told her Dennis was having a holiday for
his nerves and she was quite excited when she realized
that he was the author of 'Mrs. Prothero'. Having grown
up with that nightmare hag and her foul children I am
prejudiced against her. I know her better than my own
Uncle Beresford or Aunt Mona because I helped invent

her. Dennis gets hundreds of letters from people who seem to spend their whole time glued to that serial. We had slaved to get enough of the abominable thing written before we came away, and I was fed up with Mrs. Prothero, almost as fed up as the Parent.

I noticed a subtle change in Vicki Warren's manner when she realized I was connected with a person of note like Dennis Oberon Herrick. Vicki couldn't do enough for me, and when I said I was driving into Nithering she asked if she could come too.

'I'm really not sure about that woman the garage-man's wife suggested. She lives in Nithering and I'd better see her myself.'

So off we started and I was happy enough to have her company. Vicki's husband had taken their car and she didn't get out much. She directed me along back tracks and down on to the road to Nithering. We didn't have more than twelve miles of winding road to the town.

'Aren't you ever frightened?' Vicki asked, as we drove along.

'No,' I answered, thinking of that abandoned house. 'Ghosts don't bother me. At séances I am always asked to leave because I disturb the vibrations.'

'I didn't mean that. I meant living alone with a lot of *men*.'

Really I had hoped better things of Vicki Warren. Nothing is so boring as this harping on one string. I didn't mind men, I explained, but they were not sensible. They had complicated motives it would be a waste of time to puzzle out, so it was best to be friendly and ignore them, or if you couldn't do that, just not to take too much notice of them.

'What a lot you must miss,' Vicki said, giving me a wicked look. She would have liked to tease me, but she felt she did not know me well enough yet.

Chapter Six

NITHERING, at close hand, was very different from that distant gold-and-silver vision of the morning. When we had pursued our way along the flat land on top of the spur, we came to a downhill drop that had a notice: 'Steep Winding Road for Five Miles.' At that sign the road to the dam turned off to the right and went curving on higher and higher up. It was as though we had come along the arched little finger of the mountain's hand, and now we plunged down towards the wrist in the valley, while the dam lay along yet another finger.

Once we had negotiated the steep five miles, we came out on bends and windings of river valley, the land all tilted and tumbled about it, and before the road entered the town it passed a great camp, almost a separate town of wooden houses that had been brought in sections and nailed together like houses of cards, all an ugly mustard colour. There were offices and barracks, a canteen, a powerhouse, a laboratory for testing the concrete cores from the dam, great dumps of tractors and earth-moving equipment, caterpillars, piles of concrete pipes.

Vicki thought this new raw town exciting. 'Think of all the progress and electric light and power and thousands of people coming here.' Vicki's shrewd husband liked to think that his land might be in a strategic spot for all these new developments. There are men who can make money on a desert island, and when Nithering was drowned deep under the big dam Harry Warren would undoubtedly set up some kind of tourist centre near the great lake. He had bought the property cheap because there was still some uncertainty as to how far the reclamation would extend, although through influential friends he had made pretty sure the Warrens would be undisturbed in their possessions.

'The people here are just like the ants when you over-turn their nests,' Vicki said, as little Nithering showed, built up high round its hummock above the swirl of water. 'They've all got to go, and they don't know where or when, so of course they stay and do nothing.'

The little old post office was part of the general store with a petrol bowser in front and a wooden veranda caked with the dirt of generations. The letters were partitioned off from the jam, and a decent privacy main-tained for the selling of stamps by a screen which divided the post office section from the bacon and flour.

I sat down on a wooden seat on the store veranda to read letters from home while Vicki went off in pursuit of the rumoured housemaid. At the sight of Julie's big exclamatory scrawl on the envelope, I could see the view over the park and the water from my balcony window. We live in a huge red-brick tenement of flats, layers on layers of human beings like jam in a cake. I could almost hear the noise of traffic as I turned that letter in my hand, the eternal traffic beating like a surge around the city so far away, and now so remote and ghostly.

Julie's letter plunged across six pages with dashes in-stead of full stops. You had to turn the letter sideways where she had written in the margins throwing in some-thing important as an afterthought.

'Dear darling Mallee,' Julie scrawled, 'I'm in bed with the flu and two sweet little lovebirds that I bought myself because the flat is so lonely with all my dear ones away — and a sun seat but that wasn't expensive because I got it on time payment — I have had to put it out in the hall

77

because it won't fit on the balcony but as I have seen the house of my dreams which we will buy as soon as you get your money the sun seat will be just the thing — with Beresford as trustee I don't believe we will ever get it but it is nice to have a daughter who is an heiress — although I still feel I will win the lottery as well when Mr. Pollock finds me a really lucky day. Do not worry about my flu but I hope you are taking care of poor sweet Dennis. I suppose Nobby's friend has a charming quaint little home where you will be comfortable? Remember Dennis is not to be worried about anything and be kept from taking drink tho' I never have the heart to refuse — What I wrote about and this is *desperate* and *urgent* is that Hubert rang and says he *must* have twenty-four more episodes of Mrs. Prothero in the next fortnight because Gwen is going to Adelaide and he wants to record them before she goes. That will last until she gets back so he will not have to change the cast. He has to have six right away and my brains are just cotton wool. I am depending on you Mallee because this is our bread and butter. Do not let Dennis do it because he really has lost touch. Last time he forgot that Basil was bringing home his bride. The thought of Mrs. Prothero makes me sick on the stomach, so you *will* do it won't you? Hubert wants you to do a new serial for the Crisp Crackers morning session. "Let Mallee do it" were his very words. Isn't that a compliment? He likes your stuff he says. Do write to Hubert at once — Your *dear* aunt — how she does keep her little grasping hands on poor Beresford — rang up and seemed very sore that he had advanced you a hundred pounds to go on this trip. Do please not get yourself sunburnt as you always do. I have a wonderful new skin tonic from Madame Stein and I am sending you a bottle and do please send down Mrs. Prothero at once because you will have nothing to do but watch your bees flying about — unless as I hope

Nobby's friend has some pleasant young men learning about sheep. . . .'

'Damn!' I said, not bothering to read any farther. I might have known Julie would fall down on the job. If I had that empty shack up near Matt's place, I could slug in on 'Mrs. Prothero'. The boys could bring up the rest of the bees. They were always telling me not to lift things, so they could go and lift them to their heart's content. We had to keep Mrs. Prothero going. Her sweet wistful voice must be lifted over the air-waves Tuesdays, Thursdays and Fridays come hell or high water. Oh, for the day when my bees were making money and I could let Mrs. Prothero jump over a cliff!

Vicki came back to the Roaring Ruin. 'Not coming after all,' she said dolefully. 'Of course, you can't blame her. A girl doesn't like to be stuck out in the scrub, only driving in on Saturdays. Never mind, I may find someone else. Where do you want to go now?'

'Nowhere,' I answered, looking down the main street. There was a little shabby old shanty of a hotel and just those few houses. Then I remembered Matt's niece. I was in no mood for calling on her, but Matt had suggested it, and I had to book sites.

The Roaring Ruin skirted the town as I followed Matt's directions, passed over the bridge, the boards rumbling under the tyres. Dull, mudstained water swept round the black serrations of rocks jutting from the river bed in the channels; there were shallow warm sandbars and dark she-oaks sweeping the ripples.

We left the main road and turned up a steep track, an old road for men with horses. The truck panted, spurted upward in low gear, the pebbles flying and crunching as it crawled forward. At a gate I left the engine running while I stepped down to struggle with the wire entanglement which closed the way. Ahead was a house little

more than a hut. The sheep scrambled up the grassy
slopes, moving slowly and purposefully away from the
disturbances, stopping to snatch a head of feathery grass
and stand nibbling with their long mouths.

A young woman with two children at her skirts came out
of the shabby wooden home and stood by the gate under
a trellis sagged beneath an old grape-vine. The children
peeped out behind her while she spoke to us.

'Mrs. Hertz?' I asked. 'We are staying with Mr.
Kettrill and he told me to see you about putting some bees
in the back paddocks.'

Mrs. Hertz said there had been a man some months
before who wanted to put some bees in but he hadn't
come back. I described Fred Connelly and she nodded
when I said we were friends of his. 'That's the man.
Yes, he was real nice. That'll be all right then.'

Once the truck's engine was turned off the silence was
broken only by small noises, a cricket whirring, a locust
quivering its tiny cymbals against the trunk of a tree.

'You going back to Uncle Matt's place?' Mrs. Hertz
asked wistfully. 'Can I get a lift up with you? To
Uncle's place, I mean?'

'Sure.'

'Could you wait till I packed the kids' things?'

Evidently this young woman made her mind up on the
spur of the moment. I was not sure how Matt would take
the influx of a niece and two charming little brown boys.
It was all right with me. I told her I would like to have
a look at the country through the far gate. 'I'll call for
you on my way back.'

Apart from noticing that Matt's niece was a personable
young female, I hadn't taken much notice of her, being
intent on the gloomy prospect of coping with Mrs.
Prothero and making sure to miss nothing which would
be useful when I described this place to the Muirdens.

But when Matt's niece indicated that she was coming back with me, which meant that we might have her on our necks, I felt she deserved closer study. Standing under the shade of the grape-vine in a washed-out dress with her children peeping out behind her, she looked gentle and timid. Her colouring was beautiful, natural honey-gold hair in curls gathered loose on the back of her neck, a white skin with a faint flush of pale rose on her cheekbones.

Lon McKillop at the garage had been right when he said there were many pretty women along these ranges. Matt's niece had a long curved mouth and long, curved eyes, moth-brown, warm brown. She was going to cut a swathe like a Texas cyclone through my bee-keepers. From something Matt had said I inferred that he had no time for the absent Mr. Hertz, her husband. Nor had he spoken very favourably of his niece, Fay, who was about to add herself to the strength and yet further bulge out the walls of his homestead already bulging with guests.

'I'll wait here.' Vicki jumped from the truck. 'May I?' She turned smiling pleasantly to Fay Hertz who nodded. At least Matt's niece did not seem to be talkative.

I drove off along the creek painstakingly noting the lie of the land. I threw up rocks at the trees to bring down specimens of bud as I had seen Blaze doing that morning. This is harder than it looks. I threw sticks, I threw stones, I even tried throwing the jack handle which was too heavy. It took a long time and I nearly clonked myself on the skull with a rock. When I had a few measly specimens, I drove back to the house. Vicki was waiting with a quiver of triumphant excitement.

'I've got her,' she whispered. 'She's coming to work for me. Oh, I'm so glad I drove here with you.'

'I thought she was going to visit Matt?'

'Only because she had nowhere else to go, silly.

Couldn't you see she'd been crying? She's leaving her husband. We had a long talk.'

I stared at Vicki who looked like a fox terrier that has just found an interesting hole and is sniffing down it. Vicki liked things to happen. Inactivity bored her and the more complicated a situation, the more mischief in it, the better it pleased her. She would leap on events and shake them, trot round with them in her mouth, pounce on them. Now that she had finished painting the house she did not have enough to occupy her. Dashing in and carrying off Matt's niece was a fine excitement for her and, besides, she needed someone to do the work. She liked the little boys. There was plenty of room in the separate house at the back of the Warrens' big house for Mrs. Hertz and the boys. Vicki had it all figured out. A woman who was leaving her husband and had nowhere to go much would be grateful to an employer, wouldn't she? She would be likelier to stay on a lonely farm.

I looked at Vicki admiringly. How much quicker she was to size up a situation than I was! How much more she observed! Had I noticed the young woman had been crying? Not I. I reproached myself for my snail-souled preoccupation with my own affairs.

'She's got bruises on her neck where he tried to choke her.'

'Why did he try to choke her?'

Vicki curled her lip at me. There was a suffragette lost in Vicki. 'Because he's a brute. Anyway she's leaving him. Would you stay with a man who gets drunk and tries to kill you? And they're dear little boys.'

Mrs. Hertz came out. She methodically locked the door and hid the key under the tankstand: Aphrodite in a cheap hat and high-heeled shoes. If I were her husband a situation might arise in which I would try to choke her too. Even in Nithering looks like hers would excite admiration, more especially perhaps in Nithering, a town full of men with nothing but work to occupy them.

'Where we going, Mum?' the bigger boy asked.

'Up near Uncle Matt's place, love.'

'Dad isn't coming, is he, Mum?'

'He is *not*.' There was a formidable quiet about Matt's niece that made me think better of her. At least she wasn't helpless and she didn't snivel.

'Good,' said the boy, and climbed into the back of the truck where I stowed three gaping cardboard suitcases.

'Is there anything else you want to take?'

'No,' Fay Hertz said indifferently. 'I left him a note. He's working at the dam and sometimes he stays at the barracks, depending on what shift he's on.'

On the way through the town I bought the little boys ice cream and fruit, and when I dropped Vicki and her new maid off at the big white house, Fay Hertz was quite cheerful. 'I always wanted to live here,' she said. 'Whenever I went past I wished I lived here.'

Vicki would have had me come in for a meal, but I said I would be down next day. They shouted and waved after me happily, the little boys as glad as crickets.

Matt, hearing the story of his niece leaving her husband, only stroked his beard and narrowed his eyes. 'Always in a rush,' he murmured. 'He's the same. Bull-headed. Rushing from pillar to post. Jumping to conclusions.'

Dennis was reading his letters while I ate some food and gave them the outline. 'Isn't that like Julie?' he exclaimed. 'Well, I'm just not going to touch the damn thing, that's all.' Julie, after warning me not to disturb Dennis, had written him pages of complaint about 'Mrs. Prothero' and the demand for twenty-four episodes. 'I won't do it.'

If Matt would let me camp in the empty house, I said, I would write the abominable 'Mrs. Prothero' while the Muirden boys went back to the Pilliga for the rest of the bees. That was, of course, if they thought it worth while moving the bees. They could suit themselves. So far they hadn't expressed an opinion. Matt said I was welcome to the house. The niece wouldn't go near it again even if she didn't have a job with Mrs. Warren. 'Says it's haunted', he added with a faint scorn. Tranquilly he reviewed in his mind a niece and her warring husband circling about the board of their fate, the two sun-browned boys pawns, pushed about by their parents' gusts of impulse.

When the Muirdens came into new country, they always drove innumerable miles investigating the back roads and accessible timber land. By the time they had returned to Matt's and got themselves a meal, I was already installed, sleeping bag, typewriter and spare lamp, in the deserted shack. I had lit the fire and assembled my papers and was rolling a cigarette when they burst in. Dennis had refused to move to the shack. He said it was too cold and too far to walk after he had finished his last game with Matt. He had secret hopes that if my life was made too difficult I would come back to the city. He was cordially in favour of my accepting Hubert's offer for a new serial. Anything of that nature, provided he didn't have to do it himself, was a fine idea.

Joe and Blaze came tramping into my dear little home with Mongo behind them. I eyed them coldly. I had heard the truck roar up but hadn't bothered to come out. There they were, bed and baggage, thrusting in at the door.

'This house is haunted,' I said stiffly. 'There's plenty of room down with Matt.'

'I can't stay with all those cats,' Joe growled.

'And you can't sleep up here alone with Joe,' Blaze grinned. 'Now that wouldn't look well. And we have to bring Mongo so's we can keep an eye on him.'

Joe had already plunged into the biggest bedroom. I was sleeping in a little room off the kitchen. He slammed down his blankets and a mattress he had brought from Matt's place. I believe their intentions were kindly. They felt I might be lonely, 'perched like a shag on a rock', as they said.

'Mongo can come in with me,' Joe decided. 'Blaze can't. He's a bugger to talk in his sleep.' He walked over to the mantelpiece and smacked the clock experimentally. It gave three loud dongs.

'I keep telling you this place is haunted,' I said.

'Tell me in the morning.' Blaze yawned. 'We've been all over the place. Had an argument with a bloke on a gate at the Upper Valley Dam. He said we didn't go in without a pass because we might pinch something. "Look, mate," I said to him, "if we wanted to pinch anything why would we bother to come through the gate? Why don't we circle round a back track and come down on you from the rear and cart away the whole bloody dam? You'd never wake up."'

'So after that we didn't get in,' Joe said. 'We have to have a pass.'

'Go down to Nithering and get us one, Mallee,' Blaze ordered. 'We'll be making an early start back to the Pilliga tomorrow — bring up another load.' He began discussing with Joe what they would bring. 'Better leave the extracting house until last because we won't be taking off honey for a few weeks, but then we ought to do better than three tins to the hive. Will we wipe Fred Connelly's nose for him!'

'We could send a telegram to George the Corduroy King,' Joe said generously. 'We owe him a turn. And we might let Big Mike in on it too. Hasn't struck a flow since Adam was a pup.'

Nobody said thank you for guiding them to this bonanza.

'God bless our home.' Joe was in great spirits. 'We

don't often strike it as good as this.' He looked about appreciatively.

Hardly had he spoken when there was a report of a rifle outside and a kerosene tin fell over with a clang. Either someone had tripped and his rifle had gone off, or else his rifle had gone off and then he had tripped. A man began cursing at the top of his voice. He sounded drunk. We looked at each other, a look of speculation and foreboding. I was the only one who knew what had happened. Fay's unpleasant husband had come home unexpectedly and found the note.

I called, 'Fay isn't here. She isn't at Matt's place, either.'

The cursing stopped and there was a silence. Blaze and Joe jumped indignantly over the veranda rail and were off in the darkness running to the truck. They switched the lights on, drove round looking for the man, then down to Matt's place, but there wasn't a sign of him. When they came back I explained that the marauder must have been the husband of Matt's niece.

'Funny sort of husbands they have up here,' Joe growled. 'Scared the living daylights out of me.'

Matt had taken it very quietly. 'Come up on the horse,' he explained. 'Must have had too much to drink.'

The next morning, when Matt and I went up to the yard beyond my shack, we found a whole row of hives had been kicked over. The bees were robbing, there was broken comb, broken boxes. I was glad the Muirdens had gone before they saw this devastation.

Matt stroked his beard as he surveyed the ruins. 'That's how he always gets into trouble,' he said. 'Rushing in with his head down.'

Before that I had been willing to believe there might be good points about the unknown Mr. Hertz, but now I changed my mind.

Chapter Seven

MATT was a wonderful hand with bees. He brought up spare boxes, helped me replace broken frames with frames taken from his own hives. Of course, his bee material was not in the same street with the Muirdens', but at least we cleaned up the mess. Matt's movements were all sure and deliberate. Nervy people and frightened people make mistakes, for with bees you need rhythm and quiet. You never jerk or slam things because this upsets them. Of course you strike an occasional hive where they're savage, 'sitting down pretty hard', as the bee men say. But usually bees are just as harmless as most human beings. So would you be harmless if any time you struck at someone you lost your life.

When Matt and I had set the yard in order, we sat down in the shade and had a smoke. I was frowning over my worries, the time I had lost when I should have been going down to Nithering to fix up that pass through the gate to the dam. Then there was 'Mrs. Prothero'. Also I wanted to write a letter to Uncle Beresford explaining my need for £3,500. Three thousand to buy out the Muirdens and five hundred working capital. Getting money from Uncle Beresford was always like prising nails out of a coffin. He knew I could probably raise a loan elsewhere, but he would hiver and hover and advise and protest. When I went into Nithering I would send a telegram to prepare the way: 'Need £4,000 to buy bees. Letter following.'

'So you're going to be an apiarist?' Matt was stuffing his pipe. He sat on his heels in the grass, while I leant against a rock. He drew on his pipe with enjoyment, narrowing his eyes until they were nearly shut like a lizard's.

While we worked I had been telling him how I had come from Nobby Wallace to the Muirdens, how old man Muirden had gone to hospital, and how I had not liked to press the sale of the bees while he was laid up, but on the other hand the boys might think I had peaked on it. I had kept a careful check on what we had been spending and I would try to come to a settlement with Blaze and Joe when they came back. 'Why do you want to be migratory?' Matt asked.

'Well, I like the life,' I said defensively. 'You won't get any money just leaving bees in the one spot.' I repeated what Joe and Blaze were always saying, 'Got to move them or starve them.'

Matt slowly shook his head. 'I don't see it,' he said. Matt's bees only brought in enough for themselves. 'Anyone young wants to knock about and see the country. But you don't need to shift bees.'

This was an old argument. 'You do if you want to make money out of them.'

'You want to make money, Mallee?'

'Certainly. You see, I need to make money more than a man, because being a woman I have to show everybody I can, which is a nuisance, but there it is.'

Matt smiled his old man's kindly smile. 'How much do you have to make?' he asked.

'Well, I reckon I ought to get my capital back in three years and cover expenses. That would be fair, but it probably won't happen unless I have a lot of luck. But, Matt, I *am* lucky. Then if I were showing a profit, I could buy a little farm as a kind of foot-rest, about nine acres with sheds and places for trucks.' I sighed. 'Old Muirden said I'd only lose my dough, but I might as well have some fun with it.'

'What's wrong with this place?' Matt asked. 'You can put your gear in that shed. I used it as an extracting house. You can go tearing round the country. I'll look after everything while you're away.' He looked up in enjoyment of the day. 'I'd like to see you make a go of it.'

His generosity touched me. Here he was offering me, a stranger, the freehold of his dominions! He hardly knew me but he was recklessly ready to back me. He must have been talking to Dennis and realized that, though bee-keeping was in my very blood, my family wouldn't give me any backing, that they looked on it as a disaster.

'Matt,' I said, smiling at him, 'look out I don't marry you for your money. You'd suit me down to the ground.'

Matt smiled back. The Muirdens had shown themselves good mates, and now here was another good mate. I told him how worried I was about the Muirdens. 'Joe wants to go into the navy, and Blaze is supposed to start a harvester and tractor agency and marry a girl in his home town. Well, carting these bees about must be delaying their plans. Mongo would work for me, but he's dumb, poor old Mongo. The Muirdens have brains but they're too proud to work for a woman.'

'I shouldn't worry about those chaps.' Matt yawned. 'They're old enough to look after themselves.' He went striding back to Dennis and the chess. He never seemed to do any work except occasionally to look at some sheep he kept on agistment for other men. He couldn't be bothered, he said, waiting on a lot of woollies, crutching, shearing, ducking them and drenching them. But he would set out salt for the stock to lick.

His land lay idle, a sanctuary for trees and wild things. Matt was idle, blissfully idle. A few days later I asked him

what happened to the cane settee on the back veranda.
'Well,' he explained, 'the chooks always used to perch
on it. I reckoned they appreciated it more than I did,
so I moved it down to the fowl-house.' If anybody wanted
what he had, Matt would give it to them.

I had a great stroke of luck next day when I went down
to the new town of mustard-coloured huts and barracks,
the headquarters of the Nithering Range Hydro-Electric
Authority. Everyone was very polite, but as soon as I
explained that I wanted a pass for trucks to go in and out
ferrying bees, the men looked doubtful. They referred me
to the Head Man, the superintendent engineer, Mr.
Stollin. I didn't want a pass just for a day, but for weeks,
perhaps months. If they gave me *carte blanche* there might
be trouble.

So I saw Mr. Stollin. He was an American, one of the
international tribe of engineers who wander the face of
the earth changing and transforming it. There were
Swedes, Italians, Czechs, Danes, Dutch and fifteen other
races and sects in the camps about the mountains, but
Lee Stollin was unmistakably American. He had a smooth,
twinkling apple-face, good-humour, white hair in beautiful
waves and pince-nez of a queer shape. His clothes were as
spruce as the rest of him: corduroy velvet pants and suède
shoes and a jacket of some velvety material, all brown.

I felt shabby and undistinguished in my dusty khaki,
the same sort of garb as his men wore. Also I hoped he
wouldn't recognize me. I stated my request.

'Haven't I met you before, Miss Herrick?' he asked,
drumming his fingers on the edge of a big desk covered
with papers.

'Yes,' I admitted, 'at Mavis McKinnon's party. She's
a librarian.'

He shook hands. 'Mavis, of course, sure it was with
Mavis.' He smiled in a friendly way. There never was a

more friendly man, but I cursed him because now I would need to explain how I came to be in this setting, with typewriters ticking and telephones ringing, and models and cross-sections, with great concrete pipes outside his windows, and tractors and jeeps, and all this army camp of his. 'I remember. You gave an imitation of a ballet dancer who had trodden in something sticky and was trying to get it off her shoe.'

'It was that sort of a party. You sang.'

'A swell night and very wet,' he agreed.

I had put such things as parties behind me, but I remembered Mavis McKinnon's crowd and wondered, as I always did, where she dug them up. People you met for a night and never saw again. But here was one of them. Someone had asked, 'Where did Mavis find the Yank?' and I had replied unkindly, 'He must have been left over from the war — sort of lease-lend.'

But here he had been up in the mountains all the time. So I had to tell him about what I was doing, while his telephone rang, and his bright young men came deferentially in and out with papers. He would excuse himself to answer the telephone and put it down to hear another chapter in my life's history. Then he took me to lunch in a noisy canteen cafeteria, amid a clatter of dishes, where huge vats of food were steaming, and the heads stood in a queue with the help to have their plates filled. 'You must let me show you over the dam sometime, Miss Herrick,' he told me.

'I should like it very much,' I responded, 'and you must let me show you our bees.'

'Did you know Mavis is in charge of the shire library at Ombra?'

This was a shock. Last time I heard of Mavis she was snatching gay and frothy books away from suburban dwellers.

'She'll be pleased to know you're here.'

It was much more likely that Mavis would insist I attend her Women's Group for the Cultivation of Art and Culture. She always had some kind of organization coiled round her like a tame boa constrictor. Mavis was a pest and friend, a golfer and earnest about culture and good music, a nagger in the cause of higher things. Where Lee Stollin built concrete dams, Mavis would be building an appreciation of The Best in Literature. Mavis and I were the kind of friends who might meet once a year. When we did we drank beer together and bickered together, she taking umbrage at what she considered my sneers at golf and culture, both of which bring out the worst in me.

'Ombra's grown almost to the size of a city,' Lee Stollin explained. 'Mavis is doing wonderful work.'

She would be. I escaped with my pass, making a mental note to keep clear of Ombra where Mavis lurked and to keep clear of Lee Stollin. He looked lonely, and in these ranges a big-gun engineer would only be a complication. However, I had the pass and I promised untruthfully that I would drop in and see him again.

The trouble with a wilderness is that just as you fling out your arms and take a deep breath, exulting in the loneliness, old friends saunter up and treat you as part of their picnic. You make a pattern of your life and, try as you will, the same threads weave in. There is no escaping being stitched and pulled and woven into the recurring row. It rankled in my mind that the country wasn't big enough.

What was worse, I found myself thinking that Mavis probably had a flat with a hot bath in it, a real hot bath, not just a tin tub that you filled from a blackened kerosene tin of hot water. Dirt gets ground into your skin after a time and you can't tell whether it's dirt or suntan. Anyway, what difference does it make?

I drove into the old town of Nithering and drew up outside the post office in a bad mood. Here was I sending a telegram demanding £4,000 from Uncle Beresford; £4,000 that, once sunk, would condemn me to a life in the glare and dirt and heat and flies. Nobody mentions when they talk of the open spaces that there is always a wind blowing across the damn open spaces, usually laden with grit.

That night at Mavis's party my hair had been in short curls and I had a coral taffeta evening dress. Now I looked at my hands, hard and broken and dirty. I went in and sent my telegram: 'Need four thousand to buy bees. Letter following.' And I posted the letter.

But you don't resist temptation. It sneaks up behind you. I could so easily drive over to Ombra and drop in on Mavis for a bath, but once take that downward step . . . It was the old question that vexed the anchorites: Where does cleanliness end and luxury begin? By cleanliness and luxury Rome fell. Only a step between the baths and the circus. I would be back in the circus, the old unreal foolishness, culture and music and riding in buses and trains.

Lee Stollin had admitted to me that he had fought and lied his way out of his correct executive position in the city, where he sat all day in an office with no air, to his present job at the dam. 'It would be great here,' he had told me, 'if it wasn't for the unions There's one big buck union rep. has trouble with his wife. Every time I hear about it I give three cheers. I used to get a phone call to say that Hertz was either murdering his wife, or she was murdering him, and I'd say, "Fine!" If he takes it out of her, he doesn't take it out on me. Now this morning I hear she's left him. This means he'll probably start on me again.'

He had been so glum that I hadn't admitted to knowing

93

more of Mr. Hertz's private affairs than he did. Lee Stollin was divorced, so his views on matrimony almost coincided with my own. We had had a long conversation at that party, and agreed that you fall in love from time to time just as a hen grows broody. But then you catch influenza in the winter and that can be almost as painful. You know you will get over it, provided you don't do anything foolish to lead to pneumonia, or allow the love affair to develop into matrimony.

Once the fever and danger point is over, you are safe until next time. When I am about thirty I hope to marry a small man with a sense of humour, much older than myself, and have two sons and two daughters, but it will not be because I fall in love, but because I find an ideal working partner, someone who pulls well in double harness. Of course they're mighty hard to find, so in the meantime I can dismiss all this fluff and get on with the job, which is 'Mrs. Prothero'.

The delays were sickening. I had wasted half a day cleaning up the mess Mr. Hertz had made and getting that pass from Stollin. I sent another wire to Julie asking for two reams of paper and turned for home. On the river bank near the white bridge was a camping area of green grass reasonably flat. Willows, a high hedge of hawthorn, kept off the dust of the road. A caravan had just pulled in there, an aluminium caravan towed by a little old truck I thought was vaguely familiar. Another huge truck stood nearby, a diesel. A big woman was superintending the erection of a neat aluminium privy. Two children and a wavy-tailed dog galloped and circled and chased each other among some hens that had been released from a special travelling compartment.

The small-sized man putting up the privy was Fred Connelly. I recognized that hat, an old army hat of curious shape, blackened by age and the beeswax rubbed on it. If I had been the Muirdens I would have rushed across the river and spent the rest of the day yarning with Fred, but I remembered Blaze saying Fred Connelly had too many wives — Hilda. That caravan meant Hilda was with him, and that, instead of going to the coast, he had changed his mind at the last minute.

If he recognized the Roaring Ruin, he would be offended at my not rushing across the river to visit him, but I headed in the opposite direction to get some work done before the unholy combination of the Muirdens and Connelly began talking and tramping in and out and sitting by the fire and yarning. For they made any kind of brainwork an impossibility.

For the next three days I typed steadily. Matt and the Parent were very good about meal-getting, although Dennis was beginning to be restless again. I went to Matt's house to eat and the rest of the time was my own. From the veranda of my little house I could gaze out on the gold-green trees across the creek. Bees were already drowning themselves in the water-tank by the back door, so I put in a wooden float so that they might drink in safety. Because I was tired through to my bones, I would begin the day by basking in the sun on the sheltered veranda. A lizard came out on the splintery boards and basked too. Peace, friend, I said to him, be at ease, brother. You and I are both hypostases of the same force that drives this warmth through my flesh and pulls the grass upward.

I practised my favourite exercise, which is to imagine that the top of my head is opening so that I can pass outwards into an emptiness that is all light, with nothing in it except an ugly clot of my discarded self. Behind all these appearances, this blur of movement, was that steadfast pink light and friendship and joy. Blaze and Joe, Matt and the Parent, were just facets into which the pink light happened to split itself when observed from an angle, my angle. We moved and circled and flowed round each other like bubbles of light in a stream that was good while you knew you were only bubbles, but despairingly bad if you felt you were being whirled along without direction.

I am content to observe the pattern of bubbles and keep my own assurances. I do not know how people manage who have no friendly pink light at the back of their minds to help them when they are in a jam. The Quakers say everyone has an Inner Light and simple 'leadings'. Others would call it incipient insanity.

You could not talk to Joe and Blaze, for instance, of levels of consciousness because that would just bounce off them. But they were only a play of light and shadow and I, lying on those splintery boards enjoying the sunlight, was just another focus of light and shadow. Presently my well-being and idleness would be pervaded by a sense of guilt. That nightmare hag, Mrs. Prothero, would begin her eternal mutter in my brain:

Mrs. Prothero: But, Basil, dear, when have I ever wanted to do anything but what was best for you?

Basil: I am old enough, Mother, to know what is best for me. When Helen and I came to live with you, I knew it wouldn't work. I thought there might be a chance because you *are* different from most mothers. I *told* Helen you were an angel.

Mrs. Prothero: That was very stupid of you, Basil. I begin to realize why she . . .

Basil: Why she what?

Mrs. Prothero: Nothing. But you shouldn't have told her I was an angel.

As lousy a bit of dialogue as you would find in any serial. I would drag myself inside and rip out more of it to the same standard pattern. Mrs. Prothero was going to have trouble with Basil's wife, trouble that would last for six whole episodes if I had my way. Sometimes I think Mrs. Prothero is a kind of ooze in which my brain is choking. No wonder the Parent had his far-famed breakdown.

By the end of the third day the back of my shoulder-blades ached with typing. About five I went down to Matt's place, made some tea and cut sandwiches. There was nobody home but the cats. Back at the shack I found it chilly and lit the fire and the lamp before plugging on. Everything was still except for the typewriter talking to itself. Then there was a whirr and a plop and a great black beetle smacked against the lamp. I had been working so long that my nerves were gone.

I took the beetle up and it clung unpleasantly to my finger, waving its antennae and moving its horny wing casings. I tried to feel friendly towards it, as I did to my basking partner, the lizard. I reminded myself that killing, in itself, is not evil but the desire to kill was. The beetle was repulsive to me, and I felt like giving it a smack with a shoe. I sat for a minute wondering whether I was justified in killing that beetle and then decided I was not. I flung it out the door instead, and went on typing with one eye lifted for the beetle as it power-dived for me and the light.

Then a big black dog came to the door and panted at me. I snapped my fingers at it but it moved just beyond that circle of lamplight and looked in at me. With a curse I went back to the typewriter, aware of that confounded dog prowling and sniffing. Mrs. Prothero and Basil's bride were having a showdown.

'No woman can win against her son's wife,' Mrs. Prothero was saying. 'No woman wants to, Helen. But I don't want you to be sorry later when you think of me.

You may say to yourself some day: Now I know what it is like to have my son's wife under my own roof. . . .'

Just then something landed on the roof with a terrific report. I nearly died of fright because I suppose the gruesome details of Vicki Warren's story were somewhere at the back of my mind, below Mrs Prothero and my certainty that there was nothing in this shadow-play of life that could harm me. This spasm of fear was part weariness, part the unexpectedness of the noise. This thunderous crash was succeeded by a rumbling sound of a rock rolling into the guttering. I deduced Blaze and Joe were back.

Blaze had walked ahead while Joe and Mongo drove the truck round the circuitous track across the creek. I knew what Nobby meant when he said the Muirdens were villains. Only a villain would lob a rock on the roof when a poor weak woman was alone in a haunted house. In he came, very pleased with himself.

'In one minute' — I had returned to the typewriter — 'I'll have finished this.'

Blaze was carrying his portable radio. He now began that maddening practice of going all round the dial for popular-music programmes. He usually fell asleep with the thing on full blast and we were all glad when the battery failed.

'Basil,' I told him, to keep him quiet, 'has brought home his bride.'

Blaze made several suggestions he said I could use in the script. He offered them to me free. Any one of them would have put the station off the air. I gave it up. How was I to do eighteen more episodes with the Muirdens about? The truck came roaring up with Joe and Mongo. The little shack, after so peaceful a time, was rowdy with their voices. Joe went over to the clock and hit it experimentally. It gave three reluctant dongs.

'See?' he said. 'Still haunted.'

'What's the time?' I yawned until I nearly dislocated my jaw.

'Must be close on twelve.'

Suddenly I was dead tired. I could hardly keep my eyes open. 'Fred Connelly's here. Tell you more in the morning.' I staggered off to my sleeping bag. Six episodes in three days, I thought, that's work, Mallee my girl.

'What's the matter with her?' Joe growled.

'She's snaky because I bunged a rock on the roof.'

It was too much trouble to correct his mistake. The last thing I heard was Blaze telling Joe that what frightened him about this place was the borers, that they were working in the wood twenty-four-hour shifts and using cross-cut saws. They would bring the place down about our ears, and the noise of their gnawing was worse than Mongo's snores. He went on and on about those borers, and finally I didn't hear him any more, but even in my sleep I seemed to be aware that the beautiful peace was over and the Muirdens were back.

Chapter Eight

THE thing that fascinated me at the Connelly encampment was the electric pig-fence. This enclosed a space round the caravan and the tented awning over the caravan's wooden veranda, and you could hear the tick-tick-tick as the charge went through the wire. The idea of the electric fence was to keep the smallest child, Athol, from straying into the scrub or drowning himself in the creek. He was just past the staggering stage and a confirmed wanderer. Turn off the charge in the pig-fence, and as soon as it stopped ticking Athol was gone.

His elder brother Damien was old enough to step over the fence, but he didn't go out of sound of his mother's voice. He would have had to travel some distance for that. Hilda's voice could be heard at least three paddocks away, and when she raised it on a certain note, the hens scattered for the scrub, the wavy-tailed dog slunk under the caravan, and her husband cowered under his old black hat as though he hoped it would give him the gift of invisibility.

Matt said that Hilda Connelly reminded him of an aunt of his who had turned him off women for life. This aunt used to sit in an armchair, a fat woman too big to stir, and she kept her husband's bullock-whip handy and would send it curling round the ankles of any one of her many children. The whip could reach into any corner of the house, which wasn't very big anyway. Matt used to peep through a crack in the door, scared she would snap that whip at him. 'She started me keeping clear of women,' Matt would say, his eyes twinkling, 'and I've been running ever since.'

Hilda's kindness was of the bull-whip kind. It lashed out at you and knocked you down. She was a massive woman with curly black hair threaded with silver, light grey eyes and a magnificent estimate of her own worth. This was shared by Fred who was as proud of having a tremendous wife and sumptuously fitted caravan as he was of giving his bank manager ulcers.

Fred had theories about credit. Money, he said, was only paper. A bank manager should be made to respect you, because he only handled paper, while *you* — an apiarist — brought in something real, which was honey. He conceived it as his mission in life to tame bank managers, to bring them to heel and keep them awake at night worrying.

Fred was always ready with advice and help of the most fantastic kind, and Blaze and I had driven down to Nithering to visit the Connellys and get Fred's views on the menacing Mr. Hertz who kicked over bee boxes. When Fred had driven through Nithering nine months before, he told the locals that he was searching for a tiger that had escaped from a circus, and most of the mugs had believed him. He had camped for a night near the wooden house where Hertz and Fay and the kids were living. 'A great big bull with a broken nose who used to be a welterweight,' he told Blaze. 'Maybe you'd have a chance to knock him cold if you came up behind him with something heavy enough. Otherwise forget it. Big Mike might take him on, but even Big Mike would have his work cut out. He didn't like me camping there, but I circum-voluted him and dazzled him with science.'

'I hear his wife is a plum,' Blaze said, kissing his fingers. 'Red-haired too.'

Hilda stuck her head out the door of the caravan. 'You didn't tell me she had red hair.'

We were all sitting about on the wooden veranda under the awning. It was a dreary cold day, grey vapour blowing over the ridges and cutting off the treetops, occasional rents of blue showing like patches of water through the cloud.

'It isn't really red.' Fred always loudly expressed an admiration for red hair, and Hilda's was like a burnt log. He turned on Blaze. 'There you go, you big blabber-mouth, trying to pool me right from the start. You know Hilda's thoughts don't need no encouragement.'

'I knew there was *something*.' Hilda's eyes strayed in my direction, where I was doing my far-famed act of merging into the background unnoticed. 'Bringing me to Nithering that ought to be drowned anyway for the price of vegetables alone.'

'I've been kidding you, Hilda,' Blaze said easily. 'I haven't seen this Hertz frow. She probably has thick ankles; and, anyway, Hilda, I wouldn't like to think that anything would come between us, knowing what we are to each other.' He raised his eyebrows and gave Hilda a glance to insinuate dreadful things.

'Oh, get out,' Hilda said good-humouredly. Blaze would go away and declare that Hilda was such a vain old rhinoceros that she believed every word he said, but Hilda had him pretty well summed up. For one thing he was her husband's friend, and a wife has only to see a husband's friend to suspect him of sculduggery.

The friendship between the Muirdens and Fred Connelly was a balance of generosity and rivalry. They played terrible practical jokes on each other, scored points against each other, and rushed to help when they were needed.

'You taught those Muirden boys more than old Horace ever knew,' Hilda would complain, and Fred would grin, and reply that those boys had some natural devilment before he met them.

'Thought you were going to the coast,' Blaze mentioned, when Fred's enquiries about Horace's leg had been suitably answered.

Fred gave us a detailed account of all that had happened to him since he left the Pilliga. 'One blisthurating onpropritious obstacle after another. The bees got into some rubbish that stunk up the honey like a dead fox, a fox that's been a long time dead at that. We would have been up here before you . . .'

'We would not.' Hilda stμck her head out of the caravan again. 'We were all set to go to the coast, and Big Mike and Fred had the trucks stripped down when all of a sudden it's "Get packed, we're going to Nithering". The last place on God's earth I expected to find myself. Like to see the caravan, Mallee?'

This was a flag of truce. It meant that Hilda had decided I was not likely to lure Fred away. I sprang up and squeezed past Hilda's bulk into the tiny kitchen, admiring quite honestly the steel sink, the kerosene stove, the water storage, the refrigerator, and even the little gay curtains at the windows. The rear part of the caravan was fitted with four bunks with inner spring mattresses.

'I like a good bed,' Hilda said complacently, thawing like the refrigerator when the kerosene runs out. 'Now it sounds to me, Mallee, as though that shack where you're sleeping is *damp*. And I know those beds of the Muirdens. Hardest bed I ever slept on was a wooden table in a shelter shed when a cyclone hit us down the south coast. But that iron bed of Blaze's runs it pretty close.'

'She can share my bed any time,' Blaze called. 'I'm working her round to it.'

Hilda and I exchanged a tolerant glance which

comprehended the character of Blaze Muirden. I told her I slept on the floor in my sleeping bag.

'There!' Hilda exclaimed. 'I knew it. You'll end up with pneumonia. No, you move in here with me, and Fred can sleep on the veranda. He often does when Grandma comes with us.'

The men had gone back to their discussion of Hertz, the Peril of the Ranges, and I had no moral support in my polite efforts to explain why this generous offer was unacceptable.

'I don't see it at all,' Hilda insisted. 'This isn't really a good camp, and Fred has to go back for another load. So we'll shift the caravan up to where you are, and I can keep you company while he's away.' I kept a stiff upper lip as I thought how Matt was going to love having Hilda and what a blessing she would be to all of us. 'I didn't think I was going to get on with you, Mallee,' Hilda boomed companionably, 'but I can see what you need is someone to look after you.' Once Hilda arrived at that decision my fate was sealed. 'You need to put on a bit of weight, for one thing — all skin and bone.' She examined me critically, the queen bee of the hive making sure a strange worker would not challenge her supremacy.

Outside, the discussion had glanced off Hertz to Blaze's immediate plans. Joe wanted to stay and do some queen rearing, so Blaze and Mongo would go back to the Pilliga for the extracting house and clean up the last load. 'I'll drop in on Big Mike while I'm down that way,' Blaze told Fred. 'We're going to need all hands while the flow's on, and now that you mention it Big Mike would probably be the man to take Hertz on and clean him up.'

Hilda was preparing lunch for all of us when there was the sound of a horn tooting over by the road, and I stepped out of the caravan to see the Warrens' big car lurching towards us. I remembered that Vicki had been talking about going down to the city to collect the boys from school. There was enough luggage for a month, and in the back seat, enthroned among the suitcases, sat the Parent.

Vicki and Harry Warren and Dennis Oberon Herrick stepped out of the car and were introduced. They had the half-apologetic gaiety of a group of social workers visiting a slum settlement. They were putting themselves out to be gracious. The bee-keeping talent drew themselves in a defensive front with the effusive visitors eddying around them.

'We can't stay,' Vicki said, in a clear hearty voice. 'We're late now, but that's Dennis's fault. He suddenly decided to come with us. You won't *believe* this, but Fay' — she explained to Hilda — 'Fay Hertz is housekeeping for me — a charming little thing — but it seems she's scared to stay alone while we're away. I told her we were going for only a few days, but no! — nothing would do but we run her and the children down to Mr. Kettrill's place. And there was Dennis just frantic to get home. So we left Fay and brought him with us.'

'If I was married to Fay's husband,' Blaze observed, 'I wouldn't stay alone either. I'd be afraid he might come up some night and say, "How about it?" I'd die of fright.'

Vicki Warren laughed. 'Well, anyway, she's safe enough with Mr. Kettrill. And *you* will be there.' She gave Blaze an arch glance, at which Hilda stiffened visibly.

'Too right I'll be there,' Blaze grinned.

Harry Warren was not liking this conversation. He looked at his watch restlessly. 'Have to be getting along,' he mumbled.

'But, Harry, I had to *explain*. And Dennis has to say goodbye to Mallee.'

'You could have saved me postage on that packet of script I sent down this morning,' I told the Parent grimly.

'Have a good trip. Give my love to Julie.' It was no good telling Dennis what I thought of him in front of them all.

The Parent had a football scrum of excuses all pushing in opposite directions. 'I wanted to introduce Harry to some friends of mine in Northern Exploitations. Very important just at the moment that I should be there when there's this big merger with the Hales crowd. If I don't get back soon I might miss out on something big. You didn't tell me there would be fowl feed in the bath. And, my God! the fleas! Very decent, of course, for Matt to have us, but really — my dear girl.' He turned to Vicki. 'Can't you persuade her to leave this? Honestly, Mallee, you must keep Mrs. Prothero going. I'll be far too busy to attend to it.'

'Oh, do come, Mallee,' Vicki cried. 'Please don't think I'm trying to interfere, but really——' She turned to Hilda. 'Don't you think I'm right? If only she came down for a few days?' Hilda regarded Vicki stonily.

'Thanks all the same,' I said. 'I'm staying. I'll keep up Mrs. Prothero.'

I stepped back to indicate that the interview was at an end. The slum dwellers had been inspected by those who might do them good. But they still showed a tendency to linger. Vicki petted Athol and said the pig-fence was cute. Athol regarded her solemnly, tripped and fell on his face, showing an expanse of dirty rompers and bare legs. He had inherited his voice from Hilda and he went red in the face in giving full vent to his protests. Against that volume of sound the visitors spoke inarticulately and retreated to the car with stiff farewell smiles, waving graciously as they drove off.

'Well,' Hilda growled, 'if ever a woman got on my works! Who does she think she is, anyway?'

'Oh, Vicki is very kind,' I assured her.

'Kind!' Hilda snorted. 'A painted, dressed-up . . . Did you see those diamond rings? Now imagine wearing diamond rings in Nithering!'

Vicki would wear diamond rings in a lifeboat and she would probably come ashore the only survivor with negotiable property. I tried to explain to Hilda what a good scout Vicki was, but Hilda had decided against Vicki. Nor was the impression mitigated by Fred Connelly's expressions of coarse admiration.

'You can have the redhead, Blaze,' he announced generously. 'I'm moving up next to Vicki. Vicki for me every time.' He set his awful black hat over one eye. 'Here I come. I can't wait till she gets back, and when she does she'll find *me*. Did you notice the way she looked at me sideways, saying to herself, "Now *there* is a man I could do a line with any time"?'

He was doing it partly to annoy Hilda. She, of course, knew that if he were in earnest he would be deviously covering his tracks. She only breathed through her nose and looked stern. Anyone with a love affair in a bee camp keeps it very dark, because life can be made unbearable for him by his mates. The thing starts as a joke, but they go on and on until the victim is just about ready to knock them cold.

Blaze at once began giving Connelly a much-embroidered account of his towing the Warrens out of Cobberloi Creek. He, the hero, had made a great impression on this good-looking Mrs. Warren — according to Blaze.

'You made a great mistake, son,' Fred said, consideringly, 'in getting out of that pansy white boiler suit you go about in. You're too scrawny. Now me, I have assets. I may have put on a little round the waist, and lost me teeth and hair, but look what I've gained in *experience*.'

They were still telling each other what wonders they were when I said we had to be making tracks as I wanted to call at the post office.

'Too right we have to go back,' Blaze agreed warmly. 'There's Joe getting the edge on me with Fay. He'll be staying behind doing the queen rearing, making his marble good, and I'll be somewhere down in the Pilliga with Mongo telling me how if he was home his brother would be playing the mandolin. Come on, Mallee. Get going.'

When we left, the willows were dripping their long green leaves in the river by the white bridge, the hens were pecking about, the kids were digging a deep interesting mud-hole, the pig-fence was going tick-tick-tick and Hilda was giving Fred a piece of her mind about the way he big-noted himself on his non-existent pretensions to ardour.

I told Blaze that Hilda had decided to camp with us, and he gave a groan. 'Now what have I done to deserve that? Fred would be all right if he wasn't such a liar and double-crosser and if he didn't think he could work bees — which he can't. But Hilda! Why doesn't he cut her bloody throat?'

At the post office was a telegram for me from Uncle Beresford, saying: 'Do nothing precipitate. Did you receive my letter?' Also two reams of paper from Julie for typing 'Mrs. Prothero'. I should have told Dennis to do the damn serial himself, but I had got interested in it now. Dennis had liked the six episodes. He said it was 'King Lear' in reverse and done as comedy.

I was going to miss the Parent, and as soon as he got back to the city he would start taking too many drinks again. He had brisked up wonderfully in the clear air of Nithering with nothing to drink but tea and an occasional whisky at the Warrens' place. I had been pleased to see him making friends with the Warrens, thinking it would keep him contented.

Blaze had found a letter addressed to him at the post office. He was never the strong silent type and as soon as we were in the Ruin again, he burst out, 'Well, that's that. I'm not engaged any more. She's ditched me again.'

'Sent the ring back?'

'I never gave her one. But I rang her up from Atholfast and told her how good this flow was going to be.'

'Did you tell her I was going to buy the hives and you were coming home to start that agency?'

'Like hell I did. You'd starve those bees or else lose the lot. No, we'll cut you in on shares like the rest of the mob.'

'How much do I put in as my share?'

'You don't put in *any* money,' Blaze said fiercely. 'Any store-keeper will stake us for twelve months. We don't need your money. Charlie Wong at home'll give us credit till hell freezes over. Wouldn't take money from a woman, anyway.'

'I have my own sixty hives.'

'Oh, those mongrelly old hives,' Blaze groaned. 'I s'pose we might re-queen them and make something of them. Look, you worked in the extracting house with Joe, didn't you, while Horace was sick? We'd owe you wages if you were on wages. Mongo's on wages, but that's because he's too silly to come in out of the wet. No, you'll get your cut when we get paid, but there's one thing we better get straight right now. I'm not having any woman ·bossing me, you or Hilda or Daphne, either. While you're working with us you take *orders*.'

'But I always take orders.'

'What about the time I said, "Mallee, don't lift that heavy box", and you lifted it? What about when I said, 'Mallee, let Mongo carry those kerosene tins", and you carried them?'

We had come past the construction camp and begun to climb. Then the Roaring Ruin sheered into the middle of the road, took a dive towards a precipice and wobbled away. We had a puncture in the rear tyre. Blaze drew into the side and was out of the truck in a moment.

'Where's your jack? Where's the wheel brace? Where's the pump?' I said they were probably under the seat. '*Probably*,' he muttered. There was no wheel brace, only half the jack handle, and the spare tyre was flat. 'A bloody woman,' Blaze snarled. 'Just another bloody woman.'

'Cheer up,' I said. 'Someone will be along in a minute. I'm always lucky that way.'

'Let me tell you you need a special wheel brace for the Ruin. See those nuts? Only the right kind of brace fits them.' He said he was going to erect a statue to Dennis Oberon Herrick and inscribe on the base that he had put up with me since I was a child. 'I can tell you I've walked bloody miles sooner than ask any one to help me.'

'Well, walk bloody miles, then.'

If ever there was a nagger it was Blaze. Years from now he would be telling everyone how I threw the jack handle up at some buds in a tree and lost the damn thing.

I felt an evil satisfaction when, a few moments later, Lee Stollin came careering round the bend in a jeep with two bright young men. Of course they stopped at once, and those young engineers made no difficulty about getting off the wheel and pumping the flat tyre on the spare. I explained gracefully that it was all my fault, and introduced Blaze. He and Lee Stollin were very polite to each other, too polite. I knew Blaze was sizzling internally, like something left on a hot stove.

Lee Stollin said courteously that I might have difficulty in getting a wheel brace for the Roaring Ruin and he would have his machine-shop make me one. 'No trouble,' he said. 'You haven't been out to see over the dam yet, I'll bring the wheel brace over and we can go up to the dam one day.'

I said that would be splendid. I thought it was poetic justice that Blaze, who had been so impolite helping the Warrens out of a creek, should have someone with charming manners to help us out with our puncture. Lee and I parted on the friendliest terms, having made a date for my seeing the dam.

On the way home Blaze expressed with vehemence his views about engineers in fancy pants. He said he always hated Yanks; but as he hated Dagoes, Pommies, abos and square-heads, that was just another of his ignorant prejudices and I said as much. 'The trouble with you, Blaze, you're arrogant and you've got a filthy temper.'

'Me? I'm one of the mildest fellers going.'

When we reached Matt's homestead, Joe was in the kitchen sitting in the old cane chair with a small boy on each knee. He had quite forgotten that cats gave him asthma. The niece was finding that Uncle Matt's place wasn't so dull after all, and Joe looked like a bee drowning in nectar. He gave his brother a very sullen look as Blaze burst in and proceeded to fascinate Mrs. Hertz, talking with all stops out and being as dashing as he knew how.

One of these days scientists will discover that honey is so full of fertility vitamins from the pollen that eating it fresh is like a charge of dynamite to the human glands. Whether it is eating honey, or the loneliness, there is no doubt bee-men are always jet-propelled in matters of sex. Even Fred Connelly, who has the looks and graces of a hyena, couldn't see a woman in the distance without sparking with interest.

He once explained to me how you could tell from the way a woman waved to you as you drove past whether her husband was home or not. He considered Fay Hertz was 'an orange blossom girl', and certainly just as you can tell there is an orange tree in flower, even if you go by in the dark, so you always knew Fay Hertz was around.

I went out to the back veranda where Matt was smoking philosophically. 'Well, Matt,' I said, 'no sooner one visitor leaves than you've got three more.' I didn't dare tell him about Hilda.

'I'm one of these vacuums,' Matt said quietly. 'If you have a vacuum in nature, everything around rushes in, in a hurry to fill it up.'

Mongo was doing the washing-up. This was so surprising that I asked him if he was feeling well.

''S a matter of fact, Mallee,' he confessed, 'I got a great big festering boil on me hand. But don't worry, Mallee. This hot washing-up water is doing it a lot of good.'

We hastily took the washing-up away from him and I told him to put a bread poultice on the boil. In the morning I found he had made his poultice in my drinking mug and left the mug on the window-sill full of messy cold wet bread.

Chapter Nine

THERE were as many creeks in the Nithering Range as there are Caseys in Dublin. Ryall Creek, Cobberloi and Blott's Creek, three creeks mingling in a little gut of the hills, continue as the Cassan River. This gut made an ideal narrow place to build the Upper Dam on which Lee Stollin and his men were toiling. The water would be diverted through a race to a power-house; then there was to be another great dam below Nithering sending water through another tunnel to yet another power-house.

Nithering had become a national emergency because the rich Cassan Valley was alternately a drought area and then subject to desolating floods, when a quarter of a million people sat on their roof-tops and watched waters roll over miles of land that should have been pumpkins and corn, sheep and cattle.

In the early 1840's a hundred and eighty thousand sheep were yearly shorn and washed in the lower valley of the Cassan. The original pioneers considered its wealth in-exhaustible. They had come up the broad stream flowing under the tranquil she-oaks and had at once begun to fell the trees and clear the land. Fencing was hard work, for all the posts and rails had to be split by hand. Shep-herds every night enclosed their flocks in folds.

The improving and clearing and ring-barking went on until the foothills of the enclosing ranges were almost bare of trees save ring-barked, dead skeletons, white bones pointing upward from the sheep-nibbled sward, and they were white bones of a terrible warning.

The soil began to slip in red gashes, whole slopes at a time. Steeper land that had been used for sheep had to be given over to the less lucrative cattle. Floods which had been rare became a yearly danger on the lower Cassan. There were bad years, prices fell, labour became scarcer and the fertility of the fields declined. The farmers worked their sons until the sons ran off to the towns swearing never again to set foot in the accursed valley. Others stayed on, conscientiously sending their tractors round and round the river flats turning over soil that the next flood would wash away.

Then a rumour blew over the ranges that land cleared with what sweat and back-break only men in their graves could recount was to be given back to the trees, declared a huge catchment area. A hundred miles away, where the Cassan River ran through to the sea, the bodies of drowned sheep and cattle were floating down the main street of the city of Warnefield, past the milk-bars and theatres and hospitals and garages and furniture stores. A flood that destroyed the livelihood of a big town, that interrupted business and the running of bus time-tables, raised an outcry from a quarter of a million people who demanded to be heard where laws are made.

The huge hydro-electrical octopus began sending out red tentacles of roads from Ombra to grasp the ranges, sucking out the Nithering creeks into conduits, channelling them and stabbing them with tunnels, choking them with dams. Men swarmed like ants, digging and blasting; and the great minds who had set up all these wonders, spoke of progress and the immense opportunities of development.

There was one little point they overlooked, the quiet prophecy that these great new roads which undercut the mountains would start new landslips, would cause the trees to die back to the top of the ridge. The great minds spoke sonorously of anti-erosion experts, of erosion control.

'What it amounts to,' Lee Stollin told me, 'is that the water is running way down at the bottom of a valley, and you're on the top of a ridge. Well, you've got to get down to the water. The foreman spits on his hands and says to the gang, "There she is, boys. That's where the road's going and don't stop till you get there."'

'What about that chap who claimed that the dams would be choked with silt in twenty-five years?'

'A trouble-maker,' Lee said promptly. 'We have plenty of our own guys who say it won't.'

'You admit the roads under-cut the tree roots, that they die back and the earth scours down and exposes more tree roots, and these die?'

Lee was beginning to think I was an uncomfortable guest. He had come bustling up to Matt's place in a jeep with the wheel brace and insisted on carrying me off to see his dam. Naturally he expected the fervent praise which all other visitors gave him in a chorus.

'Any time you do anything,' he complained, 'there's always someone to tell you what's wrong with it.'

So only an impolite visitor would have persisted. We were under the stone-crushing plant on a hill above the dam. I had just been escorted up spider webs of runways where, in a tremendous dust, rocks were being churned and sorted and battered, jolting down iron chutes and falling through gratings to be mixed with cement and sand into the concrete which fell from an enormous churn into big iron vats. These were then tugged out along a wooden platform by a jeep and swung through the air on a flying fox to the dam far below.

Men were down in the creek bed scrubbing and chipping at rocks where the spillway would be. The water of the three creeks was diverted through a tunnel to join its bed farther down where it could not interfere with the big wall rising across the valley. There was something inspiring about so much activity. We had climbed all over that great wall where the concrete was spilled out of the great iron tubs and spread by men with an electric shovel that turned and tossed it.

Other men were scrubbing with wire brooms at the concrete, washing it down with hoses, like a travesty of tidy housewives at work on a giant doorstep. And behind the dam what a shouting and activity of men with grouting pumps controlling the water, men adjusting the power for the mixing shovels, men at telephones in communication with the control tower high up on the hillsides! Engineers talking and consulting and climbing, men with timber and men with wire cables and wrenches and lighting equipment, for by night the ceaseless roar went on under the great arc lamps, shift by shift all through the dark hours. I had been introduced to engineers until my handshake was weary; young men in charge of this or that, older men in charge of the young men.

'Where does Frank Hertz work?' I asked, approaching my mouth close to Lee Stollin's ear, for the concrete was falling with a shattering roar into the iron receptacle quite close to his other ear.

'Hertz?' he said, with a grin. 'I'll show you.'

We climbed the ridge behind the stone-crushing plant and there was a grateful quiet. On the other side of this rampart of stone, carved out where Bott's Creek joined Cobberloi, there was a tunnel down in a cutting where trucks ran in and out, and men with ordinary handpicks were digging and chipping the approach to the three-mile tunnel.

'Have to go very carefully and timber all the way in the tunnel,' Lee Stollin explained. 'The Norwegians got themselves killed in squads because they were not used to rotten granite, so we had to have Australian miners.'

'But I thought Hertz was a mechanic?'

'Well, he's in charge of a gang of miners, that's all I know. It isn't his shift, and anyway you wouldn't see him because he's somewhere inside the tunnel.'

There had been a dim idea in my mind that I might be ingratiating to Mr. Hertz. Just at our feet a huge shaft yawned, the shaft from which the rocks were taken to the stone-crushing plant. Lee became very technical about how many cubic tons of granite were taken every day from that large hole, and I tried to look intelligent.

Engineers are extraordinary in their pride over holes and tunnels. Nothing arouses so much enthusiasm in them as a hole, unless it is a large-sized wall. The large and splendid moraine and rubbish heap that they had burrowed for themselves was exciting, if you shared their enthusiasm for holes and walls. How impressive it looked when you stood under the high buildings above the towering dam! But when you raised your eyes to the ranges, that looked grimly down on the burrowers, their immensity was chilling. Those hills had their feet in the dam as a man might stand on an ants' nest without noticing.

'What's that sandy-looking stuff high up?' I asked, pointing to a far peak.

'Snow,' Lee Stollin said grimly. I had never seen snow before. 'Last winter we lost a bulldozer. Reckoned somebody must have stolen it until fourteen feet of snow had melted. Make no mistake, winter can be tough.'

'We'll be gone before winter is well on us,' I said, to comfort myself. 'We'll be out on the plains when the ground flora comes up.'

Rolling plains of capeweed, I thought, little yellow daisies with black hearts smiling in the early cold, pink, yellow-white, the field flowers with the chilly sunlight

and the winds over them. Then, later, the Paterson's
Curse blazing like a glowing flood, deeper blue in the
hollows, purple-red on the rises, while Nithering Range
lay grim and majestic under snow. We must get our
honey off, working against time before the cold closed
down.

'It's always a race,' Stollin said, echoing my thoughts.
'A race to get as much done as you can before the snow.
Time and weather,' he smiled at me. 'Always trying to
clutch more time.'

'We'll be going down the Cassan Valley,' I said.
'Below Warnefield. Out on the flats for the capeweed.'

Far from the beautiful mountain flowers, the golden
mountain everlasting flowers, the great violets and mauve
and pink lilies of the snow country. But the thought of
leaving Nithering was a sadness. How exquisitely the
mornings came there in a dew of promise! How heart-
lifting the purity and calm of the high ranges. But, of
course, the bees must move. If we stripped them of their
stores and sold their honey, they could not last the winter.
They must be taken from the cold hungry months. They
must move or die.

They worked for us and we worked for them, cleaning,
tending, fending for them — and robbing them. And the
honey would be shipped round the world to breakfast
tables in cities I had never seen, for householders to eat
who never knew whence it came, tons of honey going to
England to be sold probably at a loss because the prices
were pegged against us, and the English floor didn't want
Australian eucalypt honey.

Somehow the sight of Stollin's dam, instead of arousing
a just appreciation for all this progress, merely made
me sad. 'They'll get more electricity, more water for
irrigation,' I objected, 'but what's the use of it? More
cities, more progress, more roads and railways, more

people. Always more of everything cluttering up the earth. And then somebody drops a bomb on it and you start all over again.'

'Well,' Lee Stollin said cheerfully, correcting the dullard, 'if there are enough people and enough power, they can see nobody drops a bomb on them. We'll need power for munition plants, steel, blast furnaces. Make the country self-supporting.'

But what kind of a country was he making self-supporting? A country where three-quarters of the people — more than three-quarters — lived in cities and worked in offices and factories, filling up sheets of paper or transporting all the other workers to their various jobs. What a life!

'There's your friend Hertz,' Lee Stollin said. He indicated a man who had just walked into the cutting and was talking to the foreman while he put on his steel helmet. He was a man who was built for battling rocks. His whole personality was rocky. Seen from the lip of the cutting, the big Hertz dominated the scene of trucks on rails and drills and gangs with shovels. No wonder he couldn't get on with his wife. This was the life he was born for and that he understood, a masculine business of muscle and effort.

Lee Stollin took me down in the cutting and introduced me to him. 'Maybe you'd explain to Miss Herrick,' Lee said winningly, 'about the tunnel.'

Hertz expanded. Nothing he liked better than being picked out as the man who could explain about tunnels.

'It's dangerous, see?' he said. 'You've got to go a step at a time.' This tunnel would convey the water from the dam through the hill, down a three-hundred-foot race to the power-house where it would pour into the old rocky bed again. 'Trouble is the rock's not stable. Old rotten stuff. You have to timber all the way. Adds to the cost.

Then there's safety measures.' Hertz looked at Stollin significantly. 'You could bring tons of rock down on you with one explosion.'

He went on telling me about their safety measures until Lee said a foolish thing. 'Miss Herrick's in the mountains with bees. She's staying at Mr. Kettrill's place.'

Hertz gave me a look of venomous dislike, and his boastful flow dried up. 'Bees,' he muttered, staring at me. 'Bees. Yeah, I once thought of doing something with old Matt's bees myself. Know a bit about them too. And I know a lot more about the kind of coves that travel them. One come to my place, a gabby little bloke. Talk you blind. Caused a lot of trouble.' His cold pale-blue eyes summed up Fred Connelly as a possible home-wrecker. 'This place is no good for bees. Unhealthy.' And he turned away and strode from us. 'No good at all,' he called over his shoulder. 'Take my word for it.' And he bared his big yellow teeth at me in what might have been a smile.

We climbed back up the cutting. On the way home I told Lee Stollin about my part in assisting Hertz's wife to break from him. 'She's up there at Matt's place now until her employers come back.'

'And he doesn't like bee-keepers,' Lee commented. 'Well, if there's any trouble, let me know.' I had not told him of Mr. Hertz discharging a gun the first night we settled in his old house or kicking over our bee boxes. 'When you do let me know,' he added humorously, 'I probably won't be able to do anything about it.'

'Why, migratory apiarists are the most peaceable men there are,' I said loyally. 'They just like a quiet, lonely place where the bees can do well. We'll be taking off honey as soon as we get the extracting house up.'

I insisted on showing him all the yards of bees when he

drove me back, and explaining that we ought to do better than three tins to the hive. Lee Stollin shared my enthusiasm about bees as little as I shared his for ant-works, but we were both considerate and courteous to the madness of the other party. I praised his dam and thanked him for the interesting day, and then had to face, after he left, the concerted efforts at humour, the insinuations as to Mr. Stollin's intentions from those peaceable apiarists of mine. You would have thought there was something strange about a friendly engineer wanting to show me over his dam.

Chapter Ten

BLAZE delayed going back to the Pilliga for the extracting house until Joe was ready to murder him. 'We could take off honey any time now,' he growled, 'and no extractor but that brum hand-turned job Matt has.' Joe thought that Blaze was loitering around because of Fay Hertz, but it was largely Fred Connelly's fault.

First Fred wanted Blaze to look for sites round the back of the dam, then he decided to put in some bees at Lacey's Crossing. Then Fred asked Blaze to wait for him until Hilda and the boys were settled in with us.

At the thought of Hilda I think Matt turned pale in his beard. She arrived with the caravan, the hens, the dog and the kids, full of curiosity and officious good humour. The caravan was set up on the slope by the creek, and within twenty-four hours she and the niece had between them decided to fall on Matt's house and give it what Hilda called 'a thorough good going over'. Water flowed in and out the front and back doors of the house in a soapy flood. Hot water was Hilda's native element.

'No, Mr. Kettrill,' she boomed. 'It's no use you telling me not to exert myself or overtire myself. I'm a woman who likes work. You been mighty kind letting us stay here while Fred goes off, and I want to do something for *you*. Now you'll offend me if you don't let me give the place a clean up, see? And it can *do* with it. You say there's fleas, and I *know* there's fleas. Shove those cats outside, Fay. And the kids too. Don't want them dirtying the place when we've got it clean.' The Connelly kids fought the Hertz kids and the wavy-tailed Connelly dog romped with Matt's dogs.

'Well, now Hilda's settled in and is happy,' Fred beamed, 'Blaze and me 'ull be off for another load each.'

They were delayed by the arrival of George, the Corduroy King, a silent blue-chinned man with a load of bees he was dumping in on spec because Blaze had sent him a wire. George always went farther and fared worse than anyone else. He was notorious for it. He immediately decided on some sites up beyond the dam which Fred and Blaze had ruled out as too steep. It was so steep on that spur that George had to cut ledges in the hillsides to set out his bee boxes. He refused to stay more than a night or so in our shack and retired to a lonely tent on his mountain pass. He would come down, he said, for company or to borrow anything he wanted.

Finally we got rid of Blaze and Fred — and Mongo — and after they had gone the place seemed much more roomy. Mongo's boil was worse — in fact he was breaking out in boils all over — and Blaze, after the washing-up incident, had decided to take Mongo home for a spell and bring back in his place Big Mike, if he could locate that elusive character. Big Mike had worked for Fred Connelly once and for the Muirdens a couple of times, and for himself the rest of the time. They were all on the same terms of inimical friendship.

'The trouble with Big Mike,' Hilda told me, as I was sitting in the caravan with her the night after Fred left, 'is that he makes a lot of money, but he spends it. He'd take his bees to hell if it was flowering, but on the way back he'd give away all the honey to the first girl that asked him for it. He's like Blaze,' she added judicially. 'I wouldn't say a word against Blaze. You know I've

a mighty lot of time for Blaze Muirden, Mallee, but I've
never known him when he wasn't running five girls at
once or talking himself into trouble. Can't keep his mouth
shut. And he'll look in your eyes and double-cross you.
Tell you all the lies in the world if you're mug enough to
believe him.'

Hilda had been weeding Matt's garden, repairing his
wire-netting fence, waging war on the live-stock. She
had gardener's fingers and the seedlings she planted were
soon showing sprouts of salad green. She ruled us like a
female sergeant-major, bullying, shouting, suggesting and
getting her own way.

Poor old Matt was a refugee. He looked on my shack
as a place of concealment when Hilda and Fay made the
going too hot. His one-time hermitage was swarming
with women and kids, and he would come out to the bee
yards with Joe and me and stay all day.

Joe wanted to re-queen at least three hundred hives,
and Matt and I worked with him in the blazing March
weather, with the wind flashing the leaves to and fro on
the trees, making the bees restless and savage. Of course,
they are always savage on stringy-bark with its strong,
heady nectar and beautiful flourishing pollen for the
brood.

The wind would come roaring over the gulfs of trees
and the bees would roar with it. They bring in so much
pollen from the stringy that it goes mouldy, and they roll
it out of the door of the hive in little balls. They were
drunk and mad and savage with plenty.

'We'll be taking off honey,' Joe prophesied, 'just as
soon as Blaze gets back with the extractor.'

We were working against time, going through the hives.
Those that did not need re-queening were ready for
extra supers and zinc queen-excluders, so that the queen
could not come into the upper boxes and scatter eggs

through the honey comb. We were also putting matt insulators of malthoid in the lids to keep the bees comfortable. I painted my boxes in my spare time and Joe re-queened them with the others.

'Where are you, you slit-gutted bitch?' Joe would growl, turning the frame to look for the queen. 'Here, Mallee, see if you can set eyes on her.' And he would hand the frame moving and running over with bees to me. 'There she is,' and the poor old queen, the gold fur rubbed off her, shabby and black from scuttling round the comb, and old and exhausted from egg-laying, would be killed.

Or else Joe might say, 'These bees are terrible strong. Look as though they might swarm.' And, shouting to Matt for another super full of clean new frames for them to fill, he would mark the lid to tell him that this hive had an old queen due for killing next 'round'. All the boxes had private marks, bits of rock or stick on the lids, pats of dried cow-dung or dates scribbled in pencil which were the bee-keeper's records. Once Fred Connelly wrote on a hive: 'Have contacted this hive. Looks to be queenless and has been kicked over by a cow.' Big Mike, who thought scornfully of Fred's verbosity, wrote underneath, 'Love and kisses. Give name and address of cow.'

Queen-rearing is one of the trickiest jobs in bee-keeping. You are doing it all the year round, but autumn is the best time, of course, depending on the condition of your bees. With a warm hacksaw blade, the wax is cut down, then melted in a tin of hot water. By dipping a rounded stick, about the size of my little finger, first into cold water, then in the hot wax, then in cold water again, a wax sheath forms that can be slipped off until you have a billy-can full of these tiny wax cups which are called cell-cups.

The cell-cups are arranged on the bar of an empty frame and slipped into a super on a hive that has an old queen or one that is queenless. If there is a queen in the box, a queen-excluder keeps her down in the bottom where she cannot destroy the bar of queen cells. The bees come up and caress and smooth these cups. This is called 'priming' and no human hands can do it. The bar of cell-cups is left in overnight, and then, next morning, in each tiny cup a ten-hour-old larva is placed with a feather or a tiny spoon. The bar, with its living tiny specks of white in each cup, is replaced so that the bees can pack the cup with jelly and build over each the curious tower of knobbly wax which is the sign and surety of a queen cell.

Once these are wrought, the bar is lifted out, on the tenth day, and carried with the queen cells like a strange, pendulous fruit to the neuc boxes where the future queens are set up, each with a home of her own, a strong frame of good young bees and brood, and two frames of honey for their sustenance.

On the thirteenth day the queen emerges. She mates any time up to five days after that. If she doesn't mate, she becomes a drone layer and you kill her. She dances a merry measure on air with her chosen lover, and then the clock strikes, and leaving no glass slipper on the staircase of light, she hastens home, descending to the warm domesticity of the hive, and the changeless life of laying and being hustled about by her family.

When Joe let me help with the queen cells, I realized that as far as good old Joe was concerned I was passing my final test. One of the worst things I ever did was to drop a queen cell. When Joe saw my stricken face, instead of calling me a ham-handed half-wit, he said gently, 'All right, Mallee, it has to happen to everyone. We can't risk putting her in a hive, so I'll show you how she looks.'

The queen cell is always a curious, elaborate big cell,

like an acorn made of coral, and packed with royal jelly so that the tiny anonymous larva may eat and become royal. There she lay in her jade coffin, the sleeping beauty, white as a ghost in a wrapping of silk, snow white with eyes of a red cornelian, dreaming for what must have seemed to her a hundred years. I had seen nothing so lovely as that poor queen Joe showed me; and I had destroyed her, deprived that little Cinderella of her one ecstatic hour when she would have danced a measure on air with some strong-winged prince.

For her there would be no golden gloom of the hive, no ceaseless stir of progeny. I felt like the Hand of Doom, and I kept her tiny jade tower with its elaborate carving as a reminder. That queen cell went with me on my wanderings. I was always pulling it out of a forgotten pocket or turning it out of my kitbag.

Matt came over to look too, and turned the queen over gently, admiringly, in his long hard fingers. To cover my self-despisal over this blunder, he started an argument as to whether a queen could regulate her laying of workers or drones.

'Now, is it the shape of a drone cell, because it's bigger than an ordinary cell?' he asked slowly. 'Is it the shape that tells her to drop a drone egg in it?'

'It's the length of time the egg is fed on royal jelly,' Joe corrected, 'that makes it a worker or a drone or a queen. Depends on how the egg's fed. The bigger space in a drone cell means there's more space for jelly, and the bees pack it accordingly.'

'No, that's not what I'm getting at,' Matt contended. 'The queen must have some kind of storage system in her inside. She mates only once. And she goes on laying eggs for eternity.'

'Not eternity,' I objected. 'Only two or three years at the most.'

'Well, that must seem eternity to a queen bee,' Joe agreed with Matt.

'What Matt wants to know,' I summed up, 'is do all the spermatozoa unite with the ova when the queen takes her nuptial flight, so that she stores fertilized eggs? Or does she store up the spermatozoa separately and release one to unite with the ova when she lays the egg?'

'You've got it.' They both looked at me respectful of this scientific learning. 'How's it done?'

'I don't know,' I said, losing all their respect at once. 'Some of these laboratory blokes would know. They have microscopes and slides and . . .'

'Oh, them!' Joe grunted. 'They don't know anything. Send them down some leaves and blossom, and they'll tell you what type of tree it is. Send them leaves and blossom from the same tree the next year, and they'll tell you it's something quite different.'

'Well, it's easy to make a mistake,' Matt said peaceably. 'Eucalypts inter-breed like mad. Look at messmate. Look at box. Hundreds of different sorts. Cross with anything. Why, I guarantee if a Black Orpington stayed out after dark, some damn eucalypt 'ud cross with it, and you'd have a tree with feathers instead of leaves.'

So we talked and worked together in that curious and beautiful accord which is the best memory anyone can have, a memory of work done with friends, that will later glow in your mind when the troubles and storms between have quite died away, as the wind fades when the day is over, and the hush falls and the trees are still in the last glow.

Chapter Eleven

THE night of the second Battle of the Bees was an icy-cold full moon. Hilda was such a pest in her efforts to have me sleep on one of those over-stuffed bunks in her caravan that I had compromised by playing Family Coach with Matt. I slept in Matt's bed, and Matt had taken over Blaze's awful iron bedstead with the creaks in it.

Hilda was just a mite huffy over this evasion of her hospitality. I don't believe for a moment that she thought I was living in sin with poor old Joe. She just wanted to get me off the floor, out of the draughts, and she kept harping about it. Whatever she said, I had more privacy up at the shack with three large-sized men, where my small room off the kitchen was mine, sacrosanct and inviolate, than I did sharing a whole house with Fay Hertz and Brian and Bidgee, whose grubby little paws examined and ferreted my few possessions.

I could never type at Matt's place with Hilda bumbling in and out, so there was always a criss-cross of coming and going, me tramping up to the shack to type, Joe and Matt scrambling over the ridge when we beat a kerosene tin to let them know a meal was ready. The shack was within shouting distance, and we were all very cheerful together.

On the night of the full moon, George the Corduroy King came down for company and decided to stay the night, sleeping in Mongo's bed at the shack. He was so silent that he made little difference. He just sat puffing at a short black pipe, and even when he shaved he had the blue whisker-roots showing through his skin which gave him a sooty look, as though the pipe smoke had darkened him.

If ever there was a misfit of a bee-keeper it was George. He had taken to bee-keeping the way some respectable men start losing their money on the races with the idea that they might make a solid sum of cash. But to be an apiarist is just like being a horse trainer or a pearl diver. You need knowledge and flair. George never had any flair — he just plodded along. There he sat by Matt's fire, a good solid citizen bowed with work and worry, honest and ox-dumb, glad to be with us. It must have felt like a visit to the sparkling metropolis to be sitting in Matt's kitchen after George's lonely mountain spur.

Joe was in his usual place, in the sagging old cane chair. Fay was at the table sharing the lamp, while Matt and I played chess. I had taken the children out and shown them the stars, telling them stories of the Man in the Lion's Skin, and the Archer and the Great Scorpion, until Hilda swept her small tribe off to bed them down in the caravan, and Fay did the same for Bidgee and Brian.

Spider, the black tom-cat, a favourite of Matt's, was killing flies on the window pane in what had been Matt's bedroom until I moved in. Spider never allowed a fly to live. It was that peaceful lull in the evening, and the dogs, sensing the absence of Hilda, had sneaked in under the table, sending up a great scent of unwashed dog. Suddenly they scattered outside and set up a racket of barking, indicating a vehicle of sorts approaching down the slope from Matt's gate. At first we thought it must be Blaze or Fred come back, but the icy moonlight showed a big blitz wagon grinding down towards us.

Because Hilda had complained that the bees spoilt her washing by voiding on the sheets as they flew over, my boxes had been moved from Matt's slope to another site behind the Warren homestead, but there was still a homey collection of neuc boxes handy by the pine tree showing white in the glare of the headlights. At first I thought this must be Lee Stollin, but the man who stepped out was as big as a barn door. Frank Hertz, of course. With him was a dark fellow, Italian by his speech, inclined to be nervous and apologetic.

'It's Frank,' Matt told his niece.

'I don't want to talk to him.' She backed into the kitchen. The firelight shone on that wonderful red hair of hers and her pale face, which had very little expression or movement. I was always a little at a loss with Fay Hertz because she so obviously regarded me as belonging to some different species from her own. When she found the little boys accepted me, she began to relax, but she was still very careful when I was about, particularly with her grammar.

Now, although she backed into the kitchen away from her husband, I sensed that she was not really frightened of him, not in the same way she was frightened of me. But Joe straightened his big carcass to confront Frank Hertz; put his thumbs in his belt and blocked the door of the kitchen. He was not going to have Blaze come back and tell him how much better the whole situation would have been handled if he, Blaze, had been there. George, puffing his awful black pipe, moved up inquisitively, ready to back Joe in anything.

'Evening, Frank.' Matt leant against a veranda post, stroking his beard. 'That black dog of yours is still hanging round the shack. It won't come down here, don't get on with my dogs, and I think it's the one killing sheep.'

'I didn't come here to talk about bloody dogs.' Hertz had been drinking. He had a dull ferocity, and as he stood with the lamplight shining out on him, and the moonlight shining down, fixed, his head a little lowered between his shoulders, he was obviously ready for trouble. I don't think he realized at first, in the heat of his buffalo anger, that we had moved into such a compact body in the doorway. 'I've come to talk to Fay,' he went on thickly. 'C'mon out here, Fay. You listen to me. I got a few things to say to you — you . . .'

'I don't want to see him.' Fay was standing stiff by the fireplace.

'She doesn't want to see you.' Joe relayed the message, his broad frame spread across the doorway.

'Who the hell asked you?' Hertz advanced a step, swaying slightly. 'Who the hell do you think you are, butting in? I'll soon fix *you*.' He went mumbling on, 'Nice thing a man wanting to talk to his own wife and a dirty big lug like you telling him he can't. C'mon out here and I'll show you.'

'Well, if you want to pick on a man for a change,' Joe answered, 'I'll take you on. Can't keep on all your life picking on women.'

'Who the hell says I'm picking on her?' Hertz looked round him with a sense of grievance. 'Ain't said a bloody word to her. Man's got a right to have a showdown with his own wife. Clearing out and taking my kids all over the earth.'

Mr. Hertz's Italian friend had been casting quick glances at us and making little nodding and smiling movements which no one acknowledged. 'No trouble,' he pleaded. 'Frank not want trouble. His wife and kids, eh? Wants the little kids. I give him a lift up to get the wife and kids.'

'Sure I want those kids,' Hertz asserted. 'They're my kids.' He repeated it loudly, 'My kids. Got a right to do what I like with m'own wife and kids. You there, Fay? Make up your mind.' He garnished the invitation with a selection of choice barrack adjectives.

'Cut that out.' Joe stepped forward. Before he could lock with Hertz, that unsavoury visitor received a violent push in the chest from his wife who had flashed past Joe and was fronting her husband, blazing with fury.

'You dare touch those kids,' she cried. 'I'll kill you. You're not taking those kids and knocking them about. Not no more. Don't you dare lay a finger on Bidgee and Brian.' Matt's old mother cat hissing at someone who stroked the new kittens behaved just the way Fay was behaving now. She was pathetic with helpless animal defiance. Her husband fell back a step before her. 'I told you I'd leave you, and you laughed. You thought I'd never come back here because I was afraid of this place. I don't hate it as much as I hate you. Anything's better than that. You come out here bludging on Uncle Matt when he gave Mum a home. You was going to do big things.' She put her hands on her hips and laughed at him, bending forward tauntingly. No wonder he hit her. He would have hit her now if we had not been there. 'You! What have you ever done but talk big and drink and knock people about? Oh, you've got a job — digging rock — it's all you're good for. I'm supporting those kids, do you hear? They're mine. I don't want anything, only to be left alone.' She was trembling between rage and tears.

'Trouble with you, Frank,' Matt said pacifically, 'you will go rushing in like a bull at a gate.'

'Listen, you old looney,' Hertz snarled, 'you keep your face shut. I don't take no notice of you 'cause you're mad, see? You keep out.'

'I ran you off my land once,' Matt answered, 'when you came shooting here with a mob of your mates. I'll run you off again soon as look.' He jutted his beard at his unpleasant visitor.

The situation was going from bad to worse. 'You're

trespassing,' I said, from the shadows. 'If you go into that house, you're breaking and entering.'

He swung round on me. 'Well, run and tell Stollin about it,' he sneered. 'Try and get him on to me too. Everybody on a man's neck.'

Everybody seemed to be talking at once. The Italian kept repeating like a chorus, 'No trouble. Frank don't want no trouble, eh, Frank?' Hertz and his wife were having a fine domestic argument at the top of their voices. Joe was telling George that the best thing would be to show these chaps they couldn't come out kicking up a row at this time of night. Fay, usually so subdued and watchful, was going over with her husband passages in their married life which would have been better forgotten from the sound of it.

'I hate you, I hate Nithering,' she screamed. 'I was happy working in the milk-bar in Ombra, and I wouldn't have married you if I hadn't had to. You come out here trying to get Uncle Matt to let you have this farm . . .'

'You wasn't any happier living in the camp.'

'Because I couldn't look sideways but you was so jealous you'd threaten to choke me.'

'Oh, you looked sideways all right. You looked a lot more than sideways.'

'Hey, what's going on?' Along the track Hilda came tramping, swinging a hurricane lamp. She didn't really need it with that moonlight, but Hilda had theories about snakes. 'What's all this about?' she demanded. The sounds of battle had roused her out. Hilda always liked to set her caravan to rights in the evening and retire in the consciousness that everything was as it should be. She had glanced out, seen the blitz wagon didn't belong to anyone she knew, and had been arraying herself to make an impression on the strangers. She had to change her dress because, as she explained, she never liked to be caught 'all in a muck'. She felt she gave style and tone to our establishment. She had taken us under her protection and would do us proud.

I wouldn't have been surprised if she had appeared with a batch of newly baked scones in a crisp napkin, knowing our deficiencies in the matter of hospitality. But the raised voices convinced her that this could not be Lee Stollin.

'Look, missis,' Hertz swung round, harassed, pushing his pal to one side, 'I've got enough of them on my neck without you sticking your face in.'

Hilda swelled in the best dress printed with large roses which she had put on in honour of visitors. 'Well, now my face is stuck in,' she announced. 'You can want it or not.' She had decided that this must be Fay's husband. 'I've been waiting for the chance to meet you, you dirty big hippopotamus. I'm no frail little woman like your wife that can't stand up for herself. I'm not the kind you can knock down and ill-treat and trample on the way you do her.'

She breathed on him and I knew just how Hertz felt. Dulled as his perceptions were with whisky, Hilda affected him like an express train roaring into the station. She raised her voice and I realized that Fred Connelly was a hero. The Italian had sprung to one side and slipped outside the gate of Matt's garden. He raised his hands as though he was invoking the cold sailing moon.

'No trouble,' he chanted. 'No trouble.'

'Trouble!' Hilda roared. 'I'll give him trouble. What sort of man does he think he is, coming out here to blackguard and ill-treat a poor little girl half his size? He needn't think he can come the big bullying blackguard over me. Let me tell *you* I won't stand it, no, not for *one* minute. If you can't respect a good woman, you dirty big cask of fat, just get out of here — crawl back into the muddy drain that bred you, and good riddance, you big crawler, coming knocking over the bees and firing off guns and terrifying and murdering and blatherskiting and big-noting yourself among a mob of no-hopers, not worth the lifting of my little finger to knock you into the middle of next week. You and your guns and murdering.'

'I haven't got a gun, I tell you,' Hertz muttered. 'All I come for is to get a word in edgeways and I ain't been able . . .'

'Whatever you come for you can take your dirty mate and get out because you won't get it,' Hilda said fiercely. 'I'll set the dog on you.' The fluffy small dog was asleep under the caravan. 'Get out of this. Go on, I've told you.' It was the Italian shrugging and talking to himself who received the last volley. He retreated before her to the blitz wagon. 'Frank,' he called. 'Gotta go, Frank. Come on, Frank.'

What Hertz hated most was the grin on Joe's face. 'I'll fix *you*,' he said vehemently. 'Look out, that's all. I'll clear this place of bloody bees and grinning apes that cart them round making trouble.'

He turned sharply and jumped into the blitz wagon, pushing his mate away from the wheel. He revved the blitz, shot up the rise and charged at the neuc boxes. With a brutal deliberation he sent the blitz wagon smashing down the rows of neat white boxes. Joe and George were after him in a moment bent on killing him, but Hertz wasn't staying. He shot up the rise and through the open gate. George and Joe were half mad at this surprise blow. They raced over to the shack to get out the truck. They wanted to follow Hertz along the road and make sure he didn't wreck any more hives.

When they came back, Matt and I were working in the moonlight salvaging the poor bees. Not that they were worth worrying about with splintered boxes and broken brood everywhere. I could feel the back of my neck stiffen as it does when I am deadly angry. If they had told me they had done Hertz some violence I would have only approved, although theoretically I maintain that violence is ridiculous and solves no problems. Seemingly the Italian had taken over the blitz, for it had gone tearing along the road to the dam. When it was past our yards, Joe had turned back. Hertz, of course, could always claim that he had hit our neuc boxes by accident when he was turning round. He would too. He was cunning as well as malevolent.

Our pleasant evening was shattered like the neuc boxes. Fay was crying, Hilda was still congratulating herself on her forceful oratory. Matt, kind old Matt, had taken down his rifle and stood with it in his hand. I raised my eyebrows at him. 'No, Matt,' I said.

'Mallee,' he answered, 'there are some men you can't argue with. When he was out here he made things pretty tough.' Matt had been a sharp-shooter in the first world war, and he had the look of it the way he screwed up his eyes. 'If he'd come up here with just me and Fay . . .' He shook his head slowly. He tucked the gun under his arm and prepared to go up to the shack.

'Oh no you don't, Matt,' Hilda ordered. 'George is going to sleep over at the caravan to protect me and the kids, and you're staying here with Fay. We aren't going to be murdered in our beds.'

'Well, in that case,' I said, 'I'll just bunk in with Joe at the shack.' For once Hilda did not raise a squeak of protest. She frowned with her head on one side, a general disposing of her troops. She did suggest I could occupy the caravan. 'I suppose one night in Blaze's awful bed wouldn't hurt you,' she said at last.

So I retired to my sleeping bag in the hut again. Joe was grumpy and dejected. 'When I saw that film,' he grumbled, 'that "Bright Lights of Broadway", I knew how it would be.'

Chapter Twelve

NEXT morning Fay decided to go into Ombra to see a solicitor about getting a divorce, and Joe, who had been working like a fiend as long as the light lasted with never a minute to spare, found he could take the whole day off to drive her in to Ombra. The solicitor was non-committal about her chances because technically she had deserted Mr. Hertz, but it was agreed that she would try for a divorce on the grounds of cruelty.

The following day the Warrens were home with their two gangling sons, who always seemed to speak with their mouths full, were downright rude, and had not inherited, to my jaundiced eye, either Vicki's looks or brains. They immediately attached themselves to us and would come over chewing and continuing to munch until they went home. Fay must have been overworked feeding them; she said they had hollow legs. They even demanded that she clean their shoes because, as the elder boy said, 'She's only the servant.' These delightful little fellows got in our hair worse than the bees, but we bore with them because Vicki was always so generous.

But as one trial was laid another was lifted. Fred came tearing back in high spirits, swearing that the blossom the other side of Lacey's Crossing was in every way more promising than it was at Matt's place. I think he was irked by the idea that the Muirdens were resolutely set in the middle of the most bounteous flowering of stringy-bark. Hilda was delighted to move and was soon bosom friends with Mrs. McKillop at the garage, sipping tea and the nectar of local gossip in the dwelling behind the garage. Or else Mrs. McKillop was hurrying down to the caravan on the camping ground like a big, buck-toothed bee with the baby on one hip buzzing and fussing over some new-budded sensation. As Hilda said, there was always something new in Lacey's Crossing, and she rather patronized us backwoods peasants.

Joe had been cursing Blaze for not hurrying back with the extracting house, and had just arranged to borrow Fred's when Blaze arrived, not only with the extracting house, but with Big Mike. I was alone typing 'Mrs. Prothero' when the big red truck came lurching up to the shack. Joe was down at the Warren place, and Matt had gone to put out salt for the sheep, so I came strolling out to greet Blaze and his friend. Big Mike was a mild-looking character with long gorilla arms and a deceptive stoop, who could pick up a bee box with three supers and carry it the way I would carry the typewriter.

He had the innocent eye of a small boy, and wickedness to match. When the tall weather-beaten stranger unrolled himself in sections from the red truck, Blaze smirked on him fondly, and said, 'This is Mike Serrero,' with modest pride, as though he had invented him but was not taking all the credit.

'How's your dad?' I was asking, and Blaze replied that he was out of plaster but was going down to Sydney to see a specialist.

'So this is Mallee,' Big Mike said, and as I turned to welcome him with some kind and appropriate sentiment, he reached out his long gorilla arms, lifted me off my feet, and crushing me to his enormous chest, kissed me resoundingly on both cheeks.

'Why, you big ape!' I said wrathfully, my hands still in my pockets. Then I controlled my natural inclination to tell him off, thinking I would only look more of a fool.

'Yes. Very nice indeed,' Big Mike said complacently to Blaze, setting me down again like a doll. 'Gimme my ten bob.'

'You lost,' Blaze answered, strolling inside.

'Well, she didn't dong me.'

'You still lost. I only bet on certainties.'

They were still arguing about their bet when I came out of my room lugging my few possessions. 'I'm moving down to Matt's,' I said. 'So long.'

'Don't be like that,' Mike pleaded good-humouredly.

'I told you she'd be snaky,' Blaze remarked. 'She means it. Look here, Mallee, Mike was only winning his bet — or trying to.'

'How do I know what you'll bet him next?'

'That's an idea,' Mike approved. 'Go on. Bet me.'

'No sense of humour,' Blaze complained. 'Can't take a joke. He won't do it again.'

I hesitated. Matt must be fed up with women guests, but a determined stand now would save a lot of trouble later. 'I can take a joke this once,' I said, recovering my temper. Big Mike put out his hand and I shook it, looking him firmly in the eye in the manner recommended for taming lions. 'One wrong move from you,' I said, 'big as you are and ugly as you are . . .'

Mike strolled over and smote the clock which gave three dongs. 'Haunted,' he said, impressed. 'Just like you said. Where's the ghost?'

'Only walks at midnight.'

We went down to Matt's and introduced Big Mike. Matt liked him, but I kept a wary eye on that citizen and remained well out of reach. He had hands like the scoops on Lee Stollin's road-making machines, and his idea of a good jest, until I cured him, was to sneak up behind me, toss me in the air, and catch me as I came down. So although

Mike and I became friends, at first there was a good deal of coldness and misunderstanding.

Of course when we settled down to extract, we fell naturally into two opposing parties, me and Joe in the extracting house, and Big Mike and Blaze out in the yard, working against each other for dear life. Having Big Mike instead of Mongo must have been sheer delight to Blaze, for Mike was a man who could work as smoothly and as well as he did, a man who never dropped the super on his hands as Mongo did, or trod on bees, or fell over Blaze's feet. They shared their own jokes and catchwords and they kidded Joe to death. But the honey was coming off, and we were doing better than three tins to the hive, so the feeling of exultation and the pace of the work carried us headlong over any slight discords.

Besides, it was that gentle weather, with a bloom on it like a grape, the stillness of perfection when the year surveys its handiwork. We would drive out in the morning with the dew or the tender vapours of mist, and eat at noon in some sun-warmed hollow of old gold diggings, with a screaming, plunging surf of bees about us and the smell of wild roses in the short grass the sheep had nibbled. Long after dark, tired and dirty, we would come home, singing, to eat steak and boil our overalls.

The bees were all along Matt's ridge and through the Warren property. George had his hives up beyond the dam. Fred had hives at Nithering and Lacey's Crossing. The road as you drove was humming with bees, you ran through barrages of them, so it was safer to keep the windows up. The flower was patchy, and we were right in the middle of the only profuse blossom. This gave the Muirdens that ecstatic satisfaction that only comes to men who feel they have, through their own wit and cleverness, outsmarted everyone else.

Then Harry Warren, the day before he drove off with

his hopeful sons to school — for those darlings could not travel on anything so ordinary as a train — dropped off to see me with a frown on his heavy, red face. Harry was just a solid ordinary citizen, shrewd in business, keen to his own advantage, but otherwise a harmless willing poor sap.

'Look, Mallee,' he began, 'it's all right with me you putting bees in the far paddock. But that fellow Mike Serrero has dumped another load he says are his right beside the road. You can't get through the damn things. They're savage.'

I apologized for those bees. I soothed Harry down. 'Another thing,' he went on stubbornly, 'of course the Muirdens have been very decent entertaining the boys and Vic when I'm busy, but Fay — Mrs. Hertz——' He shifted and muttered to himself. 'She's in a very uncertain position. Leaving her husband, you know. She doesn't want to put herself in the wrong. Have to see he doesn't get any grounds. You see what I mean?' I certainly did. Every time Harry Warren came to his house he tripped over bee-keepers on his doorstep, or cluttering up his kitchen, talking to his womenfolk and enchanting his gaping sons with tall tales. 'Well, I just thought you might give them a hint. You know how touchy Vic is. Can't say anything to her but she flares up. Of course it's company for her.' But it wasn't the kind of company he liked himself, and he made that quite clear. 'How long do you expect to be here?'

I told him it depended on when the honey cut out or the hard cold swept up from the south. He really considered the men were more a pest than the bees. I told him I would see the bees by the road were shifted and he had to be content with that.

When I told Blaze that Harry Warren was getting hot under the collar over the excess of bees and men around his property, he only laughed, although he agreed to move the bees. 'I don't go down there to see *him*,' Blaze grinned. 'You can bet your boots on that.'

It was never my habit to enquire what any of the team did with their spare time. Matt and I were home bodies, but if the others wanted to drive in to Lacey's Crossing to see how Fred was doing or down to Nithering for supplies or a picture show, that left me all the more time to type horrible 'Mrs. Prothero'. They would go off singly or in couples, leaving me the evening clear. Sometimes Matt would come up to keep me company and sit with his feet in the fire, and his silver-rimmed spectacles perched on his nose reading, or we might have a game of chess. I left the rest to their own devices, because it was none of my business how they spent their spare time.

And then the extractor broke down. The ball-bearings in the gears just grunched into steel chips. I was in a stew because I thought I had done this, but Joe declared that the extractor had always been playing up ever since the smash on the Woodenbong Road. When a ball-bearing goes, there is nothing to be done but to ship the parts down to Pender Brothers, the big suppliers of bee-keeping equipment at Maitland, and pray fervently. They are always remarkably prompt about sending back the renovations because they know some man's livelihood depends on those parts. Joe said I could take a couple of days' holiday.

'Had to happen some time,' he assured me. 'We'll drive into Ombra with a load of honey and send the gears away.'

'I'll go in with you,' I said quickly. An unreasoning thirst for my own kind gripped me. Mavis was in Ombra. Why, you could talk to her about modern painting or Buddhism or existentialists, and she would not only know what you meant but would argue with you. Blaze and Big Mike and Joe, after you had heard their old jokes for the fifth time, could be pretty monotonous. In fact they were the biggest set of bores under the sun.

When I came out dressed to go to Ombra, in a black and white check skirt and an orange pullover, the exaggerated amazement of the Muirdens and Big Mike annoyed me. Big Mike tenderly embraced Blaze.

'Darling,' he said, tilting up Blaze's chin, 'I never thought you could be so beautiful.'

Blaze fluttered his eyelids. 'Oh dear me,' he simpered, 'let me get far from these horrid rude men to Mr. Stollin, the boss engineer.' And in a much coarser tone, 'Stockings too — and those ankles are something.'

'When you have quite finished being funny,' I said. It must have been curious when they were accustomed to me always wearing khaki shirts and trousers or boiler suits until, just as I had hoped, they ceased thinking about me as different from themselves. Now I had upset their ideas, only one minor misfortune on this unlucky day.

Chapter Thirteen

OMBRA was a town so proud that it resembled the mother of a prize baby. The baby was, of course, the giant sprawl of mustard-coloured barracks and workshops which were reproduced in Nithering on a small scale. But in Ombra was the brain and nerve-centre of the hydro-electricity scheme, whereas Lee Stollin's bailiwick was only a ganglion.

Ombra had been a wealthy old town, landlocked by sheep properties. There the graziers had come to spend their money when Ombra had slept in a fold of the hills. The railways didn't go any farther than Ombra, so the railway had made the town rich before the hydro-electric scheme constructed its headquarters. There were charming houses of well-to-do merchants and weatherboard shacks of the less well-to-do, a range of shops down the long main street with big hotels and cafés and motor showrooms, and tractor and harvester firms, barbers, bakers, chemists and forty other trades.

Some of the old cream-coloured sandstone buildings, the town hall and banks, were elaborate, carved and ornamented with overhanging bits of rock and plaster into cornices and pediments. Mavis McKinnon had taken over for her library the premises of one of the banks, a great square building, painted yellow clay colour rather like a bee box, but with enormous rooms, lofty ceilings, plate-glass doors. Inside it was all modern interior lighting, filing cabinets, grey painted shelves and comfortable reading chairs upholstered in scarlet leather.

Joe, Blaze and Big Mike followed me deferentially into the silence of the huge room where Mavis and her assistants presided at a curved desk, and we waited until Mavis had finished an argument with a borrower, an argument she conducted in her soothing purring voice with an innocent smile, saying inoffensively the most outrageous things about the poor sap who had kept a book on mechanical engineering out too long.

Mavis has the figure of a golfer, square and sturdy on the heels, with wrists of steel and deliberation and determination to match. She is always scared she will lose her sight, so she reads until midnight to make the most of her time. Now she took off her horn-rimmed glasses and shook hands. We felt embarrassed in the hush of browsing book-lovers, but Mavis did not mind raising her voice.

''Lo, Gert' — she always calls me Gert. 'Lee Stollin said you were out in the sticks. I meant to drive over and see you, but you know how it is — first, the annual report, then the new catalogue.'

I introduced my partners who were standing meekly hat in hand, but pretending to be casual and gentlemanly. They were longing to make a break for the nearest pub. When I said I was staying a couple of days with her, Mavis was pleased.

'Go through that door,' she commanded. 'Make yourself at home. There's beer in the frig, Gert. Been keeping it in case you came.'

We tiptoed to the rear door of the library and groped our way down a gloomy passage into Mavis's living quarters, which looked as though they still cowered under the gaze of a bank manager with side-whiskers. The heavy mahogany furniture, the marble vault that was the fireplace, the deep brown of the walls, were restful after the windy main street. One of the window blinds which never rolled up was propped up with a cavalry sword. There were books everywhere, Mavis's big radiogram and piles of records, magazines and periodicals, text-books, cataloguing manuals, and a very pleasant array of Venetian glass.

'You have now seen,' I said, wandering round, 'the sort of shelf I am going to share with Mavis when we are both left on it.'

I was starved for books. I had not realized how my mind was famishing. But I set about collecting a lunch for the Muirdens and sent Big Mike out for some chops. There was a big kitchen, two bedrooms, a back veranda and bathroom, and a long pleasant garden. Luxuriously I surveyed the wealth of Mavis and anticipated the fine times we would have together.

The Muirdens and Big Mike partook of their beer and their chops as though they expected a bank manager or Mavis to pounce out at them. They lowered their voices instinctively. Gone was their usual here-we-are-and-be-damned-to-you attitude. They had on their best clothes, the sports coat and creased pants that decorated a hanger on a nail in our shack. Uneasiness afflicted them, a gingerly sense of the unfamiliar hung over them like a pall. As soon as they could do so, they crept out the back gate and tramped down the alley between the library and a hotel next door. I don't suppose they progressed far beyond the hotel.

'Sorry, Gert,' Mavis called, slamming through the library door. 'I had a new assistant I'm breaking in, poor dove. Now I'm free for the rest of the afternoon, and I have only a committee meeting tonight. Where are those splendid specimens you brought?'

I was washing up the lunch plates and had set Mavis's portion on top of the stove. 'Business,' I said. 'They've gone.'

'Where did you pick up those robust males?'

I explained all that had happened in the past months, and Mavis shook her head as she always did when affronted by a defiance of her convictions.

'Lost! Lost to civilization! I gathered as much from Lee. You look like an old bone that has been lying in the grass.'

'I am all muscle, not an ounce of fat.'

'I can see that,' Mavis retaliated unkindly. 'So by day you wrestle with the bees and at night you type four episodes a week of a serial? No wonder you look beat up. It won't do, Gert. Why not live here with me and devote yourself to *real* writing. You could, you know.'

Mavis despises Mrs. Prothero because she is not Literature. I launched out on my old argument that words are always lies, that books are only lies in binding, and that immediate experience is infinitely to be preferred to peddling words. We had a long argument and enjoyed ourselves, Mavis harping on the one string that if my present appearance was the result of immediate experience she much preferred hers at second hand through books.

'And the conglomerate of bone and muscle you brought in with you,' she drawled. 'Which of them is the heart interest?'

'None of them, thank God.'

'Well, I'm pleased to hear *that*. They look as though they never read anything but comic papers. *Can* they read?'

'Don't be a snob. Dear Joe went right through high school.'

'Well, it doesn't show on him. How about you addressing the Arts Council? They're always short of speakers. You could lecture about bees.'

I told Mavis what she could do with the Arts Council, and she said that was another example of how the free life was affecting my vocabulary. Then, losing interest in apiarists, she demanded what I thought of a new work on semantics. I hadn't heard of it, so she brought it out and insisted that I just glance through it while she changed her dress. Then I had a bath and we shouted to each other about semantics and all that had happened since we left the city, while I washed my hair.

'That's better,' Mavis commented, after I had scrubbed the black ring off the bath tub and rejoined her in the living room. 'You look almost human.'

We spent a very pleasant afternoon together over Mavis's difficulties making the shire council buy books. Mavis had some new records and for once there was not the stream of visitors which Mavis always attracts, possibly because it was raining a grey drizzle.

'Only thing I hate about this place,' she said moodily, 'are floods. The dams will fix all that of course, but my first introduction to Ombra was a flood. I had to move three thousand books upstairs, and you can still see the watermark on the walls.'

She kindled a fire in the marble vault in the living-room and put on a Brahms concerto. I was telling her why Brahms, her favourite composer, didn't appeal to me as much as Mozart when a knock came at the back door, and Joe burst into the kitchen. Behind him came Blaze with Big Mike leaning on him. The three of them looked as though they had been rolled through Lee Stollin's stone-crushing plant. I led them into the living room where they bled on the carpet.

Joe had the side of his face laid open, Blaze had an eye that was going to be black, and the other was closing in sympathy. Big Mike looked horrible, a greenish colour, and he was breathing with painful sawing gasps that hurt him. He also had superficial gashes.

'We thought we'd whip in here, Mallee,' Blaze

apologized, 'when the barman rang the police. We met that bastard Hertz and some of the lower element. If you ask me, I think Mike's got a couple of broken ribs.'

'I think he'd better go to hospital,' Mavis said firmly. She rang a doctor, a friend of hers, who, when he came, called an ambulance for Mike and fixed Joe's face. He talked to Mavis all the time about the semi-finals of the golf club. He had been in Ombra too long to show any surprise at the assembly of walking wounded. He said he would keep Mike in hospital for a while to see how he shaped.

I drew Mavis into the kitchen and explained that I wouldn't be staying after all. 'Go and visit Mike like a good scout,' I begged. I snatched up an armful of the books I had meant to read.

'I shall take him some flowers,' Mavis promised, 'something to match his personality.'

For once Joe and Blaze did not protest about my driving. I climbed behind the wheel of the red international and we set off through the rain. This encounter, I thought, would embolden Mr. Hertz. He would be confident and puffed up with glory.

'How did it start?' I asked, after we had driven a long time in silence.

Joe looked at Blaze, and Blaze looked back at Joe. Neither of them said anything, so I did not press the matter. 'Just one thing led to another,' Joe said at length.

In a detective story I have always marvelled that the hero is able to swap punches with three heavyweights, be tied to a table all night, tortured by villainous Asiatics and then, after feeding himself a slug of whisky, emerge bright and shining to repeat the process. Unfortunately Joe and Blaze were not the stuff of which detectives are made. They had taken a hiding and they were in bad shape, not bad enough to stay in bed, but they lounged gloomily by the fire while Matt came up and told them of similar things that had happened to him when he was on the canefields or the goldfields in his youth.

It would be an understatement to say that Blaze and Joe were irritable. They had the tempers of cave bears. Joe couldn't talk because it stretched the cut on his face. Blaze couldn't see very well. Luckily the rain set in so they had an excuse not to work. They were worried about Mike, so I went down to Vicki's place to ring up the hospital, and of course as soon as Vicki heard the tale she was up at our shack, a ministering angel with rare foods in jars, cooing over the champions and enjoying herself immensely. If she had had any tact, she would have stayed away. No young man likes to be seen with his face in a mess. Blaze had to rouse himself to be funny, not only for Vicki, but for Fred and Hilda who called later in the day.

'No doubt we *began* it,' Blaze said, smiling lopsidedly. 'There were plenty of coves there ready to swear we did. I didn't see much of it myself because I was down on the floor with a joker on my chest that was nearly as big as Hertz. Then I heard poor old Joe yelling at this little dark bastard with a knife, so I crawled round looking for my hat. Found it too. That mob was real shocked by the feller with the knife. They stopped beating hell out of us to explain to him that it wasn't a nice thing to do. The dago couldn't see it. Where he came from, fellers always drew out a knife and he wanted to prove he was right.

'We collected Mike from where he and Hertz was mixing it, and we went through like a Bondi tram. They were hustling this Italian bloke out the back door as we carted Mike through the front. I dunno if we crawled out on all fours, but that was how it felt. We weren't dignified. If you have ever been travelling slow but in a hurry that's the way we were. You've seen that dog Pluto on the films with his paws skidding on a shiny floor? Getting no place and saying yip-yip-yip. That was us.'

'You poor dears,' Vicki sighed sentimentally, her kind eyes moist to think what they must have suffered.

'Poor dears is right,' Blaze muttered. 'Anyway, Mike landed a beaut on Hertz when it started. Hertz went back over a table and landed on his skull, but you can't dint that cove. He came after Mike and got him down and started kicking the tar out of him. Well, next time, instead of taking a crack at one of Hertz's cobbers, I will say politely, "Nice night, I remember I have to meet someone." I'll be *gone*. I am a coward from this time on. A yellow cur. I never did like a brawl, anyway.'

Hilda did not have the pleasant tact or sympathy that Vicki showed. We left Vicki to enjoy the situation as it appealed to her and went off to look at Matt's garden. The young lettuces Hilda had planted were doing well, and Hilda abstracted the best of them, saying that Matt's fowls would only have them if she didn't.

'She makes me sick,' Hilda said fiercely, grubbing about in the rain, an old sack flung over her shoulders.

'Oh, Vic's a good lass. She loves to have something happen because it's dull here for her.'

'There's no need for her to slobber over Blaze,' Hilda said sternly. 'I know him too well. Known him for years. Half that encouragement and he'd be in bed with her.' She went on grumbling about Blaze, who, from Hilda's anecdotes, must have started young and been exercising his peculiar fascination very widely ever since.

'It's no business of mine,' I said, amused. 'What Vic and Blaze do with their spare time doesn't concern me.'

Now Hilda had brought the matter to my notice, it did seem likely to me that Blaze would make a pass at

Vicki, if only to pay out her husband. Hilda was quite
indignant that I should treat the situation lightly. She
had the stern righteousness of a bossy woman.

'Yes, it *does* concern you, Mallee, and you'd better
wake up smartly. It's all very well for you to stand there
smiling at Blaze's wickedness, but that's all it is, sheer
wickedness. He'll break up that woman's home, and
she's fool enough to lose her head and let him.'

'Oh, I don't think so. Vic has her head screwed on
the right way. She just thinks migratory apiarists are a
break in the monotony.'

Hilda looked at me exasperated, the rain dripping off
her and a lettuce in each hand. 'Mallee, you make me
tired. You think you can just stroll in and out of people's
lives. Why do you suppose those boys got into that fight?
It was what that Hertz fellow said about *you!*'

'That's ridiculous! He's mad about Fay leaving him,
and he thinks the Muirdens are the attraction, particularly Joe.'

'Blaze told Fred what started it, and I'm telling you.
There's been a lot of talk — you don't know what these
little places are for scandal.'

I felt depressed. One of the most cheerful sayings, a
saying that had comforted me in many a sticky situation, was that you were not responsible for what people
thought about your actions. Your only responsibility is
for those actions. Provided the actions themselves are
blameless, no one need be bothered by the ill-advised
judgements of the idle.

'Hilda, I like bees. I like working with the Muirdens
and learning about bees all the time. The last few
months have been more fun to me than all the rest of my
life. If I had to give up and go back to the city . . .'

Hilda had recovered from her attack of virtue. 'Now,
Mallee, that isn't what I meant at all. You can always

come and live with me in the caravan, and nobody, I hope,' she added fiercely, 'would dare to say anything about *that*. If they did, they'd have me to deal with.'

'But I'm on shares with Blaze and Joe in these bees. I agreed to go with them. They'd think I was quitting.'

'Suit yourself. But it'll only make more trouble. I'm warning you. Living in a shack with three men!'

'But I don't think of them as men. They're only Blaze and Joe and Big Mike.'

Hilda said I made her tired and I had no sense. My own view was that I would look pretty silly going to Blaze and saying in effect, 'My hero, I hear you have been defending my honour at the cost of those bunged-up eyes. To save you from meeting any such fearful contingency again, I am willing to sacrifice my own inclinations and face a fate worse than death — living with Hilda.'

Blaze's answer would be unprintable. The derision of the Muirdens would be colossal. 'Mallee couldn't take it. Mallee made an excuse to get out because she peaked.'

Hilda was probably making a mountain out of a mole-hill, anyway. What Joe and Blaze thought of me was more important than what any big fool like Hertz thought. But perhaps my team would be glad to be rid of me? In their own strange way they were courteous. A stray young woman could be a nuisance. They swore at me often enough, and blamed me and yelled at me, but until Hilda stuck in her oar I could have sworn that they were glad to have me about, and that I wasn't a drag on them. I had worked so hard to keep up with them, never relaxing my efforts to be as energetic as they were. But now I would give them every chance to break free if they wished.

The cold, rainy afternoon perfectly matched my disheartened, frowning concentration on this problem. We stood there in Matt's garden with the goats prowling outside the wire-netting Hilda had repaired. The white leghorn rooster, the one Matt claimed he was training to fight off foxes, soared on top of the fence and crowed at us malignantly.

'Get out, you brute,' Hilda cried. 'Pecking all my cabbages. You're good for nothing but soup. I've got another garden going now, Mallee, down at Lacey's Crossing.'

Wherever she went, Hilda made little gardens in the waste, fiercely fighting for her greens against every pest from slugs to bandicoots. Poor Hilda would have loved a home of her own, but she wouldn't leave Fred, not for all the homes and gardens in the Commonwealth.

I will say this for Hilda. She had enormous strength and kindness and energy, but with one swift kick she could level your little house of cards and tramp the remains in the mud. When I walked back with her, I felt mean and selfish and bewildered and upset in my opinions and my morale, and my sense of humour was not functioning any more than the extractor without its ball-bearings.

'I am not one to beat about the bush,' Hilda pronounced, all in a glow. 'I go straight to the point. I sum up a situation and I deal with it. If a woman only knows what she is about, she can do a lot of good to everybody about her.'

I hoped Hilda would fall in a drain.

Chapter Fourteen

BLAZE wasted no time while we were waiting for the gears to be sent back. He wrote letters to possible buyers, or rather he dictated them to me as I typed them on the letter-head proudly marked 'Muirden Brs. Apiarists, Tembucca'. He sent off honey samples, tiny glass tubes filled with clear golden fluid, tubes that I think must once have held junket tablets. We sent down a sample to Uncle Beresford hoping to bring in an order. We went over our accounts, listing what we had spent on food, petrol, repairs, tins and sundries. Fifty pounds for a new tyre for the International, insurance road tax, oil, grease, tarpaulins, kerosene. From the way we used petrol it would have been cheaper to let Dennis find us our own oil well. I'd had some small repairs done to the Roaring Ruin at Lon McKillop's garage but that was my own affair.

'Pity nobody wants to eat this stuff,' Blaze said, holding a little glass phial of honey up so that it glowed in the lamp-light.

'Bad teeth. That's the answer.'

'They eat jam, don't they? But honey—you can't give it away. It beats me. When you think of all the people who could be eating it and they won't touch it.' He wrapped up the little sample frowning to himself. 'Makes you wonder why you go to the trouble taking it off the bees.'

Big Mike came out on one of the hydro-electric trucks and brought the new gears for the extractor with him.

We had told him to stay in hospital until the doctor gave us permission to pick him up, but he begged a lift to Nithering and then coaxed the mailman to run him up to Matt's gate. Big Mike had been X-rayed and strapped and bullied; and, he claimed, a large bunch of lilies by his bed (a present from Mavis) gave him hay fever and set him sneezing.

He was glad to be back with us, yarning to Matt and puttering about with the cooking. Then he decided to go up and camp with George. 'Won't have bloody Mallee picking on me there, fussing about if a man tries to do a hand's turn.' With George he could take life easily, not straining his ribs and his pride on jobs beyond his strength.

The Muirdens reluctantly agreed that they must have Mongo back. 'Boils or no boils,' Blaze announced, 'he's better than being short-handed. The flow won't last for ever and we've got to get off all we can while it's on.' Blaze had a habit of waving his eyebrows about as a moth waves its antennae, grimacing like a clown and twisting his mouth sideways, when he was telling us something he knew he shouldn't have done. Now, it appeared, amid the incidental comedy, that he had given Mongo such a drubbing on his shortcomings that Mongo had sworn he would sooner be dead than ever work for Blaze again. They had parted, as Blaze said, 'brass-rags'. I gather Blaze must have nagged Mongo all the way to Tembucca, although Mongo was sick, anyway.

'Mallee'd better write to him,' Joe said, scowling at Blaze. 'He always had a lot of time for her. Thinks she's the only one treats him right.'

'She ruins him, you mean,' Blaze groaned. 'Soft soap — always soft-soaping everyone. You never will learn, Mallee, that the only way to get the best out of a dope like Mongo is to keep on his hammer all the time. Why, at home, when he was down at the shed, he'd spend bloody

hours peering round the door to see if anyone was likely
to come down and make him do a bit of work. Used to
wear me out looking out the kitchen window to see if he
was still looking round the door.'

Somehow we settled back into working shape. Dear old
Matt helped us. Fred would come up and give a hand
when he could, and in return we helped Fred extract.
Fred and Blaze spent hours discussing where they would
move when Nithering 'cut out'. Hilda's mother lived
at Tembucca and she was all in favour of moving nearer
her mother. Joe and Blaze argued that they might as
well make a big move while they were about it and go
up over the Queensland border where the prospects were
good for silverleaf next year.

We had not been bothered by Hertz and I found out
the reason. I happened to mention to Blaze that Hertz
had not been around and I was glad of it. Blaze smiled
to himself. He was about to say something, stopped himself, whistled and went on with his work. I could see by
the look on his face that he was thinking pleasurably of
some devilment of his own. Then because I didn't ask him,
he decided to boast to me about it, first of all threatening
to throw me in the creek if I didn't keep it to myself.

'I saw Hertz one night. He was sneaking up towards
the Warren place. Bright moonlight, and I'd left the truck
down in a patch of shadow by the road. He didn't see
me. It was pretty late and he came quietly up on that big
brute of a horse he has and tied the horse to a tree. Well,
I was in the shadow and there was a handy pile of rocks
so I let him have it.'

Blaze is a ferocious marksman with a rock. He has a
scar on his forehead which he earned because, when they
were younger, he was once throwing pebbles at Joe. Joe
was finally tormented to the stage where he heaved a
large rock at Blaze and nearly stove his brains in.

'Well, it was funny as a circus to see him! He didn't know who was pelting him. He didn't dare yell. He made a bolt for that horse with the blood running down his face and he untied it, but I got the horse a beaut and it cleared out without him. Gave it another for luck as it bolted. Hertz is probably walking yet. I kept after him down the road — there's plenty of cover — donging him with rocks every chance I got. He was as mad as a hornet, but he ran — I'll say he ran. Funny! I nearly laughed myself sick!'

Blaze was a cruel devil. I don't know anyone else who would deliberately stand off and half kill a man by throwing stones at him, stalking him relentlessly in the moonlight, quiet and swift and ferocious. I forbore to ask what he was doing at the Warrens' at that time of night. No wonder he hadn't told Joe. Joe was convinced Blaze was trying to cut him out with Fay Hertz.

They had been bickering badly over everything, from the work we were doing to the correct amount of tea to put in the billy. I did my best to keep the rancour from breaking into open war, but as men in an isolated camp always quarrel, there was not much I could do. Joe contended that Blaze threw his weight about too much. Blaze said Joe was a sorehead, always moaning for nothing.

'I can't stand him any longer,' Joe would say to me. 'I'm going to join the navy.' But on her day off Fay would come down to visit her uncle, or Joe might give her a lift into town, and he would brighten up again.

Matt took us all philosophically. I had propounded to him Hilda's view that I was causing trouble staying with the Muirdens, but Matt only smiled in his beard.

'The real trouble is, Mallee, you're in Bandy's paddock.'

I waited for him to explain.

'You know the yarn?' I shook my head. 'Well, this cove is asking his way, and he comes on a cocky farmer who tells him he's got to go through Bandy's paddock. "First you take up the river on your right hand," he says, "and you carry it a ways. Then you pick up a mountain. Keep that over your left shoulder. Drop the river. It's no good to you. You carry the mountain on your left shoulder till you come to a fence. Pick that up and take it with you. Keep it on your left hand. Then drop it when you come to the gate. You take up Bandy's paddock from there and you'll come to a clump of trees. You don't want those. Pick them up and drop them behind you. Then you'll come on some rocks. Carry them a bit on your right hand. Then there's another fence. No, drop that, there's a gate. No, there isn't. Damn it, you're lost. You're right in the middle of Bandy's paddock and you're lost. Yell like mad for help!"'

I can't tell the story as well as Matt did. He said, stroking his beard, 'Going to make a million. All out of bees. Ho-ho!' The old devil thought we were all funny. We were providing him with entertainment.

'So you wouldn't take any notice of Hilda?'

'*I* wouldn't take any notice of her. I don't know about *you*. If it was me I would go in the opposite direction from where Hilda is and not carry her any part of the way.'

That was enough for me. I hinted round to the Muirdens that, perhaps, when they moved on, I might stay with Matt. They looked at me amazed.

'Suit yourself,' Joe snarled. 'No telling what a bloody woman will dream up next.'

'We cut you in on shares, didn't we?' Blaze demanded. 'You still harping about going on your own? Because, let me tell you, Mallee, you don't know a bee from a bull's foot. It takes bloody years to learn this game. We've

been at it all our lives and even now, sometimes,' he added
graciously, 'there's things I pick up that I didn't know
before. If you're still snaky about what I said this
morning . . .' It had been one of our usual rows. I
assured him I was not snaky at all. 'Well, if you want
to be patted on the back, Joe can bear me out that I
said to him you're shaping real well. You earn your
tucker, make no mistake. You're better than the Big
Pommy ever was.'

'Nobody could of been worse than the Big Pommy,'
Joe pointed out judicially.

'Yes. Well, I was just taking him as a case in point.
You're better than Mongo. You *will* argue. But nobody
'ull ever cure you of that. And you will keep on saying,
"Let me do that", whether you can or not. But for working with bees,' Blaze concluded with magnificent generosity, 'I'll back you against any assistant we've had, little
as you are and bloody woman as you are.'

So I was very pleased, and more especially pleased he
had said all this before Uncle Beresford appeared. For
Uncle Beresford landed on us like a jew lizard at a meeting
of the Ladies' Social. I was down at Matt's place because
the rain had started again. We couldn't work and the
tempers at the shack were ready to blow off the gauge.

Big Mike had come back puttering about and insisting
on doing more than he could. Letters had come from home
demanding more slabs of 'Mrs. Prothero', and complaining that Hubert was still annoyed because I had
refused to take up the serial for Krisp Krackers. Julie
had been shopping and studying the stars. She said there
was a strong Martian influence over me at the moment,
and if she meant arguments she was right.

Dennis had refused to return to 'Mrs. Prothero', and
was now a paid financial consultant of Northern Exploitations. His nerves were worse than ever, according to

Anita, but he was full of mystery and big plans. He said he would make my legacy look like something dropped in the church plate by the town miser.

So life at the flat must have been much as usual, and the letters always wished to know when I was coming home. I let Joe read my letters and I read his. Joe's mother always gave a full catalogue of everything growing in the garden and a report on old Muirden's leg. He had been to the city specialist and would have another operation to mend a nerve that had been severed. The nerve was the cause of all the pain. 'And all he wants is to get back to those old bees,' Mrs. Muirden wrote. 'He'll never sell them, mark my words.'

Matt was looking dreary so I suggested a game of chess before I began work. We were peacefully playing our third game when Uncle Beresford's car came roaring cautiously in low gear down from the gate. Matt and I went out on the veranda, and the dogs leaped and snarled round the car. Uncle Beresford is tall, bald and serious. He shook hands with Matt — shaking hands with Uncle Beresford is much the same as holding a cucumber — a firm, cool resistance to touch before the cucumber is restored to its rightful owner. Then he gazed about him like a man who has come to detect a gas leak.

It was nice of him not to have brought Aunt Mona on this jaunt. That would have been the limit. He came into the kitchen, and the dogs, tired of barking at his car, spattered in with muddy paws after him. There seemed to be a whirlpool of dogs eddying round the kitchen until they subsided under the table. Then he took off his raincoat, still studying the smoky fireplace and the kitchen which, freed from the ministrations of Hilda and Fay, was reverting to normal.

Uncle Beresford is a man with views and opinions. He serves on committees and boards of philanthropic institutions, raising money for good causes. But he is not the kind who gets in a fight with a carter for ill-treating a horse, and once when I had an argument with a big swine who was beating one up a steep hill, Uncle Beresford didn't simmer down for weeks he was so ashamed of me. Something unfortunate always happened if we were together. One night there was an old man rootling in a garbage tin outside the city library, and I gave him five shillings, which was all I had. Uncle Beresford presented me with fourpence for my tram fare home and said I was very ill-advised and that the man would spend the five shillings on drink. He has come round to Aunt Mona's view that the Herricks are 'bohemians' and quite crazy. It did not surprise him in the least to find me in a crack of the hills playing chess with an elderly citizen with a beard.

'Well, Mallee,' he said, sitting down in the old cane chair as though it might have a bomb under it, 'I suppose you are wondering why I should leave my business and travel hundreds of miles to look you up.'

I knew darned well it must be something he wanted very much indeed. He had a patient, quiet resignation, like the better type of funeral, but full of dignity — glass-plated hearse and flowers on the coffin.

'Come to buy some honey?' I asked.

Uncle Beresford was astonished. 'Oh,' he said, conciliating me, 'honey, yes. You sent a sample, I remember. When I go back I will ask the head of supplies to place an order. Yes, indeed, honey.'

'How much can you take? Remember you said you would take all I could produce. There's seven hundred-odd tins ready to ship at the moment.' A big order would be a feather in my cap with the Muirdens. 'Smith Health Foods ought to be able to take at least three hundred tins,' I said wistfully. 'After all, what's three hundred tins?'

At two-pounds-ten a tin it's seven hundred and fifty pounds in hard cash.

Matt was making the eternal tea. He took from a biscuit tin a mouldy old cake with cream in it that looked green round the edges, a cake that Matt had been keeping for some special occasion. His eyesight was not good, and the kitchen was rather gloomy, so he did not notice the cream looked unpleasant and I did not like to hurt his feelings by telling him.

'We can put it on the train for you,' I urged Uncle Beresford, 'or take a special load down for you by truck. If you took two hundred and fifty tins we would deliver it at the warehouse.' How Blaze and Joe would appreciate the holiday! They could stay with Julie and Anita. It might even improve their tempers, turned as sour as the cream in Matt's cake from overlong exposure to the elements. Driving down to the city with a load of honey would make all the difference to Blaze and Joe. 'How about it, Uncle Beresford?'

'Very well,' Uncle Beresford said desperately. 'I'll take two hundred and fifty tins.'

I could have kissed him. 'That's wonderful,' I cried. 'That's bloody wonderful.' Uncle Beresford winced. 'And when you've had a cup of tea,' I said, drawing up to the table as cheerful as a cricket, 'we'll go over to Vic Warren's and she'll give you a bed.'

'He can stay here,' Matt suggested.

'You know how Vic loves to have a visitor,' I insisted. When Uncle Beresford returned home, he would tell everybody about Nithering. Once he saw the Warren home, he would realize that I was not sunk in savagery. At Matt's little things might upset him and cause him to form an unfavourable opinion. Then I remembered that Dennis Oberon Herrick would have told *his* story, and that it would lose nothing in the telling.

'Have some cake,' Matt invited, holding it out. Before I could warn him, Uncle Beresford had taken a large slice. He bit into it and a look came over his face as though he had seen a vampire instead of Spider at the window. His eyes bulged. 'Excuse me,' he muttered, his mouth full of cake, and he went out round the side of the house.

He came back in a moment and took a suspicious gulp of tea. Once Mongo had made the tea out of water that had been used for boiling overalls, and Uncle Beresford drank his cup with the same air of wondering what might be wrong with it. Matt looked at Uncle Beresford perplexedly, sensing his constraint. Gentle old Matt thought it was due to Uncle Beresford's desire to have a private talk with me. He peered out into the dusk.

'Might get a shot at that dog,' he said. He took down his gun, threw on his old army hat and nodded to Uncle Beresford, who eyed the gun as though it was likely to go off.

When the sound of Matt's feet had died away, Uncle Beresford shook his head helplessly. The funeral had arrived at the cemetery and the undertakers were about to lift out the coffin. 'I could never have believed it,' he said heavily. 'Your stepfather is always inclined to exaggerate, so I didn't take notice of what he said. You are really living here alone with the old man?'

'No, no,' I replied hastily. 'Far from it. You must meet all the others.' I would rustle up Hilda and the kids and Fay Hertz and Vic. 'Why,' I said; gaily telling of the women and the kiddies, 'Hilda is always about. In and out like a draught with the door swinging.'

'And you live here?'

'Well, scarcely here,' I admitted. 'My own little place is just over the rise. Very quiet and peaceful.'

'You are there alone?' Now this caught me in a clove-hitch, because if I said Big Mike and Joe and Blaze were sharing it with me, Uncle Beresford would, to put it mildly, disapprove. If I said I was living there alone and I managed to toss the men out before he spotted them, he would probably say how impossible it was for me to live alone.

'Oh, I get along,' I said easily. 'People always coming and going. Never a dull moment. And now *you* are here. Tell me all the news. How is Aunt Mona?'

'Your aunt and I,' said Uncle Beresford, 'are going to take a trip round the world.'

'Fine. Have a good time.'

'Your aunt would like you to come with us.'

That would be great fun, the first-class funeral rolling from one cathedral and picture gallery and public monument to the next. Imagine a trip round the world with Uncle Beresford and Aunt Mona!

'Julie and your stepfather' — he always spoke as though the Parent had been brought in out of the dustbin — 'are heartily in favour of the idea.'

'Well, well, that's very nice of you, Uncle Berry. I'm afraid, just at the moment, business is going to hold me here. You see, I have a fourth share in these bees, maybe only a fifth. Mike may be getting his cut and old man Muirden, but anyway I'm on shares. I'm a business woman. And as soon as I can arrange to wind up Mrs. Prothero, there is going to be one final episode where she jumps over a cliff.'

'Mallee, I want you to drop that flippant attitude and be serious. You do not realize' — Uncle Beresford was now the funeral of a public statesman with a band and flag-draped coffin, very sombre — 'you do not realize that Mona has ambitions for you. She is going to arrange for you to be presented at Court.'

'Presented at Court!' I yelled. I must have looked very much the way he did when he bit that mouldy cake.

'Yes.' He was gratified by the impression he had made. 'She has persuaded me that you should be presented. At first I told her that it was a lot of fuss and nuisance, that as a plain Australian I thought there was too much snobbery and expense about garden parties and receptions and balls. But she is not going to spare herself. Mona is like that. She says she must do the thing properly.'

By this time the panic had subsided. All my emotions had donned their life-jackets and were stepping calmly into the boats. 'She could take Anita,' I told him.

'Anita is not a Smith.'

'Neither am I. The Parent adopted me when I was a brat. I'm Mallee Herrick. Now, look here. Wipe the whole idea. I don't believe for a moment it's your idea, because you're not a snob. You've always been fairly decent to me. Why should you want to put me through such sheer hell as mucking round being a debutante, besides me being much too old and tough? Why, Anita would love it.'

The way Uncle Beresford dropped the idea proved that it had been thought up to tear me away from the bees. 'Your aunt will be very disappointed. There has been one other little matter . . .'

Before he could get to the real meat and meaning of his visit, I heard a roar outside of Blaze blowing his top. 'Mallee! Where the hell is that bloody woman? Never anywhere when she's wanted. Loitering down here.' If he saw the car in the gloom, he thought it was only Vicki. He came on talking to himself at the top of his voice, and I hastily threw the door open.

'A visitor,' I said brightly, making a hideous face at him. 'You've heard me speak of my Uncle Beresford, the head of Smith's Health Foods? Well, he's here.'

Blaze raised his eyebrows and rolled his eyes, grimacing back at me. I led him gracefully into the kitchen, giving an imitation of how I might sweep forward if presented at Court. It was a piece of good luck that Blaze's black eyes had faded out. He was wearing a black-and-yellow football jersey and looked like what he had been once, the forward of the second-grade rugby team at Tembucca. He hadn't shaved, and Fred Connelly always said that when Blaze had whiskers his teeth reminded him of a harvester going through a field of black oats.

'How do you spell your name?' Uncle Beresford asked. 'B-l-a-i-s-e?'

'That's right,' Blaze said. 'Grandma on my mother's side was French.'

This astonished me. I had always thought of him as Blaze. I took it for granted that this was a nickname. Somehow the discovery seemed important. How strange that Uncle Beresford should have been the first to make this known!

Blaze looked embarrassed. Probably he had had to fight his way through school wearing that name, or perhaps his remarks about me, as he came down the track, were, he belatedly realized, not quite fit hearing for an uncle's ears.

'Mr. Muirden and his brother are my partners, Uncle. There is also Mr. Serrero. He recently met with an accident. If you would like to come over to the other house . . .' Sooner or later that shack had to be faced. 'But you must be tired. Let me drive over with you to Mrs. Warren's house. I'm sure they will be only too pleased to have you.'

'Very well.' Maybe the funeral air about Uncle Beresford was just that he was tired. 'I would have stayed at that hotel in Lacey's Crossing if I had known it was so far. But you will have to walk back?'

'I'll go ahead of you in my truck then.' I knew better than to suggest that Uncle Beresford leave his car in such dubious surroundings.

'No, no,' Blaze interrupted hastily. 'I'll get the International, Mallee, and drive you back. Just a minute.' He drew me out on the veranda. 'Look,' he whispered, 'Joe's gone off to join the navy.'

'I don't believe it.'

'This time he has. He took the Roaring Ruin, and he's going to leave it with Stollin. Anyway, good riddance. Matt will work with us and Fred and George will give a hand.'

'Blaze, why didn't you come and get me?'

'What the hell could you have done? Spread a lot of cowyard confetti, as usual? No, it had to come. He was too cranky altogether. Might bring him to his senses.'

Uncle Beresford was sitting patiently in Matt's kitchen while we murmured on the veranda. He looked like a man whose funeral has been a mistake and a failure. He looked as though a snake had got in the grave with him. I hurriedly suggested we set out without waiting for Blaze to bring the International.

Chapter Fifteen

Uncle Beresford brightened up when he found himself among Vic's interior decorations with Vic sparkling and sympathetic. 'Oh, I do so agree with you, Mr. Smith. No, it isn't at all the right surroundings for Mallee, but I wouldn't use the word "disreputable". If you said it was uncouth, I would quite agree.'

Harry Warren said heartily that he didn't know how Dennis had stuck it so long, and I felt hot under the collar at this chorus of disparagement. Vic had been quite cool to me lately, but I attributed this to Hilda's loving interest in other people's affairs. I stayed only long enough to fix a time to go in to Ombra next morning with Uncle Beresford. He wanted me to sign some papers at the solicitor's office there. I could get a lift back on one of the hydro-electric trucks and pick up the Roaring Ruin at Lee Stollin's camp.

Blaze was waiting for me outside the Warren house with the engine running. I could have walked back and I told him so, but he took no notice. 'You going back with your uncle?' It was a statement more than a question.

'Like hell I'll go back with him.'

He drove home very glum and savage. It was home to me, even with Joe gone, and I was going to miss him. Many and many a time Joe had stood by me and growled, 'Give the bloody girl a break, why don't you?' when I was being told off. It would be just Joe's luck to strike a petty officer in the navy with Blaze's temperament and disposition. I tried to cheer Blaze up.

'I've sold Uncle Beresford a load of honey, and you can go down and deliver it. You can stay at our flat and have a whale of a time. Chinese food and theatres and you'll meet Anita — you've always wanted to.'

'I've got friends of my own in the city,' he said grumpily. 'I worked down there once in a laundry.' Blaze had mentioned this before. He and Joe had often left home after a quarrel with old man Muirden. 'This camp is breaking up. First Mike gets beaten up. Now Joe. Did I tell you he took our last fifty quid as his share? We're mighty low on cash.'

'I can throw in a few bob. And I may get some out of Uncle Beresford tomorrow.' I had been putting in for food and petrol when I could seize the chance, but there was always an argument if I came back from town with a load of vegetables and groceries.

'Who wants your money?' Blaze objected cantankerously. 'We're not living on any bloody woman.' He was too angry over Joe's leaving to be reasonable. 'He'll never join the navy,' he growled. 'He'll spend that fifty and then turn up as large as life.' Of course, that was what Blaze secretly hoped.

In the morning I climbed into Uncle Beresford's big costly car and we rolled through Nithering very grandly. Uncle Beresford only gave a nod when I told him that this was the little town that would be drowned under the dam. I suggested we might stop and have a word with Lee Stollin, knowing Lee would make a favourable impression, but Uncle Beresford is one of those motorists who, once in a car, drive as though they are paying taxi fare. He had come all this way to see me, and instead of yarning with my friends and enjoying the scenery, he was only impatient to get away again. I was wearing my checked skirt and orange pull-over in his honour, and was neatly painted and powdered. I was even wearing stockings. He did not seem to be affected by these marks of consideration.

'What I really want to know,' he said, glaring at the road as though it was doing him a personal injury instead of menacing the shock-absorbers — 'what I really want to know is what you have been doing with that money? I thought about it all last night. You say you have a fourth or fifth share in those bees. Did five hundred pounds buy only a fifth share?'

'What five hundred pounds?' I said thoughtlessly. 'What money? You mean the hundred you lent me to come away?'

'Mallee, I sent you five hundred pounds.'

'No, Uncle Berry, you must have made a mistake. I did ask you for four thousand.'

'Which was quite ridiculous. You have no idea of the value of money.'

'Oh yes I have. I have a thirty-bob mind. Anything over thirty shillings is a fabulous sum to me. I sent you a letter explaining that I wanted three thousand five hundred — three thousand to buy the Muirden bees, and five hundred for running expenses. That was a good business proposition. Then you wrote and wired back saying that you must have further particulars and give the matter further consideration, so after that I didn't bother because I was too busy, and anyway I made this agreement with the Muirdens to come in on shares. I haven't paid the Muirdens a penny.'

'Then how was it that I had this letter — typed on your typewriter, signed with your name, telling me that you had opened a bank account at Lacey's Crossing in the name of Mallee Herrick, and asking me to transfer five hundred pounds to that account. I did that,' Uncle Beresford said bitterly. 'Somebody drew out that money, because I made enquiries at the bank in Lacey's Crossing.'

Of course the Parent wouldn't have gone to all that trouble if he hadn't needed the five hundred badly to meet calls on his shares or buy something he thought was a snip on the market. He knew I'd never advance him a penny for such a purpose. It was a pretty elaborate piece of financial juggling. No wonder he had departed so hastily when his pleasant little scheme paid off.

Uncle Beresford ground his teeth and his gears. 'Forgery! False pretences, sheer robbery! He always was a waster and a loafer. Your mother never had any brains or she wouldn't have married him.'

'He's always been very kind to me. Please don't go making a fuss about it.'

'Fuss! Why, he can get years in gaol. The bank would prosecute. I'll have that money out of him if it's the last thing I do. Look, Mallee, it comes to this. Either you come back to your home and leave this tomfoolery, or I will inform the police of what your stepfather has done. You can suit yourself. I have some concern for your good name even if you have none. Living in squalor in a hut with four men! That's a nice thing to have said of one's niece.' He groaned in a moving manner. A forger for a stepfather. He'll take your last penny and squander it. I won't have it. Living with a set of ruffians in the scrub! Oh, Warren told me all about them —— My own niece!'

'Uncle Beresford, if Grandfather hadn't fallen out of that cart and broken his neck, he would have lived at least till eighty-five.' It had been just a bit of bad luck. The horse moved off suddenly while he was standing up in the cart. How was he to know that he'd land across a stump just where it would knock the back of his skull in? 'If Grandfather had been alive, he wouldn't be wailing about me living with four men. He knew all about it. He said everyone had a place where they fitted in best, and the only thing was to find it.' Uncle Beresford did not seem at all touched by my reference to Grandfather. 'You know he never interfered with people. He never interfered with *you*.' Uncle Beresford still looked implacable. 'Now, the Parent's native element is oil, and he probably saw a chance of diving in with a big splash. He knew I wouldn't give him a red cent for oil shares. So he lost his head.'

Despite all my arguments, my amiable relative was determined to make trouble. He drove up to the solicitor's office in Ombra, the same solicitor that Fay Hertz had consulted. That solicitor's manner to me was amusing. Uncle Beresford sonorously explained that he had come to put my affairs in order — 'for *I* am not the kind of man, Mallee, to do anything underhand'. What he wanted was for me to transfer to him some of the shares in Smith's Health Foods, shares once belonging to my grandfather and now to me. These would give him a controlling interest. That was fair enough. There would be no Smith's Health Foods if it was not for Uncle Beresford's work as managing director, and he was willing to pay me the full market price for the shares, less the five hundred pounds he had sent to Lacey's Crossing and the hundred I owed him.

'You understand, Uncle, that in consideration for my selling those shares you are going to forget all about the Parent's little effort on his own behalf?'

Uncle Beresford hesitated. 'Very well,' he said; 'but I shall get that money back for you if it kills me. You don't object, I hope, to my getting the money back?'

'Oh, if you can,' I said. 'He probably hasn't got it

now. Besides, he shouldn't be worried. His nerves are in a bad state.'

I congratulated Uncle Beresford on his despatch as executor. I had thought it took years to fix up a will. Uncle Beresford admitted the will was by no means settled, but these documents would give him power to control the company. 'You can't touch the rest of your capital,' he snapped. You would have thought I was prowling round and round that capital stealthily by night. 'You will receive your dividends regularly.'

'But what about if I want some money?' The solicitor and Uncle Beresford exchanged a look which, if they had been Blaze, would have been translated into the exclamation, 'Bloody woman!' 'I would like to know exactly how much Grandfather left me.'

The solicitor also looked as though he would like to know. His dusty office was tense with enquiry.

'Well,' Uncle Beresford admitted, drawing a memorandum from his pocket and giving the solicitor a sour look, 'your shares in Smith's Health Foods and your other capital, invested as it is now, will give you an income of nine hundred and fifty a year. Probate has been met, but it will be six months before you receive your next dividend.'

I was a little disappointed. The Parent could drop nine hundred and fifty down a hole in the ground and never notice it. 'So I'm flat broke and nothing to show for it? Well, that means I will just have to stay by those bees until they make a profit.'

'No, no,' Uncle Beresford said hastily. 'You have the money for those shares. Don't you understand that?'

I had another look at the cheque which seemed seamed and crossed in every possible manner to make it uncashable. In fact it looked so formidable I felt it would just vanish into a bank and never be seen again.

'Smith's Preferential,' the solicitor murmured. 'Listed at eight and fourpence ha'penny. Four thousand shares.'

So I was rich again. We could buy a new truck and swap the red International in. I could return the Roaring Ruin to Nobby and get a table-top truck of my own.

From the solicitor's office we went to the bank, and I signed madly after being introduced to the bank manager. As a class my views on bank managers were derived from hearing Fred Connelly discuss his overdraft. Fred's idea of an elaborate good joke was to write to his bank manager saying that he had just credited him with a thousand tins of honey that had been sent to England to be sold, and he had instructed the heads in England to leave it on the floor and wait for a rise in price. The bank manager then wrote back to Fred begging him not to do this thing, and saying that all he wanted was a little cash money, not some lumbering old tins of honey which would probably never be sold anyway. Another of Fred's capers was to have three overdrafts at once in three different banks, and when one manager became too plaintive he would draw some money out of an overdraft in another bank and pay him with it. What Fred could do to an overdraft was worse than a big black tom-cat in a chicken farm.

The bank manager at Ombra was kindly and intimate and tender with a love of little children. He also played cricket, and on Sundays he clipped the grass in front of the bank in a pair of shorts and an old grey shirt. I've seen him do it.

Now that Uncle Beresford had his shares — I think he had been afraid I might want to hold out on them — but why on earth should I want a controlling interest in Smith's Health Food Company unless to sell it honey? — he was more like a funeral on the way home with the mourners gradually reviving and taking an interest.

'Nice woman, Mrs. Warren,' he remarked. 'I wish you'd be more like her. More feminine and attractive.'

But my mind was set on food, and although Uncle Beresford wanted to eat at a hotel, I assured him that Mavis had a kitchen and the prices of hotel meals in Ombra were sheer ruin. So I had my way and bought some cutlets. Mavis was pleased to see me. She said she had the week-end to herself and had intended to forgo her golf to drive out to Nithering.

'Lee Stollin has invited me to go over the dam, and I thought I might look you up as well. I suppose you could give me a bed?' Mavis has a small car known as Primrose.

'Certainly,' I said, thinking of Blaze's crazy old iron bedstead. The boys could bunk in with Matt for the week-end, and Mavis could have Blaze's bed.

'My dear Miss McKinnon,' Uncle Beresford was shocked, 'you don't know anything of the conditions under which Mallee is living.'

'Well, if she can take it, I can.' Mavis had to listen to a rancorous recital of the cream-cake incident, and I could see her shaking inwardly while she extended sympathy and politeness.

'No, I certainly won't eat any cake. But look here, Mr. Smith' — Mavis treated him like a book borrower who wanted *Sins and Satin* instead of the works of some sorrowful Russian — 'a man of your liberal mind and advanced philosophy ought to be the first to see that Mallee is doing a very remarkable piece of pioneering. Would you condemn a young man who wished to follow his chosen career, just because he might come into the company of women? Would you tell him that this was no profession for a man? Of course not. You would be the first to realize,' Mavis purred, 'that the evil mind can see harm in everything, but a man of intelligence

177

just recognizes and takes for granted circumstances which, in themselves, might be misleading.' After this oratorical effort on my behalf — for which I could have hugged her — Mavis continued, 'Certainly it is a hard life and a rough life. You should honour your niece for her courage.'

'Nice work, Mavis,' I murmured to myself. 'Keep it up.'

'I can't see that at all, Miss McKinnon.' Uncle Beresford was somewhat mellowed by food and the successful conclusion of a piece of business. 'It's just not the life for a young woman.'

'One of these days there will be hundreds of young women like Mallee, and then nobody will be disturbed. Why, look at the outcry over the first woman doctor! It wasn't possible for a woman to do anything so immoral.' Uncle Beresford murmured something about primitive living conditions. 'What about a war?' Mavis came back at him. 'People will do exactly as their own principles incline them, whatever the living conditions or the circumstances. You should be proud of Mallee, Mr. Smith.' She painted a picture of me as the head of a big honey business with trucks and men working for me all over the West. 'But, of course, she must start at the bottom, mustn't she, Mr. Smith? Unless she has experienced the life these men live, how can she do anything to improve the industry? When Mallee is the first woman president of the Commercial Apiarists' Association, you will be proud — you will be pleased that you encouraged her in the beginning.'

What a friend! I took back everything I had ever said about Mavis and her bent for culture and the Best in Literature.

'There is a reporter on the *Ombra Times* who is breaking his neck to interview Mallee,' Mavis told my uncle.

'The Arts Council has invited her to address them on "Bees as a Career for Women". Her work has aroused a great deal of interest in Ombra.' I kicked her under the table, knowing the sort of interest, but Uncle Beresford was lapping it up.

'I don't know.' He looked at me incredulously. 'Perhaps there may be something in what you say.'

'I can assure you, Mr. Smith,' Mavis said gravely, 'that I have met all Mallee's partners and they are men of the greatest rectitude. Gentlemen to their fingertips. Perhaps,' Mavis caught the look on his face, 'a little rough. Not exactly drawing-room types. But while Mr. Serrero was in hospital I had a talk with him. I took him flowers and books, you know. And nobody could have a greater respect for your niece. Why,' Mavis exclaimed, 'I'm looking forward to this week-end. I've even given up my golf!'

Uncle Beresford was really impressed. When he left, he wished me every success. Honey, he said, was a health food, and any enterprise which improved the diet of the nation had his full support. I could send him three hundred tins instead of two hundred and fifty. He was going to make the best of it: 'My niece, you know — a very strong-minded young woman — lives completely alone competing with men on their own grounds — managing her own business on a large scale — honey-producing. Interesting work — skilled work. She went through all the mill labouring with her hands at the roughest jobs. President of the Commercial Apiarists' Association.' Poor old Uncle Beresford! All he needed was the right feminine touch which I never seemed to supply.

Chapter Sixteen

WHILE Mavis was at our camp everybody mingled sweetly, like last year's honey that is being treated to be sold as First Grade, Best Table Quality. Even Hilda and Vicki were charming to each other. Matt was buried in books that Mavis had brought. He had never had such a feast. Lee Stollin came visiting, and a general air of picnic and holiday prevailed.

Then, as soon as Mavis, who congratulated me on the pleasant life I led with my friends, had sped away in her small car, a kind of coarse granulation set in on the honey of our dispositions.

Blaze must have been chafing at the interruption, for all his gracious good-fellowship dropped away like a coat of bark. He suddenly decided he would work with me in the extracting house, but I never knew a man who took up so much room in a confined space, and I couldn't do anything right. He and Joe were both fastidiously clean and scrupulous, which made them easier to live with in our shack, but Blaze hated the extracting house, watching the gauge and the honey pump and the level of the wax reducer, all the details that were second nature to Joe. Blaze worked like a fiend. He quarrelled with everyone and nagged at everyone, not just me.

'I wish he was in gaol,' Fred would say. 'Three months might cool his temper. No it wouldn't. I'd send him urgent telegrams saying, "Honey flow. Advise shift to here immediately. Sites available. Stop. Keep your trap shut. Connelly." '

Fred was working with us, when he could, out of sheer friendship, and George the Corduroy King, because he was flat broke, but Blaze would have neither of them in the extracting house. Yet he hated to be there and wanted to be back at his own job in the yard. So by craft, importunity and persuasion, I finally arranged that Matt Kettrill should work with me. Matt and I worked beautifully together. There was the peace and rhythm of two people who knew each other's minds and movements. We could stand side by side, hour after hour, talking pleasantly, while Matt's steady working pace fitted with mine. We would grin at each other when we heard Blaze out among the hives roaring at George or arguing with Fred in a stream of sarcastic but usually good-humoured insults.

Perhaps it is being stung that makes apiarists so nervy, but irritability is certainly their occupational disease. The acid seems to get into their blood. Fred said Blaze should keep his mouth shut more often. Blaze said Fred was under the thumb of that mischief-maker Hilda. George resented Big Mike, and they all agreed that George was too slow, that snails raced past him. Oh, a happy camp, a delightful camp! It resembled a sore thumb under a hammer, and the hammer was Blaze.

'Here I am,' Blaze would snarl to me privately, 'with one bloody woman, Mike crippled up, an old cove like Matt, and that half-wit George.' He didn't count Fred.

Personally I thought we were doing pretty well. The honey, strong, beautiful, clean honey, was flowing into the tank and being tinned off. But I will admit that Blaze did more work than the rest of us put together; and he planned the work, gave the orders, thought and organized and bullied and drove us like a team of bullocks.

It was coming colder and I made excuses to move down to Matt's place. George and Mike and Blaze would be more at ease, I said, on their own in the shack, and Matt was all by himself down at his house and happy to have me. I was surprised that they all took this in such bad part, as though I was insulting them. They discussed this shift of mine as if it was something important, although we had all been moving round like pawns on a chessboard ever since we came to Nithering.

But the way those three men looked at me you would have thought I had dealt them a treacherous blow. What was wrong? they demanded. Had anybody said anything, done anything, to make me feel I had to move out? So, at last, in desperation, I had to tell them the truth.

'No, it isn't anything to do with *you*. It's the house.' Once the words were out of my mouth, although I felt a fool and they would laugh at me, I was easier in my mind. 'I'm sorry, but I just can't stick it any longer.' I knew what Fay meant when she said the house crept up on you. You could swear something you could not see was just about to speak, was hinting and menacing. Lately it had been getting worse, until I would wake in the night listening, stiff with apprehension. It was not my friends I was afraid of. But there was something about that shack that made me eager for Matt's homestead, where there was nothing to bother me but the fleas.

'Have it your own way, numb-wit,' I said angrily, when Blaze began to be comical at my expense. 'If you had any sense, you'd know I wasn't talking through my neck. You'd be down at Matt's place with me.'

'If I move my good iron bed down to Matt's place, will you go me halves in it?' Blaze teased. We had chipped each other so often about my refusal to accept

Blaze's bed that it was one of our standing jokes. 'Now she's got to the stage,' he told the others, 'where she's scared to sleep alone and wants someone to keep her company. It's got so cold that if a ghost got in with me these nights, I'd be glad of the warmth. I'd just hope it was a female ghost and say "Move closer, dear".'

Fay was down at Matt's that evening. She claimed that once that house began to 'get bad' I was doing the most sensible thing I could do to get out. She swore that lights used to glow round it and voices talk in it, but she must have been exaggerating, because I never saw any lights or heard any voices. I just sensed something there. 'I didn't notice it at first,' she agreed, 'but then it got so I couldn't stand it.'

I could have done without Fay's support and encouragement. I felt a fool but I was stubbornly determined to go on being a fool, no matter how much they laughed. Matt didn't laugh, but he had book fever and was reading even at meals. He liked travel and politics and accounts of new inventions, things that satisfied his curiosity. So he was quite happy to have me because I didn't interrupt his reading. When Fay and Big Mike and George and Blaze were all gathered in his kitchen he would look up from time to time in a puzzled way, put a word in and go back to his book.

I think Matt liked working with me in the extracting house. He liked to work hard for a spell and then take a rest and do nothing. He knew we were only in Nithering while the flow was on, and then we would all go away and leave him to his mountain-top again. We amused him with our comings and goings, 'tearing round the landscape herding a mob of bees'.

Fay had come down that evening with a purpose. She wanted to go into Lacey's Crossing on Saturday and thought she might pick up a lift if anyone was going over to Fred's camp. She was restless and fidgety.

'I'm tired of being stuck up here,' she said. 'There's going to be a dance Saturday night in Lacey's Crossing. A big dance. Everybody'll be there. Nance McKillop will put me up, and Lon would drive me back Sunday morning.' We discovered that Matt and I were picked for the role of baby-sitters. She planned to leave Bidgee and Brian with us. 'Unless you want to go too, Mallee?'

I assured her that a dance in Lacey's Crossing meant nothing in my life. I was tired enough of bee-men without having a lot of drunken dam workers treading all over my feet.

'Sure we'll go,' Blaze suddenly decided. 'We'll give you a lift, Fay. We've been working like steam and it's high time we had a bit of a break.'

Blaze didn't realize that Fay's restlessness was partly hope that she would see her no-good husband. She had found out that he went over to Lacey's Crossing to see the McKillops and made himself at home in Lon's garage. If she encountered him quite by accident something might come of it. She didn't know her own mind. I think she just missed fighting with him. And if she didn't see him it would at least be a change.

'A bit of life,' Fay called it. She had an appetite, a thirst for 'life', for the movement and swirl and eddy.

Matt marked his place in his book when they had all taken themselves off. 'She wants to start something,' he said. 'Frank hasn't been around, so she has to start something.' He said it beat him why people always had to be stirring up trouble, but he'd given up the human race long ago anyway. So, shaking his head, he burrowed comfortably back into his book.

I could feel that dance in Lacey's Crossing brewing up like a thunder cloud. No sooner did Vicki hear that Fay was

going than she decided that Harry must drive her in to the
dance too. Harry was not keen about it. He was having
some trouble with the two men who worked with him as
share farmers, and he would sooner have stayed at
home. But he wanted to see a man about some fencing
over in Lacey's Crossing, so he finally agreed to drive in
and put up overnight at the hotel. Everybody would be
there, Vic said, and why should they miss it? If the
share farmers could go in and take their wives, why
shouldn't the Warrens go?

It was Vic who brought Bidgee and Brian down in the
car on Saturday afternoon. I was doing some washing
because we had knocked off early. George had gone
off to camp above the dam and look at his bees, which
weren't doing any more than feed themselves, just as
everyone had predicted. Blaze and Big Mike were
up at the shack making themselves beautiful and shaving
off a week's growth of whiskers. Matt was home and
happy to have the two boys. Bidgee would follow us
around saying 'Bees, bees!' and he would eat the dead
ones if no one was looking.

Matt tossed Bidgee in the air and went off to show the
small boys a goanna in a tree. The horse, as soon as it
saw Matt stroll away from the house, tossed up its head
and came cantering over to be with him. The dogs and
some of the pussies joined the procession, and even the
goats came jostling up too. Wherever Matt went, all
the animals followed, and he talked to them and rubbed
their noses.

Vicki seemed just as restless as Fay had been. I wondered whether they were still getting on as well together
as they did at first. Vic followed me into the kitchen,
exclaiming at the grime. She drew her finger down the
top of the sideboard and showed me the black dust.

'Now, Vic,' I pleaded, 'what would be the use of making

Matt unhappy? I'm a guest here and it isn't my place to be polishing and casting aspersions on my host's way of living. Matt likes things left alone. He hates dusting and scrubbing.'

Matt had cocked one eyebrow at me only that morning when I swept the kitchen. 'Wasting your time,' he said, keeping his face straight. 'When the wind's from the east I open the kitchen door and it all blows out through the bedroom. If the wind's other way round, I open the bedroom door.'

He had to spread sheets of newspaper on his bed because the swallows came through the window every year and built their nest in the same old place over his bed. He said they did it because they knew he would look after the young ones while they were away. One year he had kept the window shut so they couldn't get in. But they flew in through the kitchen and he vowed they must have beckoned in every swallow in the neighbourhood to help them build that nest in one afternoon, because they knew he wouldn't knock it down after it was built. So after that he just gave up and let them have their own way.

Vic had plenty of time to clean house. 'Well, I think it's simply frightful,' she said, and then apropos of nothing, 'I don't know why a man should think he's being entertaining talking all the time about another woman. "*She* did this", or "*She* did that". Why, even in bed when he should pay some attention . . .' She stopped, probably thinking she had said far too much. If Harry Warren had been casting his eyes in the direction of his pretty housekeeper, it was none of my concern. 'Fay says you refuse to live in the shack. Is that right?'

'I must be losing my nerve, Vic. That's about the strength of it.'

'Sometimes' — Vic discontentedly followed some idea in her own mind which was more important than my change

of abode —'sometimes I feel I will just throw everything
to the wind and go off honey-gathering or bee-tending
and really *live*.'

'But you couldn't do that, Vic.'

'Oh, couldn't I? *You* do. Those bees — ever since
those bees came here humming and flicking about in the
sun stirring round the range — you talk about a honey
flow. I look out the windows down at those hives at the
end of the paddock, and it's been just as though the honey
flow was in my veins. A sort of restlessness and sweetness.
You'll say it's a bit late in the day. I ought to know
better. But the trees never know better when they flower.
They just toss their heads and forget old leathery leaves.
Drunk and crazy with nectar. Silly of them.'

I had never known Vic talk like this before. 'When do
you leave here?' She tapped irritably on the window
pane.

'I don't know. When the honey gives out.' Now that
she had put it into words, I realized that our camp must
soon break up. 'Why don't you ask Blaze? He's the
boss.'

'You take altogether too much from Blaze Muirden.'
She swung round from the window as though she wanted
to quarrel with me. 'I'm really sorry you're taken in by
him, Mallee. He's just a self-opinionated, bullying, bad-
mannered tough. A loud-talking liar and double-crosser.'

'But I thought you liked silly old Blaze?'

'Silly old Blaze!' Vic returned to her usual good-
humour. 'Silly old Mallee, you mean. Oh well! If you
will be so blind!' She walked to the kitchen door to watch
Matt and the children in the sunlight under a big old
tree. 'Don't take any notice of me. I had a row with
Harry because I wanted to go to this dance. It will be
terribly boring, I know that. But why should we always
just drowse along doing nothing, never going anywhere?'

I must have been terribly dull not to realize that she and Blaze Muirden had been working up more than a flirtation. But if I had known all about it, I would have kept my mouth shut because anyway it was none of my business. If the stealthy footsteps round the shack at night were just Blaze returning from some expedition, it didn't worry me. I would only be relieved to think they were honest human footsteps, and that one of the gang was doing a bit of good for himself, and good luck to him.

But if Blaze was slipping out at night to meet Vic and losing his sleep, that might account partly for his bad temper. It seemed pretty hard that he should go off gaily and act like the hero of *Rouge et Noir*, and then blow hell out of Big Mike and me for forgetting to sprinkle water on the stack or for using the wrong bucket.

Vic was still there when Blaze and Big Mike came down the track ribbing each other about what a swathe they were going to cut at that dance. They had shirts with collars and ties; their hair had been wetted and brushed. The best sports coat, the hat Blaze was always losing ('Where's my hat, Mallee, have you seen my hat? I hung it behind the door or I left it on the table and some bat's-brain put it somewhere else'), the trousers with a genuine crease, the polished shoes.

When Blaze and Big Mike were working around in boiler suits, they were men. When they dressed in their best, they looked cheap lares, the type you see leaning against the hotel or the general store. They would get as drunk as Chloe and probably end up in a fight somewhere, but, poor saps, that was their idea of fun, so they might as well enjoy themselves.

'Well, bless your dear little rosy faces!' I said, walking round them. 'Can these two film stars be Whiskers Muirden and Feather-faced Mike?' Mike reached out one gorilla arm and I jumped out of grasping distance.

'See you at the dance,' Blaze said to Vic. 'If we don't have to pull you out of Cobberloi Creek.'

Vic went over to the car and stepped in light-heartedly. Blaze leant on the side talking to her while Mike and I strolled over to see what Matt and the kids were doing. One of the cats had found a tiny flying squirrel possum, a furry little thing, quite dead, about the size of a rat. Bidgee and Brian had never handled one before, and Bidgee was determined to wake it up.

'Sleep,' he said. 'Him's asleep.' Mike took it from him, but Bidgee squealed for it. That squirrel possum was his and he was going to take it back and have it to sleep with him. By the time we had convinced Bidgee that we must leave the squirrel possum in the grass where his mother could find him, the Warren car had started up the rise and Blaze was waiting with his usual impatience to be off.

'Have a good time, boys,' I shouted, waving after them. I looked forward to a sleepy, easy-going week-end.

Chapter Seventeen

THE LITTLE boys were quite cheerful until it came to their bedtime. Then Bidgee said he wanted his mother. 'And I want my daddy too. Where is my daddy? I want him. Please get my daddy.'

It was one of those corny situations straight out of 'Mrs. Prothero'. Finally he consoled himself by pulling Matt's beard and trying on his spectacles until he went to sleep in Matt's arms.

I was telling Brian stories about the mice. There was a family of mice up at the shack and they had become quite tame. While I was working there on 'Mrs. Prothero', the mother used to bring the little ones out from a hole in the side of the fireplace and I would scatter crumbs for them, much to Blaze's indignation. He was always threatening to get Matt's cats, but while Joe was there, Joe's dislike of cats acted to the mice's advantage. I told Brian about the mother mouse finding a great treasure just when she was afraid winter might be coming and her babies have nothing to eat, how scared that mother mouse was of the big giants and how she crept about and stole their treasure while they were asleep.

'I'd kill that mouse,' Brian said firmly — a true male. 'Why do you wear trousers, Mallee?'

I said I was really an Eskimo and Eskimo women always wore trousers. So we had a story about Eskimos killing whales which was gory enough even for Brian.

When they were both in bed, I wiped my brow and

remarked to Matt that baby-sitters earned every penny of their money. Stepping outside into the dark where the stars showed over the black tree-tops, I breathed in the crisp air, enjoying the beautiful night, peaceful with just a red glow over the rise. Then I gave a yell as I realized what the red glow might be. The shack was on fire!

'Matt!' I shouted. 'Quick!'

Matt came out and we started up the rise at a run. We knew the track so well, every jutting rock of it. I was thinking of our honey tins stowed in the shed behind the shack. Besides the tins there were spare tyres, each worth twenty pounds, lids, bottom boards, excluders, all the extra gear that usually lies around in the wet or under a tarpaulin.

When we reached the shack it was blazing so that there was no chance of saving anything. The wind was blowing the flames away from the shed, but by morning nothing would be left of the shack except twisted corrugated iron sheets and blackened timbers. Matt looked at it philosophically.

'Well, maybe it's just as well she burnt down,' he said quietly. 'Always a temptation to someone to go and live in her.'

Blaze and Big Mike would have only the clothes they stood up in. Their tucker boxes, most of our groceries, were down at Matt's, but their bedding, their small possessions, Blaze's radio, were all under that belching mass of fire. We stood there helplessly.

'Buckets,' I said. 'Why didn't we bring buckets?'

'No use.' Matt moved farther back from the heat. 'See that tin?' An empty kerosene tin lay shining in the glare of the fire.

'The bees?' I said quickly. 'I wonder if he's done anything to the bees?'

'No. He'll have sloped off by now.' Matt bent down looking for traces of Hertz's horse in the grass. The dogs had come up with us and were moving restlessly considering the fire as though they had never seen one before.

For about an hour we stood around making sure the fire did not spread. When we retraced our way down the track and came into the kitchen Frank Hertz was waiting for us. He was sitting with Matt's rifle between his knees. He had been drinking and he had a gash under one eye. The look on his face was worse than the rifle.

'Hello, Frank,' Matt said mildly.

'Siddown — both of you,' Hertz muttered. How he must have brooded down in that dark tunnel where he worked with the water dripping on his helmet, making crazy plans of revenge, mad schemes of wreckage! 'I don't care what I do,' he said dully. 'I'm finished. So siddown.' The dogs had gone up to him recognizing him. He took no notice of them. 'You got some nice friends, Matt, you old mongrel. Nice friends. Met them down at the pub. That bastard of a Muirden knew I'd had too much in — I could hardly see him. So he piled into me and knocked me rotten. He laughed. Well, he can laugh! I'll fix you too, Matt. You've always had a set on me.'

'I've no set on you, Frank,' Matt said. 'It's the other way about.'

We stood there in the lamplit kitchen with our backs to the open doorway, and I knew how a man must feel when he faces a firing squad.

'That looney that lived up at the shack had the right idea,' Frank Hertz said in his pathetic monotone. He killed the kids, see? Didn't have to worry about them any more. No trouble. I got enough bullets for them and you. And I got a steady hand, Matt.'

He was trying to nerve himself for the second when the rifle would explode and he would have gone too far to turn back, so we had very little time. I took a long breath as though I was diving under water and walked across the kitchen. I never knew before how far across it was.

'Stand back,' he said, raising the rifle. 'You're the one. You brought them here.'

I dared not look at him. I walked into the dark of Matt's bedroom and groped those two children out of Matt's bed. They were warm and heavy with sleep. 'Come on, Brian,' I said. 'Daddy's here.' I picked up Bidgee and carried him out wrapped in Matt's greatcoat which was at the foot of the bed. My heart was choking me it had come so high in my throat. 'Here's Daddy,' I said to Bidgee, 'come to see you.' I dumped Bidgee on his lap where he held the rifle. 'Daddy,' I said. 'Your own daddy's here!'

A woman who has dealt for years in 'Mrs. Prothero' and received hundreds of letters from parents ought to have some small knowledge of what a parent will do. Maybe he could have killed those kids if they had been lying in bed asleep.

'Hello, Pop.' Brian yawned. He went over and jealously shoved his younger brother aside. 'We liked it up here for a while. Mr. Warren let us have a lamb each. Can we take my lamb when we go home?'

Hertz glared at me uncertainly. I went over to the table, sat down and rolled myself a cigarette, helping myself from Matt's tobacco pouch. I was pleased my hands were steady.

'You think you're pretty clever, don't you?' the man said helplessly. Bidgee had his arms round his neck. Through his haze of drink he looked puzzled.

'Why, hell!' I said. 'You're not *mad*, are you?' I thought of our shack and wondered whether he was. 'You know, Fay's just breaking her neck to come back to you.

Why do you suppose she went to that dance tonight if not to see you?'

'I never went near any dance. I would have knocked her damn face in if I'd seen her at any dance.'

'Well, it's just as well you didn't go, isn't it?'

'Don't you worry about that old shack, Frank,' Matt said peaceably. 'It caught alight. That's right, Mallee?'

'That's O.K. with me,' I said.

'Is there a fire?' Brian demanded. 'Lemme go and look.'

'Not just now,' Matt said.

'You going to stay here, Dad? With us? Aw, go on, Dad.'

'Your daddy's going away tonight,' I said. 'But he's going to come and take you and Mummy home. He wants you all back with him.' I might be able to use this, I thought callously. Hubert would eat it up. Run it for about ten episodes.

The man in the chair began to cry. He sat there clutching those small, snub-nosed whelps of his and sobbed. Matt, deciding that there was no more trouble, went over to put the blackened billy on the fire. He blew the red embers on the hearth, brought in more wood.

'Cigarette?' I said. Hertz shook his head. He went on crying and hugging the little boys. They began to be bored when he didn't answer their questions. Bidgee jumped down and went over to the sideboard where the kittens — there was another litter now — and another mother cat — were curled down in safety. The mother cat spat at him.

'Don't you hurt them pussies, little feller,' Matt said, coming back into the kitchen.

'What am I going to do?' Hertz repeated to himself. 'It's the stone finish.'

'Why, you hold all the cards,' I said cheerfully. 'Doesn't he, Matt? All night long we've had, "I want my daddy. I want my dad." Poor Fay must be crazy if Bidgee keeps on at her the same way.'

'Poor Fay!' he said, with a twist to his mouth under his fair moustache. He used some unpleasant adjectives about his wife.

'Well, the kids need both of you. It's a shame that they've got to suffer. Why don't you make it up?'

'Oh, she's doing fine. She thinks she's well off with that mongrel friend of yours.' He gave a lurid and imaginative account of what he believed to be the relation between his wife and Blaze. 'You don't know her.' He was working himself up again. 'It's been the same everywhere we'd go. She don't want anything but men.'

It was no use arguing with him. I did my best to convince him that he was wrong about Fay. Matt and I talked to him reasonably, soothingly. I was getting very tired. The effect of all this excitement was to make me drowsy. Bidgee had fallen asleep again curled up on his father's knees. Brian had drawn up a chair close enough to put his feet on his father.

We seemed to have been there for hours. Hertz wouldn't have any tea, but Matt and I drank some. He talked. He kept on talking, repeating the same things over and over again, going on and on, but there was no more to be feared of him now his fierce resolution was broken. He had come out on that long-suffering horse which was tied up somewhere handy, I suppose. He had vindictively and with malice burnt up the shack. Certainly, I think, he would have tried to murder us. He must have gone up to the Warren house first and found it all dark and silent. But now he was like a needle that had stuck in a crack of a record. He just repeated his anger and hopelessness over and over.

'Well, give it another go,' was Matt's advice. 'You and Fay could make a go of it if you wanted to. I used to tell you that often enough when you were living here.'

'Why don't you,' I said, sitting up with a jerk, 'make a clean break? Why don't you go away — you and the kids and Fay?'

He stared at me with suspicion.

'Now, don't be dim,' I urged. 'Think of the kids. Fay wants to get away from Nithering. Everybody will have to go when it's drowned. Why don't you go away now and make a new start?'

I was worried that Blaze and Big Mike might come back while the man was still talking, but Blaze and Big Mike were quartering themselves on Hilda, I do not doubt, too overcome with their wassailing to drive even half-way home. Hilda would be censorious about that. Hertz suddenly remembered that he had to be on the midday shift. He stumbled to his feet, carried Bidgee off to bed and came back into the kitchen. He mumbled that he had to get some sleep.

'Tell her,' he said, 'that I'm willing to go away. Tell her I don't care where I go. I'll go away from Nithering. I ain't been so happy here that I couldn't go somewhere else and make a better fist of it.' He glanced at the clock and saw it was after midnight. 'So she went to a dance,' he said bitterly. 'She left her little kids and went to a dance. You see the sort she is?' We told him how different everything would be. Everything would come right. We were worn out, as though that man had been a heavy dead weight we had carried up a steep hill. He would start over again, talk about going away to get some sleep. He needed sleep. He'd feel better when he'd had a sleep.

'I'm sorry I burnt your things,' he said to me.

'There were none of my things at the shack.'

196

'Well, I'm glad of that. When I've done my shift I'll come back. I'll make it all right if you say. You think I can square everything?'

'You can square everything, Frank. You'll see. Everything is going to sort itself out, and you'll wonder why you ever thought you had to try anything like this.'

'Maybe,' he said wearily. The poor devil went off to his barracks at Nithering. He probably had only enough sense to leave the horse to take its own way. Going down the steep mountain road in the dark he stood in some danger of his neck, and Matt and I begged him to stay, to get into the bed with the boys.

'I'll sleep here by the fire,' Matt offered. 'I don't need much.'

But no, there was that shift he felt he had to work. Perhaps he did not care to stay to face the dwellers in the shack when they returned. We went out and held his horse for him.

'You been pretty good to me,' Frank Hertz said. 'Shake hands.' So we all shook hands and he leant down solemnly from his horse to do that. 'You think I'm going to square it all?' he repeated, as the horse began to move away. 'Square it all . . .' We heard the horse's shoe strike against a stone.

The first big drop of water fell. The sky had been clouding over while we had been listening to that poor fool talking himself out. 'Shouldn't be surprised if it set in,' Matt said.

The rain fell all night, drearily, on the blackened ruins of the shack, ruins smelling of burnt sodden cloth. Cobberloi Creek was already swollen and running strong, so we gave up hope of seeing the merrymakers back. They would probably be cut off on the far side of the creek, all of them, Fay, the Warrens, the truckload of workers from Nithering. Nothing for them to do but come round thirty miles through Ombra or wait until the creek went down.

That was the last we saw of poor Frank Hertz. He made back to the barracks, he caught the bus up to the dam at eleven o'clock the next day. The weather had cleared, the twelve-o'clock shift went down the tunnel as usual. Then immense purple clouds piled up, angry lightning splitting them. As the storm came over, it was like looking up a great whirling funnel that was green in the middle high up, staggeringly high and violent with floating masses of vapour going up and up in a spiral of strange light.

We shut all the doors while the lightning flared and the thunder ripped and crashed on the tin roof. The little boys watched out the window, shouting at the hail dancing in the grass. There was hail piled up in round pebbles in a drift a foot deep against the door where it had pelted across the wet veranda. The boys brought in a basin full of hail to put round the butter.

As soon as the storm eased we all drove over to the Warrens' place. I was worried about the bees and wanted to do a round of the yards. Almost at the gate we met Lee Stollin in a jeep. He drew in to the side of the road and I jumped out of the Roaring Ruin and went over to him.

'There's been an accident,' Lee said. He looked old and tired and haggard. All his spruceness seemed to have gone from him. 'That cloudburst came so suddenly they didn't have time to get the men out of the tunnel. We always get the men out if there's a storm. These ranges — the lightning . . .'

'Was it bad?' Somehow I knew what he was going to say before he said it.

'Four dead. The lightning ran in and exploded the detonators. Static electricity is like that. Hertz was trying to get the detonators out. Is Mrs. Hertz up at the house?'

I told him they had all stayed overnight in Lacey's Crossing after the dance.

'Yes. That dance. Some of the men didn't get back for their shift. They were lucky.'

If Hertz had stayed for the dance perhaps everything might have been different. He might have seen Fay, made up their quarrel, though after the fight with Blaze there was probably little chance of that. Fay had missed him — and forever.

There would be no work done in the tunnel that day or the next. The flag would be flying half-mast at the dam. There would be the funeral in the little cemetery at Nithering on the high rise of ground by the church, the hill that would be drowned so deep under the water of the great dam when Nithering was abandoned.

Somehow there was a weird and gruesome side to burying those men in Nithering, as though they were twice lost — lost in their own graves. I drove the little boys back with Matt, feeling sick and depressed. It was no use now Bidgee asking for his father. That fierce, drunken man had 'squared' it in the only way one can finally balance accounts in this world. For if it is true that we take nothing with us, it is also true that the last final addition leaves a credit balance, that all mistakes are erased, all wrong totals cancel out. Poor fierce Frank Hertz! I can still see him sitting in Matt's kitchen with his two little boys. He never got away from Nithering after all.

Chapter Eighteen

THERE is never any instant when you can cry: 'Here it was that the shadow began, the light died out, there was no more laughter.' When, that first morning, I had wandered out and looked down with Blaze at the little gold and silver town of Nithering, far down the valley, I had an exultation in this ragged wilderness; it was all my hopes gathered up in one promise. This was the land of honey and tossed blossom, of unending birdsong and bright morning.

Now, after all these months, we had the honey. We had taken off over a thousand tins, but we had, little by little, been turned from a happy-go-lucky set of good mates into what more nearly resembled survivors. A few emotional cannibals can suck the marrow of enjoyment out of your days while you are wondering where all the fun has gone, and the simple casual pleasure. They have eaten it up.

Matt knew about that. He had had Fay and Frank Hertz holding their cannibal feasts before. Probably he cursed the day he had ever suggested I call and see his niece about some bee-sites.

With Frank Hertz gone, perhaps, one would have thought, the strange atmosphere that hung like smoke about us would clear, but that angry and troubled spirit haunted the ranges for us. His taking-off made no difference now that we no longer wondered whether he was meditating some new attack.

There was such a horrible unexpectedness about Frank

Hertz's death that for all of us, except possibly Matt, it struck at the certainty and order of our existence. Old Matt, refusing my offer to drive him in to Nithering, harnessed the horse to the old green sulky and set off slowly, but with a kind of dignity, for Frank's funeral.

The Warrens made a point of driving down with a wreath of flowers Vic had made from her garden. They were presenting a united front and doing the right thing in the wrong way as usual. I think it was a mistake on their part to try to face out publicly the strange rumours that had rippled into a major scandal. Nithering was only a little place with not enough to talk about, and the most part of that conjecture. Harry and Vic Warren had not been long enough in the district to have overcome the suspicion attaching to newcomers.

They were out of place at a funeral that was masculine, black and grim under a grey sky, with the silent men come in from the dam, taking the day off for the funeral, talking to each other of their own concerns, with curious glances for strangers and the heads of the hydro-electric administration who had driven from Ombra. They must have murmured that this man and his wife were the two who had sheltered Frank's no-good woman when she left him. The fact that the Warrens had been at that dance in Lacey's Crossing, and Fay had been there with those bee-keepers, did nothing to help.

The inhabitants of Lacey's Crossing were there in force. Frank's own relatives could not come all the way from the coal-mining town near Newcastle where Hertz had been bred. But he did not lack acquaintances and mates to whom he had become a champion and a hero, all the more because he was dead. To us, he had been a menace, a night prowler whose undeserved animosity had been something to reckon with like the weather; he was part of our emotional climate in our lonely spur of the range.

Big Mike had taken one glance at the burnt shack and declared he had to go home for more clothes and gear. He had only what he stood up in. 'Won't be able to do anything, anyway, this weather,' he said. 'And Blaze has gone to Tembucca with Fred to look over some sites.' Mike was queer and tight-mouthed and tired. For a long time he had been wanting a break home, and this sudden move by Blaze had given him his chance. Big Mike was not employed by Blaze. They were only on yet another share arrangement, and he did not like being told by Blaze to go back to the camp. 'Just hard lines, Mallee,' he said. 'I'm sorry for that poor bugger Hertz, but I'm not going to burst into any tears.'

While Matt and the Warrens were at the funeral, I went over to keep Fay company. She was pale and silent as ever. The trouble with Fay was that there was a gap between her thoughts and her speech, and that no spark leapt the gap. She could never explain what she was feeling, so her actions were likely to take you by surprise. In the Warrens' beautiful kitchen she went mechanically about her tasks, stopping by the window to look out at the grey drift of rain or, when it cleared, the shafts of sunlight that fell between the clouds. It must have seemed to her that she had spent most of her lifetime looking out the windows of lonely houses on grey rocks outcropping among the small wild flowers where silence walked with the visiting wind.

The tears ran down her pale cheeks and, dully, like some trapped animal turning its head to escape, she ranged round the inescapable despair that hunted her along her fences ever closer to that emptiness ahead. She began to talk in short commonplaces — jerkily — just for the relief of talking.

'Mumma couldn't go because of her heart,' she said. 'I rung her up. I could go to Ombra, but Mrs. Warren wants me to stay until she can get someone and she's been good in her own way.'

I had settled the little boys to a game with the fine railway Vicki had just given them, one which had belonged to her boys when they were younger. 'It's too soon to think what you'll do, Fay. Let it unfold. You know Matt will help.'

'I've got to get away from here — right away. But there's the kids. I can't leave them.' And she began to cry again.

I had to think of something to cheer her, anything. To divert her mind I told her how, when my father had died, Julie had worked for the two of us in the bar of a city hotel. Fay listened curiously, fitting in the pieces of my background she had not known. I think, from Dennis's overblown assertions, she had regarded me as a fantastically rich young woman. I kept talking to her, telling her of my ambitions and how some day I hoped I might have a thousand hives and manage them all myself.

'Blaze Muirden'll never let you,' she said suddenly. 'He cruels everything for everyone.' Her face twisted into an ugly mask. 'It was him. Oh, if ever I get the chance, I'll *fix* him.'

She began to talk of that dance and I realized it must have been quite a field-day for Blaze. Why Blaze thinks he can fight nobody knows. He isn't built for it, he has never learnt to box, he hates getting hurt, and he always is hurt and plunges in just the same. He had found Frank Hertz drinking steadily to drown his wrongs. Anyone knows it is a lousy trick to beat up a man who is so drunk he can hardly see straight, but that hadn't worried Blaze. Then, quite pleased with himself, and probably two sheets to windward himself, he had appeared at the dance very gay.

Anyone except a woman who has had her observation dulled by writing 'Mrs. Prothero' would have known long before that it was Vic he was chasing, not Fay. At the dance he had made a bee-line for Fay, insisted on dancing with her while she watched nervously over his shoulder, hoping her husband would not choose that time to appear. No one told her anything of the fight; and terrified because some of the dam workers would be sure to tell her husband about Blaze whirling her round the floor of the hall, she had left the dance and gone to the McKillop garage where she shared a bed with the eldest McKillop girl.

About midnight Harry Warren caught Blaze and Vic in each other's arms behind the dance hall, and Blaze had his second fight for Saturday. Harry had not been drinking, and it was no wonder Blaze so suddenly decided to go to Tembucca. What Fay could not forgive was the way he had deliberately used her as a blind. The Warrens weren't speaking to each other in private, but were putting up a united front in public — and very necessary too.

I was not surprised later when Harry Warren asked me to see all the bees were shifted off his property as they were worrying the stock. He explained that he was bringing in more cattle and the new mob were wild and hadn't settled down. He didn't need to be so long-winded about it.

But to Fay I kept saying apologetically, 'Well, yes, Fay, I suppose that was pretty rotten of Blaze.'

'I know how it was with Frank.' Fay began to cry again. 'It was my last chance, I see it now. And he spoilt it.'

'He didn't realize, Fay.'

'Yes, he did. And before that he made poor Joe think I had fallen for him — for Blaze, I mean — and Joe went away. He tormented Joe — he thought it was a joke. Joe told me about the way he got their father so he just made up his mind to sell the bees. He was the same with their uncle. *He* got out, did you know? There's no one — ask Fred Connelly — that can stand Blaze Muirden. He's the best-hated man, Fred says, anywhere where there's apiarists. Can't get anyone to work with him.' She looked at me squarely. 'And I've heard the way he bosses you about — swears at you and treats you worse than a horse.'

'Oh, come off it, Fay. I can look after myself.'

'That's what you think, Mallee. But Hilda doesn't think so . . .'

'Oh, Hilda!'

'And I don't think so either.' Then she relapsed into her listless staring out the window.

'Well, never mind all that, Fay. Think about going away and taking the kids with us. When I go down to the city for a holiday, you could come too. You could stay with my mother until you got a job and a little flat of your own.'

'I can't stay here.' She began to pace along that fence in her mind where she had worn a deep track trying to break through the invisible wires. 'I can't stay with Mrs. Warren. She doesn't really like me now.'

How she hated Nithering with the ragged trees, the broken rocks, the rainy vapour in the valley and winter grinding its knuckles into the backs of our necks. All the distances and depths, the small bird flight and monotony of nature that filled me with such exhilarated delight.

'Promise me you'll take me when you go,' she said desperately. 'Anywhere — I don't care where it is.'

'I promise,' I said. I stood up to go. I couldn't think of anything more that would comfort her and I didn't want to be there when the Warrens came home, now that I knew their differences were so deep. More than anything, I couldn't bear the questions of Bidgee and Brian, who had been twisting my heart with bad imitations of Mrs.

Prothero: 'Where is my daddy? He said he would come back. If we are good can we go where he is?'

When Blaze came back a week later, and he came driving back quite brisk and cheerful as though nothing had happened, I repeated to him what Harry Warren had said about the bees worrying the new cattle. He cursed Big Mike for leaving us. He had no interest in any emotional entanglements he might have caused. He was interested only in getting the honey out, moving the bees — planning a retreat before winter overtook us.

Blaze had a low opinion of Tembucca, but it seemed to be the best place offering. But we could not get out because of the weather. The rain kept on until the flooded creeks could hold no more water. It slashed down viciously on a slant, driving in and drenching everything. The wet chooks roosted on the veranda. Matt's horse and the roan gelding that had belonged to Frank Hertz came and stood against the wall of the house for shelter. That gelding was a solid big horse with the temper of its former owner, but Matt would go out with a sack over his head and stand in the rain talking to it and rubbing its nose.

He said the horse was lonely. And certainly it followed him about with the other animals as though it liked his company. You could see Matt sauntering round when the rain eased off, with his little court of animals and maybe the small boys. The dogs ran on in front, the pussies came leaping over grass tussocks and jostling the dogs, the cow lumbering behind, and the goats running bleating up to him. He had so many things to occupy him, small nests and burrows and tiny wild animals that he knew by name. To him the forests were never lonely but a city crowded with interesting life.

Chapter Nineteen

THEN came the wild weather, and the cold sleet froze into flakes of snow.

'Snow!' Blaze declared incredulously. 'There oughtn't to be snow for six weeks at the very least.'

'I've known four inches of snow here in December,' Matt drawled. 'Right in the middle of summer.'

Matt and Blaze had been out in the gale and the snow, nailing down the lids of bee boxes. They came in with their teeth chattering.

'We've got to get out of here,' Blaze said. 'I saw an Abominable Snowman this morning. Tracks like an elephant's and a face like Matt's. He recognized Matt too. Thought he was a brother or a relative. Yes, we've got to leave this warm little corner.'

But a landslide had driven a wedge through the Ombra Road and thrown a slice of it down into the valley, and the Cobberloi Creek cut us off from Lacey's Crossing. Blaze started to worry about George up on his mountain top.

'We've got to get him out,' he growled. 'We told him not to go, and now we're the mugs. Lovely weather for building a road in to him. George never can pass up the chance to make someone build a road.'

George had followed along a track made by a land-rover when some crazy engineers had gone careering across country. On a good day it would raise your hair, but in the wet and cold it was unspeakable. We took both trucks so that one could tow the other out. The cold made you feel that your hands had fallen off at the wrists. We managed to turn in along a track where some big pipes had been laid to bring a watercourse down to the dam. There were places with a drop of hundreds of feet where one skid would take you into the tree tops far below.

Up towards George's hideout the ridges were bare moor with trees down in hollows, and those trees on the bare crown that did resist the blast were riven and stunted. But on the steep valley slopes they were definitely good. Of course this cold meant that the blossom was finished. The hard casing of the bud would protect the bloom that had not yet pushed out. The caps that fit over the top of eucalypt bud are practically armour plate. But if you had any more hope of flower you could kiss it good-bye. We had just flashed in on the run of honey and now for months, probably, although there would be thaws and warm periods, the cold would keep the sap from flowing fast. There is always a dead period in winter, and in the roaring heat of the summer when the hot winds shrivel the flowers off the trees. The best flowering periods are in between, when the trees decide to make the leap. But it is a hard life being a eucalypt, nearly as hard as being a woman, a matter of holding on grimly, and good judgment.

Stubborn old George, when his tent blew to tatters, had rigged himself a sort of dog-kennel with bee boxes and a tarp. He came crawling out of it shivering and blinking and coughing. Blaze called him for everything for being such a fool. We couldn't get the trucks down the slope and had to carry all the boxes up. I carried the neuc boxes and was sworn at for doing that.

We had to get George's truck out from the place where he had bogged it. In all, we spent three days dismantling

George's little home. As usual when the going was tough, Blaze was gay. He made us laugh describing how George would have washed down into the dam. His head, Blaze said, was so thick that he'd probably have stove a hole clean through the dam and gone floating along down the valley until someone fished him out and pickled him in alcohol for a sideshow as the fabulous bunyip of the ranges.

We bedded George down in my room and I slept by the kitchen fire. Somebody had to get up and change him in the night when he was dripping with sweat, so I did. Poor old George was half delirious. He thought I was his wife.

'You're right,' he kept muttering. 'A man's a fool. You're right those bees would take the best of me. They get you in. No kind of life for a married man. But this time I'll do well — see if I don't. Listen, old girl, I've only got to get one good season and we're in the clear.'

I told Matt he ought to have a doctor and he ought to get home to his wife. But the bridge at Nithering was under water, we couldn't get through to Ombra, and Cobberloi Creek was running a banker, so it was no good trying to go through Lacey's Crossing.

'We'll get him out,' Matt said. 'Easy.'

He rummaged in the bathroom and produced two big axes, tested the blades, and said disgustedly that you could ride to Bourke on them. So he went to his old grindstone in the shed and had sparks flying from it as he sharpened the axes. Then he found some heavy chains that I think must once have belonged to the hydro-electric authority. Probably found them somewhere because the gangers were very careless.

He harnessed his old horse to the cart and stood in it straight and gay as a charioteer, the dogs barking round him. Blaze and I followed along in the Ford. Cobberloi

Creek was sliding along with a purposeful swirl, a menacing headlong motion that was more sinister than all the mud and foam. Matt pulled in to the side of the road and we drew in behind him.

'You follow along slow where I turn off,' Matt ordered. 'We don't go right down to the creek.'

He wheeled the horse off the road to the right, along a hardly perceptible track made through the trees by his sulky tyres. The dogs loped ahead gaily, the bushes snapped and scraped against the mudguards, and wet drops from the boughs flicked our faces.

'I think I pretty near cleared her of stumps,' Matt shouted.

We took it slowly, Blaze spinning the wheel frantically on the sharp turns that were all very well for a horse and cart. Matt hadn't cleared that track of stumps by any means, but we managed not to bash the sump off the truck. Finally we came out on the creek bank about a quarter of a mile above the road crossing.

Matt smiled at the look on our faces. 'I don't go into Nithering much,' he explained. 'Don't like the old horse looking round at me when I ask him to pull up that hill. And the Cobberloi's a bit careless the way it comes down, so I built this bridge.'

There was an overhanging lip of rock, and from this Matt had laid across the narrow deep cutting to the far bank a rough collection of tree trunks. He drove the cart over to show us, the old horse breathing suspiciously, testing that bridge with its front hooves, trusting Matt of course, but careful of its shoes.

'You old dingo,' Blaze said. 'Letting us bog in that crossing and never splitting you had a bang-up bridge.'

'Well,' said Matt mildly, handing him the spare axe, 'it isn't a truck road. And as soon as you use it the mob from the dam will get wise and tear hell out of it. Like enough cave the bank in on me. They'll go blasting out trees and mucking the place up properly.'

Matt was one of those axemen who make it look easy. He sent the chips flying from a big messmate on the far bank, laying it neatly across the creek so that it came crashing down, tangling its boughs in the bushes on the opposite side. Then he walked across and he and Blaze felled a tree he had marked as a possibility for the day he needed to strengthen his bridge. Some of the trees we dragged with the cart where we couldn't use the truck. They were clenched together with the heavy chains, and when the approaches were levelled, that bridge was a job any gang would have been proud to acknowledge as all their own work. It was getting dark when we finished.

'I wouldn't risk taking a load over it,' Blaze said thoughtfully. 'But you could unload your bees this side, take the truck across and load up again the other side.'

Already he was calculating on getting out as soon as he could take his bees away. It's funny how a camp breaks up. One week there is just an uneasiness, and then the next everyone is so sick of the place, so desperate to drive off and away that they'd do anything to go. It is as though the bees, robbed of their honey, communicate their own complaints about poor conditions to their human slaves.

'I'll have George over to that doctor in Ombra tomorrow,' Blaze promised. 'Go through Lacey's Crossing and take the Ombra Road. Then I'll go straight on to Tembucca and pick up some clothes I need and find out what's happened to Mike. Be there tomorrow night. You come, Mallee? There's nothing to do here.'

I thought this over. I wanted to see Horace Muirden, but I knew now the old villain was never going to sell those bees. We drove off in the Ford, leaving Matt to follow, jogging slowly along in the cart.

'Blaze, are you going to take that load down to Uncle Beresford?'

'He can wait. George can't. I'll have a word with Mongo when I see him, by God! Sitting nursing his boils when he could be useful. I'll blow him so high he'll think he's a rocket.' He looked sideways at me. 'By cripes, you're wet and mucky. I never knew a woman that could get muddier. Here — have my coat.'

'It'll only get mud on it.'

'Take it, blast you!'

It had been left in the truck so it was dry at least, but I made no move to put it on. Blaze pulled up the truck with a jerk. 'When I say put my coat on, you put it on.'

'I'm all right, I tell you.'

He jerked the coat off the back of the seat and draped it round me. 'I get so mad with you,' he said savagely. 'Never doing as you're told, bullocking about in the wet, carting rocks. Look at you. You think you're some kind of alligator. If you'd get yourself dressed up like other women . . .' He was kissing me. 'Damn it,' he swore. 'It must be that bloody creek. First time I ever wanted to kiss you was when you were sloshing about in it.'

'I suppose someone bet you,' I said, pulling away.

'Hell, no. Just a nice idea of my own. A very nice idea.' He kissed me again. 'Makes this a decent kind of day after all.'

I was very tired from all the work I had done, too tired to be bothered making a fuss or acting like a professional spinster. I could only talk myself out.

'What a wonderful time you pick,' I said, 'to start anything. It's funny how a man thinks any girl will be offended if he doesn't make a pass at her. Nice of you,

Blaze. Well, now you've paid me this pretty compliment, we'll forget it.'

'Like hell we will!'

'Well, everybody's tried their luck, except Matt. Big Mike — Joe — now you.'

'Joe?'

'You bet your socks Joe tried. But he's nice. He takes a knockback without any wounded vanity.'

'But then Joe isn't me. I'm persistent.'

'Drive on. Matt will catch up with us.' He looked at me to see if I meant it, then sullenly started the engine. 'Of course you realize,' I said bitterly, 'that you've kicked over my gay plans for being an apiarist.'

'Now don't go acting like a silly squarking hen. And don't hand me any guff about this being the first time you've ever been kissed, because I've kissed enough women to know better.'

'I'm not handing you any guff. I'm just saying this dissolves the partnership. You can keep my share.'

'Well, you expect too bloody much of a man, that's all.'

'Listen, Blaze, I know you too well to stick around after this. Either you've just run out of women, or else you think I'll do for the time being, or else you're just keeping your hand in.'

'How many times do you think I wanted to kiss you and haven't done it? Why, the way you're abusing me, anyone 'ud think I was sharing my beautiful bed with you that got burnt up in the shack.'

'Thank God, it's gone. Look here, Blaze. You know I *like* you. But I'm not a fool. Stuck away in the scrub you get to the stage where anybody of the opposite sex . . .'

'The opposite sex! Who's talking about the opposite sex? If I'm big idiot enough to fall for a stubborn army mule of a woman, you talk about the opposite sex.'

'What about Daphne?'

'Daphne is nice,' Blaze said judicially. 'She certainly is gorgeous. If I were home. But I see her point — I'm not home often enough.'

'What about Vic? What about Fay Hertz?'

'Mallee, if you're going to sit there running through a list of women I might take an interest in, I can give you a list as long as your arm. I'll tell you something about Fay though. She doesn't want a man, she wants a little boy — somebody like Joe who needs mothering. That Joe — he's a big sook — always be the baby of the family.'

'You might be right about Fay.' I was pleased that we were talking casually.

'Right? Of course I'm right. And let me tell you, I was right to kiss you. Otherwise you'd be kidding yourself and everybody else that you were just a cross between an alligator and a mule.'

'Well, anyway,' I said scowling, and settling my hands in my pockets, 'we're through. I don't see myself hanging around. Somebody who didn't know you well might make that mistake.' I wasn't exactly flattered. Blaze wasn't getting the chance to try any of his technique on me.

'I'll marry you for your money, dear,' Blaze said. 'I'm always hearing about your bloody money. You ram it down my neck.'

'Thank you. That's a damn lie. And I wouldn't marry you if you were the last man left alive.' I started to laugh. 'As Big Mike says, "Any bee-keeper who's five miles from home is single again." Oh God, Blaze, you're an idiot!'

Blaze got down to open the gate of Matt's place. He climbed back into the truck and kissed me again. 'That's for talking a lot of bull,' he said. 'Ever since you walked into our camp I've been getting worse and worse about you all the time.'

'Stop kidding,' I said, losing interest. 'Keep it for someone who likes that line.'

The trouble with Blaze was always vanity. He thought he was irresistible. Well, my fine friend, I said to myself, you have a big shock coming. The more I thought the matter over, the more sure I was that I had come to the parting of the ways with the Muirdens. When Blaze and George left next morning, there would be one other person planning to go in the opposite direction, and that person would be Mallee Herrick.

Right up to the minute he left Blaze was certain I would go with him to Tembucca. He did his utmost to persuade me. He seemed to regard carrying me off to Tembucca as important. He had some plan in his head, some scheme of his own, but I was determined not to fall in with it. Finally he drove off in a bad temper, with George unshaven and dejected beside him.

'Give my love to Daphne,' I said sweetly.

Blaze only gave me a dirty look.

Chapter Twenty

NOWADAYS the idea prevails that bad temper can make you ill, and that various diseases are associated with undesirable states of mind. But everyone who has a cold knows that your disposition and character can change as soon as you are sick. To be thoroughly miserable and cantankerous, you need the kind of feverish cold I developed building and levelling the approaches to that bridge of Matt's and sitting round in wet clothes on the way home.

Of course, Hilda had another theory just to contradict me. 'You caught George's flu,' she accused, as though I had done it on purpose. 'Just like George to give everyone his germs and then clear off. Now somebody'll have to shift his bees as usual. And as for his fool of a wife letting the baby drink out of a bottle of kerosene when she wasn't looking, I told her what I thought of her.'

Hilda was all in favour of kidnapping me to Tembucca with her in the caravan, but I said I couldn't be moved. I would enjoy my ill-health where I was. Matt didn't bother me, apart from recommending a mixture that had stood on a shelf in the shed since he used it on the horse. Hilda smelt it and said it was half kerosene and the rest creosote.

Hilda had come up to say farewell for now, because she was going back in the caravan to Tembucca. She settled down comfortably to a complete dissection and analysis of the scandalous conduct of Blaze Muirden at that dance in Lacey's Crossing.

'It's all very well for you to laugh, Mallee.' I couldn't laugh because it made me cough. 'But it isn't any laughing matter to have Blaze going around breaking up people's homes.'

'Oh, get out, Hilda,' I gasped, trying not to cough and laugh at the same time. 'Vic must be ten years older than Blaze.'

'It wouldn't be the first time,' Hilda replied, settling down on the foot of my bed so that it sagged sideways, 'that some fool of a woman has encouraged him.'

Luckily just then Fay came in. Fay was wonderful while I had that cold. I had not realized before that Fay had any assets, apart from her looks, but she was a domestic genius, an aura of protection, a cooling soothing competent presence. A magnificent hospital sister was lost in Fay. No wonder she got on so well with Hilda. Fay came down to Matt's snuggery, and without actually disturbing the fine Rembrandt brown or even the texts and wasps' nests, she made me comfortable. She would walk all the way up that road after she finished work to wait on me, bringing fabulous fruit like lemons to make into drinks.

Now she took Hilda out into the kitchen with her while she warmed some soup she had brought. Witches, I muttered to myself, stirring up bats' wings and toads' blood, poisoning each other's minds. I was in that state when everything was an affront and a deliberate offence. I was disgusted with myself for existing at all, for being such a miserable object, for losing my sense of humour and my grip and common sense, and even the ability to stagger out of bed.

Nobody wrote to me, not even Nobby, who had been pouring out advice and counsel from a distance in inde lible pencil. I seemed to have existed for uncounted centuries in the Nithering Range with a pack of savages, and I was homesick and disgruntled and fed up, just like George. Bees! I hated them. Nobby and I used to potter about with bees, peaceably, without any driving and bad temper.

If I had come straight up to the Nithering Range with my sixty hives, Matt and I would have continued to potter about peaceably, not getting much honey perhaps, but enough to make us feel quite happy and excited. My big mistake had been trying to buy the Muirden bees, and then getting tied up with the Muirdens. All apiarists were not like them. Others I had met were easy-going men, friendly, pleasant, kindly. Why did I have to pick on the Muirdens? Anyway, why had I ever thought of being a migratory apiarist? Mad, absurd, utterly incongruous, just as everyone had told me. I was a competent script-writer, and I should have stayed at my trade.

In this mood of dejection Lee Stollin found me. I was at the crawling-into-the-sun stage, and looked like something that had been dug up as an interesting antique. Lee Stollin sat down beside me on the edge of the veranda with that air he had of being completely clean and well-dressed and intelligent. He listened to my lamentations with patience and amusement, and suggested he should drive me to Ombra to see Mavis. He had come up our way to see Fay about some papers she had to sign in connection with her husband's decease, and Fay had told him I had the 'flu. But in my lassitude and self-pity I couldn't even rouse myself to seek sanctuary with Mavis.

'I'm quitting,' I told Lee. 'I'm through.'

He looked at me understandingly. 'I've had it too,' he said. 'You feel like playing Russian roulette with a loaded gun.'

'Bees! Who wants bees? Who wants honey? Damn sticky stuff that gets in your sore tooth.'

'Where's your outfit? And the dark young fellow who bossed the concern?'

'Gone for the time being, thank God. I couldn't have coped with them in my present snivelling frame of mind.'

'I was sorry for those guys,' Lee said, chuckling mischievously to himself. 'I never saw any set of men that kept a closer watch on each other. You could see them slide their eyes sideways in a warning sort of way, seeing that the others kept strictly in line.'

I sat up straighter and glared at him through my bunged-up eyes. 'Meaning me?'

'Like jaguars in a cage waiting for the lady to relax just one little minute. Poor devils, they had my sympathy.'

'You're all wrong,' I said with a sniff. 'You've got a nasty mind, Lee.'

Lee chuckled again comfortably. He saw he was annoying me, so he changed the subject, no doubt thinking he was leaving me with my illusions. But I hadn't any, not even about Lee. Maybe the isolation was affecting him, but he was as often up at Matt's house as his job would let him. And he was comfortable to have around. He could talk, for instance, impersonally, and that is something men like Joe and Fred and Blaze seldom do. He had fine manners and Matt enjoyed arguing with him.

Indeed Lee contributed more to my recovery than the break in the weather. He had Fay's competence, and he wasn't either obtrusively masculine or effeminate. He was the kind of man as steady as a rock and as deep as a well. And he was moving in. Oh my, yes, he had his intentions. I could see I had to hasten out of Nithering, but I still felt too feeble to make the effort. And it had started to rain again.

I was tottering about just being something Matt had around, like the cats or the cow, when Vic came whirling down full of brisk concern to say that Dennis had just rung from Ombra to say that he was on his way out. It was a grey, mist-drifty day, and if you think the Parent was prompted by any concern that he might be inconveniencing us, you have greatly mistaken his character. No, he wanted to be sure that someone cleared out of the best bed and had it all ready for him.

'Oh, poor Mallee,' Vic said, 'you do look awful. What a shame!' I think she had been keeping tactfully away because she knew that tidings of the dance in Ombra would have drifted over the grape-vine. 'Can I do anything?' she asked solicitously.

'Yes, cut my hair.'

So Vic draped a towel around me and the pussies formed a ring, and Matt watched while she snipped my locks with Matt's beard-trimming scissors. Of course she refused to cut off as much thatch as I wanted removed, but in the argument she forgot to wonder how much I knew, and we were easy and friendly together. We speculated what the Parent was doing in this part of the world.

'I'll take down some of that honey to Uncle Beresford when I go,' I decided.

'You are going then?' Vic asked.

Matt was blunt. 'They'll plant her in the graveyard if she doesn't get rid of that cough. I don't want the horse straining into Nithering for another funeral.'

'You don't get rid of me as easily as all that, Matt. If you'll keep an eye on those hives of mine, I'll be back later.'

I wasn't coming back until the Muirdens had quitted the neighbourhood. Matt said that he had enjoyed the last few months, and if he ever found himself alone again it would probably get on his nerves. I didn't believe him, of course. He must have felt like a railway goods yard with all the shunting to and fro, and people sleeping on his bedroom or kitchen floor.

'Dennis can stay with us,' Vic offered, so I judged the domestic situation was now stabilized.

'He can sleep in the shed,' I said cruelly. I thought the Parent should suffer. There was that matter of my five hundred pounds. He really had a cheek coming back to the scene of the crime, after committing forgery, bank deception, criminal malpractice and, I think, felony.

Vic was still there chatting to us when Dennis swept down from the gate in a car which gleamed through the mud. He must have stopped outside the gate and wiped it off so that we might admire its beauty. The Parent can drive if he has to, but, particularly when his nerves are jittery, he prefers to have someone else do it, and he sits beside them carping all the way. He was driving all alone in this glorious car; beautiful travelling rug, beautiful travelling clothes. He posed beside his automobile.

'Where'd you steal that?' I called.

He greeted Vic gracefully. He wrung Matt's hand; the prodigal who has made good, returning to lift the mortgage. But I noticed he didn't come close enough to be coughed on. Vicki cried out flatteringly at the Parent's grandeur.

'And where am I sleeping?' he asked boyishly. 'Out in the rain, I suppose?'

'In the shed,' I said maliciously. 'The shack burned down.'

Of course Dennis didn't believe me at first. They had to take him and show him the ruins. When Vic went home, we gave him chapter and verse for all that had happened. He heard about Frank Hertz and registered the correct emotions and strewed flowers of appropriate words.

'You really are gaunt, Mallee, my good girl,' he said at last.

'Matt thinks I'm about to grace the graveyard,' I said, laying on the pathos. 'So I think I'll come home with you, Parent. And Fay and the kids will come down too.'

'But I'm not going home,' Dennis cried. 'You haven't given me time to tell you why I'm here.'

'You mean to say you've shaken the city off your shoes?'

We were having the inevitable cup of tea together.

'Corned beef,' Dennis said. 'I haven't tasted corned beef since I was here last, with apologies to Matt. I'm sure it's very good corned beef.'

'I notice you don't intend to tucker yourself,' I pointed out sourly. 'You didn't bring any goodies for the little ones. No caviare, no black olives or oysters?'

'Mallee, if you'll give me time to tell you my plans, how I was held up by these ghastly roads and hastened to be here this afternoon, never stopping for supplies lest the light fail before I reached Nithering . . .'

'And then you were so frightened of the prices in Nithering that you didn't bother? Fire ahead.'

'Why don't you stop picking on him?' Matt drawled. 'He means he don't intend to stay.'

'That's just it. I'm on my way to Queensland. I have been appointed resident superintendent at Brannigan's Bend for Northern Exploitations.'

I felt that a place called Brannigan's Bend couldn't be much chop. 'Why Brannigan's Bend?' I asked. 'What's Brannigan's Bend?'

'It's our most important development to date,' the Parent said importantly. 'Why, when it rains there, the oil oozes out from underground and rolls down the creek, staining it with rainbows. You know how in India the biggest oil show of all time was discovered by whites who found that the natives had for generations been scooping the oil off the river? Well, that's the way it is at Brannigan's Bend.'

It began to sound better. Matt and I could both see those rainbows and the natives scooping them up; the kind of place I was always hearing about from Dennis, where nobody dared to light a match for fear the river caught fire.

'What river's it on?' I asked.

'Well,' Dennis seemed rather dashed, 'it isn't really a river. It's called Hellhole Creek.'

'I'm just trying to get an idea of the locality,' I said patiently.

'I was up that way in nineteen-eleven,' Matt said. 'This Hellhole Creek, what's she run into?'

Dennis coughed. 'Well, Hellhole runs into Cut-throat Creek, which runs into the Elizabeth, which runs into the Condamine.'

'Now we're getting somewhere,' Matt nodded. 'We're within a hundred miles or so of it anyway.'

'Half-way across Bandy's paddock,' I muttered. I got out all my maps, but of course Brannigan's Bend wasn't marked on them. The nearest town was Caterpillar, which didn't sound promising. A thought struck me. 'What made you call in here?' I asked. 'You could have whizzed straight through on the main road.'

'I remembered that I owed you some money,' Dennis said, very much the son lifting the mortgage from the old roof-tree. 'Here's your cheque. And let me tell you, Mallee, that the way your uncle has behaved about what was only a temporary borrowing has been outrageous.'

'Well, now that you're managing an oil-well,' I said, pocketing the cheque without looking to see if it was genuine, because only the bank could reassure me on that point, 'now that they're paying you a fat salary and giving you this car . . .'

'Oh, the car!' The Parent waved his hand. 'I bought the car, and the superintendent's position is by no means well paid, at the present. But I had a great stroke of luck.' He paused dramatically. 'I sold Mrs. Prothero.'

'Sold her?'

'Film rights and television!' The Parent almost shouted. He had been keeping it to himself and mystifying us. 'All that last section I wrote — I made it into a separate sequence from where Basil brings home his bride, and I sold it to Bertrand Spellman, under the title of "My Mother's Roof".'

I gazed at him dazedly. Maybe the 'flu was making me a little stupid, but I was under the impression that I had written all that slab of 'Mrs. Prothero' myself. Then I glared at Dennis. I was sure of it. 'Listen, Parent, *I* wrote all that part.'

'You may have had a hand in it,' Dennis said smugly. 'But I was the man who thought of selling it to this picture magnate and pulled the deal off. Surely, Mallee, you don't grudge Julie any little extra luxury that this may have brought her?'

I had to take time to simmer down. It is all very well to despise the non-essentials and the fripperies of existence, but it is another thing to have a loving stepfather pinch your hard work without as much as by-your-leave or thank-you. I got up, took the lamp; the cold winter dusk had closed down on us while we were talking and eating.

'I'll see what the shed's like,' I said.

Matt rose up with me. 'I'll go,' he said. 'Dennis can have my bed. There's clean sheets.' I didn't care if the Parent didn't have any sheets at all.

'Mighty nice of you, Matt,' Dennis responded gracefully. 'I really appreciate it. I'd sleep in the shed, but I'm still a mite delicate. Got to look after myself. That was why I called in to see if Mallee would come with me to Queensland.'

'I'll come with you,' I said, 'on one condition.'

'I suppose you want me to take those sixty bee-hives,' the Parent said. 'Or some other bee-hives or bee-men. Well, I have no objection. Let them all come. Muirdens, Connellys, George or what's-his-name. Makes no difference.'

'I'm leaving my bees with Matt. But I'm taking Fay and Bidgee and Brian.' Matt and the Parent looked at each other. 'Fay wants to leave Nithering. Well, she's going to leave. She's coming with us.'

'I see.' The Parent sounded dubious. 'But — d'you think it's wise? I mean — probably rough conditions. Hellhole Creek, you know. Cut-throat Creek.'

'Anywhere you can live, Fay and the kids can. So that's settled. Plenty of room in that outsize buggy of yours. I'll just walk up to the shed with Matt. I need the air.'

We took the hurricane lantern. When we reached the shed, I sat down on a box, rolled a cigarette and threw it away, muttering angrily. Matt sat down on another box. He knew I couldn't smoke because of my cough, so with his usual good manners he didn't smoke himself.

'So you're leaving the bees?' he said.

'Yes, if you'll look after them for a while. And if you'll get Lon McKillop to bring the Ruin out I'll arrange to send it back to Nobby somehow. One of the gang might run it down with a load of honey.'

Matt looked at me curiously. 'Thinking of giving up bees?'

'Oh no,' I said hastily. 'I'm not pulling out. But

I'm curious to see what the Parent has up his sleeve, and
— oh well, Matt, what's the use? What does it matter?
I'm probably not cut out for even a mug apiarist, anyway.'

'Everybody feels like that with the 'flu,' Matt said
quietly. 'Trip'll do you good.'

'And one thing, Matt,' I said. 'I'd think it a favour
if you didn't mention to anyone where we are going.'
Now Matt was the kind of man you could ask something
like that, and he just nodded. 'You don't have to tell
a lie, Matt. No harm saying we're going somewhere up
towards Queensland, but Queensland's a big place.'

'Yes,' Matt said. 'I've been there.' Then his eyes
twinkled. He began to laugh to himself.

'All right, you old devil,' I said. 'If you won't tell me
what the joke is . . .'

'Going to make a million out of honey, ho! ho!'
laughed Matt.

I left him pulling off his boots and still shaking his
whiskers in his evil joy. Personally I didn't think it was
very funny. When I returned to the Parent, who had
found the clean sheets and made Matt's bed for himself,
I didn't say anything of my disagreement with Blaze.
I just let the Parent think he had persuaded me to go
to Queensland. I gathered he hadn't been able to persuade Anita or Julie, although they might travel up
later for a pleasant holiday, if Brannigan's Bend turned
out to be other than its name implied.

The Parent had picked on me as the mug, the buffer,
the chauffeur, the housekeeper and comforter in his new
splendour as resident superintendent of a promising oil
town. But imagine the optimism of the man going to a
place called Brannigan's Bend on Hellhole Creek! I
marvelled at him.

Chapter Twenty-one

'Now you quite understand, Mallee,' the Parent said, feeling his oats and looking like a big executive, 'you are coming with *me* this time. I will pay your expenses, but none of this camping. We are putting up at hotels, and you are to *dress*.' He emphasized the word. 'Your mother has sent your clothes, and if I see those dungarees once on this trip, I shall — well, I shall be utterly disgusted. You must at least pay me the consideration of not looking like a dirty youth from a garage. People will expect me, my dear girl, to at least look the part, and I trust you will do the same. If you want to bring a maid . . .'

'Less of the maid. Fay just wants to get away with the kids and start somewhere else.'

'Well, bring her, bring her,' the Parent said impatiently. 'I don't know how they'll all fit in the car.' He realized I wouldn't go without Fay.

'How's the road?' I asked, looking at the map I had spread on Matt's kitchen table.

'The road is filthy. Luckily we will be on the highway once we reach Ombra, but even driving up here played old Harry with my nerves. Mud, water, stretches of water all the way. There are floods at Warnsfield, I hear, but luckily we won't be going near there.'

Matt took our projected departure with a fortitude that was partly relief. 'You'll be back,' he said quietly. 'Won't be far from young Muirden for long.'

I gave him a cold look because he was drawing the wrong deductions from the wrong premises. He chuckled to himself.

We were giving the Parent a day's rest after his drive up from the city, so I had time to go over to Lon McKillop's garage in the Parent's car to see about the Roaring Ruin. Lon got the surprise of his life to have someone actually pay him. He needed to go down to Sydney in a week's time and offered to take the Roaring Ruin down to Nobby's place for me. We agreed the Ruin wouldn't last out on a trip to Queensland. My idea was to buy a new truck — none of your second-hand jobs — that is, of course, if I continued as an apiarist; and Lon and I discussed the different makes and their advantages and disadvantages.

We walked all round the Parent's beautiful new sedan. Lon crawled underneath and surveyed the mudcaked underpinnings. 'She's too low slung for Queensland roads,' he announced, crawling out. 'What did she stand him in? Near enough to two thousand, I'll bet a dollar.'

'As much as that?' I was aghast. Probably Dennis hadn't paid for that sedan yet, and here he was driving off to Queensland, where it would be knocked to pieces. 'He'd have done better,' Lon decided, 'to get an older model, higher off the ground, or a light truck or a Ute.'

The Parent had persuaded Matt to drive in with us for a farewell beer, so Lon and I joined them at the pub. The Parent gracefully waved away Lon's doubts about his beautiful new purchase.

'Comfort and speed,' he said. 'I have had my fill of driving in trucks. I have no intention of departing from the highways, and I was assured by the salesman — who is a friend of mine — that there is *nothing* this car is not built to stand.'

'Powerful job,' Lon agreed, turning his glass in his great fist. 'Been a lot of rain, of course.' He mumbled to himself. 'More predicted. Those Queensland rivers . . .' But he could see Dennis was as proud and fond as a young mother, and had just as much sense about his darling. She was the first offspring of his wedding to Northern Exploitations, the first-fruit of his new opulence.

The Parent went down to Harry Warren's place and spread himself and shone before Vicki and Harry. Nobody said a word to him about any slight difference of opinion over bee-keepers. I drove down to see Lee Stollin, but as he wasn't at the camp I left him a note. So we were all ready to leave early in the morning, and my last stop was at Ombra to say farewell to Mavis.

'Wouldn't have known you, Gert,' Mavis declared, surveying the garments that Dennis had decided would be suitable for the daughter of a big oil man. Anita and I are much the same size, and Anita had replenished my wardrobe with generous contributions from her own. Our flat must have been overflowing with new frocks. Mavis listened to my hasty outline of our plans with a preoccupied air. 'I think I'd better clear all the shelves up to about five feet,' she mused. 'Last time the flood was about a foot over the kitchen refrigerator. If you're getting out of here, Gert, you'd better be going while the going's good. Warnsfield's cut off, you know?'

Of course, in Nithering we didn't read newspapers often and the battery of Matt's radio had been out of action. We had taken it for granted that all the rain we had been having was purely a local affair. Mavis and I gave each other a hug for luck. 'I'll be seeing you,' she called after me. Nobody seemed to take this Queensland trip as anything but a short interruption to my sojourn among them. I returned to the car in the rainswept street in a thoughtful mood.

'Parent,' I said, 'Mavis has been giving me the flood warnings. Do you think we'd better press on or turn back?'

'I've already told you I should have been there a week ago,' Dennis complained. 'I have so many things demanding immediate attention. I have to Make a Report. I've got to wire to Head Office as soon as we arrive. I can't have everything going to rack and ruin while you loiter here. I should have gone by air if I hadn't wanted to bring you too — and the car, of course.'

He was driving because the newness of his car had not worn off yet. It was his toy and he wanted to play with it. Fay and the kids and the luggage were in the back. There was more luggage stored in the enormous boot. The Parent grumbled that the car was overloaded, but it certainly sped over the dreary, sodden country, sending out a spray of brown mud and water at any low-lying part of the road.

The kids chattered to their mother excitedly. They took it for granted that Queensland was a heaven for good little boys. Fay was silent and thoughtful. It must have been a desperate venture for her, setting out into the unknown, poor Fay. One of the reasons I had not pressed Dennis to turn back was that Fay and the kids would be disappointed. Besides, I have always hated to turn back myself.

We had to stop for flocks of sheep jostling along the road, being driven to higher ground, sometimes by a woman on horseback, or children on ponies, self-contained, self-reliant. Then, coming round a bend, we saw the water stretching before us in brown swirling ripples, flowing across from a swamp on one side to a lake of flooded fields on the other. Far off, the dripping willows indicated a creek that had broken its banks and was now flowing over the countryside at large.

The Parent, determined to outface my silent judgment, churned into it and proceeded bravely almost as far as the middle. Of course he couldn't get through. I hitched up my skirt and was peeling off my shoes and stockings almost before the car stopped.

'Well, I hope you're satisfied now,' he said pettishly. 'You've been waiting for this for miles.'

I lifted the mud-spattered bonnet of the car, wiped the spark plugs, got the engine going by great good luck and backed her out. 'Home, James,' I said, letting him take the wheel. Without a word he turned the car round while I put on my shoes and stockings, and we started back to Ombra.

'Why are we going back, Mallee?' Brian asked.

'Because there's too much water,' his mother answered for me.

'Oh, I don't wanna go back,' Brian grumbled. 'Why do we have to go home again?'

I was studying the map. 'If we go back to Ombra,' I suggested, 'and take the road east, we might get round it. Anyway we can find out.'

But getting back to Ombra sounded easier than it was. The pools on the road were now sheets of running water and it was difficult to judge their depth.

'Good thing we aren't in a real flood.' I tried to cheer up the silent passengers. 'Think how comfortable and warm we are in the Parent's nice car. Soon we'll be back in Ombra and we'll have a hot dinner at a café. What will you have, Brian? You choose.'

The Parent hunched grimly over the wheel, looking like A Race With Death. There he was, with two helpless females and two little children, the hero. When I offered to drive, he snarled at me.

'She's doing well,' I encouraged. 'Positively sailing through it. Good old Queen Wilhelmina.' I did not realize that I had christened the car, but Brian and Bidgee called her Wilhelmina from that time on. The water, as I have said, was deeper, flowing from one side of the road to the other, and when we came to one low-lying stretch with two culverts it didn't look so good. I offered to take the wheel again, tactlessly, and was treated with the scorn I deserved. Sure enough, there we were with the rain pouring down, sogged and stuck, like a piece of toast in a plate of soup.

'This,' murmured Dennis, 'is the finish.'

'Horse feathers,' I said, peeling off shoes and stockings again. 'Gimme a go.' I shifted over into the driving seat and began to give the car some choke to see if I could dry out the plugs. Very often they will dry themselves if you leave them alone to steam.

Behind us, in the pouring rain, a big red truck was coming up. Of course, being much higher built, it had just surged through the spreading stream. It was a red International and as it drew up a voice yelled, 'You're not stuck, mate, you're just panic-stricken.' I knew that raucous, insulting voice and wound the window down. I was as mad as a hornet to think that he had to come along just at that particular time. I had shaken myself free of Blaze with dignity and just that aloof indifference that I felt the situation demanded, and he had to come pounding through the floods to make me look a silly.

Not only was Blaze peering down at us with a grin, but with him in the truck was old man Muirden, and a girl. I stepped out into the road. Of course Blaze hadn't expected that that plushy-looking car contained the Herricks and the Hertz family.

'Thought you were in Tembucca,' I said.

'Bloody lucky for you I'm not. Daphne, this is Mallee.'

I shook hands with Horace Muirden and asked after his leg, while Blaze examined the Parent's car.

'I thought Blaze said,' Daphne's voice commented to old Muirden, ' that you couldn't tell Miss Herrick from a man. *I* could tell her from a man.' She inspected my wet green dress.

'Well, you won't be able to,' I replied, 'just as soon as I get some real clothes out of the car.' I walked round to the front of Queen Wilhelmina where Blaze was peering rather admiringly under the bonnet.

'Start her up, Dennis,' he ordered. 'Well, mug,' he said to me, 'I suppose you were taking the kids for a picnic?'

I didn't bite. Let him find out where we were going if he thought he was so clever. I wasn't returning to Nithering whatever happened. Ordinarily I would have launched out in a long explanation of how we came to be there, but I was annoyed. 'Anything up with her?'

'Pistons,' Blaze said provokingly. 'They knock.' I ground my teeth and climbed into the car.

'We'll tow you through the worst bits, Dennis,' Blaze decided. He lashed his tow-rope to the front of Wilhelmina, and in that undignified fashion we proceeded towards Ombra.

When we reached Ombra the whole force from the great barracks on the high land was out sandbagging the banks of the Curran. The river was creeping up behind them through drains and billabongs. Old Muirden and Blaze conferred together.

'We won't get through to Nithering now,' Blaze said. 'The bridge on the other side of the town will be too deep under. This must have come down in the last few hours. We'd better leave Dennis's outsize buggy up here.'

'We'll put up at one of the hotels,' Dennis announced.

'Suit yourself. You'd better hop up on the back of the truck.'

Fay and the kids went in front with Daphne, and Dennis gracefully inserted himself in with them. Horace and I climbed up on a pile of tarpaulins, leaving the Parent's new car looking pathetic, locked and empty, by the roadside. It was an ominous start for Wilhelmina. If I had known how often that sumptuous fat car was to strand or betray us or wallow in sand and water, I would have abandoned her forever there and then.

Old Muirden told me his leg was quite healed now. He had insisted on coming to Nithering even if the road was, as he said, 'a bit tacky'. He wanted to be there when Blaze moved those bees, so he could tell him what to do. The old chap was wresting the business away from his loving son in his own forthright fashion. 'Knew he'd have a bust-up with Joe,' he growled to me. 'Wouldn't be the first time.' He plied me with questions about how much honey we had taken off, how many neucs we had. We jolted into the deserted main street of Ombra and stopped at the first hotel. That hotel was full up and so were all the others. Mavis was the obvious victim.

'Well, I thought I might be seeing you, Gert,' was Mavis's greeting. 'There are fifteen people in the top storey and one Primus stove. Take the kids up and then you can help me shift books. This is going to be lovely.'

I changed into some shorts and a pullover in her bathroom. The water was only in the back garden, but by the time Blaze had carried our goods and chattels up to the top floor of that old bank building the water was up to the back doorstep.

Blaze went out scouting for food and got himself cut off. He slept in the truck on a patch of high ground that night. The caretaker, who lived in the top flat with her son and daughter-in-law and the baby, started everyone peeling potatoes. They had a sack of potatoes which ought to last until the water went down.

It was a foot deep in Mavis's kitchen when we stopped to snatch a meal. There were kids and mothers everywhere upstairs. Nobody worried about Blaze, least of all this girl Daphne with whom I shared potatoes and sardines on the stairs. One of the sights I most enjoyed on that trip was Dennis Oberon Herrick drearily peeling potatoes in that camp of refugees. The water was now running three feet down the main street, and the people who had taken shelter in the Town Hall opposite waved and shouted to us, and exchanged news with the hotel further down the road. They were improvising a track across the roof-tops and taking everything with a mixture of anxiety and hilarity.

'Won't be more than a day or so,' I apologised to Daphne, as we sat in the gloom on the staircase, surrounded by books.

'I spent a whole night once on the roof in Tembucca,' Daphne said. 'Dadda got swept into a tree.'

It struck me she had served the right apprenticeship for marrying Blaze Muirden. She was a small dark girl with silver rings in her ears, and a charm bracelet with everything on it but a miniature kitchen stove. Now I cannot bear metal on my skin, and that charm bracelet fascinated me. It had a silver windmill and a silver elephant, birds, small animals, little men. The children thought it was wonderful. Daphne said she collected ornaments for her charm bracelet, and some had come from Japan and some from Europe and America.

She was a definite girl. Every movement she made was quick and exact. She was a telephone switch girl in Tembucca. Knowing how apiarists are always ringing each other up and flirting with the switch girl while they wait for their long-distance connection, I could see how she must have first fallen into Blaze's clutches. Her voice was charming. She was not plump, but her curves were very taking. She probably danced like a feather. She had the temper of a cyclone when roused and her dark eyes snapped and sparkled. Holidays had been due to her and there seemed no reason why she should not pay a flying visit to Nithering with Blaze and Horace Muirden.

I approved of Daphne. She seemed to me the right mate for Blaze. She could stand up for herself and was no meek dove to let him bully her. Of course she quite naturally suspected me of tampering with her property, and was ready, at first, to take me apart. In her place I would have felt the same. She was a girl of character. There is a curious unspoken agreement among women that masculine persons roving at large, but with a brand on them, must be returned to the owner. Until some private treaty is signed concerning the transfer or exchange of such movable property, any woman appropriating it becomes a dangerous outlaw and is given as short shrift by her comrades as a horse-stealer would be in a camp of horsemen.

By the time we bedded down for the night on the top landing with Fay and the kids, Daphne and I were friendlier than most sisters are. We sat up, Mavis and Fay and Daphne and I, embayed in books. Fay and the kids had a mattress. Mavis and I and Daphne had a blanket each. The books cut off most of the draught, and it was peaceful enough save for two small babies crying in the front bedroom. Our forces had been augmented by another family splashing in, so there were twenty-one people, counting children and not counting babies, in that top flat. The sewerage system was holding out nobly and we shared our cigarettes.

In the darkness — the electric light had failed — you could hear a faint lapping noise from the flood waters downstairs. It was chilly, and Daphne and I sat back to back with our blankets wrapped round us. I had on my lumber jacket and woollen socks and, of course, my old boiler suit.

'Well, Gert,' Mavis said cheerfully, 'I stopped worrying when we got the radiogram upstairs. The books are safe and if the frig has to be repaired again, the council has to pay for it. I wonder what happened to your young friend Blaze?'

'Oh, he'll look after himself,' I said.

'He certainly will,' Daphne agreed.

'So you're the girl that's going to marry our Mr. Muirden,' Mavis purred. 'I wish you luck.'

'I don't know about that,' Daphne said sharply, stiffening her spine against mine. 'I'm not going to marry any bee-keeper.'

'Apiarist,' I corrected.

'Bee-keeper. You know Hilda Connelly? She waited seven years to marry Fred Connelly, and look at the life Hilda leads. A caravan! And it's worse if you stay home. Remember I live in Tembucca and there's twenty families there whose men talk nothing but bees. Bees! I hate them!' Daphne shook her head firmly.

'Well, that's a bad look-out,' I said disappointedly. I had it all arranged in my mind that I was going to be godmother to Daphne's first daughter. 'Couldn't you rescind that? After all, you're engaged to him, aren't you?'

'Off and on,' Daphne said bitterly.

Fay rose up from under her blanket and adjusted Bidgee, who had sprawled across his brother. 'I wouldn't mind marrying a bee-keeper,' she said wistfully, 'if I really liked him. You'd be moving about, not stuck in one place.'

'That's all you know,' Daphne said sharply. 'You're stuck in some clearing with nothing to do for weeks at a stretch, no one to talk to but men. Nowhere to go. Oh, I know *all* about it. Why, Hilda's my mother's cousin.'

The Ways and Means Committee for Marrying Bee-keepers was really launched.

'And then,' Daphne went on, ominously, 'look at the way they go on if you let them out of your sight. And home they come with their dirty clothes done up in a bundle for you to wash, spoiling the kids and making work and then off again into the blue. No, thank you. I like to know where my husband *is*. I like to think he'll be in to his dinner at the proper time. Victor,' she paused, 'Victor works at the bank. He's a boy who saves his money. And what is more, he is *there*. Tennis on Saturday afternoon, church on Sunday. He sings tenor in the Presbyterian choir. I'm a Presbyterian myself. There are plenty more men than Blaze Muirden, although he has this idea he is the lord of all he surveys.'

'There's only one thing you've overlooked,' I pointed out.

'What?' asked Daphne.

'You wouldn't have come all this way with Blaze and his old man,' I lowered my voice, because Horace Muirden was sleeping along the corridor between Dennis and the caretaker's son, 'you wouldn't be going to Nithering unless you took him seriously.'

'Well, it was my curiosity,' Daphne admitted. 'I wanted to see *you*.' I snorted incredulously. 'Yes, I did, and now that I've seen you I think it'll be much better if you have him.'

'I don't want him,' I said, raising my voice. 'Wouldn't have him at any price.'

'Gert doesn't want him,' Mavis, the umpire, announced, in the tone of one calling the score.

'Ssh!' Fay exclaimed. 'Of course she doesn't want him. Why, he was sleeping with Vic Warren all the time he was at Nithering.'

'Oh, Fay,' I said reproachfully. That was so mean of Fay. I never would have mentioned a thing like that. Fay had some very feminine habits.

'I wouldn't be a bit surprised,' Daphne said. 'You see what I mean about bee-keepers?' Daphne pretended not to take any notice of that cat Fay, but she would take it out of Blaze Muirden. I don't suppose I had shared a conversation like that since my schooldays. 'Mallee likes bees,' Daphne contended. 'She really likes them. Why don't you marry Blaze, Mallee?'

'Mallee wouldn't marry any man who can't spell,' Mavis said coldly. 'And his grammar is appalling.'

'Mallee doesn't know anything about engines.' Daphne defended the subject of the committee's deliberations. 'Blaze says so. And she's a fool about money.'

Fay had been trying to edge back into the conversation. She felt that as the only married female present we should listen to her words of authority. 'Any man with a bad temper is a washout,' she declared. 'Look at poor Frank. I thought when I married him that he'd get better, but he didn't. I feel sorry he's dead. I think often and often that I ought to have been nicer to him, but I know if he was here we'd be quarrelling again. Why, Blaze Muirden and Mallee argued and bickered all the time, Daphne. You ought to have heard them.'

'Well, let's not say any more.' I curled down on the floorboards and settled a volume under my ear, testing it for size. It was a little too high so I chose another. The conversation seemed to me vulgar, embarrassing and quite without point.

'You leave those books alone, Gert,' Mavis commanded.

I found two thin ones were better than one thick one and settled down, taking no notice. 'As soon as this excess of water removes itself,' I said peaceably, 'I am going north with the Parent. Don't worry, Daphne. You are stuck with old Blaze, so you'd better make the best of it. Victor!' I said scornfully. 'Ha! ha! to Victor and the choir! You will marry Blaze Muirden and he will have bees in the backyard and bees in the front garden and you will be *delighted* when he brings his clothes home for you to wash.'

He would tell her how to wash them, too, and complain about the way she raised the young and nag her and order her about. I didn't care. When the coast was clear of Muirdens, I would come back and move my sixty hives from Matt's place up to Queensland. I was beginning to like the sound of Brannigan's Bend. Probably silverleaf, blue-top and bimble-box on the claypans. I might pick up another hundred hives. There were plenty of bees along the border.

If I ran down through Texas, where there is good yellow-box country, I'd be sure to strike apiarists all the way. Yes, indeed, the future was promising. But I was sour about Fay. She lay there telling Daphne things about her fiancé that must have made his ears burn. I was shocked at her. No reticence! Good taste alone should have kept her silent. I blamed Daphne for listening. She should have shut Fay up.

'Move over, Gert.' Mavis distributed her golf-player's carcass over the top landing. 'Remember, I'm counting on you to help move the books downstairs.' That was like Mavis. You never even shared a draught on the landing with her unless she found some way of evening the score.

I fell asleep with Mavis's elbow in my ribs and Blaze's affianced curled into my spine. What made me laugh was remembering Dennis's saying the previous day: 'And we will stay at *hotels*. No camping.' Of course, he would blame me for the flood. He would be quite sure I did it on purpose to spite him.

Chapter Twenty-two

JULIE explained later that Mars-opposition-Neptune always means violence associated with water, and that on the Thursday of the flood this interesting conjunction had taken place. But whether it was an adverse conjunction of planets or just the natural cussedness of things, I thought we would never get away. We would spend years in the top storey of that old bank building looking out on the same view of submerged houses. The gloom and chill settled into one's bones, the misery of a countryside paralysed and thinking in terms of debt, mortgage, repairs, fences and drowned stock.

The townsfolk of Ombra were insulted by this flood; they were outraged by it. Here they had the most expensive and best-publicized hydro-electric scheme in the country, great dams a-building almost on the town's doorstep, and just the same Ombra was flooded. Of course, Warnsfield down on the wide river-plain was used to it. Once every year, on an average, Warnsfield was submerged and hit the city headlines with illustrations of telegraph poles projecting from a sea of sullen grey water. But that was Warnsfield, and the people of Ombra felt a peculiar sense of injustice, although they knew this flood of theirs would go sweeping down on Warnsfield, adding deeper woe to that city's dejection.

As the water went down, and the main street of Ombra emerged in its abominations and filth, everyone, from the housewives who had just finished paying for some sodden lounge suite to the shopkeeper with ruined stock, was in a mood to blame someone. Dennis, as I knew he would, blamed me.

'It is a peculiar thing, Mallee,' he said bitterly, 'that events always match the people to whom they happen. Now, left to myself, I live a life of casual distinction and energetic sociability. Whenever I venture out with *you*, I find myself in something *stark*, some battle with the elements.'

I pointed out that if he had stayed in the city he might never have anything more stark than a bus strike, but that if he would go to Queensland nobody could blame me.

All the books on the lower shelves seemed to be reference volumes and encyclopaedias weighing a ton, and I had staggered up and down stairs carrying books until I was played out. The sooner we took to the road the better I would like it. But, of course, we had to wait until we were sure the road was open for traffic. From the radio reports, there were still people marooned on railway stations and roof tops, and large impolite holes had been torn in the great concrete highways. The water cared nothing for the Parent's appointment with an oil-well.

When we descended into Mavis's mud-caked flat, I saw the advantages of dark-brown wallpaper and woodwork. Scrubbing brushes were issued to all hands, and Dennis developed a toothache and had to look for a dentist reputed to live on a height of land over towards the hydro-electricity camp. Fay and the kids betook themselves to Aunt Jess's place. Fay had been worrying off and on about Mumma, and what this would do to Mumma's weak heart. The old lady found it tremendously stimulating and enjoyed every minute of it.

When Fay arrived Mumma was drinking tea with Blaze Muirden, who had camped the second night in

Aunt Jess's kitchen. Fay, thereupon, I discovered later, launched out and told Blaze how he had been auctioned off on the top landing with no bids. I thought I heard the receding flood murmuring 'Bloody women', but it must have been telepathy.

When old Muirden found that his hopeful son was within wading distance, he departed with Daphne. He shook me warmly by the hand that wasn't holding the scrubbing brush; Daphne kissed me on both cheeks. I promised falsely to call at Tembucca and meet Mrs. Muirden and the whole far-stretching clan of married Muirden sons and daughters. But I had no intention of doing so. Muirdens were not for me. Bees were my interest and not bees mixed with Muirdens. I had wanted to buy their hives and that had been complicated and criss-crossed. I had been quite willing to work the bees on shares. That position had become untenable. There was no use humbugging myself that the Muirdens and I could work together.

Blaze drove up to collect the spare effects Horace Muirden and Daphne had left. I went out and stood by the old red International in the evil-smelling street, in a grey, greasy sunlight that was as unlike real sunlight as my civil farewell was like the rude way I usually spoke to Blaze. The Parent had not returned from his quest for a dentist, but I knew he would pick up Wilhelmina on his way back. I slapped the old International, wistfully thinking it was probably the last time I would see that huge truck. I would never ride in it again.

'Good luck,' I said. 'Hope you take off plenty of honey.'

'I hate women,' Blaze said. 'I always have hated them. I don't know why they ever happened.'

'I rather agree with you that women are hateful. A great pity. Well, good luck, anyway.'

'And what's more, you're a quitter. You've left me in a hell of a jam.'

I raised my eyebrows. Mavis had come out on the front step of the library and beamed at us, so I couldn't, if I had wished, do more. 'So long,' I said. We did not even shake hands. The red truck roared off to pick up Horace and Daphne.

'I have found a bottle of sherry in the bottom of the cupboard,' Mavis announced. 'No use waiting for your Pa. You look as if a sherry would do you good.'

'Seriously, Mavis,' I told her, as she uncorked the sherry, 'what I am looking forward to is being a nice old lady, one of those humane old women with hands knotted round a crochet hook, who say, "Yes, my dear," and think their own thoughts. I shall have a stick with a silver knob and a pussy cat and I shall collect old china. Here's luck!'

'Just as long as you don't marry him,' Mavis warned me. 'Don't ever marry him, Gert, or I'll disown you.'

'Don't be bloody silly,' I said. 'You heard young Daphne the other night? That girl worships him. A splendid piece of face-saving on her part, but not convincing enough.'

I quite agreed with all the people, including Hilda, who had warned me that it was not possible to be friends with men. The mistake I had been making all my life is that I always thought you could. I like friends. I like being friends with men, but only a fool will go trying to do the impossible. No, men and women should live in separate worlds with the doors locked between them. Centuries of training are needed before men and women can be civilized to the stage where they can be friends. I don't mean equals. I don't care about who is better than whom. I mean friends.

Mavis and I drank two sherries and discussed flood

damage. The following morning the sun was once more a ghost in grey vapour, an unholy steam was rising from the sodden fields, waterlogged, but like something you would see from Ararat. There was that big pale dove, Wilhelmina, roosting in the gutter ready to take off, and I had only to assemble the Hertz family and negotiate some seven hundred miles to central Queensland.

There was nothing very eventful about the trip. Dennis allowed me to drive, saying he was too shaken by his sufferings at the dentist's and his sleepless nights with children crying in the top flat. He satisfied his longings to put up at hotels where he could expand to commercial travellers after dinner and occupy a single room down the corridor from the bath. Fay and I and the kids bedded down in one of those large chambers kept by self-respecting hotels for the stowage of families, accommodating six children with attendant parents if necessary.

The little boys behaved beautifully. Certainly Bidgee spilt a glass of water all over the table and the Parent's grey trousers, but that was an accident. Dennis said we stopped at every tree while one or other of the party made good the intake of lemonade and ice-creams. He fussed about the leatherwork, but I was able to prove it was his suitcase that was rubbing against it, not small feet in sandals. The more I saw of those two little boys, the better I loved them, and Fay — well, she was Fay. The presence of the Hertz family made the trip enjoyable. Blaze had been right to ask if I was taking the kids for a picnic. That was what it was for them. Bidgee was sometimes homesick and whimpered a little, but Fay would soothe him and cuddle him until he fell asleep.

We had to go slowly because the roads were in one hell of a mess. I was so dizzy from driving that at night I just went to bed after dinner, shut my eyes and watched mile after mile advance towards me through my eyelids. The last stretch was the worst. I had decided not to try to reach Brannigan's Bend by nightfall, but to do the final thirty miles early in the morning. I wanted to reach Caterpillar at sundown. There is a prodigality about Queensland hard to explain. The country is wider or bigger, or it seems to be so. The huge skies roll over unending miles of wonderful rich land, glossy with crops and grasses.

My own theory is that New South Wales is in the belt of eternal winds. It is blown on by every wind from the Antarctic and the Pacific and the desert. Maybe Brannigan's Bend was sheltered by the tremendous stretches of forest. Not forest that goes up and down at a tilt as the landscape did at Matt's place, but forest that seemed to be flat.

The main road was a level strip like a race track, mile after mile of perfect going, where Wilhelmina soared like a bird, smooth and superior. But as sunset was falling I came to a turn-off that said 'Stock Route to Caterpillar', a turn-off with perfect concrete, and without thinking I curved the car off the main road and up the stock route. 'Now why did you do that?' Dennis complained. In the middle of nowhere the concrete ended suddenly by the only house in sight. I got out and went over to interview a citizen who was peacefully sawing wood outside his solitary dwelling.

'Well, it might be a bit muddy,' he admitted. 'But you won't be able to get through on the main road at all.'

I found later that a deep, swift-flowing creek crossed the main road about half a mile beyond where we had turned off. 'Now there's your best way.' The man pointed across a swamp with two wheel tracks showing in the black mud.

The picturesque sunset was dying in the distance blood-red beyond the she-oaks, and the frogs were croaking among the reeds. 'Man came through there in a tractor this morning. Once you're over the Five-Mile Swamp you're on bitumen all the way to Caterpillar.' I thanked him, but I did not dare tell the Parent there were five miles of swamp.

The tyres went suck-suck in the black mud, and if we were stuck, there was no dry land to camp on. We would have to sit in the car all night. There were private tracks turning off to homesteads somewhere over that five-mile swamp, but I grimly kept my eye on the marks the tractor had made and followed them, paying no attention to Dennis's prophecies of doom. But before darkness fell we were out again on the bitumen and I drew a long breath of relief.

We spanked into Caterpillar, a clean, white-painted town with a butter factory and bougainvillaea over the verandas. The hotel was as clean and self-respecting as the other buildings in the main street.

Dennis, his destination almost attained, was jubilant. 'Well,' he said, 'you must admit, Mallee, that when you travel with *me* there is a difference. It is quite possible to maintain the decencies and yet get over the country. The thing to do is to decide where you will be at nightfall and make sure that the hotel is passable.'

Fay had hurried off to the post office. I had never known her move so rapidly. She had just left us sitting outside the hotel in the car and shot off into the gloom. A man came out of the hotel bar and lounged over to us. The little boys greeted him with rapture.

'I've been watching out for you,' he announced. 'Where's Fay?'

It was Joe Muirden. He helped to carry our bags in, and when Fay came hastening back he gave her a slow smile.

'Got your letter,' he told Fay. 'I've been hanging

about. Mallee's got that car in a hell of a muck. It's roaring like nobody's business.'

This flow of chatter from Joe was to cover his embarrassment. He was very busy moving in our gear and taking the car round to the yard behind and tossing the boys into the air and hugging them.

'So you didn't go into the navy, after all?' I asked wearily.

'Well, it doesn't look like it. Have some sense, Mallee. How would I be in the navy when I'm *here*?'

'That's true,' I admitted. 'Do you know, Joe, I'm glad to see you?' I was too. The strain and responsibility had all fallen away from me. There was good old Joe, on whose capable shoulders my troubles would be lightly borne.

Dennis, however, was disconcerted. He drew me aside. 'How does it come about,' he asked, 'that the first person we meet is young Muirden?'

'Fay,' I answered. 'She must have been writing to him all the time. I should have thought of that.'

Dennis sniffed. 'Somehow,' he said, 'I gained the impression that you were through with the Muirdens.'

'What gave you that idea?'

'I'm sensitive to atmosphere.'

Chapter Twenty-three

ON the drive up I had plenty of time to think. By deadening my ears to the monologue from the Parent on how important it was for him to make a success of this executive position, and ignoring a certain plaintiveness in Fay, and by yelling 'Take your ice-creamy hands off my neck' at intervals to Bidgee and Brian, I managed to preserve the vestiges of my reason, and spend long periods just driving and, as the Parent would have said, 'analysing the situation'.

The conclusion I arrived at was that I had made an unholy mess of my attempt to become an apiarist, and that it was my own fault. No one overcomes obstacles by ignoring them. I couldn't work bees without men. I couldn't get men to work with me on ordinary friendly terms, in isolated places, apparently, until I turned forty and looked like a horse, and that was too long to wait. To be a lady bee-keeper and putter around with a few hives as a hobby was not my ambition. I wanted to be a commercial apiarist with a big outfit.

What about old men? Not strong enough, and they would complain of the hard going and rough living. Mugs like Mongo were strong enough but inefficient. The obvious suggestion had been made by Daphne that I could marry into the game, but from all I heard of apiarists' wives they never came out of the kitchen. They stayed home with the children. As for marrying Blaze Muirden, I was not big enough fool for that. One could live with Blaze Muirden just as long as one didn't take him seriously or let his jibes get under the skin. Wherever he was Blaze would live in a whirl of quarrels and upsets and violence. I admired his vitality; he made me laugh, but he loved to nag and torment. He came under the fiery sign of the Scorpion, hard and brilliant and cruel, and the people of the Scorpion are sensitive to their own poison and sting themselves to death, whereas the people of the Poor Fish are given to deep unfaltering devoted friendship.

Although I laugh at Julie's astrological nonsense, a good deal of it has seeped into the cellars of my mind, so that I did not believe in any fixed, unalterable fate, but in a sparkling moving sea of invisible tides in which there was no accident but exquisite order. I had a hearty trust that whatever happened was good and fit for me. See how pat this journey with the Parent had fallen out? I could sit tranquilly in my mind as people sit quiet in church. But Blaze Muirden lived in the Diasmos, the flux and flow and undirected Chaos. The prayer that says, 'Lead us not into temptation,' means, in Greek, 'Lead us not into the Diasmos,' or as the poet put it, 'From the wheel and drift of Things, Deliver us, Good Lord.'

I determined to forget all about bees. If they were my right calling, they would come to me without any killing effort on my part. When Wilhelmina heaved herself over the last pothole and came to rest outside the hotel, I had my affairs sorted out. Then old Joe loomed out of the murk as unexpected as an elephant. Fay was lonely, terribly lonely, but I wondered whether she was the right partner for Joe. She would mother him, and the little boys were very fond of him. But her former state of domestic warfare, a mingling of antagonism and attraction with the fierce Hertz, made me doubt that

Joe was quite up to her weight as a life partner. However, that was their affair, not mine, and Joe made no concealment of his intentions to annex Fay.

Now that the Parent was in sight of Brannigan's Bend, he began to look more critically upon his entourage and wonder whether his arrival with a pack of women and children might not spoil the dignity of the occasion. The leading citizens of Caterpillar all had shares and expectations in that oil-well, and soon after breakfast, word having drifted round that the big oil magnate was among them, the mayor, who was also the owner of the cordial factory, called to offer Dennis rights of divot and fairway on the local golf course. So Dennis decided to drive out to Brannigan's Bend with the mayor, leaving his feminine followers at the hotel.

'And just one thing, Mallee,' he said, before he went off. 'I don't want all the riggers and drillers calling you by your Christian name. You're always too chummy with the help — look at that oaf, Mongo. Far too familiar.'

'Since when have you developed into a haughty hidalgo? You used to be a good mixer yourself. I⁺ was part of your charm.'

'That's all very well for a man. It's different for a woman.'

This annoyed me. 'How did you know that one of my great dreams was to lasso myself a beautiful big rigger and have him for my own?' For a moment the Parent believed me and was quite panic-stricken. 'Anyway, suit yourself, my fine-feathered friend. I'll stay so far away from your oil-well that I won't hear it clanking in the distance.'

The Parent was nervous about his first interview with the two men who controlled operations at Brannigan's Bend. One was the foreman, or chief oil plumber, Mel

Staines, who was supposed to see that the well was bored; and the other, Hasselfors, was the office manager. But as neither Staines nor Hasselfors would speak to the other, and nobody could sack them, the work had come almost to a standstill, each man blaming the opposition. Staines had all the men on his side and Hasselfors had a laboratory with an assistant who didn't do much except give him moral support.

Although I try not to dislike people on sight, I felt, when I met Hasselfors later, that I would make an exception in his case. He had long yellow teeth always smiling, and yellow-brown eyes which he rolled about, and his face always seemed to be opening and shutting and never still, until it reminded you more of a muddy pool than a face.

The Parent's job was to make peace between Staines and Hasselfors and to see the work went forward. Staines was too valuable to be dismissed. Hasselfors had been taken over with some stock from the parent company, and was well entrenched and had the ear of the directors. 'It all depends on my Report,' the Parent said unhappily, as I carefully brushed him down and picked fluffs off him and sponged a spot on his tie.

'Well, off you go,' I said, having recovered my good humour, and I went to change into my old slacks and shirt and lounge in the sunny backyard with Joe.

Fay was doing some washing, hanging out small-boy pants. Bidgee and Brian were contemplating the turkeys in the fowl run and there was a smell of cooking from the kitchen. The maids were calling to each other from the upstairs bedroom, and that peace which can best be enjoyed in a little country hotel was all about us as we sat on the tankstand, smoking cigarettes.

'Give me the news, Joe,' I commanded. It was always harder to make Joe talk than to clear a blocked drain. He contemplated the pleasant rear view of Fay stretching up the line on tiptoe. She had clothes pegs in her mouth, and she half turned and looked at us. Even with clothes pegs in her mouth Fay looked ornamental. Joe and Fay had sat on the darkened upper veranda the night before, talking in low voices for hours after the boys and I were in bed. So Joe knew everything that had happened at Nithering. I bet Fay had given him a vindictive account of Blaze's doings. As Blaze's future sister-in-law she would be running true to form. Give her time and she would have a stand-up fight with the whole Muirden family.

'How did you know to wait at this hotel, Joe?' I asked, trying another tack.

'I figured Dennis wouldn't pass it up. There's a mean sort of blood-house at Brannigan's Bend, but this is the last real hotel.'

'You must be in the money to stay at hotels.'

'Only drove in from where I'm camped yesterday afternoon.'

I was exasperated by his reticence. Surely he had given Fay a better account of himself. She finished pegging out the washing and came to sit close to Joe. She was wearing a blue dress that was a little tight on her, or else she'd been putting on weight. Joe looked at her, lost and dreaming, and I didn't like to interrupt his thoughts. In fact I felt like a third party and decided to steal tactfully away.

'Siddown, Mallee.' Joe roused himself as I rose to join the two boys. 'Fay and I want to talk to you.' He had evidently been turning over in his mind what he wanted to say. I sat down again and he began to talk.

Joe's attempt to join the navy had been spoiled by a friend — the one who kept a laundry where Blaze used to work. He took Joe to a chiropractor who found he had a slipped disc in his spine. No wonder poor old Joe had complained of an ache in his neck. He had gone working on with a slipped disc, and it must have been agonizing. Anyway, this quack had found it out and went to work on him. By the time he had pushed Joe's neck-bone into place, the urge for deep water had left him.

'So I thought I'd look Uncle Col up,' Joe continued. 'He's at Boona, just the other side of the border. You remember, Mallee, when we were at Nithering we were talking of moving up into the silver-leaf ironbark? Col has a hundred hives at Boona and about seventy scattered about, some on stringy-bark over towards this range.' He began drawing a map of the country with a stick in the dirt. 'Here's where we are. Broadleaf iron-bark on the ridges, gums on the flats along the creeks. Over here — say, thirty miles — there's a flat, puggy class of soil with grey box, and stony ridges with desert gum, wattles and stringy-bark. South, there's a better class of box on the flats, narrow-leaf ironbark on sandy loam, stunted ironbark on the foothills. Now, down over the border where Col is, you come into better country with forests of silver-leaf.'

I wasn't really listening to him as he laboriously listed the results of his wanderings and searchings. He was making his own way towards what he wanted to say by back-tracks and by-ways just as he would drive across the country.

'Where are you camped?' I interrupted.

'At Brannigan's Bend, just near the first timber mill on the creek. Dennis's oil show is out a few miles the other side and, my God, wait till you see it.'

'Bad as that, is it? I thought it would be.'

'Couldn't be worse. Look, are you going to let me tell you, or do you keep cutting in?'

Somehow I knew what was coming. Bees. Where Joe was there would be always bees. A deep contentment filled me.

'Now you may not have heard me mention Uncle Col.' Joe hesitated. 'He and Blaze never hit it off somehow. Funny, when you think of it.'

'I don't think that's so funny,' Fay said sharply.

'Oh, Blaze is all right,' Joe said tolerantly. 'Gets on your works at times, but you've just got to leave him alone and he'll come round. Well, anyway, there was a bit of a bicker and Col quit.'

I remembered that I had heard about this uncle from Blaze who, when he wanted to illustrate how lazy anyone could be, would say, 'Like Col the Zombie, walking in his sleep.'

'Mind you,' Joe went on, 'I don't say Dad and Blaze were wrong. Col wanted to use carbolic acid. Said that all this business of brushing bees off the comb was too much trouble. Dad said carbolic acid spoilt the taste of the honey. Col said it didn't. With carbolic, you only need some sacking pasted inside, say, fifty lids, sprinkle a weak solution of carbolic and water on the sacking and put the lids on the hives. The fumes drive the bees down out of the super into an empty box you put underneath. You can lift off your frames without a bee on them. One man can do the work of three with carbolic. They're all using it now.' He sighed and shook his head.

I rubbed my forehead. There seemed to be some fatality about it. Here was another Muirden with bees when I had come clean across New South Wales to get away from them.

'This is the point,' Joe said, bending forward. 'Col never stays interested for long in any one thing. First, it's fowls, then it's fruit trees. D'you know what he's had me doing? No, I won't tell you. I'll let him tell

you himself.' He laughed. 'You wouldn't believe it. **Bats!** Mongo was working for him too.'

I thought he was referring to his uncle when he said 'bats', but I found later that Uncle Col had obtained mining rights over an underground cave and had been digging out and vending the bat guano. He had Joe and Mongo digging and moiling underground, bringing up the fine fertile white dust. But Joe and Mongo had grown tired of working in those dark caves while Uncle Col drove round persuading farmers to buy bat dung. Joe had taken a holiday and, borrowing an old truck, had come to Caterpillar to meet Fay. He said he still sneezed every time he thought of those caves, and Mongo was fluttering like a bat.

'Now here's the point,' Joe said. This was about the third time he said he was coming to the point without doing more than circle round it. Fay took the words out of his mouth.

'If you want to buy bees, Mallee, Joe will work in with you half shares. His Uncle Col has seventy hives he wants to sell and an extracting house and gear. He never uses them because he won't travel his bees.'

I caught my breath. 'What about Mongo?'

'Mongo 'ud come like a shot. I know where there's another hundred hives going for a song. The postmistress at Brannigan's Bend — her father died — he had a hundred hives there and they'll be no good to anyone in twelve months. I could get them for a pound a hive.'

'There's a catch in it, Joe. I'll have to stay and keep an eye on the Parent. You know that's why I came up here.'

Joe said reasonably, 'Mongo and I could carry on by ourselves, Mallee. We just haven't the finance.'

Fay called the boys and the committee of ways and means drifted over to the old bomb Joe had borrowed.

'We'll take a look round,' Joe said as we bumped out the gate. In my mind I was fitting together a jigsaw puzzle of hives. Seventy, Col Muirden would sell; say, three pounds a hive. Sixty I had down at Nithering needing to be moved. A hundred at Brannigan's Bend. The five-hundred-pound cheque I had back from Dennis would cover it all, if the cheque was not a dud. 'Joe,' I said, as we jolted out of town, 'we'll need a truck.' I was sitting in the back seat so that Fay and the boys could sit with Joe. Bidgee was perched on his knee helping to drive the car. I could see the tracks where Wilhelmina had ploughed through the creek. We didn't have any trouble, because this old teetery car was high up with plenty of clearance.

'What's up with the Roaring Ruin?' Joe shouted.

'I didn't think she'd make it. Besides I told Nobby I was only going to Nithering in her.'

'There's no need to lean over backwards being straight,' Joe growled. I think he had been counting on the Ruin. However, he decided it wouldn't be hard to find a bigger and better truck in Caterpillar.

As the smoke-coloured forests eddied past us we shouted to each other about trucks. Six months ago I would have been bored by a long dreary analysis of the different makes, their performances and petrol consumption. Now I listened with an eagerness and interest that matched Joe's own. I was surprised to find how well Fay fitted in. We were the makings of a team, Fay and Joe and I. You could feel us dovetailing our minds and sentiments. There was none of the exasperation you felt with Blaze.

'It's a good thing we found Joe, isn't it, Mum?' Brian observed, and added ungratefully, 'Mr. Herrick said no more ice-creams in his car.'

The forest had that elusive, innocent-seeming sameness that made you feel like an insect in the grass roots. It was all cut and carved into squares by firebreaks, like a chessboard, but it was just as easy to lose yourself on those squares as it would be to go round in circles. For weeks I would drive off and stumble on some landmark like a broken timber jinker or an old engine boiler just where I least expected it.

Brannigan's Bend was a scattering of tents and wooden huts and barracks among the trees. The road snaked through the dense forest right up to the houses and the sawdust pile. There was a railway track along which a small engine shunted trucks to be stacked with lumber at the mills. Just before you came to the creek there was a U-shaped bulge of land with the creek round three sides of it. Joe had his camp there in a clearing by an abandoned hut from which he had cleaned out the tins and broken bottles.

The hut had a mud floor and a tiny veranda with a tin roof. Fay's eyes widened with the glance of a woman who is about to make a home. Just across the creek was the high yellow sawdust pile, and you could hear the whine of the saws, the toot of the whistle for knock-off time, and the thumping jarring squealing of trucks on the rail. But there was one house I knew must be the post office. In the paddock behind it there were white rows of hives ranked neatly, and I counted them as though I was counting my heart-beats. They made my fingertips tingle and my lungs expand. I suppose a painter feels like that when he smells oil paints or a sailor when he sights the sea.

'Bees,' Bidgee said, pointing his finger and tugging at my slacks. 'Bees, Mallee.'

Chapter Twenty-four

I T was at Brannigan's Bend that I finally came to grips with the Parent and realized that my egotism was at long last just as strong as his. Most of my life I had regarded Dennis as a minor deity who condescended to dwell among us; and his moods were the weather of the working day. How often had he deplored his lack of a son, and how wistfully had I realized when I was a child that Dennis's kindness to me and little Anita was no consolation for the disappointment that we were indubitably female.

I had propitiated him by doing my best to lighten his work. Under a microscope you can see the indeterminate amoeba flowing round some small, swift, darting object and absorbing it, putting out pseudopodia as tenuous as cloud to engulf the free-swimming morsel. That was Dennis. He wrapped his charm round you, and you found you had no life of your own, you were just part of Dennis. Emotional tension was the medium in which he moved and breathed. It was so hard not to be sucked in and exhausted by his belief that his affairs must be the sole concern of what Julie would call his 'dear ones' that he made me more matter-of-fact in sheer self-defence than I might otherwise have been, harder, and more critical.

His nervous breakdown had come just as I was making my break for freedom, and, although it was inconvenient, I had taken him with me to get him off Julie's and Anita's hands. He had returned, braced from his hard living, not to the kind of work he could do, handling dramatic situations and producing soap opera, but resolute to show me that he was the big man of affairs. I am quite sure that bringing me to Queensland was not solely prompted by the idea that I would be useful; he just hauled me along at his chariot wheel.

Now I had to face telling him that I was buying a hundred hives and a large green Commer truck that Joe had decided was a bargain at four hundred pounds. It had done twenty thousand miles, was registered for the next twelve months, all new tyres, and it had a table top. Joe and I went to have a look at it and played a kind of poker with the garage owner who had it for sale. I would have put down my money and driven the thing away, but Joe despised such unorthodox procedure. We had to walk away despising the truck, to show that we were not interested. Then we would come back next day and beat the owner down another twenty pounds. I pointed out to Joe that the time we were wasting was probably worth twenty pounds if you took in our hotel bill and paid us for our labour.

'That's not the point, Mallee,' Joe said wisely. 'If you're impatient about one thing, you're impatient about others. There's all the time in the world.'

Joe was right. You had to let him go his own pace, which was that of something fitted with caterpillar treads.

Dennis was flashing to and fro digging up the dust on the road, and he had, so he said, located 'a quaint little inn' only three miles from the oil bore. The 'quaint little inn' was what Joe had called 'a mean kind of blood-house at Brannigan's Bend'. Joe said that the barmaid, Patsy, put him off his beer by lifting up her stomach and resting it on the bar before asking what he wanted to drink. She was a fat, pig-faced wench with a voice like the sawmill whistle, but not so musical.

The son of the house, Eric, had the shakes and went around red-eyed and nearly weeping, because Patsy wouldn't let him behind the bar, so he had to hang about waiting for someone to shout for him. The mother was a grey woman, bent with work and arthritis, so Patsy bossed the show. Inside, the pub stank of paint because brother Eric had just been bullied into painting it, or rather slapping on a coat of chocolate or mud-coloured mess. I have been abused for painting bee boxes much better than Eric painted that hotel.

The windows wouldn't lift because they had been painted to the frames. The doors had to be burst open by force because Eric had painted them to the door frames. And the clientèle of the hotel justified Patsy's take-it-and-get-out attitude. I understand that in Brannigan's Bend there was a logger, a New Australian, who was the nearest thing they had to a teetotaller because he drank only a quart of wine a day. Other well-thought-of citizens allowed themselves a little more latitude and three quarts of beer was average.

I asked Dennis what had become of the superintendent's residence about which I had heard so much. Dennis explained that Hasselfors and his wife and children had taken possession of that. 'Well, can't you boot them out?' I asked callously. 'Hasselfors seems a total dead loss anyway.'

Dennis reiterated his request for me to keep my nose out of his oilfield. Mrs. Hasselfors, he said stiffly, was expecting an addition to the family. How could you sack a man whose wife was about to present him with a fourth child? Anyway if the hotel wasn't good enough for me, it was good enough for Dennis Oberon Herrick. It was good enough for Mel Staines, an engineer, who had worked on oil shows all over the world. There were only barracks for the men at the field and the men complained about them. They had to line up in a queue for a shower. The latrines alone, Dennis said darkly, were enough to explain the unsatisfactory state of affairs on that field.

'Well, don't worry about us, Dennis,' I said, knowing full well that he wasn't worrying about us. 'We'll be away for a couple of weeks visiting a Muirden uncle, and if you haven't brought in a gusher by the time we get back . . .'

'It has to be brought in under control,' Dennis explained seriously. 'If the oil came in in a gusher, Mel Staines would get the sack.' Anyway, he went on gloomily, there was little chance of a gusher yet. They had lost the drill-head down the hole and had been fishing for it for months.

'Why don't they just leave the drill down there and dig another hole?' I asked.

Dennis glared at me, contemptuous, and sniffed knowing that they might be driven to do that very thing. 'Mallee, you know nothing about the technical side. You have always done your best to thwart and obstruct my efforts to break into the game. You would have me writing scripts — damned hack to the end of my days — on a pittance.'

'All I was trying to say was that we'll be camping on Cut-throat Creek just below the Bend when we come back.'

'Camping?' Dennis cried. 'I can't have you camping.' His idea was that I could attend to the correspondence in the dusty shed that served as an office on the field, and be at the pub in the evening with a sympathetic ear when he could tell me of the trials of the day. For a man who wailed so much about his lack of a son, Dennis was very dependent upon female companionship. He

asked suspicious questions about this trip to Boona to see
Uncle Col. 'By the way,' he said carelessly, 'could you
let me have that cheque back?'

'What about all the money you made from Mrs.
Prothero?'

'Oh, that went into Northern Exploitations.' Dennis
was surprised that I should even ask the question. 'Apart
from what Julie seized, I'll be in deep water if this well
doesn't come good.'

I told him I had spent the five hundred on the Commer
truck and the postmistress's hives.

'That truck! I thought it belonged to Joe.'

'Well, it doesn't. It belongs to me.'

'Bees!' groaned Dennis. 'I've *had* bees. I hate the damn
things.'

'If you knew how grateful I am to you, Parent, for
bringing me here among all this splendid silverleaf and
blue-top! We might never have found it but for you.'

'Mallee,' said the Parent, 'I am not going to have a
pack of tough bee-herders up here and my daughter
among them. I couldn't stand it. Just at the time when
I am counting on you for a little moral support, you go off
wallowing in squalor and apiarism. I've a position to
keep up. I'm the boss here. I'm not going to have the
men talking behind my back about my daughter camped
with a lot of hoboes. You *must* — you really must realize
that this means everything to me.' He smiled at me
winningly, the old charm turned on like a searchlight.
'My dear girl, I've always been able to rely on you.
You're staunch — you're loyal. You always have been.'

'Well, I'm not any longer,' I said firmly, making an
effort to break away from the amoeba. 'Sorry, Dennis.
I'll clean up the correspondence. I'll do what I can to
help, but I've got my own life to live just as much as you
have.'

We looked at each other in silence. It was a crisis and we both knew it. I had been firm before when I refused to lend Dennis money to put into oil, but he always managed to make me feel just as mean and low then as I did now.

The astute old amoeba withdrew his tentacles. 'Just what do you intend to do?' he asked pleasantly.

I fell for it, and eagerly told him that Joe thought so well of the forest that he was booking sites with the Forestry Office in Caterpillar. 'But, of course, we have to get the permission of the grazier who leases it for his cattle. That's the rule here. He's a man called Studwell who thinks he owns the earth anyway, so we'll have to butter him up a bit.'

'Indeed,' the Parent said, smiling. His first move was to locate this Studwell and impress him, over a few drinks, with his importance as an oil executive. He explained that a set of no-good apiarists had planned to descend on his forest. Studwell, who had blood pressure anyway, went purple in the face and swore that our bees would come into Settunga Forest over his dead body. He had already promised a Queensland apiarist called Ken Musselton the sites in Settunga, and as soon as he sent a wire to Musselton he would be up there with flame issuing from his ears.

Queensland apiarists resent their fellows from New South Wales making forays over the border. Studwell, a typical cattleman, resented the idea of anyone so much as breathing in that forest without his permission.

But we went gaily ahead making our arrangements to go down to Boona, though Joe wondered why he was never able to find the cattleman Studwell at home.

Dennis made one more attempt to flow round me. He drove me out to that oil show and did his winsome best to arouse my enthusiasm. That oilfield looked about as hopeless as the Brannigan's Bend Hotel, but not so moist and prosperous. Just a bare stretch of baked clay, a wide clearing in the scrub with the big steel rig and the huddle of machine shops and engines at its base. The living quarters were over towards the forest, and the superintendent's house stood in splendid isolation with a bed of red geraniums in front.

Hasselfors was the optimist of the outfit. He had a house, an easy job and a good salary, and while the work kept loitering along all these pleasant things continued. He had a line of humour that would raise your hair. Living among bee cockies accustoms anyone to off-colour stories, but Hasselfors could leave Fred Connelly standing in the road. Of course, he covered his natural bent with politeness and the hard living conditions for his poor wife who detested the forest. He made it sound as though he was doing Northern Exploitations a favour by staying there.

Dennis had not given up hope. He said privately to me that he only had to make Hasselfors and Staines pull together, get the rig in operation, fish up the drill and everything would be plain sailing. Naturally, to get Staines and Hasselfors to work together he had to drink with both of them; and it was a question which would set in first, goodwill between the manager and the engineer, or ulcers in the Parent.

Mel Staines, too, complained about that forest. He was a big Canadian with a cleft chin and a grim expression. 'I'm used to sand, Miss Herrick,' he told me. 'Sure, there's oil gas here because they tapped it. Had to plug the hole because they didn't know what to do with it, and were afraid of setting the hull forest on fire. The oil sands are there, but if there's only gas when we bottom, that means we have to set up a cracking plant, which is mighty expensive, to turn the stuff into petrol.'

The Honey Flow

If Mel Staines had had his way, he wouldn't be putting a hole down there at all. Settunga Forest with its rolling monotony of trees was not his kind of country and it got on his nerves. Give him a desert, and he knew where he was, but to be crowded with trees was, to him, like having someone breathing down his neck while he worked.

'There's nothing much to an oil show,' he told me, indifferently, when I tried to extract some information. 'We're down about one thousand seven hundred and we ought to bottom at three thousand. But we haven't skilled men. Everything depends on that and, of course, your mud. If the density of mud is incorrect nearest the hole, your hole will collapse and the drillpipe is stuck. And if you're coming into the gas zone and the weight of mud is incorrect, you're likely to blow out. But apart from that' — he waved one hand — 'nothing to it. You jack up, level off, raise the mast, and the machines do the rest.'

Pumps and rotary tables and cores of grey mud for testing may be fascinating to people born under an earth sign, and I listened respectfully while Mel explained why the rig is made a certain height to take the weight and what tests you use on the core, packer test, production and perforation tests. They worked twenty-four hours in eight-hour shifts — when they were working. There was a tremendous overburden and no indication what the underlying strata were like except the geologists' guess, which was as good as mine.

Mel Staines's ruling passion was mud under pressure, eight hundred pounds to the square inch, mud that sifted into oil sands and might take weeks of washing and analysis. They had a gun that fired armour-piercing bullets through the casing when they reached the gas sands. Somewhere down there was the shoreline of an ancient sea with the minute organisms that had died and become oil or gas. They could miss it by feet. Trying to thread a needle in boxing gloves in the dark was easy by comparison.

'Wonderful, isn't it?' the Parent said modestly. He still hoped I might develop a vocation for oil. 'If I had had a son . . .' he began.

I almost snarled at him. 'Well, you haven't a son, thank God. If you had and he took after you, he'd be a prize blister. We wound up Mrs. Prothero, remember? So save your sobs.' As usual I felt mean as though I had wronged the poor amoeba when it tried to swallow me.

Joe was dissatisfied with me too. It worried him that I had insisted on letting Fred Connelly know that Settunga Forest was so well-budded. I had always promised myself I would do Fred a good turn some day, after the way he had toiled over the Roaring Ruin when we were down at Pilliga.

'Mallee, I keep telling you Fred wouldn't have the money for a big move. He didn't do as well as we did at Nithering. The cold caught him soon after he came. There isn't a bank will trust him after the way he's messed about juggling overdrafts. He can't get credit. He's as near sunk as makes no difference. And if he did come up here, we'd have Hilda giving us all hell.' This, of course, was Joe's real objection.

'I like Hilda,' Fay spoke up. 'And she's got those little boys.'

Privately, when I sent that telegram off to Fred, I had decided to offer him a loan. We either all struck it lucky or we went broke together.

'Fred can't keep his mouth shut,' Joe complained. 'Tell Fred and you tell the world.' But when he read the answer to my telegram, he just growled.

'Outbreak of American foul brood here,' Fred wired. 'All burning hives. Thanks for offer, Fred.'

You must have a clean bill of health to move hives, and the inspector would be at Tembucca if there was an outbreak of foul brood. I wondered if Horace and Blaze had moved the bees to Tembucca. American foul brood is one of the diseases that the apiarist dreads most. In its early stages it is hard to detect, and by the time it gets a hold the infected hives must be burned to prevent it spreading. The bees all die out in the hive and then other bees start to rob and catch the complaint and that is the end of your bees.

When I said goodbye to Dennis, I asked him to let me know by telegram if there was any news from Fred. 'Fred too?' Dennis commented. 'Why not invite all the old gang? What about Blaze? Isn't he coming? I thought you would like to have him. Don't tell me you had some kind of lover's tiff.'

That was from the man who said women were cats!

Chapter Twenty-five

I NEVER discovered whether Col Muirden was the genius or the discard of the Muirden family. He had interesting theories about honey sections, and had patented a contraption which would give you perfect sections of sealed comb, if you ever got a flow big enough to fill them. As soon as he heard about my difficulties in lifting bee boxes, his one good eye lit up — there was something wrong with the other one — and he began planning a mechanical hoist which could be wheeled like a trolley from place to place. It was a Heath-Robinson affair with a kind of iron spade which dug under the bottom board, levelled off and held the bee boxes on a small platform. Another spade arrangement of steel plate slid under the platform and jacked it up so that the bee boxes could be pushed off on to a truck. With that trolley — known later as Col's Curse — I could certainly move boxes and be sworn at for getting underfoot by people who were just picking them up in their arms and dumping them.

Col had a contempt for apiarists, and I never heard any-one, not even Blaze, so soundly curse the whole tribe for a 'half-baked set of weevil-gutted crawlers' — his own words. Men who ran a little store and couldn't make a success of it went off part-time bee-keeping. Others, he hinted darkly, were religious. Yet others wanted to get away from their wives.

Since the day when Col had tossed his brother Horace for first chance to propose to Elsie, he had never looked at another woman, and only proposed to three or four of them. If Col had won the toss and proposed first, I don't think it would have made any difference, except that Elsie might have taken to the scrub. Col looked like a man who should have found his ambition satisfied in embalming bodies, or catching spiders. He was a water diviner. In fact, he was a little uncanny.

He was crippled up with some kind of bone complaint which not even honey could cure, and he hated to have anyone sympathize with him. It made him angry. He lived in an unpainted wooden house which was pitifully clean. Ordinarily a morose man, with the worst temper of all the Muirdens, he would talk by the hour when he had someone interested. I was interested because I felt he might have been a better apiarist than any of them.

'You don't need a heap of bees,' he insisted. 'You need bees that are well looked after. And you don't need to move them once you find a place where there's a cycle of blossom — see what I mean?' He always said, 'See what I mean?' at the end of every speech. 'Now if a man has too many bees, he's got to keep moving around — see what I mean? They strip off every last skerrick of honey, and then wonder why their bees are poor. Like feeding a poddy calf skim milk — meanness, that's the answer. A hundred hives is enough for any man — if he looks after them.'

Col was a gnome and anything that could be mined fascinated him. He would go fossicking for sapphires, and he took me with him, driving over to an old field that was supposed to be worked out. He always had phenomenal luck. His collection of uncut sapphires would make your eyes open, and he kept them in a linen bag, and would spill them out carelessly on the table, taking one up and turning it to the light to show you the depth and how it would be when cut. I picked up one black sapphire which I still carry with me for luck.

Mongo distinguished himself by spilling a pan of hot fat on his ankle the day after we arrived at Boona, and was laid up and could hardly hobble. So Fay and I and the boys caught crayfish in the creek, or went fossicking with Col, while Joe busied himself rummaging out a complete trousseau of old iron, ropes, tins and spare boxes from Col's sheds.

The country around that rich, well-drained pocket where Col had his orchard was geologically very interesting. There must have been some meeting and twisting of strata, for in a space of miles the changes rang from the rich tobacco fields of Texas to the wild bushranger outcrop of savage hills broken and split and crumbled into splinters. The lazy life of fossicking in the sun suited me, and I lost my cough. Col Muirden hated hard work, but what Blaze said was laziness was really this bone complaint of Col's making his life a misery.

All over the country there are independent old men like Col or Matt or Nobby Wallace making do on the old-age pension, or managing from pride to support themselves without it, men who have been left behind from an age when they said exactly what they thought, and ranged where they pleased, from the Gulf to the Bight; but, now, what they thought no longer matters, and they give life a hard, amused glance as it passes them by.

Col was deeply interested in all we could tell him about the Parent's oil bore. When he and Joe had struck a price for the bees, the old extracting house, and the piles of equipment Col threw in as part of the deal, he suggested he might come back with us to Brannigan's Bend. This would save a second trip, as Joe could tow the extracting house behind the Commer loaded with the seventy-five hives. Fay and the kids could ride with him and Mongo.

I would go with Col in his truck loaded with all the spare gear.

No one was more anxious to reach Brannigan's Bend than Mongo. He did not think much of Col's inventions, particularly the flying fox for winding up tubs of guano from underground. He said digging bats' dung had turned his hair grey. He looked in the mirror and there it was — grey. But it washed out.

Col drove like all the Muirdens — one swerve away from heart failure. But he would pull the truck in to the side of the road to teach me how to judge different stages of bud. He talked of mineral deficiency and the way sap responded to the absorption, differences of clay and sand, how each class of soil had a different vegetation. He even tried to clear up my confusion over why the Forestry Department call a tree grey box and the apiarists call it gum-top box, and why there were sometimes three different names for the same tree. He had the apiarist's unholy love for what farmers call weeds, and would tell me about the virtues of African box thorn for brood-rearing, how you can have no better pollen than that from wild turnip.

'Of course, it's a curse to the cockies — it taints their milk. I almost caught a crack with a hoe from one joker when I worded him about cutting it on Her Majesty's highway. He told me it tainted his milk, and I told him by the look of him his milk was sour already.'

It was useful, Col explained, to run your tyres over weeds by the roadside because then they would carry seed to some part where the cockies thought they were rid of that weed. Come back in twelve months, and you had good pollen for the young bees; bull-thistle, Paterson's Curse, Mexican Poppy — Col spoke of them with approval that would earn him more than a crack with a hoe at a Graziers' Conference.

When I entered some of his information in the black notebook I always carried, he complained that I must keep it in my head. 'You should be able to go into new country, find out the rainfall for the past twelve months, take a look at the trees and predict what they'll do.'

I enjoyed listening, and Col enjoyed talking, so it was late afternoon when we sped into Caterpillar and pulled up in the main street to stretch our legs and drink a milk shake. Almost immediately we were met by a deputation headed by the mayor who owned the cordial factory and had made such a point of welcoming Dennis. The most excited member of the deputation was the stationmaster, a bald anxious man with a swollen eye. It seemed he had done his best to intercept Joe, but Joe had said to look for us as he had a load of bees and couldn't stop. From the way that deputation treated us as public enemies and criminals, I could see why Joe was in such a hurry.

'Those bees have been in the goods yard waiting for you for two days now,' the stationmaster snarled.

The big railway bogey was marked all over: 'Bees. Urgent. Deliver M. Herrick. Despatch Express. Handle with Care. F. Connelly.' Nobody wanted to handle them. They had chewed their way out and were working the cordial factory handy to the railway yard, falling into the syrup and drowning themselves, crawling over the sacks of sugar, menacing the men round the vats.

They were a pretty sight, sweeping up and down the station platform like gold rain, keeping it clear of intruders. We had our veils with us, and Col always carried a sack of fibrous wallboard which he claimed gave a better smoke than narrow-leaf ironbark. It was his 'own invention'. Also we had Col's Curse on the back of the truck, so I looked forward with pleasure to helping move those bee boxes.

But that deputation kept threatening us with legal proceedings and arrest. They were not grateful. The things the stationmaster said as we unloaded our gear in the goods yard to take those bees on the truck made us think better of offering him a tin of honey to quiet him. If anyone had offered him honey he might have spat in it.

Just as we were getting our first load out of Caterpillar towards Settunga Forest, we were stopped by Studwell, the cattleman. Someone must have rung him on the phone. 'These your bees?'

'They belong to a friend of ours.'

'Have to have permission to put them in the forest. I won't have it, d'ye hear? You can get to hell out of here with those bees.'

'Listen, Mr. Studwell,' I said. I had been preparing for this. '*I* own the only standing apiary in Settunga Forest. I've bought the postmistress's hives. By law, three miles around that apiary belongs to me. Nobody can bring bees in there without *my* permission. But if I want to bring in bees, you can't stop me. These are not migratory bees. They belong to my standing apiary.' I hoped he would not spot the name 'F. Connelly' on them. If he did, I would tell him I had bought them.

'You there!' Studwell bellowed at Mongo. 'These your bees?'

'Who, me?' Mongo shook his head vehemently. 'I only work for Miss Herrick.'

'And I'm just driving the truck,' Col said blandly. 'They're not my bees.'

Studwell looked nonplussed. 'We'll see about this,' he fumed. 'I've warned you. I've refused my permission. You're illegal. I promised the sites in Settunga to a friend of mine. He's on his way up from his camp.'

'Bringing his bees with him?' I asked. 'Don't let him put them within three miles of mine or we'll take him to court.'

Col let in the clutch and we went off leaving Studwell fuming in the road. It took us until after dark to move those bees, and Joe came back to help us. We just dumped them hastily, without clearing the sites, because we would be moving them again, either farther into the forest or, if Studwell had his way, right out of it.

We were all tired and looking forward to a hot meal, but when we reached the camp Fay was in a state of terror from two large drunks who had come down demanding a drink and who wouldn't go away. Every camp has some disadvantage, whether it is blowflies, black snakes or mosquitoes in football jerseys who come at you in a scrum and can suck the blood through a thick tarpaulin.

Our camp at Cut-throat was free of all these pests, but it had drunks. Someone must have circulated the rumour that it was a good place to sleep off the D.T.s. Fay blamed fat Patsy at the Bloodhouse, and suspected that Patsy had deliberately given the impression that we were a couple of good-hearted girls who craved a little masculine company. For quite some time we were troubled by men who had the fixed idea that there was a keg buried somewhere in the camp. They begged us to be hospitable, they abused us when we refused.

We cajoled our drinking water out of the staff at the Forestry Office, who were always surprised at the amount of water we drank. Nobody else in Brannigan's Bend had much use for the stuff. A red-eyed, unshaven character would stagger into camp and begin pleading, in broken English, for just one drink. When you thought you had got rid of him there was another of them.

There is nothing more disconcerting than having a large drunk stagger into your tent in the dark. Saturday night was hellish with squalling and fighting in Brannigan's Bend, and the *haute noblesse* such as Dennis and Mel Staines always drove into Caterpillar on a Saturday. One night a tractor driver decided to demolish a whole row of tents with a bulldozer. His mates stopped him at the sixth tent. Another night someone tried to burn down the Bloodhouse.

The language barrier was a nuisance because it wasted time crossing Cut-throat Creek to look for someone who spoke the language of an inebriated visitor. One of these New Australians would be sacked from the timber mill, and instead of leaving town, he would lurk in the scrub and steal. Joe bought some mill timber and made a door and a wooden shutter for the hut, but even then they broke in, made off with our stores and turned the whole camp over searching for money or wine.

Patience with drunks is a quality that everyone should learn, but my patience often ran out. Afterwards I found that the man I pushed into the creek was once the champion wrestler of a dockyard, and that the other little bloke, who ran away when the gun went off, had only come to borrow some nails. Joe forbade me to touch the gun after that, because, he said, I would only blow my feet off. Certainly no one was more surprised than I when it exploded.

However, the incident had its good effect, because after that the mill-workers gave us a wide berth. Even if we had the most beautiful keg in the world buried in the banks of Cut-throat Creek, we were too inhospitable, too savage and uncivilized in our behaviour, to make it worth anyone's while to cultivate our acquaintance.

Chapter Twenty-six

THERE is always one person who sets the tone for a camp, and in our camp — or rather Fay's camp — it was Fay. She would suggest quietly that we needed a new frying-pan or a set of shelves. Mongo, the untidiest boy who ever lived, didn't know at first what hit him. No more soap left out in the rain, or old towels hanging from the limb of a tree. No more boiling clothes in blackened kerosene tins.

We had a copper; we had a petrol iron, starch. The mud floors were swept neatly every morning; there were no more boots mixed with the bedding in the men's tent. The tent I shared with Fay had a mirror on the dressing-table which was made of two boxes and draped with a piece of cretonne. Of course, she did it all by degrees. I was paying Fay a token wage, and she spent it on canvas folding chairs to replace the old oil drums we sat on. Leave her there long enough and you would have a homestead.

It was Fay who made friends with Mrs. Balancovitch across the river, whose husband was the mill foreman and able to exercise some influence over our visitors. Mrs. Balancovitch would mind our camp for us while we were away. She was a plump woman with gold rings in her ears. She appeared in our camp one day, perspiring and excited, because her ducks had left home.

'More than a mumma I have been to those ducks, and when the creek flooddit them blasted ducks coom in my

kitchen and quark because they are afrait. But now they
svim down the creek and coom home they vill not. Coom
then, Mr. Muirden, with that gun and shoot them ducks
vitch sit in mittle of the creek and laff at me.'

The sight of Joe with the gun was enough to send those
ducks waddling home, where Mrs. Balancovitch forgave
them and was 'more than a mumma' to them all over
again. She was a good kind friend to us, and Fay had
somewhere to visit besides the post office if she needed
company. Fay even made friends with Mrs. Hasselfors
and went out to visit her at the oilfield.

Fay was changing, taking on authority. She was
plumper and it suited her. She was silent as ever, but she
had her own way. I didn't notice Joe progressing in
his courtship any more than a stranded whale. Evidently,
until he was established as an independent honey pro-
ducer, Fay was just there for the air and the scenery.

Some of those hives I bought from the postmistress
were not worth the pound I paid for them, but the seventy-
five I had from Col were full of good brood. Our first
job was to re-queen and make up neucs. We had to
paint boxes. We sent away for new frames, foundation
comb, paint, excluders, gauze screens, bottom boards,
carbolic, tar, and the hundred and one other oddments an
apiarist needs, down to nails and wire.

Col was the chief hindrance to work. He was, I was
ready to agree with Blaze, a bad influence. He found an
army ammunition dump hidden in the forest, forgotten
from the last war, and for a time he convinced Joe there
was a fortune to be made out of becoming a gun-
runner. 'Talk about the mystery of the *Marie Celeste*,'
he told us excitedly, when they came back from their
investigations. 'There it is, with a barbed-wire fence
fourteen feet high all around it, and not even a caretaker.
Joe just struck the padlock in the right place and we drove

in, getting the shudders from the silence. We picked up some pink stuff we thought was soap, but it was high explosive. There were concrete underground cellars and rooms and gas dug-outs and God knows what all. Creepy as hell!'

Col began to believe he owned that ammunition dump, and Fay and I were always frightened he might bring home some little souvenir and construct a drunk-trap on the creek without telling us. He had set up an elaborate set of trip wires round the camp, but after Mongo and a cow fell over them by night and set off the alarm, we disconnected the gong and used the wires for hanging clothes.

When Col wasn't exploring his ammunition dump, he was taking an interest in the oilfield and nearly driving the Parent deeper into drink. The Parent's genius for getting his own way had served him yet once again, and he had achieved the impossible by persuading Staines and Hasselfors to sign a truce. Now they both came to him complaining that his one-eyed friend was telling them how to do their jobs. The Parent was building a small refrigeration plant, and Col told him how he should build it. The Parent was cementing paths around the barracks so that the gluey mud was not walked in. He had put in orders for fly-screens. Col took a deep-devoted interest in it all.

'Too utterly primitive,' Dennis explained. 'You can't expect men to live under these conditions.' He had Hasselfors' wife eating out of his hand. I think he flirted with her, and there is nothing like a flirtation to cheer a woman with one foot in the labour ward.

While they were still fishing for that drill, he had men at work clearing and levelling the ground for the Number Two Test Hole, eight miles away. Perhaps his shrewd friends in the city were not as insane as they seemed when they sent the Parent out to revive their ailing oil-field.

He and Col Muirden would drive out in Wilhelmina, change into dungarees and set to work, telling the men with the bulldozer where to go, taking a shovel to dig a boundary trench while the help stood around and marvelled at so much energy and determination. If they went home, the whole gang would lie down in the shade, or, if it was a cold day, in the sun. So finally Col was tired of that oilfield and bossing navvies, and he decided to buy a geiger counter and make a fortune out of uranium. But, in the meantime, the Parent, by the use of a little charm, had a great deal of work out of Col, absolutely gratis.

Dennis found me work, too, in the dusty shed of an office where Hasselfors hated me to be because I found out all kinds of inconvenient things. I did not want Hasselfors' company, so I was glad when Fred Connelly arrived, for now I hoped our own work would speed up.

'By God, Mallee,' Fred exclaimed, when he had eaten an enormous meal and finished a long story about how he was held up by the main jet shaking loose and petrol pouring into the engine oil, 'if this isn't better than Nithering I'll throw you into the creek. We've had a lousy run ever since Nithering. Saddest-looking lot of bee-cockies you ever saw round Tembucca with that foul brood. Everybody selling out. Most of the state under water. I've been every place that should've budded and didn't. I've been to a hell of a lot of places I shouldn't.' He eased his weight into our new canvas chair and sighed happily. 'Best thing that happened was me giving Blaze Muirden the slip when he wanted to come up here with me.'

This was the first news we had had of young Tarquinius Superbus. It was Fay who asked quietly: 'What's Blaze doing with himself?'

Quarrelling with Pa as usual. He can't quarrel with me. It's just a permanent state of hostile incivility and impoliteness between us. Of course, he had that bust-up with Big Mike — you remember — at the dance at Lacey's Crossing.' So that explained why Big Mike had left so unceremoniously! 'Anyway, forget about Blaze. One of these days he's going to destroy himself through my machinations.'

Fred estimated that the bees would go along quietly until the end of July and, by August, we should be 'stuck into it'. 'We might just as well go broke here as anywhere else,' he said in a tone that meant it was really good. He had sent word to Hilda to start with the caravan.

The day after Fred's arrival our second battle for the bees in Settunga opened with Ken Musselton driving up to our camp. Col, Fred and Joe — and Mongo — all gathered round him as though he was just an ordinary visitor, and for an hour they talked about the Commercial Apiarists' Conference which Ken had been attending. That explained why he had not been up with drawn sword before we settled in.

Every beekeeper with the fare takes the slow season in the middle of May to attend a conference in the city and mingle with other apiarists and stay at the Great Southern Hotel. They air their views about the supply of drums and quotas and the Forestry Department, returning to the scrub much refreshed to think of that excellent and impressive speech they made on the subject of the sales tax.

So only after they had worked through all the commonplaces of polite gossip did the men come to the hard and disagreeable statement that Ken Musselton could go and leap in the creek if he thought they were clearing our bees out of Settunga at his say-so.

'You know you blokes are dumping in on me.' Ken Musselton raised his voice. 'You come charging up here without please or thank-you and shove your bees in on my sites.'

'We booked these sites,' Joe said, 'at the Forestry in Caterpillar.'

'I'd got permission a year ago. The only reason I didn't book sites was because I didn't want every little bee-cockie in New South rushing up here with his ears back.'

Fred's contention was that Ken never meant to use those sites, and was just a dog-in-the-manger keeping everyone else out. 'Look at you now,' he contended. 'If you'd wanted these sites, you would've rushed your bees in six weeks ago instead of waiting till now.'

The argument grew hotter, but Ken knew he was out-numbered. It ended with them all going up to the Blood-house, and they were still there when darkness closed down. When they came back, Ken Musselton held Fay's hand and said nobody understood him, and it was a lonely life. If he had only met a good woman before it was too late, he would never have been an apiarist. 'A lonely country,' he said. 'Old Joe and I won't quarrel. Not even quarrel with bloody Fred. I'll tell you something. They're good blokes. Even Col. The one that gets my goat is that bastard of a Blaze. You know what he did to me once?'

It might have been a good story if he had not been interrupted by the others who wanted to tell him what Blaze had done to them. Nobody was going to argue about us being here, they decided, as long as that bastard Blaze Muirden didn't come stirring up trouble.

Ken Musselton had some hives he was willing to let us have — good hives that were on mintweed, and Fred and Joe were going to drive back with him next day and look at them. They were all friends together and Ken was accommodated with a shakedown in the men's tent.

Next day, they didn't bother to start, because they had to take Ken out to see the ammunition dump. They returned, disgusted, because someone had put a new padlock on the gate. When finally they did go, leaving Fay and Mongo and me to mind the camp, it was peaceful enough except for a Saturday party somewhere across the river.

'Fay,' I said, as we were sitting in the lamplight after supper, 'why the devil do you stay here? I've told you you can go down to the city any time to my mother. You always said you hated the loneliness and trees. Don't think I'm trying to get rid of you, but this camp is enough to drive anyone nuts. You're scared of drunks. You don't really like bees. Is it Joe?'

I might have known better than to ask her questions, because she had no talent for answering them. There she sat sewing, beautiful enough to bring those mill-workers over the creek just to look at her. Her talents were domestic and ornamental. I had given up waiting for an answer and was thinking about painting some boxes with Mongo tomorrow, when she said:

'At least, Mallee, there's no snakes. And I might as well wait for a while.'

'Wait?' I asked. 'What for?'

'Oh, I don't know,' she said. 'I'll wait and see.'

Chapter Twenty-seven

THE thin creeping question that blows in under the corner of your mind: 'What am I doing here?' had begun to chill my collar-bone again. In our flat there had always been Dennis tearing his hair and saying, 'For Godsake, Mallee, nut something out — Julie, can't you think of anything? This has to be done by Tuesday, Tuesday I tell you.'

I was used to working to a deadline, and the idea that it wasn't desperate to finish painting boxes by 2 p.m. on Tuesday took a long time to register. Of course we had heavy waves of work ahead of us, but Fred and Joe and Mongo worked at a large, leisurely, dignified pace like draught-horses. There was no studio ringing up to say they were all set to cut a record; where was the script? I think the Parent secretly felt there was an empty place in his mind where the worry of 'Mrs. Prothero' used to be, but of course he wouldn't admit it.

Now the difference between a hack and amiable people who 'know they could write a book because they have had such an interesting life' is that the hacks, the paid professionals, hate writing. They won't sit down to the typewriter until the messenger is pounding on the door, and the nagging and cursing start. They will not face the moment when they have to crank up the tired brain and set it ticking over.

So when I, of my own free will, was beginning to think about plots and scripts, something had to be done, some excuse found, or I would begin typing from force of habit. Why, dammit, I told myself indignantly, here I am an apiarist at last, I'm not even broke yet, and I'm beginning to think of a plot. So I would go up to that dirty office on the oilfield and clean up the mail, and bully Hasselfors, but it was only a means of stopping the draught, that persistent question: 'What am I doing here? Why am I doing it?'

I have come to the conclusion that all the work human beings do is ultimately only a barrier against that chilling question, that blowing wind from outer space that freezes us into insignificance. We have come into this world as prisoners, we are isolated in our separate bodies that are padded cells, dooming us to silence, and our thoughts rush round our bodies trying to move the walls, trying to get back to the significant life from which we are all cut off.

When I die, I am quite sure I will only emerge and say: 'Why, of course, how could I have forgotten all this?' Just as the bees on their first flight into the sunlight must know the ecstasy of recognition. But meantime we just whirr about the enclosed comb of this world, very busy exuding our wax, and tending the young, with no idea that somewhere there is a great open range of happiness and unknown possibilities in blossom.

I suppose the young bees, when the draught blows in the hive door, must whirr their wings just as fretfully, fanning to keep it out and saying: 'Why is it like this? Why am I here?'

Anyway, whether it was just being born under the Sign of the Two Poor Fish who are tied by their tails while they go in opposite directions, when I was a script writer I wanted to be an apiarist, and now I was an apiarist I was hankering to start writing again.

Fay was summoned dramatically to take over the Hasselfors homestead while Mrs. Hasselfors was in hospital — 'swarming', in the vulgar bee-keeping phrase. Hilda arrived, complete with dog, kids, chooks and caravan, and immediately. began making a vegetable garden where it was most convenient to park the trucks. 'I hardly see you, Mallee,' she complained. 'You're as bad as Fred and Mongo, never anywhere when I want someone to cart manure.'

I decided I had to drive down to Ken Musselton's camp on the other side of Chillings because he had some Boultons that he was ready to part with, as he was converting to full-depth hives. Joe and Fred hadn't bought them when they were there before, because they argued the Boultons were a curse to handle when you were extracting; but thinking it over on the way home, they had come to the conclusion that we should have those Boultons. Boultons are little half-depth supers and quite handy to have.

Joe decided he would go with me so he could do a dicker with Ken Musselton for an engine boiler and motor Ken had that were better than ours. Ken received us royally and we stayed as long as we dared, returning with the motor and boiler and a hundred Boultons. We passed through a little town called Casing, which seemed to be an important centre for the trucking of old bones and the skulls of cattle. There were trucks piled with bones and skulls in the railway siding, and not another sign of life, not even a dog or an old man. What was stranger was that it was Saturday afternoon and the hotel was shut, the only street swept by the bitter wind that goes before rain.

Far away over the flat, in a large paddock, we sighted a flapping banner and rows of cars and trucks. In the lulls of the wind a loudspeaker was blaring. It looked like a race meeting, and when we drove over it was a race meeting sure enough. The bar was a little wooden stall roofed with brushwood completely surrounded by men and dogs, the women huddling in the cars for shelter from the sleety blast. A roar and a thumping of hoofs and the excitement of the loudspeaker made little impression on me. There in the neatly parked rows of trucks and cars by the racetrack fence was the Roaring Ruin.

Joe went over to it with me. We walked round it. 'That's George's port,' he said, and made for the bar.

'No,' I told him. 'You wait here. I've got a better idea.' I left Joe and pushed through to the loudspeaker to ask the man in charge if he would put out a call for George. 'Would Mr. George Fulton please come to the microphone,' he proudly blared all over the racecourse. 'A young lady would like to speak to him. Mr. George Fulton, please.'

Sure enough, presently George came strolling up. He was as blue-chinned as ever, but the rest of his face was blue too — with cold. He had only a thin shirt on, and his teeth were chattering.

'Good God!' I said. 'You'll have pneumonia again.'

'Hello, Mallee,' he mumbled. 'What you doing here?' I was pleased to see he looked awkward. 'Come on,' he said, and shouldered his way off towards the bar. I thanked the man with the loudspeaker and followed George. He only grunted noncommittally when I spoke to him, and then, reaching over the rows of drinkers, he prodded one of those in the front row. The chap he prodded was loudly holding forth to the assembly about what he thought of the horses they had gathered there as a means of robbing unsuspecting strangers. When he backed out, still talking, and turned round, there was the angle-ironed carcase of Blaze Muirden.

'Hello, Mallee,' he said. Like George, he had only a thin shirt on and he wrapped his arms round him to keep out the wind. 'George and I did the last of our dough on that race,' he explained to me.

'Joe is over by the truck.'

'He is, is he? Have a beer, Mallee? Christ, it's cold.' Where George was blue, Blaze had a greenish-yellow complexion and a cough you could hear half across the racecourse. 'I'd better get my coat,' he said when I declined the beer, and he made off towards the Roaring Ruin. 'Hello, mate,' he said to Joe.

'Hello!' A smile spread over Joe's face at the sight of his brother. 'How'd you be?'

'Good! How's yourself?' They nodded to each other casually. Blaze and George got into their coats. 'That's better,' Blaze said. 'I didn't notice until just before the race that it had come up chilly.' The blast whistled past us and the rain began to beat on our faces.

'Where's your camp?' I asked.

'We haven't got a camp. We've been sleeping on the school veranda. But I'm not sleeping there tonight. We'd do a freeze. I always did hate schools. Gave me a nightmare.'

'The best thing,' Joe said, considering, 'is for us to drive on to Brannigan's Bend. No sense wasting money on pubs.' Now he had his brother back, I could see, Joe was determined to keep him. Once he got Blaze to Brannigan's Bend Blaze would settle in. I wondered how Fay would take it when she returned from the Hasselfors' establishment.

'Who's there?' Blaze demanded.

'Hilda.'

Blaze groaned. 'Bloody Hilda!'

'Fred's there and Big Mike was supposed to be arriving some time.'

'Well, I don't mind having a yarn with Fred,' Blaze said generously. 'He was keen for me to drive up with him, but I couldn't make it at the time.' They walked over to the Commer and leant on it, discussing its points until I was frozen stiff. Then Blaze had a look at the load. 'Not Boultons!' he exclaimed. 'Don't tell me that burglar Musselton unloaded a heap of lousy Boultons on you.'

Joe grinned. Nobody had sworn at him for a long time as Blaze was swearing now. I looked at Joe, wondering if he remembered how keen he had been to be quit of Blaze, but if Joe had been a dog with two tails he would have wagged both of them. Then they had to discuss the boiler and the little engine that we had bought to replace those on the extracting house.

'Trust Col to palm off that old extractor of his on the first mug that comes along,' Blaze commented. 'Did he say anything of the forty quid he still owes me?'

'Come on, George,' I said impatiently. 'You and I will ride in the Ruin.' It looked as though the Muirden brothers would stand in the rain until darkness closed down. 'We've got to find a place to get petrol if we're going through to Brannigan's Bend.'

Joe gave me an apologetic glance and that was all. I could have put my foot down then and there. I could have told Blaze to go to hell and get warm and take George with him. But of course at the sight of him all my sense of being lost and at a loose end had departed. I was just as pleased as Joe to see the most villainous of the Muirdens. Yet I realized that my brief span of authority was now at an end. Once Blaze reached Brannigan's Bend, I would be one of the slaves again, on no better footing than Mongo when it came to taking orders.

'I'll ride in the Ruin with you, Mallee,' Blaze decided. 'Got to sweeten her up a bit. She's got a face on her like a judgment summons.'

We climbed into the Roaring Ruin, while Joe and George roared off in the Commer. 'A new radio!' I said, lifting it off the seat. 'Now we'll have blues till midnight.'

'And you needn't be a bigger liar than usual, Mallee, and say you're not pleased to see me.' Blaze drove fast after the cloud of dust that was Joe ahead of us. 'How far is it to Brannigan's Bend?'

'About seventy-five miles.'

'An hour and a half,' Blaze exclaimed, with satisfaction.

'Did you ever take those three hundred tins down to Uncle Beresford?'

'Mallee, how the hell do you think I would find time to personally drive down with three hundred tins for your bloody uncle? There I was short-handed, shifting bees on my bloody lone. You bugger off, leaving me in a spot with Daff breathing down one ear and Dad gnawing the other off. If it hadn't been for Matt I would've perished. I hand him a medal. And your best boyfriend Stollin prowling round like a dingo, acting like I'd eaten you and buried the bones. I even had a go-in with *him*. And the first thing you ask is: Did I take Uncle Beresford his honey? No, I did not. For one thing, I was waiting for a rise in price, instead of rushing in with my ears back to get rid of it the way you did. . . .'

'What you mean is that you neglected a man who controls twenty-three stores and one of the biggest distributing businesses in the state. After all the trouble I took, you just wipe him. He'll never take another tin of honey from us in his life.' I felt a deep pleasure to be sitting beside Blaze again, as he switched on the headlights and the Ruin shot through the yellow dust that had still not enough rain to lay it.

'Sa-ay that you lo-ove me,' Blaze sang. Then, reverting to the voice of a member of parliament at question time, he said sententiously, 'You will be pleased to hear that I shipped his lousy honey by rail. So *now* are you satisfied? Now will you shut up about it?'

'There's just one other little matter,' I admitted. 'I left the Ruin with Lon McKillop, who was going to drive it down and return it to Nobby.'

'But we *needed* it!' Blaze was surprised. 'I *told* Lon that. I said you must be out of your mind.'

'I left it with Lon because I thought it wouldn't stand the trip to Queensland.'

'Don't be bloody silly. It's been all over the earth since, and as for standing the trip to Queensland,' he mimicked me, 'imagine that! Why, Queensland is the place where cars like the Ruin spend their old age! I was going to lend her to George,' Blaze went on, 'and then I thought I might as well come up with him. Every bee-cocky in New South Wales is pushing over the border. This is the wettest year in the whole history of the universe. It's too cold on the highlands, everywhere is flooded. There's cyclones on the coast. We thought last year was a hell of a year, but it's nothing to this.'

He didn't ask me how the prospects were in Settunga Forest. He would not have considered my opinion was worth having. He went on talking, telling me about his father and mother and the foul-brood at Tembucca. What the inspector had said to him, and what he had said to the inspector, about the man he suspected of spreading the foul-brood. Then there was a long, involved story about what the suspect had said about Blaze, and the argument which nearly ended in a knock-down-drag-out battle. 'Fred was there, but did Fred say anything? Not on your life. He just kept dodging round, excited, saying, "Wait a bit, wait a bit, no need to take it that way!" "Listen, mate," I said to this bastard, "I was the man who worded Jack Pearson" — that's the inspector — I told him straight out. "Now what have you got to say about *that*?" He had a lot to say about it . . .'

I felt the old sense of exasperation and irritation at the way he prosed along, boasting and self-centred, and with the same pugnacity.

'Oh, and about *you*!' He put the old Ruin into low gear to growl up a hill. 'I've got a bone to pick with you. Thanks to you shinning off and leaving me, I'm engaged.'

'Get out,' I yawned. 'You're always engaged or breaking it off.'

'But this time it's serious. I'm getting married, you mug.'

'Fine. Congratulations. Congratulations to *you*, not Daphne. When?'

'September.'

'And don't kid me you're not tickled pink,' I said contemptuously. 'Best thing that could happen to you. You've been dying to get married.'

'You think?' He took the Ruin down the other side of the hill at a breakneck pace.

We must have done pretty well out of that honey at Nithering if Blaze was marrying on it. I did a quick addition sum in my head. Say, two thousand eight hundred tins of honey, and Blaze said he had been waiting for a rise before he sold. There would have been hardly any honey on the floor except ours, if he had only just trucked it all down in the last month. The rain would have ruined everyone else, but we had just snapped in between the drought and the flood, and struck it lucky.

Blaze began talking bitterly about the fine time he had had getting that honey to the railhead at Ombra. He had had snow, and I hated to remember what the road through Nithering was like without snow. 'First we had to get the bees out, and I didn't have time to bugger around with the honey. Besides, as I say, I was waiting for a rise. Then I realized it wasn't going to be much good frozen solid, besides being heavier to lift. . . .'

'Why would it be heavier?'

'It *feels* heavier. Try it when you're freezing and you'll find out. And I had to leave the bees with the Old Man. Now how they got infected, I don't know — there must have been an old hive somewhere, neglected, and when the bees die out from foul-brood the other bees start robbing — then they cop a dose. The wild bees only have to get it and it's all over the place. Anyway,' he added carelessly, 'we weren't badly hit. Got it in time.' He always made light of his losses.

We reached Brannigan's Bend about ten o'clock because we stopped to eat at a Greek café in Caterpillar, and Joe had so much to tell Blaze that I suggested they swop over and let me and George drive in the Ruin. George had nothing much to say, but I found out from him it *was* Blaze who had suggested they come this way. So he had been hovering in our direction of his accord. George had just come for the ride. His bees, he said, were doing no good, but then neither were anyone else's.

Hilda and Fred, after their expressed hostility, welcomed Blaze as though he had brought them a handsome present. We sat around talking in the hut until a late hour. The pleased and affable face of Mongo loomed in the background like a large red benediction.

'Gee, I'm glad to see him,' he breathed to me. 'Now we'll really get cracking.'

It occurred to me that this was the unanimous sentiment. Blaze was the man to see we got cracking. Without him we lacked a sense of direction, we just wandered along; but with Blaze yelling in your tracks, you sped.

'Just tottering along,' Blaze snorted to me next day. 'Fumbling about like a blind man with a stick.'

First he had to go round and round the forest like a dog circling to flatten the grass, then he would organize a shuttle service as soon as Big Mike arrived, trucks roaring off to pick up bees from Tembucca, trucks roaring in with bees that were being moved to sites Blaze liked better than the ones we had already cleared. We pulled up our socks and snapped to attention, and when I offered a suggestion, instead of Joe saying, 'O.K., Mallee, we might do that,' I would hear, 'Now, Mallee, you know perfectly well I never take the least bloody notice of what you say, because you haven't enough brains to come in out of the wet.' The radio played Blaze's favourite tunes whether anyone wanted to sleep or not.

I drove up to the oilfield to announce the news. 'The place is like a fun-fair already,' the Parent commented. 'I suppose young Muirden will be out here, no doubt, telling me how to run my affairs. Keep him off my neck, that's all. He talks too big.'

But Blaze admired Dennis. 'That's what I like,' he said. 'When Dennis goes broke, he's going to go broke in a big way. Nothing penny-pinching like Mallee saving a pint of petrol here and there.' He knew I watched the petrol bills with the face of a chief mourner. 'Dennis does things in a big way if it's only digging a hole in the ground.' He whisked all financial arrangements out of my hands with the airy remark that the overdraft would take care of the bills in future. 'That was what the overdraft was for.' He even mentioned something about paying me my share of the honey cheque from Nithering, but I told him to shove it in the kitty, so he did not press the matter. He had his pride, but I guess if I had demanded my pound of flesh, even his airy talk about the overdraft might not have been quite so airy.

When I went out to the Hasselfors ménage and told Fay that Blaze was back with us, a shade of colour rose in her face but she said nothing. 'Joe's very happy to see him,' I told Fay. She went out to hang a dishcloth on the back veranda and removed Bidgee from the ash-can where he was pouring ashes on his hair.

The Honey Flow

'He'd have real nice curls,' she said, taking out her temper on Bidgee, 'if he wasn't filling them with dirt.'

'Joe likes working with Blaze. You can't get over that. Big Mike's just blown in, and you'd think they'd never had a split. All brothers and friends. Of course Big Mike and Fred and Joe and Blaze have always been a team. They get along together in their own strange way.' I was chatting to fill the silence. 'Hilda agrees that you might as well let them go until they have their next big row. By that time let's hope we have some honey off. We can all take a holiday from each other — say, by Christmas.' The Parent would either have struck oil or got the D.T.s and cut his throat. We could go down and stay in Julie's flat, as I planned originally, and Fay could get a job there if she didn't want to marry Joe. But you never knew what Fay wanted.

'No sense holding old scores,' I blundered on. 'Daphne's going to marry him — good luck to her.' I contemplated this prospect all the more contentedly because it would mean that Blaze kept his mind on the job. He would need a handsome bank balance to get married to Daphne.

'I'm not going to say anything to him,' Fay murmured; then she added bitterly, 'You think the sun shines out of him, don't you?'

I was disconcerted. 'Well, I wouldn't say that, of course. I've got a lot of time for the old Blaze.'

She gave me that sidelong glance of hers that could mean anything. 'And Joe just let him walk in,' she said sardonically, 'and put his feet on his neck?'

'They were all over each other. "Hello, mate." "How's it with you, mate?"'

She nodded. 'I thought that's how it would be.' Joe had done no good for himself. Fay plainly thought that Joe had no more backbone than a jelly-fish.

Chapter Twenty-eight

I TOOK one trip down with Joe to Tembucca to see Daphne and Mrs. Muirden. She was a woman with whom I got on exceptionally well. She had a sense of humour. You wouldn't have thought so to look at her, for she spent all her spare time in her garden or putting up pickles or making clothes. She had grey hair which she wore nearly as short as mine, and hard-working hands, but her mind had a lively sparkle to it, and I could listen all day to Elsie Muirden describing the funny things that had happened at a meeting of the Ladies' Social of the Methodist Church, for humour is not in large affairs, but the wry and dry and odd little twists of human behaviour.

We would go for a stroll along the main street and Elsie Muirden would carry on a running commentary about the people in the houses we passed that lit them up like a searchlight in all their absurdities. She did it without ever moving a muscle of her face, or changing her expression from one of mild amiability. Elsie writes to me now and I look forward to those letters, in a neat hand, giving the small details of her family. Elsie wanted so little from life.

'The pleasantest thing of all,' she told me, 'is to have a mob of grandchildren and them all drawn up eating at the table, knowing it's your own eggs and butter and milk, your own vegetables and chicken that they're eating.' Joe was her favourite, so she was anxious to hear all I could tell her about Fay. 'Sounds as though she'd suit Blaze better,' she said dryly. 'A woman that fights with her first husband, she needs someone who'll fight back to her. Joe's the only one with any kindness in him.'

But she was dead keen to add to the number of her grandchildren, and I could see that Bidgee and Brian would be welcome at that ample table where Elsie sat down and fed the eddying numbers always alighting and departing in trucks.

The Muirdens had a battered-looking weatherboard house on the outskirts of Tembucca, across the river, with a good stand of yellow box and an orchard. The house itself was nothing much to look at, but the huge barn behind was the size of a small church and fitted with tools and benches, saws and vices, hoists and garage equipment. There were stacks of wood for making boxes and frames, handy pieces of iron that the Muirdens had picked off some junk-heap, spare batteries and tyres, and of course there were bees in boxes here and there, almost to the back doorstep.

I missed Daphne, who was visiting an aunt somewhere out on a farm. We drove back to camp with neucs Joe had picked up about twenty-five miles out. He grumbled about the vegetables with which Elsie had loaded us. 'Hardly any room on the truck for the bees,' he claimed.

'Oh, you and your bees,' his mother said lightly. 'You take that other sack of carrots and be grateful.' We had two plucked fowls, eggs, and a ham. I told Else when I kissed her goodbye that it felt like Christmas.

'Take care of yourself, Mallee,' she said. 'Don't try to do too much, my dear. Keep to the track across Bandy's Paddock.' I had told her Matt's story about the traveller seeking directions because I knew she would enjoy it. She stood waving to us until we swung round the bend and over the river bridge through Tembucca.

We camped that night with Horace and picked up the bees early in the morning, and reached Brannigan's Bend after driving most of the night. We were pretty tired and travel-worn when we finally made camp. Fay had returned from her brief rule over the Hasselfors establishment. Big Mike and Fred were out at a yard fifteen miles south, but Blaze was in camp looking as smug as a rogue horse.

'Had a friend of yours up here,' he greeted me. 'He's gone now. Lee Stollin.'

'Well, that's a nice thing,' I exclaimed. 'You might have told him I was due back.'

'It was Fay he came to see.'

But when I went up to the Bloodhouse to talk to Dennis before turning in for a sleep Lee Stollin was still there. He hadn't taken any notice of Blaze's assurances that I would be away at least another week. He had had some holidays due, he said, and the business of Fay's compensation had to be finally settled. So he thought he would attend to it personally.

'Compensation?' I asked, mystified.

He hesitated, then decided that there was no secret about it. Fay was in receipt of worker's compensation until the final arrangements were made for a settlement over Frank Hertz's death. The Hydro-Electricity Authority carried its own insurance. I didn't ask him what the payment would be, but he told me — seven thousand pounds. It sounded pretty gruesome to me, but a good thing for Fay. Lee said that, if the widow agreed, he was empowered to sign on behalf of the Authority.

'She just wandered off,' he told me. 'Her uncle seemed quite cagey about giving her address. Even her mother didn't know where she'd gone except that it was some place in Queensland. Then I put two and two together and realized she must be up here with you.'

Evidently Matt had overdone his promise to say nothing about where I was going. Not that it mattered. I wondered why Fay, with all that wealth in prospect, was still with us, camped on the creek and roughing it, instead of going somewhere she could enjoy life. Maybe she still had an interest in Joe.

Lee Stollin looked tired and quiet, sitting on the back veranda of the Bloodhouse after the Parent went off to work, telling me small scraps of news about Nithering and Matt, for whom he had developed a humorous affection. 'I drive up and have a yarn with him sometimes,' he said. 'They're snowed up at Nithering just now. The work's practically at a standstill. How are you doing up here?'

'It would take a whole book to tell you,' I said, yawning. 'One of these days I'll write it — only the things that would interest you.'

'Well, anything about you interests me,' he said quietly. 'I came up to ask you to marry me.'

This was a jolt. I was looking like something that had crawled out from under a log and I wasn't expecting to have any heavy shock fall with a thump on my neck. I wavered feebly, sparring for time. 'Why, Lee,' I responded, 'I wasn't contemplating any move like that.'

'I hoped you'd think it over,' he said, still in the same businesslike quiet tone. 'You'd have a free hand with your bees. Go and come as you please. *I* haven't any prejudices against women in business. All I want is that sometimes you'd say, "Well, now I'm going home."'

That would be pleasant, to have somebody who was home, some place that wasn't just the balcony of my mother's flat where I had a bed and a desk. But I felt rather aggrieved that Lee had sprung this on me when I was fuzzy from night driving and had just strolled up not even expecting to see him.

'Take your time, Mallee,' he said. 'But if you've got a proposition, it's no sense letting the opposition get in ahead of you.'

'No opposition, Lee.' I rubbed my face, feeling blurred like a glass someone had breathed on. 'When I was writing scripts,' I told him, 'I used to fall in love occasionally. Usually with the wrong men — or married, and I had to cherish my unrequited passion in silence. Or coves as old as my father.' Lee rather flinched at my tactlessness. I could have kicked myself on the ankles. I hadn't been referring to him. 'Lee, how would it be if I told you at Christmas? That's if you don't mind. By Christmas I should have had nearly twelve months trying to set up in business. I'd know whether I could make a success of it. I really don't know. . . .' I hated to be so irresolute. Lee had that kindness and consideration which are so rare in men. The more I thought of it, the more I began to believe I might learn to take an interest in concrete.

'I haven't any intention of getting married unless I know it's to someone I could work with for life. Everybody wanders around and falls for one or two no-hopers but marriage is a different matter. I couldn't be bothered chopping and changing.'

Again I had said the wrong, the tactless thing. I had meant to indicate that I was a serious character, and instead I had reminded Lee he had made a hash of his first marriage.

'Mallee, it's a damned lonely life being a construction stiff. I'll never be anything else. And an engineer needs a special type of wife. Josie' — that was his first wife — 'was bored stiff. That was the whole trouble. She liked city life. I can't stand it.'

I rubbed my knuckles in my eyes trying to keep them open. 'I hope you won't get the idea that I think of you as a kind of alternative to fall back on if all else fails,' I said, rousing myself. 'It isn't that at all.'

'I don't care as long as you don't waste yourself on that loud-mouthed ape.' Lee spoke with a viciousness that made me think well of him. He had been far too restrained and good-natured. 'If I had that guy on any job of mine, I'd have him somewhere where a wrench would drop on him.' I felt much better. Why, the man was quite lovable, he was charming.

'Dear Lee,' I said fondly. 'I do like you. But be at rest. Blaze Muirden is to be married to a girl in Tembucca.'

'I wouldn't trust him as far as I could kick him.'

'That's very sweet of you. Write to me often.'

'And don't go making a joke of this with that human meat-ant,' he said savagely.

'Why, Lee, I wouldn't do any such thing. You do think badly of me.'

'No, I don't. I just know that lousy sense of humour of yours. I've stuck my neck out. Well, it stays stuck out.'

'And very nice it looks that way.'

He glanced at his watch. 'I'll have to beat it,' he said. 'I've hung around too long. I should have gone early this morning, but I had a hunch. I'm glad I didn't go now.'

'I'm glad you didn't.' I walked with him back to the car and he said he would give me a lift back to camp. 'Oh, I do hope,' I told him, as we sat in the car, 'that I'll have worked out a way by Christmas. Nithering would be too cold for bees all the year round. It wouldn't be a good base.'

'I don't stay up there all my life. On the other hand,' he smiled, 'I can't take a job just because it's a good climate for bees.'

In the conversation we had had I had not said one thing right. What I should have done, instead of leaving as nice a man as Lee dangling on a rope, was to tell him that much as I appreciated the sentiments already expressed, he had better go build a dam. For a minute I thought what a good idea it would be if he would marry Mavis, and then I realized that Mavis wouldn't look at anyone who didn't make a dry rustling noise and have an index at the back and good binding.

'You don't have to apologize if you want to forget it.' He dropped me off where our trucks usually turned in over the stretch of grass from the road.

'You know, Lee, you've unsettled my mind.'

'That's the best news I've heard.' He smiled at me and I thought how very much I liked him. You could go all round the earth and not find a man with more character and intelligence than Lee Stollin. Any other man would have stayed around and pressed his suit and my hand, and taken me driving, but Lee just stated his proposition, take it or leave it, six months allowed for termination of notice, otherwise the contract was signed.

He had never even seen me dressed in my finest female clothes, and I determined I would give him such a surprise when he saw me with my hair curled and my warpaint on. To hell with bees! I was tired of being brow-beaten and hectored. I would be the first lady of Nithering Upper Dam, as from the 1st of January, and I would keep that dynamite up my sleeve and explode it under the person referred to by my intended as 'that human meat-ant'.

When I got back to camp Blaze was painting lids. 'Did he propose?' he asked.

'Go to hell!'

'He'll dedicate his next dam to you. I can just see him writing in the concrete: "Lee loves Mallee" with a couple of hearts and arrows under it.'

'Where did Hilda get the ducks?' I asked, by way of turning the conversation.

'Bought them from Mrs. Balancovitch. They keep

going home. But *did* he ask you to share his dam? Go on, tell me. I'm interested. I'm not kidding, Mallee. Honest to God, I wouldn't kid you.'

'Go and drown, will you?' I walked away, leaving Blaze behind me still painting those lids and talking to himself, a monologue full of scandalous insinuations, a fantastic reconstruction of what he imagined Lee Stollin's style might be.

I had known I was in for a ribbing of the worst kind, but the fiendishness of Blaze in the following weeks made even Hilda sorry for me. I held my tongue and smirked to myself, knowing he was only guessing. He was trying to get me wild; and if he did, that was a score to him — 'getting a bite, hook, line and sinker' was his term. If he did get a bite, not only would he roar with laughter but the rest of the team, Big Mike and Joe and Fred, would chuckle with him. So I didn't bite. I knew better.

Chapter Twenty-nine

THE PARENT was on top of the world because they had actually fished up the lost drill. Now they had to take all kinds of precautions against a cave-in, and they could go ahead with their groping down towards the gas sands. The bees were doing 'extra good', as Joe said, and we were still building up colonies and getting ready to extract. Big piles of shiny new tins were stacked at the camp. The honey tank had been cleaned.

Blaze went off to conduct an argument with Col about the forty pounds he claimed Col owed him. Col had borrowed forty from him a few years ago to replace the back axle of his truck. There had been an unpleasant misunderstanding when Col sold the truck to another apiarist, who came to his camp to find the truck propped up on bricks, because Blaze had removed the back axle which he claimed he owned. He was finally induced to return the back axle, but the matter of the forty pounds had never been settled, Col insisting that Blaze had had it 'in kind' twice over. 'Might get a truckload of vegetables out of Col as interest,' Blaze decided.

This matter of borrowing to-and-fro meant that before you knew where you were all the oddments in the camp were in a common pool. George had taken some drums he wanted. Fred had helped himself to bottom boards because we had some of his lids. Big Mike's new inner tube had gone into the tyres of the International. Of course, everybody's boxes were painted a different colour, and suitably branded, but even so our Boultons were on Fred's boxes, and Fred complained everybody used his beautiful aluminium privy in preference to the sacking-covered erection Mongo had set up in a little grove of black cypress much too near the creek.

But on the whole we rubbed along well enough. Bidgee and Brian had a stray kitten which always seemed to find its way to the foot of Joe's bed. We were a little squeezed when George's wife arrived with a charming little girl. George's wife was a sensitive woman who did not get on well with Hilda, so the Fultons set up their camp the other side of the clearing and came over when they wanted to borrow anything. Blaze also decided to have a tent to himself. Joe complained about the radio and the way Blaze talked in his sleep, so Blaze came back in triumph from Boona with an auto tent he had borrowed from Col, four sacks of swede turnips and a case of apples, all pure blackmail that Col had paid to get rid of him.

But the great excitement was Dennis dashing down to the camp waving a telegram to say that Anita and Julie were coming up on a plane that would deposit them on a bare little aerodrome forty miles off. The Parent claimed they should stay in Caterpillar because the Bloodhouse had 'certain undesirable aspects'. I knew that Julie and Anita would like to be with us. Blaze offered his tent, and Mrs. Hasselfors, home with the new baby, insisted that the wife and daughter of the superintendent must accept her hospitality. Hilda said they should come with her in the caravan, and Fred could sleep in the tent with Joe.

'Julie doesn't even say how long she is staying or why she's coming,' the Parent complained. 'I thought she was quite happy because she was writing articles for *The Astrological Survey*. Of course, they don't pay her anything, but it takes her a long time to work out all her calculations. Someone will jump in and take away all her trade in horoscopes.'

We looked at each other forebodingly. We were so accustomed to have 'our dear ones' at a comfortable distance that the possibility of having them with us did not bring that gush of affection they had a right to expect.

The winter weather had been glorious; great, wide, sunlit blue skies and a dash and sparkle to the days. The blossom, so confidently expected, was breaking, and they could not see the forests under better aspects.

'You can drive over with me in the car and pick them up,' the Parent decided unselfishly, knowing the state of the roads. We would have to go by back tracks across country, and those back roads were grim; but Julie would expect me to be there waving when the plane came in.

It was a potty little plane that looked as though it had been made of left-over dustbins beaten out and painted silver. I had had to dash round and borrow an iron from Hilda and rummage in the suitcase under my stretcher for suitable garments so that I would not have too many complaints about my appearance. Julie rushed cheerfully in her high heels down the rickety gangway, in a black suit and small black hat, with Anita following, holding the excess baggage. Anita paused automatically in the plane doorway to give us the full effect of her travelling outfit in soft grey and gold. We were successively folded into hugs and kisses. You sink into Julie as into a feather cushion, losing your breath. Anita's embrace was interrupted by her asking how I liked her travelling coat.

'Slashing,' I said, kissing her again. I hadn't realized how much I had missed them both. We talked all together to overcome the disconcerting moment when you view your nearest relatives as strangers, when you have not regained the family vision of them, and they are separate and different people, not part of yourself, taken for granted like breathing.

'Dennis, you need a haircut,' Julie exclaimed. 'Mallee, my darling sweet daughter, how brown you are! I couldn't wait, Dennis, to write — I had to rush up here, although we hardly had our fares, and it was terribly expensive, and I will probably have to borrow from Mallee to get home — but wait — I haven't told you. I could have sent a telegram, but it would have taken any number of telegrams and, anyway, I wanted to see my dear ones — I have been so lonely, and Anita had her holidays, so what could be better?'

'Will I put the rugs on top?' Anita asked me. Anita was always the practical level-headed Libra, born under the sign of the judgment and the scales. She weighed values and kept the balance. I drove Wilhelmina with Anita beside me holding her breath when we plunged through gullies and negotiated the patch of mud where the timber junker was stranded. At that place you just take off between the trees and make your own road through the grass. There is one tricky culvert where someone has made a bridge by throwing saplings across the deep ditch. It saves a couple of miles. Anita gave a surprised little hiss, but Julie screamed and clutched her hat.

'I have to go fast,' I explained. 'Deep sand. She wallows in it.'

'Oh, look at the dear little parroquets,' Julie began. 'Like so many feather hats flying about. Anita, where did I put my glasses?' She fished them out of her pocket and put them on, looking for a letter she had in her hand-bag — at least she said she had it there, but after an argument with Anita that it was in no such place, she found it in a zipper-bag containing cosmetics and face-cleaning tissues. 'Here we are, Dennis,' she said triumphantly. 'I told you before that you would never succeed under an earth sign. Air, I said — you are definitely an air type, and always have been. The idea of positively delving is ridiculous. And, sure enough, just at the Uranus conjunction, this letter came. I rang Hubert and said I would be coming up to see you, and I would let him know at once.'

'Julie, you were always a hell of a talker.' Dennis was beginning to run his hands through his hair. 'What's gone wrong now? Just spit it out, don't keep hovering.'

'I want to read you the letter.' Julie waved it at him.

'Here, give me the damn thing.' The car flung them together and Dennis almost snatched it.

'But you can't understand it unless I explain,' Julie wailed. 'Sam Kainsberg bought the rights and they were going to get a team to work to turn "Mrs. Prothero" into television and film. Now they're not happy about the hash these fools have made of it. Hubert is a friend of Sam's and he suggested they get you to do the job. It would be a wonderful chance for you, Dennis.'

'What? Not on your life! Wouldn't have it at any price.'

'But unless they get that film they won't pay you any more money. You remember the clause in the contract that you put in yourself that the script was to be personally supervised by you, and you had the right to make any alterations, and for your services in supervising the writing you got a royalty? Dennis, *dear* — we are so broke again.'

'But you can't have spent *everything*. Why, I was just going to write down and tell you to pay something off the car. They'll be screaming.'

'I'm afraid, dear,' Julie said winningly, 'that it's all just trickled away. But Mallee will lend you some.'

'Not a hope.' I gave all my attention to my driving, not bothering to listen to the detailed financial statement from the back seat.

'You know what Mother's like,' Anita said, under cover of the mutual recriminations in the back seat. 'Nothing but the best.' Anita had probably forgotten that those beautiful clothes didn't come out of her salary.

'But where did it *go*?' Dennis was demanding. 'Yes, I know there were the debts, but you've been playing baccarat again, Julie. You always do if I'm not there.'

'We won't say anything more about it. You've been writing to me for money, and I've been sending it — not that I can understand what you spend it on in this wilderness. By the way — is there a hotel?'

'There's the Bloodhouse,' I said, 'where you can share a room with Anita next to Eric who is sick and groans all night. He tried to cut his throat. You can have half Hilda's caravan — I wouldn't if I were you. The best bet is Blaze's tent.'

'Well, dear,' Julie said placidly, 'we came up determined to rough it, didn't we, Anita? We said if dear Dennis can make do we will just contrive for the time being.'

'The superintendent's cottage has three kids and a baby and their mother and father. But you are invited to sleep on the veranda if you care to.'

'Suppose we wait and see,' Julie said sceptically. She didn't believe it could all be as bad as that.

When we reached the camp, nobody was doing any work because their curiosity had kept them where they could view Mallee's mother and sister. Anita walked, delicate and smiling and light-footed, through the oil drums and children and hens and ducks and the washing on the line, and Julie said it was 'very picturesque and pastoral'. After viewing the Bloodhouse and the Hasselfors homestead, they agreed that the camp on the river bend was the best bet.

'Of course, Dennis,' Julie reminded him, 'we can't stay here long. We haven't the clothes. I suggest we could all drive down in the car together.'

'No chance,' the Parent objected. 'I came *up* in the car. We'll go back in the plane, thank you. I don't see why I shouldn't take a week or so off and then dash back here. I'd have to leave the car with Mallee, of course, and she'll tear the guts out of it. You are not to lend the car to anyone, Mallee. Remember I have to realize on it, and I don't want the upholstery knocked about any more than it is now.' He shook his head pettishly. 'I don't know why you had to come up here, Julie. You could easily have written.'

'But I wanted to see it all with my own eyes.' Julie gazed affectionately about her. She repeated this to Blaze Muirden.

'You mustn't go,' Blaze assured her, with his gaze on Anita, 'until we've shown you the place. There's the fire-watching tower, and the explosives depot. There's a good swamp for duck-shooting. And the bees, Mrs. Herrick — we'll be extracting next week.'

'Yes, indeed,' Julie said sentimentally. 'Mallee's dear bees. She has written so much about them, Mr. Muirden. I think you are so brave to handle them.'

Blaze swallowed hard, but made no answer. Anita and my mother were a new interest in our camp. They added an exotic touch that had been missing. When Anita emerged from Blaze's tent in the harlequin-patterned slacks and the emerald-green shirt she had bought for the rough life at Brannigan's Bend, Fred and Big Mike just looked at each other with a wistful expression, and Joe stood still without noticing the cat rubbing against his ankles.

Of course, Blaze got in first and suggested he show Anita the sawmill. Julie wouldn't go because she wanted a 'nice long chat with Mallee', so Blaze was able to lead Anita off, talking all the time and helping her over the stepping stones.

' Bloody opportunist,' Big Mike growled. I was avoiding that nice long chat with Julie, because I had an instinct that I was going to be the woman who used to have a bank balance when it was over. However, I drove her up to the top yard where Mongo and George were setting up the extracting house and explained how we went about taking off honey.

While we were away, Big Mike went over to borrow another mattress from the Fultons, and Hilda contributed extra spoons and knives and forks. She even sent over two cups and saucers because she said you couldn't expect a lady like Mrs. Herrick to drink out of an enamel mug like the rest. Fay dashed over to Mrs. Balancovitch for another mirror to put in Blaze's tent and a mat for the bedside, and there was a scurry of apiarists all bent on showing the best side of their natures in contriving little comforts.

When Anita decided to wash her hair, nobody offered her creek water, and she used up a substantial quantity of drinking water with the shampoo. We were now trucking it fifteen miles from a clear stream because the Forestry Office had finally jibbed at our inroads on their tanks. It had been a dry winter, they said. Where would they be if there was a fire? Not that water would be any good to them if a fire started, but they said they wanted it for the beaters.

'These men you employ,' Julie remarked when we were alone, 'they all seem very interesting and obliging.'

'I'm not employing them, darling. My bees are only a very small portion of the total. Didn't you read my letters? We all work in together.'

'Well, who actually is in charge?'

'Nobody's in charge. Blaze Muirden shouts the loudest, so he mostly gets his way, not always. Sometimes Joe and Fred gang up on him, or Big Mike moves his bees down to a place he likes better. Everybody's always coming and going.'

'Then there's nothing to stop you from coming back with us?'

'We'll be extracting,' I said quickly. 'That's my main job — in the extracting house.'

'You always did have the queerest friends,' Julie commented. But she was on good terms with all of them. Blaze told her she was a witch, and pestered her to tell him his fortune. When he found she would not look at the lines on his hand, he wanted her to cast his horoscope. Fay and Hilda, who were just as superstitious, were very respectful to Julie when they heard she was paid five guineas for each horoscope she predicted. She good-humouredly settled down to forecast.

'But hasn't she ever done it for *you*?' Fay asked. 'Gee, if I had a mother like that I'd see she did mine.'

'I don't want any horoscope,' I explained. 'Every day is a lucky day. Nothing ever happens to me anyway.'

That camp was astrology mad, and even Mongo was bustling up with questions about his future and prospects. Anita and I had been bored for years by Julie's hobby, so we went off by ourselves.

'Your friend, Mr. Muirden?' she began. 'He has quite a line.'

'He's giving you the rush tactics because he's afraid you may dash off before he really gets down to business.'

'Is he like that all the time?'

'Well, he's young,' I said handsomely. 'And he's engaged. And he's a long way from home.'

'He was telling me about this engineer who came all the way up here to see you.'

'Ask him to keep his face out of my affairs, will you?'

Anita looked injured. 'I only brought it up because I was quite thrilled to think you had found someone at last.' Anita paints water-colours and I have never known a water-colour painter yet who wasn't romantic. She was sitting on the creek bank making a wash drawing of our camp.

'It's fun to have a talented family,' I said. 'Don't forget to put in Mongo's latrine.'

'But truly, Mallee, about Lee Stollin . . .'

'You've got the name right. Is Julie as broke as she says she is?'

'So-so. Mallee, I wish you'd come home. I can't stop Julie spending when you're not there. I'm away all day and she dashes out to the shops and comes home in a taxi because she can't carry all the parcels. Of course I like parties too, but it isn't the same without you and Daddy. The flat is always full of people, but if the flow of food and drink ceased,' she shrugged her shoulders cynically, 'they wouldn't be there. It's such a restless, rackety way to live. Honestly, Mallee, if Daddy did make a tremendous amount out of this oil concern I'd never believe it was real. We've been broke so often that I'm always wondering if the man will come to cut off the gas.'

That is the trouble with the kind of childhood Anita and I had. It makes you very careful.

'I love clothes,' Anita sighed. 'I may become a designer. I'm trying to get a leg in with the television people too.' She smiled in her self-contained way. 'Life's very interesting, isn't it?' I admired my beautiful sister and she admired her wash drawing. 'The trouble is always the light,' she added. 'It changes all the time. And the shadows alter so. Mallee, you are a pig. You never tell me anything. Here comes your boy friend.'

'He isn't my boy friend.' Blaze Muirden was making

313

across the flat in the direction of those harlequin pants and green shirt.

'No-o,' Anita said critically. 'He's the kind that runs through wives the way Mother runs through money.' Which was good observation for my small sister.

Before they departed for the plane, Julie kissed me and folded away the cheque in her handbag and promised that she would use it only for outstanding debts. 'You know I hate to call on you, Mallee darling, but it's all I can do to make ends meet. Dennis just doesn't realize how the cost of living has gone up, and I certainly hope he strikes oil soon. Personally I would prefer to see him with these television people, because that's the kind of thing I can understand. I am not very happy in my mind about Brannigan's Bend. I will have to place the whole matter before Mr. Pollock.'

Julie's round of farewells was a series of mysterious injunctions: 'Remember what I told you — do nothing before the end of September' — this was to Mongo who never did anything he could avoid — 'because you have adverse aspects under Mars.' He would have adverse aspects if any of us found him doing nothing until the end of September.

'You must be very proud of your mother, Mallee,' Hilda said reverently. 'That woman — she knows, I tell you. She knows! I only wish I had her mind.' I saw I would bask in reflected glory until the astrological fever wore off.

Julie was especially reluctant to break off her last little talk with Fay. Dennis was in a fever of impatience by the car, while they drew to one side and Fay's bright head bent deferentially towards the source of wisdom, plump in its black suit.

'Yes, Mrs. Herrick,' Fay murmured, clasping her hands. 'That's just it.'

'Well, follow your instincts,' my mother called, breaking away. 'Don't let what is called conscience spoil your life. You have every opportunity and you are born under Venus, you know. Yes, Dennis, I'm coming.'

I felt quite lonely driving back over the darkened road from the airport by myself. Nobody in camp could talk of anything but what Mrs. Herrick had said. They were like dram drinkers deprived of their stimulant. Now they would have to go on from day to day without Julie peering over her horn-rimmed glasses — I'm sure she only wore them because Mr. Pollock did — and making everybody feel that there was a special dispensation waiting round the corner. Why, a lucky day might occur, and they wouldn't even know it! They might treat it just like any other day.

Blaze was especially glum. 'Here I am,' he moaned, 'stuck at Brannigan's Bend with the best part of my life gone, and all I have in front of me is: What I think is going to happen won't happen. That's a nice thing to look forward to. But no wonder Dennis does so well with a private witch in the family.' He looked at me darkly. 'Do I ever come into wealth? No, I don't. Do I get what I want? No, she says, I get what is good for me.' He added importantly, 'Big changes. That's what the witch said.'

You could see that you wouldn't get any sense out of them until we started extracting.

Chapter Thirty

THERE had been hardly any winter. The wattle was out at the end of July. First the gold began and the magnificent blaze of wildflowers followed. All the white flowers tossed together in a wind that was getting warmer all the time, and the bees began swarming out of season.

In New South Wales they take off about September–October, and you find magnificent, goldy-brown clusters, some as big as two armfuls, in the whippy bushes round the clearing or, worst of all, hanging up in a tree where you had to climb for them. When I got the vapours, I would say I was going to look for swarms, and stroll off for an hour or two to recover my temper. I began to have quite a reputation for finding lost bees.

Joe would bring the boxes when I went back to report, climb up to shake down the swarms, while I stood by to clap a lid on them. We were putting on extra supers all the time, trying to prevent them swarming, and giving them room for the honey they brought in; and we were extracting from daylight until after dark — long after dark.

Joe and I still worked in the extracting house, with Blaze and Mongo or Fred and Big Mike out in the yard. This season we were using carbolic lids, which were more efficient because you could stack the boxes of comb, and deal with them as you pleased.

We shuffled those bees about to take advantage of the different species as they came into flower, leaving the weak hives behind to build up. We were slinging the honey in, but for some reason the bottom had dropped out of the market. However, while the bees were doing so well, and the burr comb a-building in the lids because they had so much honey and didn't know what to do with it, we were happy enough.

Fay still considered she was house-keeping for me and that her position in camp was that of a kind of companion and keeper. What she found to do was little enough, but she did the cooking and tended Bidgee and Brian. At the week-end I would do my washing and take a share of the cooking, and every night I boiled my own overalls and rinsed everything I wore, so Fay wasn't exactly waiting on me. She made up for it by defending me against Hilda, or driving out to spend the day helping Mrs. Hasselfors.

I had rather lost my grip on that oilfield and all my information came through Fay, or Mel Staines, who formed the habit of spending his spare time with us. There was no sign of Dennis, who evidently found the lure of the bright lights too strong. I knew if he left he would be too caught up to come back, but I wrote to him faithfully, reporting what little activity there was.

I would have been perfectly happy if it had not been for Blaze Muirden, who was working harder than anyone, and keeping his eye on a dozen things at once. As long as he kept his eye on a dozen other things that suited me, but his eye had a tendency to stray in my direction. We neither of us ever referred to that rainy day in Nithering. I was assured that my swift action in leaving for Queensland had convinced Blaze there was nothing doing.

But I might have known that unscrupulous customer better. He was just waiting his time. I had been so cheered by the news that he was getting married that we were back on the old footing exchanging cheerful insults.

I worked with Joe because we fitted in well together, but I rode in the truck with Blaze because he always insisted on driving and I had the seat of honour in front. Or when I went pottering off looking for swarms when work was slack for a time, I would find Blaze, instead of Joe, following with the boxes. Joe could swarm up a tree like a cat, but Blaze was unhandy at it and inclined to stand and curse.

We were turning over one swarm to make sure we had the queen, with bees circling about us everywhere and a drift of smoke to keep them at bay, when Blaze launched the big barrage.

'Mallee,' he began, 'why don't you take an interest in something besides bees? I know for a fact that you're just as big a bloody villain as I am, and that I'll get you sooner or later — see if I don't. But you put on this act of being all cool and aloof and I'm just about ready to scream.'

'Look, Blaze,' I said, peering into the bottom of the box for the scuttling, long-bodied beauty we were searching for, 'if your glands are giving you trouble, for Pete's sake take a trip to Tembucca. You've been pretty bad-tempered lately, and I suppose the celibacy is getting you down.'

'There you go again. My glands! The way you say that. Would it occur to you that I've always been struck on you since the first time I saw you?'

'Me and a few others,' I suggested. 'Just a few.'

Blaze moved in my direction with the intention of trying a little direct action. I gave one swift glance in the direction of the bee-yard in the distance, and realized that we had wandered farther than I thought. I took up that bee-box and bounced it.

'Look out, you fool,' Blaze yelled. 'You'll lose the swarm.' That was the bee-keeper coming out. In his anxiety at seeing me maltreat those bees, he forgot his intentions for a moment.

'There she is.' I clapped the lid on the box. 'Safe inside.'

'Honestly, Mallee . . .'

'Honestly, Blaze, you can keep your predatory paws off.'

'All right, Mrs. Stollin,' Blaze murmured. We left the box and he took up another empty and followed along as I tramped ahead.

'Somewhere round here,' I said, gazing about me, 'I marked the tree.' I went bird-dogging around looking for it until I found it. 'Here we are.' The bees had clustered in a sapling and all we had to do was shake it. Blaze just stood there with the smoker in his hand.

'I've never known it fail,' he said to himself. 'I'll work you round to the idea.' I was not weak-minded enough to ask what idea. 'I just persist and persist.'

'Has it ever occurred to you that you are a louse? You know that I've given myself till Christmas to learn this game. By Christmas you'll be married to a girl I like to think is a friend of mine.'

'So I've only got till Christmas.' He sighed and gave me what was meant to be a heart-rending look. 'I'll have to work fast.'

'Well, if you start acting the goat I'll just remove my bees down to Col's farm. Mongo would come with me. There's some good silver-box there.' I tried to speak reasonably.

'I can always cry. I've had some real good results by sobbing out loud.' He gave a splendid imitation of a damsel relenting. 'There, there, darling. Let me hold your head in my arms.' He reverted to his own manner. 'You shed a few more tears and wipe your eyes, and you're home and dry.'

I couldn't help chuckling. 'I used to know a chap who tried that. It made me want to hit him. He *always* cried.'

'Tell me about him.' Blaze was interested. He gave the bees some smoke and shook the tree while I held the box. To keep his mind on the job I told him about the man who used to cry. 'It's no use, Mallee,' he said, as we walked back. 'As I said before, you're just as big a villain as I am. I am not going to pay you the compliment of putting on any fancy act. I can always rape you and save you the responsibility of saying, "Yes."'

In a few well-chosen words I gave my opinion of this line of conversation.

'I won't have to,' he assured me. 'You'll weaken.'

'I wish you'd get it into your head that I have some self-respect, if you haven't.'

'Doesn't make a damn bit of difference.'

When we got back Joe was growling impatiently. 'You took a hell of a time just picking up a few swarms.'

'Your brother talks too much.'

'Don't need to tell *me* that.'

So we got to work on a stack of comb that was waiting. Blaze was tinning off and he sang to himself and kept Mongo working like a dog, and generally acted as the boss of the job, but by the end of the week he had me jumping in the air when he suddenly started out under my feet like a quail just where I least expected him.

I took to riding on the back of the truck instead of in front, and I took good care not to be left alone with that menace. But Blaze was giving the orders and every now and then I found myself stranded with him, and the campaign would start all over again. I was pleased it wasn't October because that is a bad month for me, when I am apt to lose my head.

Now and then I would review my plan for carting my

bees down to Col's place, but they were doing so exceptionally well it would look queer to move them and be apt to excite comment. Besides, I didn't see why Blaze should upset me, or drive me away. Big Mike was aware that Blaze was out to cut the ground from under my feet. He had a way of looking at Fred as much as to say, 'Get a load of Muirden. He's certainly making the pace hot,' that made me hopping mad. Sooner or later everyone would wake up.

Nobody could say that Blaze made any secret of his sentiments. He overdid it; he exaggerated, he clowned. He would stare at me across the mess table when we were eating and shake his head pityingly, and say, 'Mallee is simply pining away. I can't believe it's dear Mr. Stollin she's interested in, so it must be me. Of course, I know I'm pretty good, but what does she see in me?' So far they took it just as a development of his old line of ribbing me. 'You can tell by the way she looks at me.' I was giving him a furious glare. 'Poor girl! She just can't hide her feelings.'

'Pull your ears in, Muirden,' I would snarl. 'They spoil your fatal beauty sticking out.'

'Really, Mallee,' Hilda would chime in sympathetically, 'I don't know why you put up with him.'

'She thinks she's going to marry Lee Stollin,' Blaze said, complacently eating. 'But it's really me she's struck on.'

Hilda tried to pour oil on what she thought was the makings of a pretty row. 'Blaze gets worse every day,' she told me privately. 'He never has been very careful what he says, but he goes beyond a joke. Is it true that you're going to marry that engineer up at Nithering?'

'Don't you start on me too, Hilda. One is enough.'

Occasionally Blaze would torment Fay instead of me. He never got any change out of Fay. She would just smile and never answer but it gave me a much-needed respite. We went on working until we all looked like ghosts and were so tired we could hardly stagger. Blaze drove us and he drove himself.

'Come on,' he would yell. 'We've got to get another five hundred tins off. Dreaming on your feet. The flow won't last for ever. We've got to keep going and take off while we've got it. Get those supers on, Mongo. What are you waiting for?'

His language was enough to make a bullock blush, but if he hoped to make me blush he was underestimating my admiration for his flow of language. I had heard cursing, but nothing like him when a bee crawled up the leg of his pants. It wounded him, he said, in his tenderest feelings, and we were happy all day to think that bee had returned Blaze some of his own medicine.

Then one night we came home to find a pile of mail waiting for us, and, of course, we all fell on it like starved wolves. Nothing was heard while we read our letters. Blaze thrust his savagely in his pocket and went off with a scowl. Next day, instead of swearing and singing, he hardly spoke.

'What's up with him?' Joe asked.

'Search me. Bad news from home, d'you think?'

'Could be,' Joe considered.

Blaze said shortly, 'I'm driving in to Caterpillar. Lend me the car, Mallee?' and off he went leaving us staring at each other.

The next day after breakfast, which was just after daylight, he said, 'Mallee, we'll take a look at those bees of yours in the yard up on Hellhole.'

'What about the extracting?'

'That's right. Argue with me,' he snarled. 'Fred can go in the house with Joe, he's only repairing his bloody truck.' He started slamming supers on to the back of the Commer, still in a black temper.

'What have you done, Mallee?' Fay asked.

'Damned if I know.' Everybody sensed there was something wrong. 'Will I bring the tucker boxes?' I asked.

'Suit your bloody self.' So I packed some cold meat and bread and butter and the usual allowance of tea and sugar. Fay hovered round helping. She seemed nervous. 'What's wrong with you, Fay?' I asked.

'Oh nothing, Mallee. I was just giving you a hand.' She was quite humble and propitiating.

While we were driving the twelve miles to the yard on the bank of Hellhole Creek, Blaze said nothing about what was worrying him. I kept quiet. When we reached the yard of neatly painted boxes he made no move to put on supers or see how the bees were doing. He sat down on the top of the nearest hive. The bees were not unaccustomed to people using their home as a seat and they went in and out and circled round without worrying about it.

'Take a look at this.' Blaze fished that letter from out of his pocket. It was, as I had suspected, from Daphne, and if Blaze had been twice as unscrupulous as I knew him to be, it would still have been a very stiff letter to receive from the girl you expected to marry. I turned it over, hoping there was some postscript giving him a hope.

'I rang her up from Caterpillar yesterday,' he said glumly. 'Had to wait a hell of a time for them to put through the call.'

'What did she say?'

'She finally hung up on me, but she made it plain enough. Now read *this*. It was enclosed with Daff's letter.'

I have never liked anonymous letters and I had seen a few of them at the radio station, where they come about two a week. The letter was not only unsigned but it gave Daphne to understand in the plainest terms that her

affianced was not true to her in any meaning of the word.
I daren't tell him he deserved it. 'While you are home
getting your trousseau ready,' it concluded, 'he is sleeping
with Mallee Herrick.' I handed him the letter back without comment. It made me feel low in my mind.

'Surely she doesn't believe that. She couldn't be so
stupid as to believe it. You'll just have to belt down to
Tembucca and convince her it's a lie.'

'Oh, let it go,' he said indifferently. 'I'm sick of this,
anyhow. I'm damned if I'm going down there to patch
it up all over again. Even if it isn't true, I've tried hard
enough. *You* can swear to that.'

'Who do you think wrote it? Hilda?'

'Who cares? Well, I'll tell you something you never
will believe — it doesn't matter that much to me.' He
snapped his fingers.

'What a lie! That's just your vanity talking.' I leant
against the mudguard of the truck and rolled a cigarette.
'I'm sorry, Blaze.'

'Well, don't be sorry. I chewed it over wondering if
I should say anything to you. Then it struck me I should
put you wise, because, after all, it concerns you as well as
me.'

If Fred had been there he would have abused Blaze
for me. He would have told him that he should keep his
mouth from opening so wide, that he had brought this all
on himself and he needed a kick in the pants. I remembered the way Fay had hovered round that morning.
The more I thought about it the more certain I was Fay
had written that letter. It wasn't like Hilda, who always
said straight out what she thought, and would give you
the rough edge of her tongue on the slightest provocation.
Fay was much more devious.

Blaze took some supers and carried them up to the end
of the row. We began working in silence, lifting off the

lids to see how the honey was coming in. If the hive needed another super, I would slip one on neatly and Blaze would adjust the lid back. We went right through the yard without more than a word or two about the bees. When we finished we scratched some sticks together on a patch of bare ground to boil the billy.

'This forest is too dry for the time of the year,' Blaze said thoughtfully. 'All very well for those forestry blokes to talk about standing-by around Christmas. If we got a spark now it'd run like gunpowder.'

He had given me a lecture the night before about being careful with cigarette butts. In fact, he had dressed me down in front of the whole company, and finished up with a monologue on the evils of smoking directed to me and Mongo and Joe, who were the only smokers. Joe had told him to go and boil his head.

I was so cut up about Blaze's busted marriage that I hardly dared say anything. I liked Daphne very much indeed, although I thought she was wasting herself on Blaze. But I would have done anything to pick up the pieces.

'All right, Mallee,' he said good-humouredly enough. 'You don't need to act as though it was your girl had run out on you.'

'It wouldn't matter so much if it was me, because I wasn't born under a fire sign. If you are born under a cold, watery sign with a different nature . . .'

'Oh, don't *give* me that. You hand me that bull all the time. Anyway, the witch was right about me not having anything happen to me that I thought was going to.' He had really taken a knock and he kept on talking about Daphne and all the time he had known her, with a few curses thrown in for luck about the gullibility of girls, and how they would believe anything of a man when they ought to know him better. He was recovering and

325

licking his wounds and talking himself into a state of mind when he could believe he had quite decided this for himself instead of being slung out on his ear.

'I never would've got engaged to Daphne that last time,' he said savagely, 'if you hadn't skidded out on me. You know it was you I wanted.' Here it came again. He hadn't recovered from one love affair before he was trying to clinch the next. 'I believe you *are* in love with me, but you won't admit it. Damn you, I wish I knew.'

'That's right, Muirden,' I said. 'You borrow my truck, you help yourself to brood from my hives, and you think you might as well borrow my carcase into the bargain.'

'Answer me. Would you ever just act human? Would you come to my tent some night and say, "Well, you bastard, you win. Move over"? Because if I thought that would ever happen, Daphne and every other girl on earth could go out of my life for keeps. I mean it.'

I really did think he meant it then. We gave each other a hard, steady glance through a cloud of bees. 'Just so that you could prove that letter-writer was correct in every respect?'

'What of it? Do you really worry about what anyone says about you?'

'I don't suppose I do. Not that sort of letter-writer.'

'Well, then, what about it?'

'Are you going to do the next yard down or leave it?'

'You're yellow,' he said contemptuously. 'You exasperate me. You do. Tell you what would explain it. You've never slept with a man in your life and you're scared.'

I was outraged by this accusation. 'I don't pretend to have your wide experience,' I said sweetly. 'Nor do I go about giving everyone an earful of my conquests. At least I can keep my mouth shut.'

I sighed because I did so hate the prospect of packing and leaving. Blaze would keep on harping and nagging. We drove back to camp, and those present, respecting our lowering looks, tip-toed around as though it were a death-bed. After supper Blaze was hilariously gay. He began teasing Fred about some old quarrel, and they shouted each other down and argued it all over again. I yawned and went off to bed.

However, I lay awake in the dark until the camp settled down and there was only the sound of Blaze's accursed radio. I was tossing pennies in my mind, heads I move, tails I cut across and prove to that villainous character I'm not as windy as he thinks I am. It would be nice to give Blaze a pleasant surprise. Well, I thought, what does it matter? Maybe I am being a rotten kind of worm to the old Blaze. If he's working himself into a state about a little thing like finding out what my style and tactics are in a state of nature, am I fair to hold out on him? It means something to him. I'd like to see him happy, poor devil. And then I told myself not to be so damn patronizing. Not at all the right spirit, just trying to screw yourself up to the required pitch. With a little sigh I slipped out, taking every precaution so as not to wake Fay.

I slid across that clearing like a shadow, trying to tell myself that I wasn't in a low, dejected frame of mind, but that I liked the prospect immensely. Anyway, I was resolved to do my best. I might not be up to Blaze's standards, but he would find that out for himself, blast him. I flattened myself against the wall of his tent and took a deep breath. Then I realized Blaze was talking to someone.

'And don't try to kid me you didn't write that letter to Daphne,' he was saying. 'Because I know damn well it was you. You did the same thing down at Nithering, didn't you, and put Harry Warren wise to me? What a lovely move that was! All I can say is that you needn't have brought poor bloody Mallee into it.'

There was a muffled murmur in response. I had taken that deep breath and now I didn't dare to breathe it out. If I trod on a stick or made a noise, I was in an embarrassing position, just the most embarrassing position I could be in. My obvious course was to steal quietly away from there, but the trouble is that once you decide to steal quietly, and you have a desperate reason for stealing quietly, you trip over a tent rope.

'What was that?' Blaze said sharply.

'Mongo, I suppose.' Fay was not in the least disturbed. 'You know how he blunders about.' I didn't dare move.

'Well, anyway,' Blaze resumed — I could see he was a talker-in-bed, a confirmed talker-in-bed; as Joe said, he talked even in his sleep — 'anyway, I suppose now we square Joe somehow and we skid off and get married. *I* don't mind. Joe will be sore for a while, but he'll come round.'

'When I'm married to you,' Fay said quietly, 'you will never look at another girl, because I will see to that.'

'I know damn well you will.' He laughed to himself, contentedly enough. 'If you catch me.'

'I'll always find out. And I'll take good care, see if I don't, to make you stay put.'

'I still think you're a bitch, Fay. I think you're a double-dyed bitch.'

'You like it. And it serves you right.'

This time I *was* stealing away. I crossed that clearing as though it was red-hot and shot back into my sleeping bag like a case moth recovering its casing, even drawing in my head.

Then I started to laugh with the edge of the sleeping bag in my mouth, so that I could only laugh silently. Even when I had subsided into just a broad grin, it still occurred to me that this was the joke of the century. The trouble was that I had no one to share it with me. Mavis would appreciate it. I could just see myself describing to Mavis how I had hot-footed out prepared to make the supreme sacrifice, and discovered that Fay had got in first. I meditated on the pleasure of looking that elder Muirden boy in the eye and letting him know I had over-heard his conversation; but if I did, that would pool me, because what was I doing outside his tent so late at night? No, I would keep my face straight. By no word or flicker of an eyelid must I ever let Blaze Muirden know that his innocent domesticity had been on the point of being disturbed.

Then it occurred to me what a good pair Blaze and Fay would make. He would be a wonderful father to those boys. He liked children, any sort of children, and he was stricter than Joe. Fay would certainly see to it that Blaze didn't stray, and if he did she would deal with him. I shouldn't be surprised if he made a model husband. Perhaps, after all, Daphne had been too straightforward, too quick to pounce out. Fay would wait her time and deal her loving spouse a thump under the ear when he was least expecting it.

But what surprised me was my own half-wittedness in not realizing that Blaze would always try to play two women at once, or three if there happened to be three about. Dear old Blaze! How I like that man! A heel if ever there was one.

Chapter Thirty-one

I was quietly prepared to break the news that I was leaving with bees and baggage, when Mel Staines came down to the camp in what would have been a state of tension in a less craggy and stern-faced character. The drillers were just ready to come into the gas zone, and Staines had been sending telegrams to Dennis to bring him up for the great event. The Parent was chartering a special plane, and all the heads of the concern would be descending on Brannigan's Bend like a flight of angels or galahs, complete with pressmen, photographers and a member of parliament.

That oilfield was being groomed for the occasion. Of course, they wouldn't stay at the Bloodhouse, which might give the wrong impression, but they would drive over from the hotel in Caterpillar. The mayor of Caterpillar wanted to lend the oilfield a flag, and Mel Staines asked me if I thought that was the right touch. He could get a couple of men to cut a pine sapling.

'All they'll want is booze,' I suggested. 'Alert the Bloodhouse. You'll find they'll all be down there anyway.'

Staines said that the gas coming in was not one of those things you could bet on. They didn't know what would come in, but they were hoping for oil in commercial quantities. Under his stone-bound exterior he was as nervous as a prima donna before the Big Night. So many things could go wrong. He hadn't expected Mr. Herrick to bring a whole gang of people; they must get the holes filled up in the road. Was there anything else I could think of?

I went up to the office with him and found Hasselfors showing his big yellow teeth. 'You're quite a stranger, Miss Herrick,' he greeted me, making it sound sinister.

'Well, you only had to put out a call' — I swept dust in his direction — 'and I come running.'

We looked at that oilfield with the idea of doing something to pretty it; but there is nothing you can do about an oilfield. There it is, take it or leave it, mud, dirt, engines and weatherboard sheds, with the steel rig looking bony and forbidding in the middle. It was as bare as a dancer's bosom.

So after cleaning out the office I went down to the Bloodhouse and had a word with fat Patsy, who agreed to turn on the beer freely for the great day. These gentlemen who were so importantly descending on us didn't realize that they all had to be fed. Hilda and Fay and George's wife went up to consult with Mrs. Hasselfors. Northern Exploitations would foot the bill for the banquet, but we would have to get out meat and bread, slay Mrs. Balancovitch's ducks, if it came to the pinch, borrow knives and forks from the canteen. Of course, knowing the Parent, I should have realized that he would see that lobsters packed in ice, caviare and desserts, would all be sent by air — and champagne. Nothing but the best for Dennis Oberon Herrick.

The mayor of Caterpillar offered to lend the band, but Mel Staines vetoed that. He said the bandsmen would probably drink more than even the member of parliament. Poor little Brannigan's Bend, excited over the idea of being the centre of an oil industry, hummed with new excitement, and there was some resentment that Caterpillar seemed to be taking the cream. The mayor, who had quite forgotten the coldness between himself and me over Fred's bees, made a special trip out with some of the Caterpillar notables and was important and genial. The postmistress at Brannigan's Bend hardly left her switch, the conversations were so exciting to listen to.

We reviewed our wardrobes and courted fat Patsy with the aim of getting a bath at the Bloodhouse in real water instead of creek mud. When the news came through from the post office that the great men had arrived in Caterpillar even George and Mongo, who were not dressy at the best of times, were borrowing shoe polish.

The men were working at the oilfield with flaring arc lights, and at midnight the gas blew in with an explosion that could be heard miles away.

Next morning Mel Staines had a man stationed by the gate to warn people in cars to put out their cigarettes. He wasn't taking any risks on his precious oil show. He had timed the whole thing beautifully so far. Of course, there was nothing special to see, only a hissing noise and a strong smell. He couldn't keep anyone out because they might be one of the official party and take umbrage. People strolled in, had a look and drove off again.

'I'm so damned scared of setting the whole forest on fire,' Staines told me, 'I've got the forestry brigade standing by. If we only get gas, we'll just have to pipe it off and burn it the way we did before.'

'Any oil?'

'There's still a hope. We haven't bottomed yet, you know.'

For the Parent's fiesta there was the bitterest wind of the year, and I had wasted my time cleaning out the office. The wind had a rum-and-red-nose quality; it was the epitome of the winter we had missed, suggesting 'flu, chilblains and seven rugs.

When the magnificoes arrived — and they were late — the Parent was in the second car, fretful at eating dust all the way from Caterpillar. He gave me a piercing glance, no doubt relieved that I had not turned out in my boiler suit, but inspecting me like a drill sergeant to make sure I would do him credit. He had phoned and had me called to the post office the night before with special instructions as to what I was to wear — 'that wine-red thing because it has the small hat to go with it and that will hide your hair. And, please, dear girl, plenty of make-up. There will be photographs for publicity. I expected you to meet me in Caterpillar.'

'You didn't even wire to say when you were coming.'

'But you *knew*. I told Mel Staines to pass the word on to you.'

In the first car was the member of parliament with the chairman of Northern Exploitations, who was enormous and vital and unaffected — one of those men that even creditors trust — with a streamlined personality. Of course, Northern Exploitations was only pickles to him, just a little side gamble to amuse him between really big deals. He kept it as he might keep a racehorse in his stables that just conceivably could win sometimes.

'Hello, H.D.,' I said.

'Mallee, my darling girl, how are the bees? Dennis has been telling me about them. Meet the Honourable Charles Fairborough, member for Settunga. His hobby,' he told me in his deep voice, 'is orchids.'

'There's some food, H.D., when you've looked at the works.'

'Fine, fine. Who's the beautiful creature with the red hair?' That was Fay, so I introduced him; and H.D. kept as close to Fay as a postage stamp to an envelope, until he was cut out by a wiry journalist with an insolent expression and a cold eye. I was left with the member of

333

parliament on my hands, and they all wandered round in groups looking intelligently at pipes and mud and casings, the rotary table and the engines and the clanking drill, until they had some excuse to get in out of the wind. The member had brought his secretary; H.D. had brought his secretary. There were representatives of the big press syndicates, and news-reel men who took a pessimistic view, and photographers who trudged round with leather plate containers hanging from their shoulders.

H.D. made an impressive speech about the hardships which one faced in developing the potential assets of this glorious land; and the .paid hands stood out of the way of the cameras and made low remarks to each other out of the corners of their mouths.

'All good publicity,' the Parent said cheerfully. He was hoping it would come on the screen with the announcement: 'There has been a Great Oil Strike at the Settunga Oilfield in the North. Just before the great news the member for Settunga spoke of the tremendous possibilities . . .' and so on.

I was so bored I could have cried. Here was the old Diasmos whirling round and sucking about, the pretence, the long pretence. 'How deep is that death,' I repeated St. Augustine's words to myself, 'in vanity and futile strivings.' Just pushing about in the Diasmos.

When the bones of Mrs. Balancovitch's ducks had been removed from the back veranda of the superintendent's house, the toasts were in order and even the news-reel men were looking human. There were more speeches, one from the mayor of Caterpillar. I slipped away, and the Parent joined me later and abused me for helping with the washing-up when I should have been minding the member for Settunga..

'If only there was some oil,' the Parent sighed. 'But never mind. There's gas.'

'Plenty of gas,' I said.

I had promised the news-reel men I would take them out to look at the bees. Fred and Blaze would be secretly thrilled, but putting on a great front that they hated it all the time. I didn't want them to feel left out. But in that wind bees have a nervous tendency to eddy about, so the news-reel gang took some hurried long-distance shots and sped down to the Bloodhouse. Those chaps liked Brannigan's Bend. They were still there when the rest of the cortège had rolled off towards Caterpillar. They had their tongues in their cheeks about the oil show though.

The journalists were down at the camp with Fay, and they had a case of whisky which was their own private case donated by Dennis Oberon Herrick, who had called in to retrieve Wilhelmina for the duration of his stay. Half the population of Brannigan's Bend was down with the journalists having at long last realized that dream of striking a deep, rich stream of liquor in our camp.

By dusk the oilfield was deserted except for the shift on duty. We packed the last pressman into the car and rounded up the film unit. The wind had increased and was now a gale. After so much drinking we were all inclined for an early night, pleased that everything had gone off so well. Tomorrow the member for Settunga and H.D. and the film unit and the pressmen would be something we could talk about as an event receding into the past. We were awakened at two in the morning by the sawmill whistle blowing. The forestry gang were shouting and climbing on trucks with spray-gun outfits on their shoulders. On the wind was the smell of smoke and burning gum leaves and the fire was coming with a roar down on Brannigan's Bend.

Nobody ever found out exactly how it started. My own view was that the night-shift on the rig had found some left-over champagne. By a miracle nobody was singed except the fire-fighters. They got the Hasselfors family out in their nightwear.

Before dawn the film unit came tearing out from Caterpillar again, heroic and enthusiastic. This was something they really seemed pleased about. They took shots of the cars and trucks loaded with portable property conveying people out of Brannigan's Bend. With the wind there was no hope of stopping the flare that blew through the tree-tops and lit up the scrub behind the beaters, so that they had to run back for their lives.

All the men from our camp were out beating, also the men from the sawmills, and volunteers kept arriving from Caterpillar, so that the road surged with men and vehicles. It was only a narrow road at best, and how Hilda drove that caravan through the stream of traffic was a sight to see. Fay and I and George's wife worked getting down the tents and loading the Commer and the International. The grey Ford and our extracting house were ten miles the other side of the oil-well. Fay couldn't drive, worse luck, so I took the Commer down to our bee yard on the Caterpillar road and dumped the load, got a lift back and took out the International. George's wife brought their truck back close behind to pick up another load.

By that time there was no hope for Brannigan's Bend and the fire was creeping round by the creek. Their only hope would be if the wind dropped. There were piles of bottom boards, tins, excluders, boxes. I was heaving them on to the International when Joe and Blaze came running.

'Leave it, you fool!' Blaze yelled. 'Where's the others?' I told him everything we could save was down at the bee yard.

'Don't stop here,' he ordered. 'Get down to the farm with all the cleared paddocks five miles from Caterpillar. You'll be safe there.'

'Hilda has all the kids in the caravan.'

'You go with Mrs. George, hear me? Take the Ruin. Leave us the International. We're going to need it.'

The fire was nearly to the edge of the clearing the other side of Brannigan's Bend. Mrs. George was a slow, nervous driver, so I kept with her. We had to get ahead of the firemen from Caterpillar who were preparing to make a stand at the clearing round the forestry office down the road. When the last truck got away from Brannigan's Bend — and it was our red International — the flames were either side of the track to Caterpillar and Brannigan's Bend was burning with a crash and crackle.

It was lucky in one way the wind changed. It left Brannigan's Bend a twisted, blackened stretch of smoking ruins that smouldered for days. But it was unlucky for us. We had all our yards of bees, except the one on the Caterpillar road, spread out through the forest. The wind took the fire away from Brannigan's Bend, when it was too late to matter, and poured it like a flood of flame travelling south on our bees. The men did their best, driving zig-zag along forestry tracks to reach the bees and get them out. When the ammunition dump blew up, that gave the fire a fresh start.

I still think of those poor bees, suffocating in the smoke, not going away from the hive where the brood was, because the brood is the most important thing of all. Right to the last they would be protecting the brood, the scouts out, the bodyguard on duty retreating from the landing stage, the nursing bees dropping from the comb; and the poor white grubs in a sizzling mess of hot wax, blackened and unrecognizable.

There were four hundred hives belonging to Fred Connelly, a hundred and fifty of Big Mike's, three hundred owned by the Muirdens, the grey Ford and the extracting house — and mine, of course. The fire kept

337

going with a good wind behind it for two days, and then when the wind dropped they were able to halt it at the breaks.

The Parent was like the fire. First he blew in one direction wanting all the publicity he could get, and then he was working very hard indeed to keep the enquiry within bounds and guide it the way he wanted it. 'Of course,' he said, 'we'll begin again. Now that we know there is gas in Number One we will be able to push ahead with Number Two Well. The ground is already cleared.'

'They'll probably lynch you,' I said wearily, 'and the mayor will hold the rope.'

The Parent insisted that it was sabotage. Every precaution had been taken to guard against fire, the most extraordinary precautions. Someone had deliberately burned up Northern Exploitations Number One Well. 'It couldn't be anything but deliberate intention on the part of vast overseas interests,' and that was what he expressly stated in print.

'Stuff,' I told him. 'The only possible saboteur out that way was Hasselfors and he wouldn't endanger his own family and set his wife's bedding on fire in the middle of the night.'

'Mallee, you don't realize how important this is. You don't realize that millions — millions, I tell you — hang on the outcome.'

'What about our bees? Do you realize that your damned oil-well burned up our bees?'

'That is a mere bagatelle compared to my own loss. I wish you wouldn't keep mentioning those bees. And the people who are pressing for the enquiry are the defence authorities who have suddenly realized they had an ammunition dump up here ever since the last war. I can swear they had forgotten all about it. Really, Mallee, to go harping about a quantity of bees shows a complete lack of any sense of proportion. What about Brannigan's Bend? Three sawmills and a railway. Work that one out.'

What surprised me was the attitude of those apiarists of mine. Because they could not bear to think about the desolate, burned-up yards, they made a great joke of it.

'The man who engineered that fire was Mongo. He just wanted to get out of work.'

'You know damn well it was you, Blaze. You wanted to get nearer home.'

'Well, anyway, we're always getting our hives burned up. Nothing new in that. Last year we lost a lot. What beats me is that we come out of New South to avoid the floods just so's we can have the best bang-up fire for years. Nice work, boys! Shows real brains! We make a long, expensive move, and belt hell out of our trucks hurrying to get here. We were afraid we wouldn't make it, but we made it all right. And we built up those bees, by God — got them in splendid nick. There wasn't a weak hive, except those on the Caterpillar road that got saved. We'll get a nice little honey cheque, and we'll be just as deep in with the banks as ever. But if it wasn't the bloody fire, it'd be something else. Always something, so what the hell!'

Chapter Thirty-two

WE SET up our camp at the Fifteen Mile Creek from which we had been carting water. It was isolated, mosquito-ridden; but, at least, it wasn't charred and blackened. The hives on the Fifteen Mile had escaped, besides those on the Caterpillar road. George's, of course, were at Fifteen Mile, that being the most inaccessible place.

'You know there *is* something damned funny about that fire,' Blaze said. 'Much as I hate to agree with Dennis.'

I was putting some triple-dye on Mongo who had blistered ears, and his hair burned up the back of his neck. He was beginning to look like a savage painted with woad.

'You must have turned your back to it, Mongo,' Blaze said suspiciously. 'How'd that happen?'

'When my coat caught alight,' Mongo said heroically. 'But I put it out. I didn't say anything when I came back to camp. You were all talking to those journalists, so I went straight to bed without any tea.'

'Journalists?' Blaze said. 'But that was before the fire started.'

'That's right, Blaze. You know that pile of oil drums you bought from the forestry? Well, you told me to pick them up and bring them back to camp and you said, "Clean them, do you hear?"'

'Go on, Mongo,' Blaze said gently. 'That was the dump about a quarter of a mile up the road from the oil-well.'

'That's right. So when everybody was up there that day, I thought I'd clean a few before I brought them down. That's how I got the burn.' Mongo looked shifty. He had a feeling that he was going to be cursed when he deserved commendation. 'But there couldn't possibly have been a spark got away because I had a look round before I came back.'

Just as you can't get stringy-bark to grow on flat clay soil, so you couldn't get an idea into Mongo's head that survived the shock of finding out where it was. He had been told to clean those drums sometime, and a patch of scrub with a strong wind blowing didn't make any difference to the faithful worker.

'Let me tell it,' Blaze said, with a moan. 'This idiot is up there on his own, so what does he do but start cleaning a lot of old oil and petrol drums. He lights the oil in the bottom to burn it off — that right, Mongo? Then what did you do?'

'I threw in a little petrol, Blaze, but the drum was still alight,' Mongo said simply. 'Luckily I had stepped back before the flame and soot and sparks shot out. There was just this little hole in the top about four inches wide and another little hole about an inch, so I couldn't see properly. There was a bit of an explosion.'

'Now, if you had been bending over it,' Blaze suggested, smiling, 'you would've got your head blown off.' He dropped his own face on his hands and said wearily, 'You and Joe hired Mongo. It's *your* job to kill him.'

'But, Blaze, you can't be *certain* that Mongo started the fire. He says that when he'd put his coat out he looked round to make sure . . .'

'I did, Mallee,' Mongo said eagerly. 'I swear there wasn't even a little coil of smoke. But I was feeling a bit sick, so I left the drums there and came back to camp. I put some dripping on the burns, and I wasn't going to say anything with all those people about, so I just lay down and had a rest and I went to sleep.'

We both looked at him without speaking. 'Somebody ought to let Dennis know,' I suggested later to Blaze. 'You do it.'

'I've got to go down to Col's place and see what I can scrounge,' Blaze said hastily. 'Besides, Dennis will have left by now.'

Dennis had sold Wilhelmina before arranging his plane booking. I said I would write to him. It seemed the most tactful way of conveying this interesting piece of news. I funked telling Mel Staines, who probably would have organized a pogrom against apiarists and shot us all down in cold blood.

'By now,' Blaze said, 'there'll be hundreds of miles of Paterson's Curse in flower. We can move what we have left, and those down at Tembucca, out on to the plains.' In his mind's eye he was already looking over great purple sweeps of colour flooding the fields, deeper azure in the hollows, misty over the rises, miles and miles of pollen and honey, blue pollen that the bees brought in so that their legs looked as though they had tiny blue bags tied to them. The bees rubbed themselves all shiny, burrowing down into the great bells, and it frayed their wings working the Paterson's Curse, but it was certainly beautiful, pale clear honey and wonderful pollen.

'Then there's white box in the Warrumbungles,' he continued. 'We might try a few yards there. Of course with so much rain down that way, the white box may have too much water in the nectar, and white box plays merry hell with the bees sometimes. I'll have to go and have a look at it. Take Joe with me. Hilda's keeping Fay and the kids with her in the caravan for now. They'll be staying at Col's place.'

'Col will like *that*.'

'Col isn't home,' Blaze explained. 'He's out with his geiger counter on the ranges. But he ought to be pleased to have somebody mind the place for him while he's away. Joe will drive the Commer. Good thing we've got it.'

'I can drive the Ruin,' I suggested.

'Suit yourself, Mallee.' He was being too polite to ask what my plans were. 'I'll be glad to get out of this. I never did like this Settunga Forest.'

'You didn't like Nithering either, did you? But we took off honey . . .'

'Look, Mallee, in one way we've had a bumper year, and in another we've lost more hives than any five years I know. We'll have to spend everything we've made replacing what we've lost.' This was beginning to be a full-blown post-mortem. 'Twice I've gone against a sixth sense I have. I've let you plump into some place that never in a hundred years in my own judgement I'd have touched. I've followed you round this country getting burnt and froze like a fool. I've said as much to Joe.' Of course Blaze was heart-broken about those bees, but he was unjust. 'It's all very well for you. You've got plenty of money to play with.'

'Sure,' I said, thinking how I would have to go back to work until my next year's cash came in. I had private loans out to Fred and George which they wouldn't be able to repay, and certainly I wouldn't ask them. As for Julie and the Parent, I never expected to see any money they borrowed.

Blaze was hammering out tin strips, getting ready to extract with Fred's extractor which had been at the Fifteen Mile taking honey off George's bees. Then they would move.

'I think I'll leave in the morning,' I said. 'As soon as I get the Roaring Ruin checked over at the garage in

Caterpillar. I'm going down to look at those sixty hives I left with Matt.'

'Those!' Blaze snorted. 'Forget them. They'll have starved to death or be eaten with wax moth. Besides, you can't travel all that way in the Ruin. She won't take it.'

'If you can come up here in her, I can go back.'

I didn't bother with too many elaborate farewells. In a camp someone is always coming or going. Surprisingly enough, Hilda and Big Mike were the two people who seemed to realize they were seeing the last of me. Big Mike did not try any of his rush-and-grab tactics. He shook my hand quietly. 'Been nice to know you, Mallee,' he said. 'You're a great girl.'

Hilda hugged me. 'Don't think it's the money, Mallee,' she said. 'Although that'll be a godsend and you'll get it back, see if you don't. I'll keep Fred up to it.'

'Don't worry Fred,' I cautioned. 'He's got plenty of other things to worry about.'

'What I mean, Mallee, is I'm going to miss you for yourself, apart from the fact that you're the only one that can keep Blaze Muirden in order. I'll be pleased to have Fay for the company because Fay and I get on well — but it won't be the same. The men will go their way and we'll go *our* way and there won't be any missing link.'

'Thanks, Hilda,' I said, smiling to myself. 'It's nice to be the missing link.'

Hilda said in a rush, 'Oh, we'll see you again, but by that time a lot of things could've happened. You know you can always come to me and Fred.'

Fay and I kissed each other. 'Good luck, Fay,' I said. Fay blushed with that faint rise of colour under her white skin that was always so delightful to see. She knew what I meant.

'Thank you, Mallee,' she said sedately. She told me she intended to keep her settlement from the Hydro-

Electricity Authority untouched. 'That's for the boys,' she said firmly, and Fay was the kind of woman who'd never lend a cent of it once she made up her mind — not even for bees — especially never for bees.

The Ruin and I made the return trip uneventfully enough. I came through Nithering, and it looked the same as ever — gold and silver in the distance, and rather ramshackle and forlorn close to. As I passed the construction camp I thought I might drop off to see Lee but I was too tired, so I drove on up the range to Matt's place in the golden evening, humming under my breath.

I was glad I was not going back to the flat, where the Parent would be dramatic and tragic and spectacular. I needed something slow and peaceful. Matt was sitting smoking on the back veranda with the dogs at his feet and the cow looking at him affectionately over the gate. The slope from the old pine tree on top of the rise was all greeny-gold, and his little old house had the same look of being too frail and patched to withstand the first wind.

Matt came over to the truck stroking his beard. 'Thought it might be Blaze and I nearly had heart failure,' he greeted me.

'Mind if I stay?' I said. 'There's only me.' I got out and dusted myself. 'Well, Matt,' I said cheerfully, 'I started out with sixty hives and the Roaring Ruin. I've done my dough just the way everyone said I would. How are my hives?'

'Doing all right,' Matt said quietly. 'I've only damper and tea.'

'Damper and tea is all I want.'

After we had had a meal and a smoke, I told him about the trip north. At first I wasn't going to mention anything about Fay, but I did hint that she would probably team up with Blaze Muirden. Matt chuckled. That appealed to him very much indeed.

'You've had a bad year with fire,' he said. 'Fire here, fire up there.'

'Yes,' I admitted, rested and soothed by his old pleasant quietness and the smoky draughty kitchen. 'Julie would probably explain it. Her Mr. Pollock said nothing ever happened to me, and I suppose nothing ever does. How's Lee Stollin doing?'

'He isn't at Nithering now. No end of a big bug. They've got him in Ombra at the head office there driving out overseeing all sorts of dams.'

It occurred to me that Lee Stollin had better remain in ignorance of my whereabouts for a while longer. 'Matt,' I said, 'I have it in my mind to write out a sort of account of this trip. I'll be in pretty low water financially for a while, but I've still got enough to pay board.'

Matt was indignant. 'If I can't have a friend come to stay,' he grunted, 'might as well give the place away. Been damned lonely all the winter. Good place to write, Mallee. Nobody to disturb you. I've got a lot of Warren's cattle on agistment at the moment, and I'll be out looking after them half my time.' He was anxious to assure me that I was welcome. He was really interested in what I was going to write.

'Who knows?' I said. 'If I manage to sell it . . .'

'What'll you do with the money?'

'Put it into bees,' I said, without thinking. Matt chuckled. 'Come on, you old devil. What else would you do with money?'

'Going to make a million out of bees,' Matt murmured. 'You and the big feller and all the rest. You know, I've got a theory that the bees are awake to you mob. "Come on," they say. "We got to get somebody to look after us. Give them a little bit of honey for their trouble and kid them along." Bees have been dealing with us for thousands of years now and they just about got us taped. They *need*

346

us. And they know that once you get to like bees and understand them they're good company. Can't do without them any more.'

As he spoke I felt the kind of prickling at the wrists you get when you shake off a whole swarm of the little daughters of the light, the feeling of their tiny feet and their whirring wings and their living bodies. How strange it is to *love* bees — to love them so that when you are away from them you are lonely!

'There isn't a worse organized business in the world than the migratory apiarist's,' I told Matt, sharp and bossy. 'I've learnt now. I know the groundwork. What it needs is to be put on a proper footing. Not just this aimless careering round the country. When Connelly and Fulton and a lot more owe me so much money they have to listen to me, I'm going to have the biggest bee business in this continent. A decent costing system — a central exchange where information can be gathered — distributing centres — men posted at strategic points to take delivery and handle the hives when they arrive. Those big bogeys on the railways take a hell of a lot more bees than you can truck on even the biggest trailer. If only my grandfather were still alive he would have been the man for it. Funny he'd never have it on. He said bees had sent him broke when he was young. Still, if he were alive now . . .'

I am still working out how much we made and how much we lost, and what the percentage of profit ought to be over an average three-year period. Why, the possibilities, as H.D. said about that oil-well, are enormous. Even if you aren't dodging the banks and the income tax, like Fred, you still ought to be making a hell of a lot of money. But of course we're selling at a loss overseas and the home market buys dearer honey to pay for the loss on the stuff shipped away.

I looked up from my papers to see Matt sitting with his feet up on the old cane lounge he had rescued from the chook-house and scrubbed down. He felt, he said, that with his rheumatism he needed it more than the chooks.

'Going to make a fortune,' he murmured over his pipe. 'All out of bees.'

With those sixty hives for a start, gradually building up, and a new extracting house; and maybe I can get Nobby Wallace to work for me, and that fool Mongo — oh dear me, yes — next year — why, next year ought to be, as Blaze would say, 'extra good' — marvellously good, with burr comb in the lids and bees hanging out the front of the boxes, and the forests surging with flower.

There will be the faint blue drift smelling of gum leaves from the smoker, and the hum, and the bees chasing away a dusky wood swallow from the hives. The dusky wood swallows love nothing better than a feed of bees, and you will find them dead with hundreds of stings in their bodies. The smell of honey and smoke — the trucks roaring away for hundreds of miles carrying the bees to blossom. This time — oh, this time I'll be on my own!

THE END